PRAISE FOR
ILLEGAL

★ "Moving and informative, *Illegal* puts an unforgettable human face to the issue of immigration; it is recommended for all readers of middle school level or higher."

— *Foreword Reviews*, Starred Review

★ "[An] achingly poignant graphic novel."

— *Publishers Weekly*, Starred Review

★ "Action-filled and engaging but considerate of both topic and audience, Ebo's story effectively paints a picture of a child refugee's struggle in a world crisscrossed by hostile borders."

— *Kirkus Reviews*, Starred Review

★ "The horrors Ebo witnesses, the impossibilities he survives, are haunting testimony to the human spirit. Artemis Fowl series creator Colfer (who taught elementary school in Italy, Saudi Arabia, and Tunisia) leads the team...in transforming staggering statistics into a resonating story about a single boy and what remains of his family. Italian artist Rigano's gorgeously saturated panels—rich in details, affecting in its captured expressions, landscapes made spectacular as if a reminder of everyday beauty despite tragedy—prove to be an enhancing visual gift to the already stirring story. A creators' note and quotes from real refugees close out this illuminating, important volume."

— *Booklist*, Starred Review

★ "The narrative...[moves] back and forth through time, depicting every new, painful trial—murder, poverty, dehydration, repeated dehumanization—with sensitivity and nuance. Rigano's illustrations show the beauty of the unforgiving landscapes and the individuals desperately seeking a better life; Colfer and Donkin's text is deep and evocative. *Illegal* is not an easy read, but the creators have made the story both approachable to and captivating for a young audience. With the timely subject material and back matter dedicated to both the refugee experience and the art of creating a graphic novel, *Illegal* is sure to be a bookseller, librarian, and teacher favorite."

— *Shelf Awareness*, Starred Review

FOR JACKIE, FINN, AND SEÁN. -EC

FOR VIV, LEXIE, AND FISHER,
WITH LOVE, ALWAYS. -AD

FOR PAOLA. WE ALL DESERVE A
BETTER WORLD TO LIVE IN, AND
ONCE AGAIN YOU'RE MINE. -GR

GLOBAL

EOIN COLFER
ANDREW DONKIN

ART BY GIOVANNI RIGANO

LETTERING BY CHRIS DICKEY

sourcebooks
young readers

First published in the United States in 2023 by Sourcebooks

Lettering by Chris Dickey
Cover design by Jordan Kost/Sourcebooks

Line art created by ink on paper and digital colors from Photoshop were used to produce the final illustrations.

Published by Sourcebooks Young Readers, an imprint of Sourcebooks Kids
P.O. Box 4410, Naperville, Illinois 60567-4410
(630) 961-3900
sourcebookskids.com

Originally published in 2023 in Great Britain by Hodder Children's Books,
an imprint of Hachette Children's Group, part of Hodder and Stoughton Limited.

Cataloging-in-Publication Data is on file with the Library of Congress.

Source of Production: RR Donnelley Asia Printing Solutions Limited
Date of Production: October 2022
Hardcover ISBN: 9781728257235 Run Number: 5027764
Trade Paperback ISBN: 9781728262192 Run Number: 5027765

Printed and bound in China.
HUK 10 9 8 7 6 5 4 3 2 1

ACKNOWLEDGMENTS

RESEARCH CONSULTANT, VIVIEN FRANCIS

MANY THANKS TO ANTONIO SCRICCO
FOR HIS TECHNICAL SUPPORT. —GR

AND THANKS TO THE
AMAZING TEAM AT SOURCEBOOKS

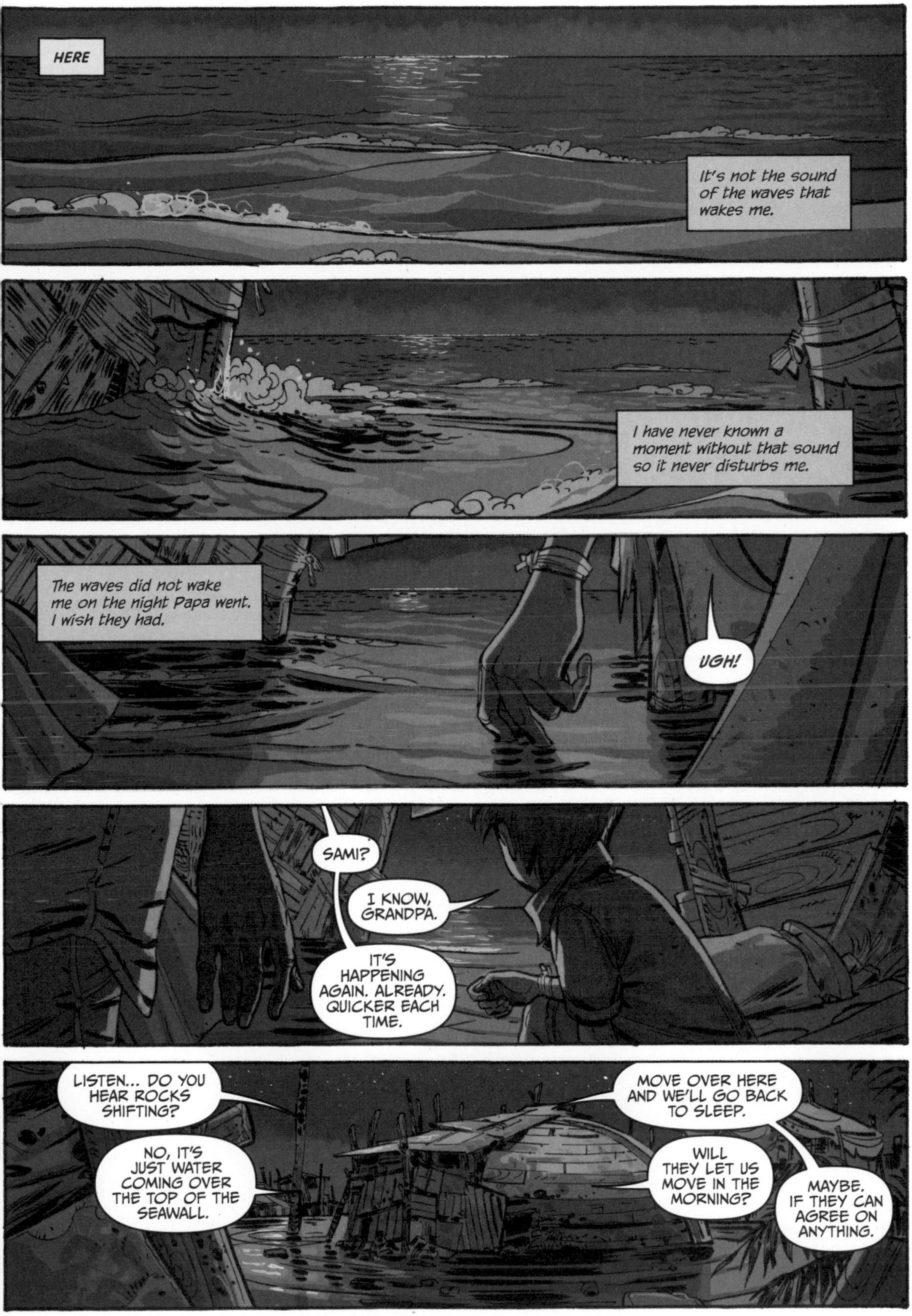
HERE
It's not the sound of the waves that wakes me.
I have never known a moment without that sound so it never disturbs me.
The waves did not wake me on the night Papa went. I wish they had.
UGH!
SAMI?
I KNOW, GRANDPA.
IT'S HAPPENING AGAIN. ALREADY. QUICKER EACH TIME.
LISTEN... DO YOU HEAR ROCKS SHIFTING?
NO, IT'S JUST WATER COMING OVER THE TOP OF THE SEAWALL.
MOVE OVER HERE AND WE'LL GO BACK TO SLEEP.
WILL THEY LET US MOVE IN THE MORNING?
MAYBE. IF THEY CAN AGREE ON ANYTHING.

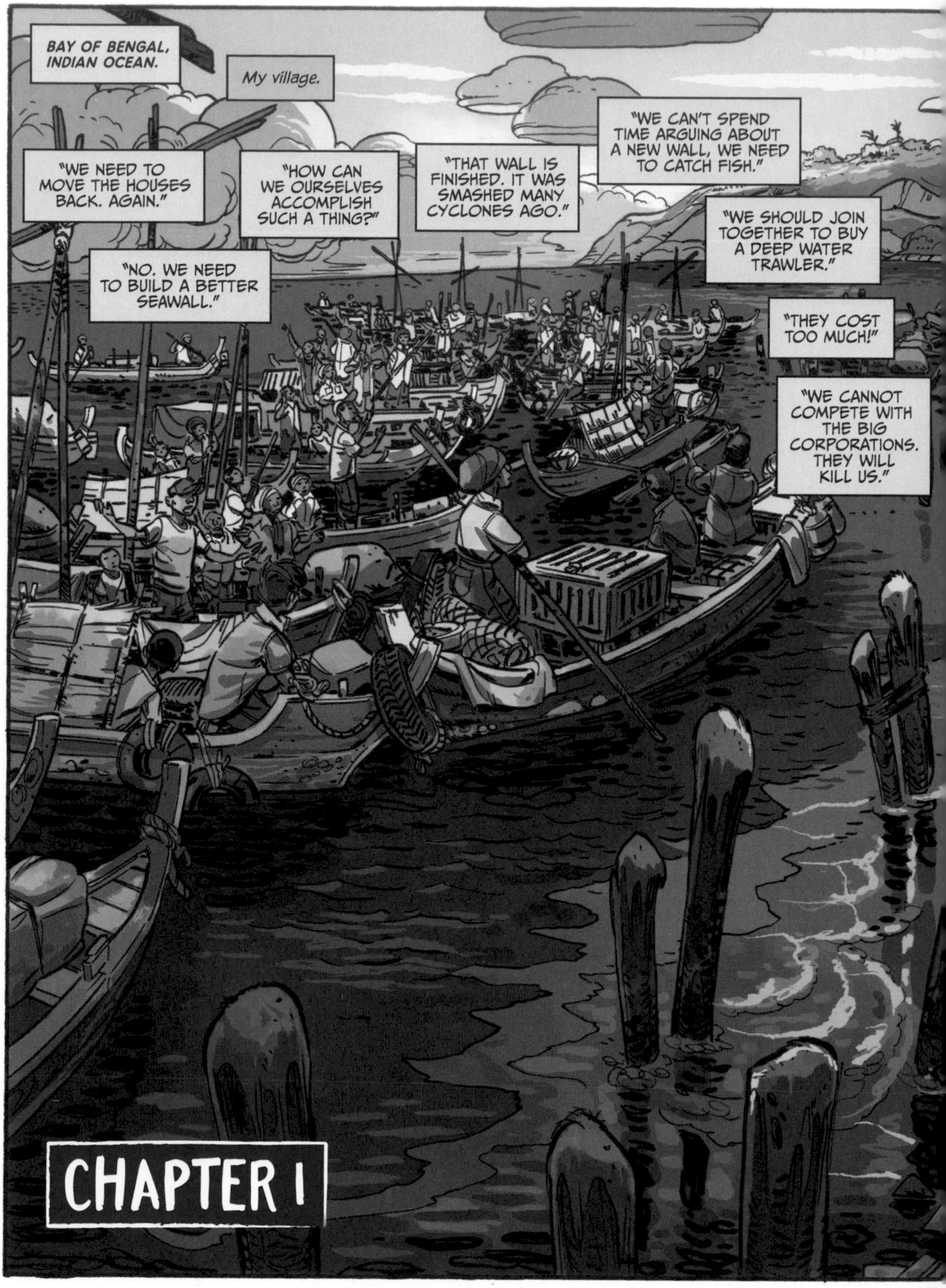
BAY OF BENGAL, INDIAN OCEAN.
My village.
"WE NEED TO MOVE THE HOUSES BACK. AGAIN."
"NO. WE NEED TO BUILD A BETTER SEAWALL."
"HOW CAN WE OURSELVES ACCOMPLISH SUCH A THING?"
"THAT WALL IS FINISHED. IT WAS SMASHED MANY CYCLONES AGO."
"WE CAN'T SPEND TIME ARGUING ABOUT A NEW WALL, WE NEED TO CATCH FISH."
"WE SHOULD JOIN TOGETHER TO BUY A DEEP WATER TRAWLER."
"THEY COST TOO MUCH!"
"WE CANNOT COMPETE WITH THE BIG CORPORATIONS. THEY WILL KILL US."
CHAPTER 1

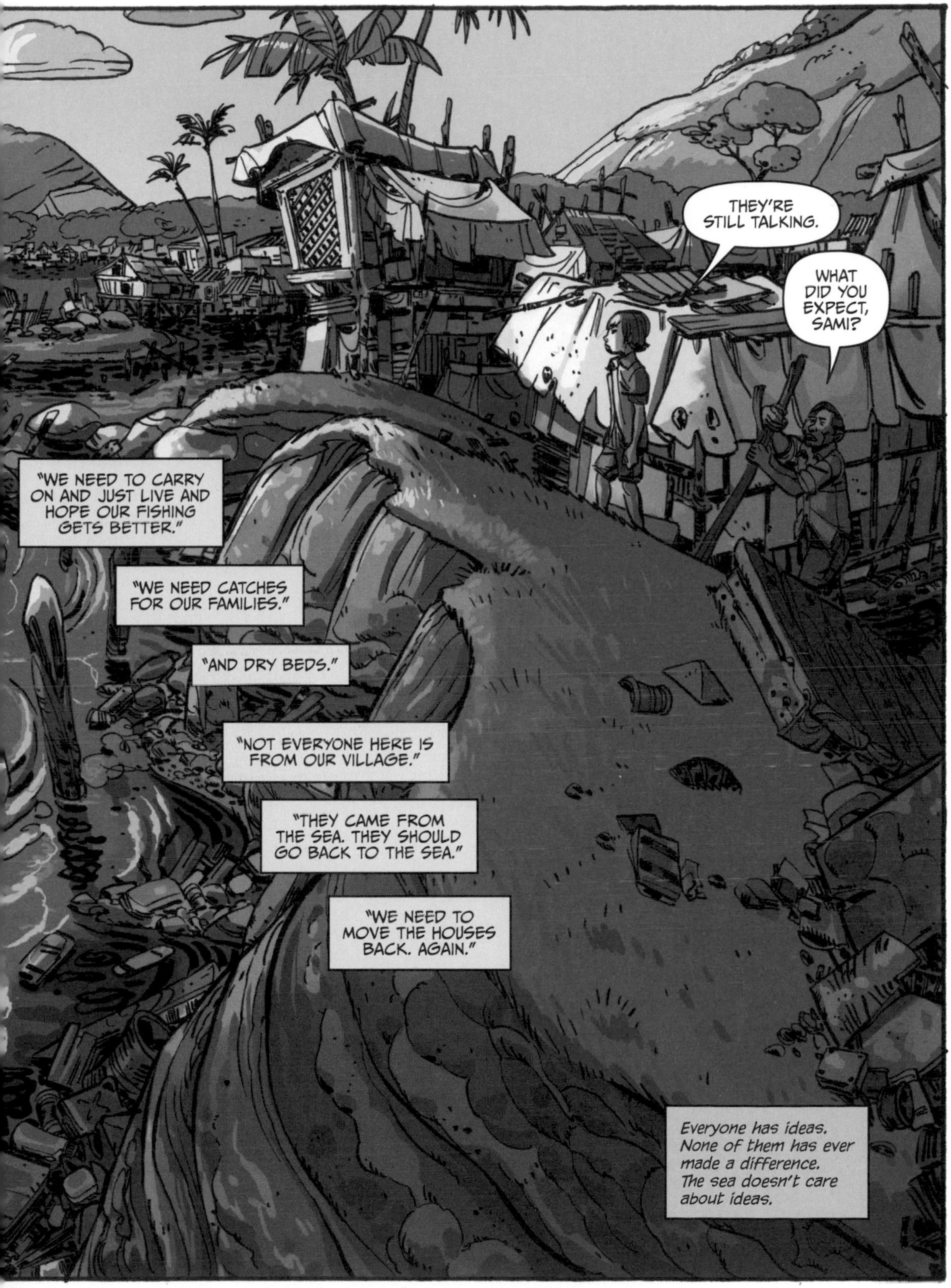
THEY'RE STILL TALKING.
WHAT DID YOU EXPECT, SAMI?
"WE NEED TO CARRY ON AND JUST LIVE AND HOPE OUR FISHING GETS BETTER."
"WE NEED CATCHES FOR OUR FAMILIES."
"AND DRY BEDS."
"NOT EVERYONE HERE IS FROM OUR VILLAGE."
"THEY CAME FROM THE SEA. THEY SHOULD GO BACK TO THE SEA."
"WE NEED TO MOVE THE HOUSES BACK. AGAIN."
Everyone has ideas. None of them has ever made a difference. The sea doesn't care about ideas.

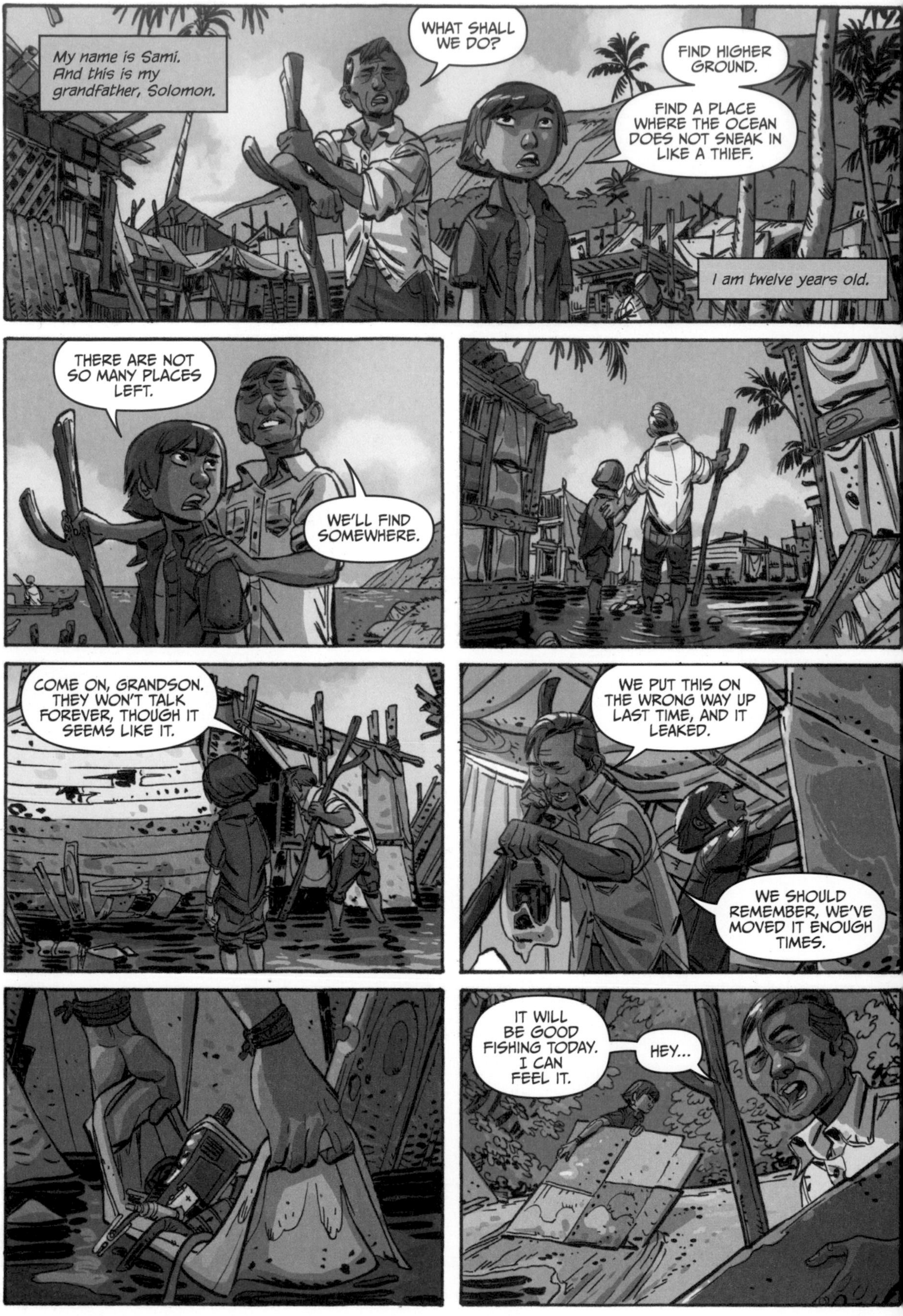
My name is Sami. And this is my grandfather, Solomon.
WHAT SHALL WE DO?
FIND HIGHER GROUND.
FIND A PLACE WHERE THE OCEAN DOES NOT SNEAK IN LIKE A THIEF.
I am twelve years old.
THERE ARE NOT SO MANY PLACES LEFT.
WE'LL FIND SOMEWHERE.
COME ON, GRANDSON. THEY WON'T TALK FOREVER, THOUGH IT SEEMS LIKE IT.
WE PUT THIS ON THE WRONG WAY UP LAST TIME, AND IT LEAKED.
WE SHOULD REMEMBER, WE'VE MOVED IT ENOUGH TIMES.
IT WILL BE GOOD FISHING TODAY. I CAN FEEL IT.
HEY...

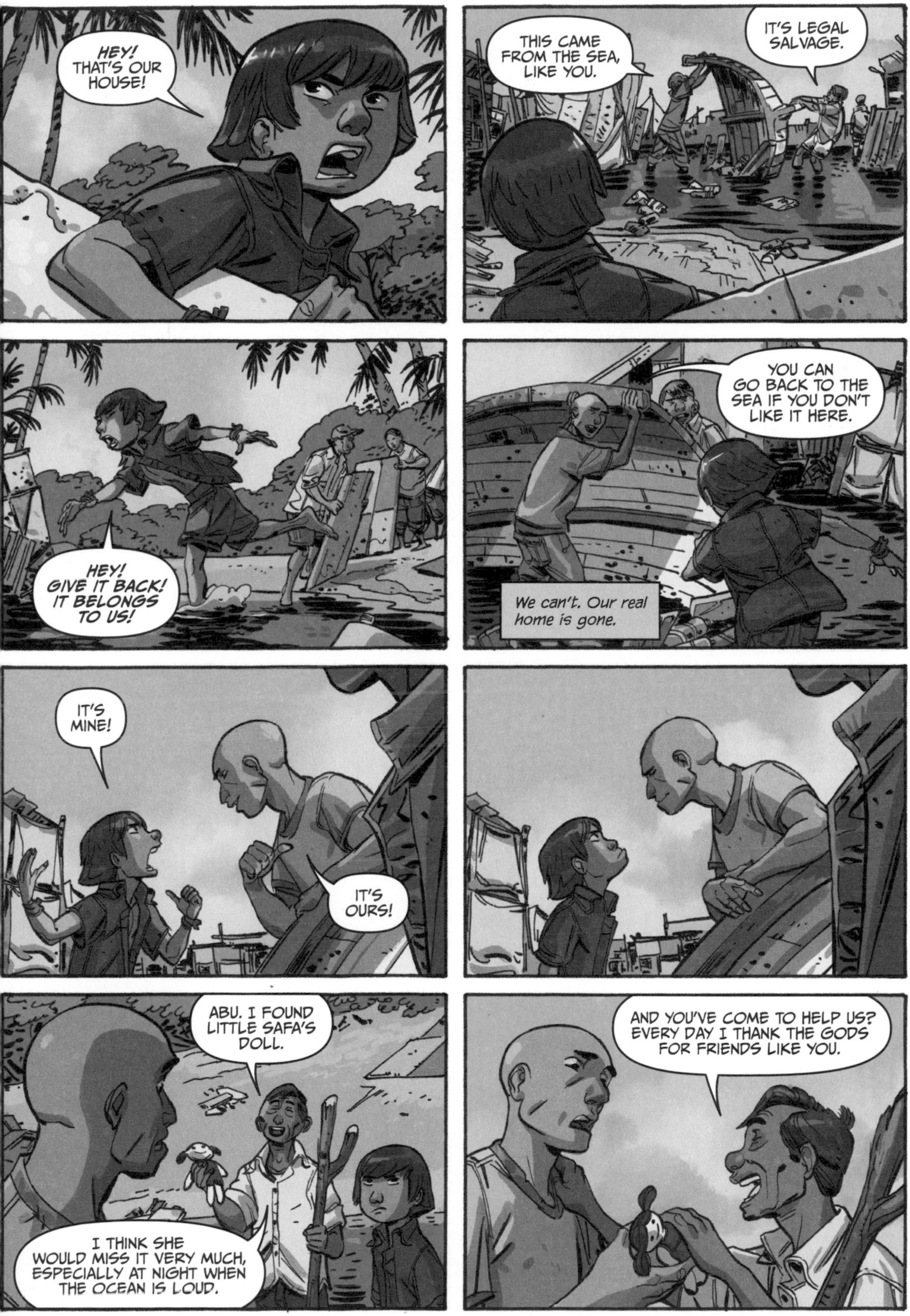
HEY! THAT'S OUR HOUSE!
THIS CAME FROM THE SEA, LIKE YOU.
IT'S LEGAL SALVAGE.
HEY! GIVE IT BACK! IT BELONGS TO US!
YOU CAN GO BACK TO THE SEA IF YOU DON'T LIKE IT HERE.
We can't. Our real home is gone.
IT'S MINE!
IT'S OURS!
ABU. I FOUND LITTLE SAFA'S DOLL.
I THINK SHE WOULD MISS IT VERY MUCH, ESPECIALLY AT NIGHT WHEN THE OCEAN IS LOUD.
AND YOU'VE COME TO HELP US? EVERY DAY I THANK THE GODS FOR FRIENDS LIKE YOU.

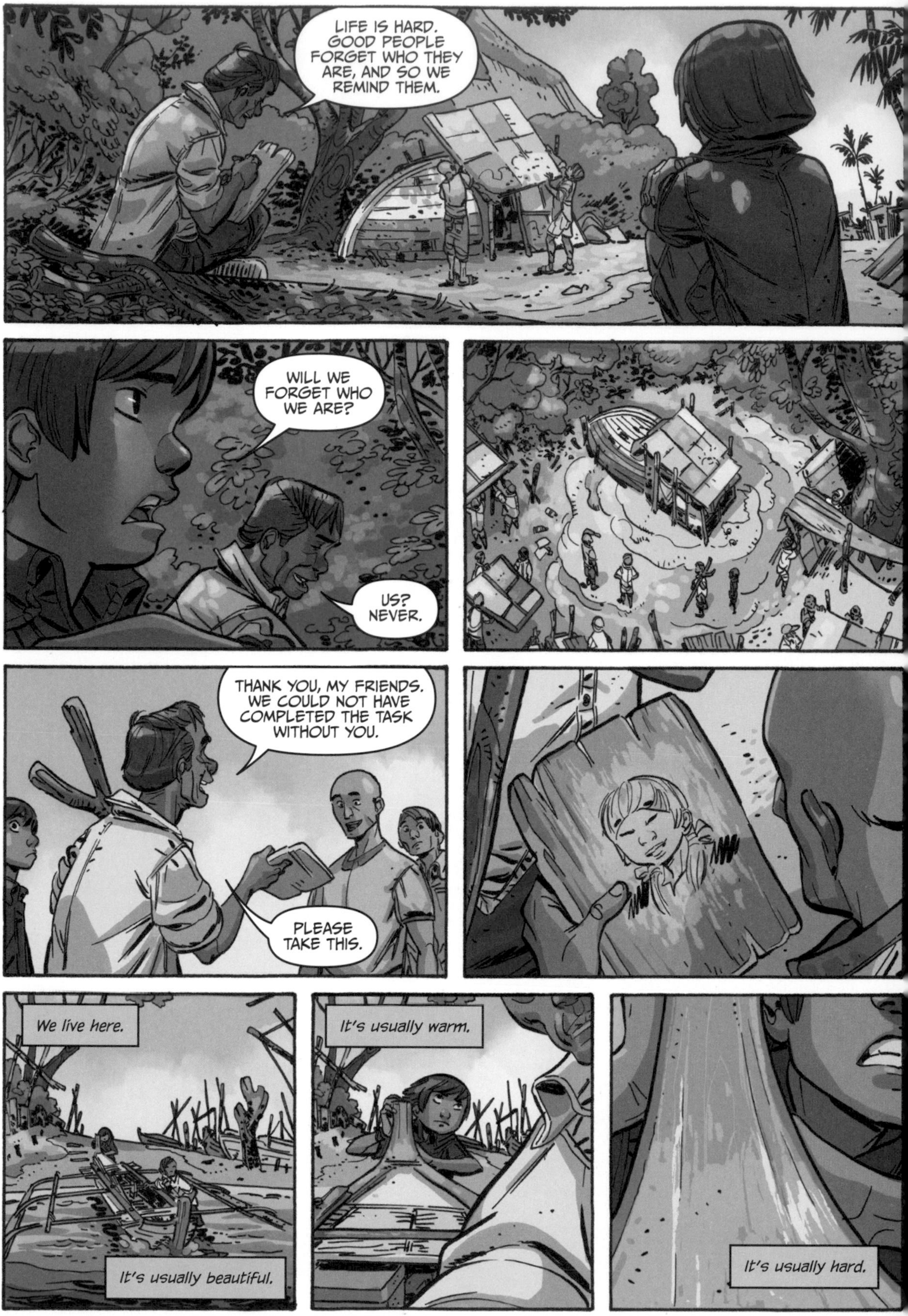
LIFE IS HARD. GOOD PEOPLE FORGET WHO THEY ARE, AND SO WE REMIND THEM.
WILL WE FORGET WHO WE ARE?
US? NEVER.
THANK YOU, MY FRIENDS. WE COULD NOT HAVE COMPLETED THE TASK WITHOUT YOU.
PLEASE TAKE THIS.
We live here.
It's usually beautiful.
It's usually warm.
It's usually hard.

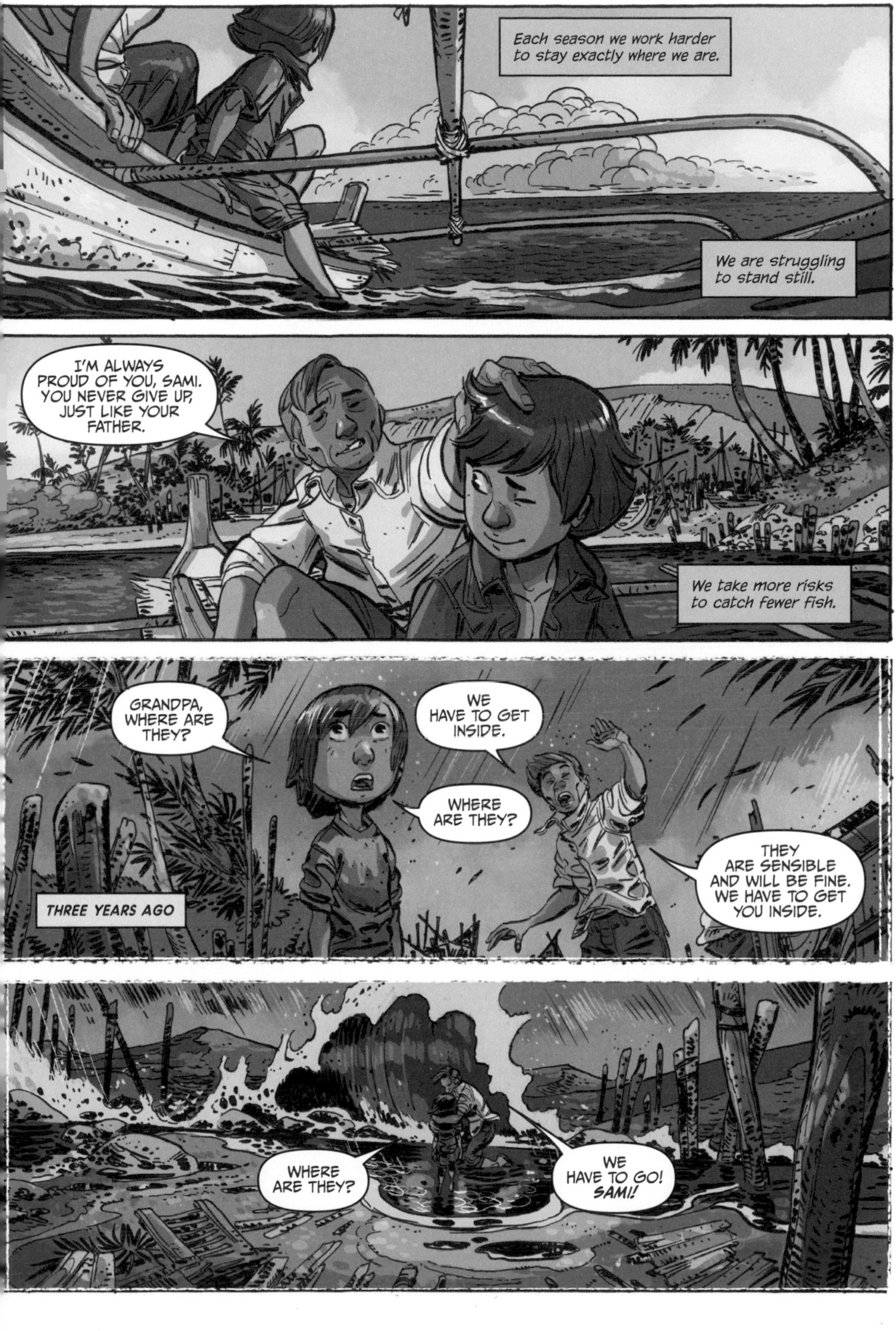

Each season we work harder to stay exactly where we are.
We are struggling to stand still.
I'M ALWAYS PROUD OF YOU, SAMI. YOU NEVER GIVE UP, JUST LIKE YOUR FATHER.
We take more risks to catch fewer fish.
THREE YEARS AGO
GRANDPA, WHERE ARE THEY?
WE HAVE TO GET INSIDE.
WHERE ARE THEY?
THEY ARE SENSIBLE AND WILL BE FINE. WE HAVE TO GET YOU INSIDE.
WHERE ARE THEY?
WE HAVE TO GO! SAMI!

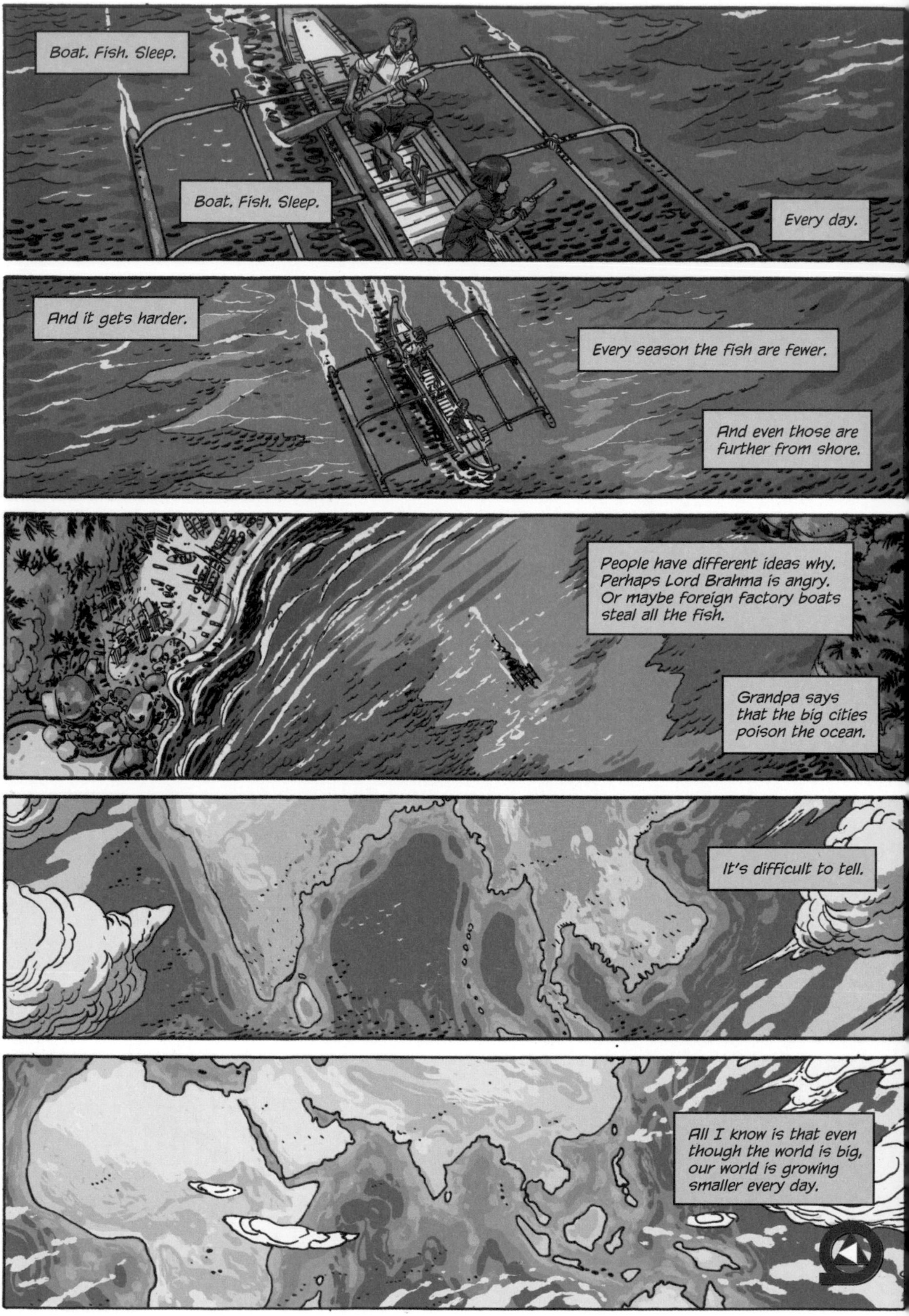
Boat. Fish. Sleep.
Boat. Fish. Sleep.
Every day.
And it gets harder.
Every season the fish are fewer.
And even those are further from shore.
People have different ideas why. Perhaps Lord Brahma is angry. Or maybe foreign factory boats steal all the fish.
Grandpa says that the big cities poison the ocean.
It's difficult to tell.
All I know is that even though the world is big, our world is growing smaller every day.

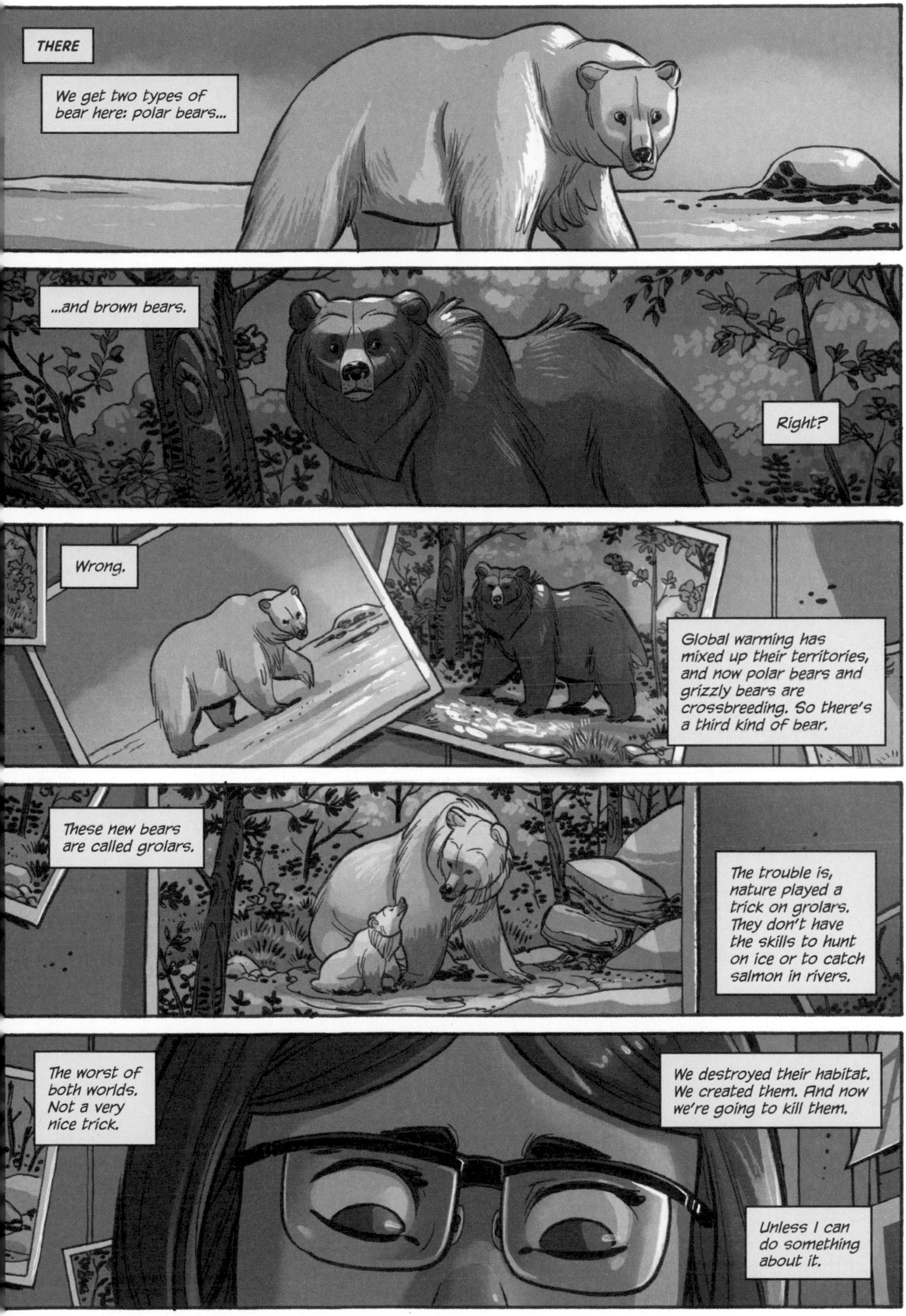
THERE
We get two types of bear here: polar bears...
...and brown bears.
Right?
Wrong.
Global warming has mixed up their territories, and now polar bears and grizzly bears are crossbreeding. So there's a third kind of bear.
These new bears are called grolars.
The trouble is, nature played a trick on grolars. They don't have the skills to hunt on ice or to catch salmon in rivers.
The worst of both worlds. Not a very nice trick.
We destroyed their habitat. We created them. And now we're going to kill them.
Unless I can do something about it.

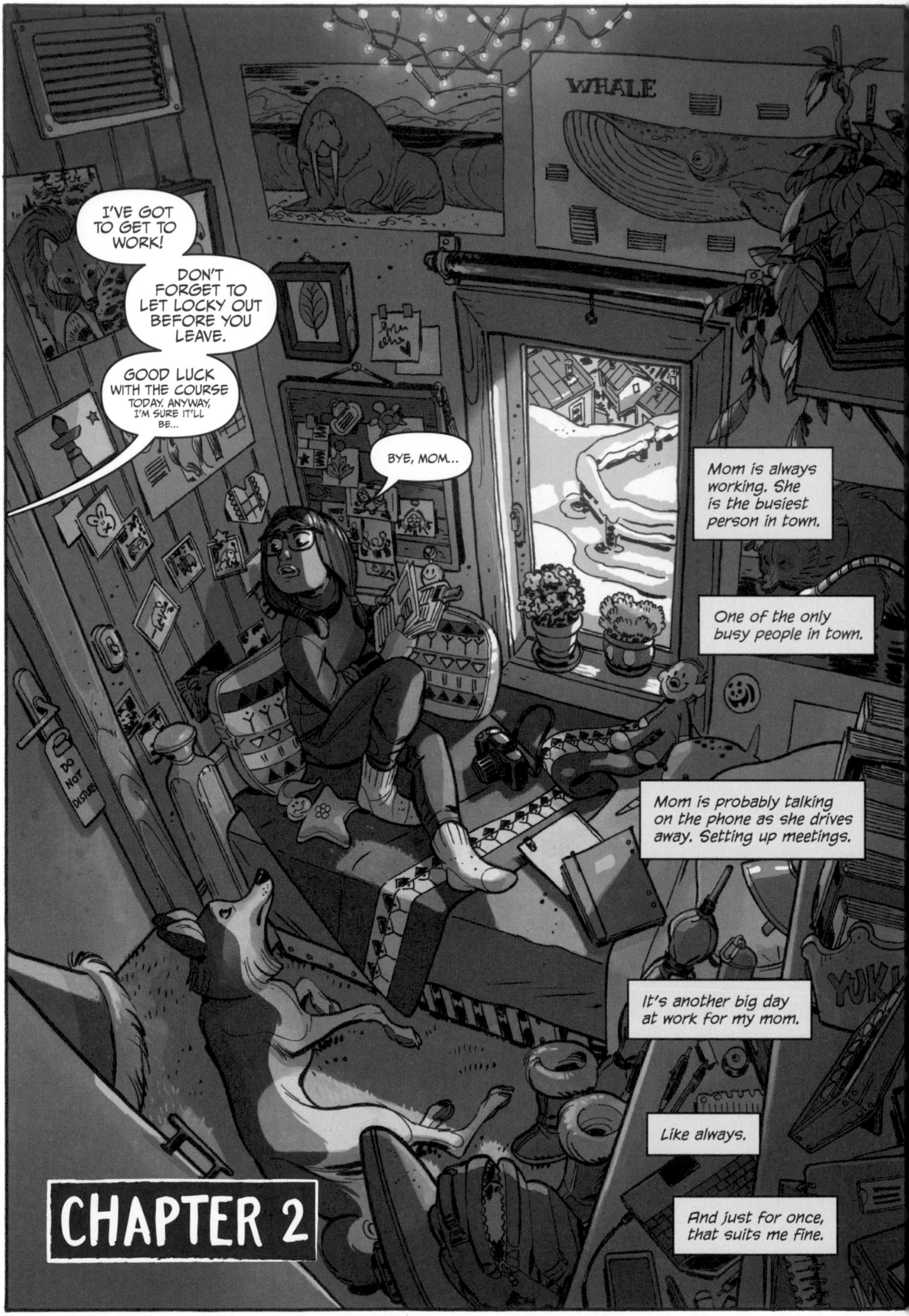
WHALE
I'VE GOT TO GET TO WORK!
DON'T FORGET TO LET LOCKY OUT BEFORE YOU LEAVE.
GOOD LUCK WITH THE COURSE TODAY. ANYWAY, I'M SURE IT'LL BE...
BYE, MOM...
Mom is always working. She is the busiest person in town.
One of the only busy people in town.
Mom is probably talking on the phone as she drives away. Setting up meetings.
It's another big day at work for my mom.
Like always.
And just for once, that suits me fine.
CHAPTER 2

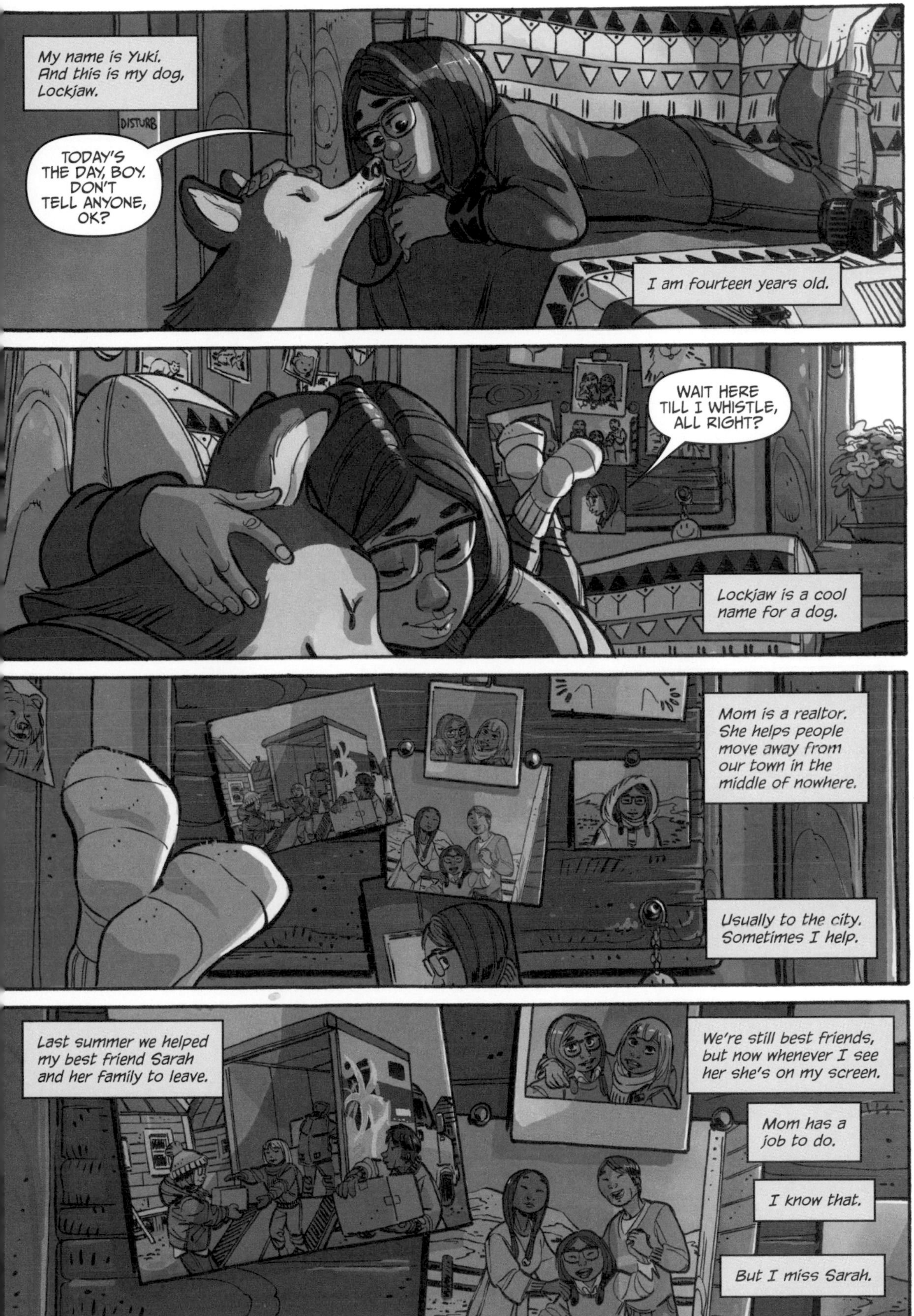
My name is Yuki. And this is my dog, Lockjaw.
DISTURB
TODAY'S THE DAY, BOY. DON'T TELL ANYONE, OK?
I am fourteen years old.
WAIT HERE TILL I WHISTLE, ALL RIGHT?
Lockjaw is a cool name for a dog.
Mom is a realtor. She helps people move away from our town in the middle of nowhere.
Usually to the city. Sometimes I help.
Last summer we helped my best friend Sarah and her family to leave.
We're still best friends, but now whenever I see her she's on my screen.
Mom has a job to do.
I know that.
But I miss Sarah.

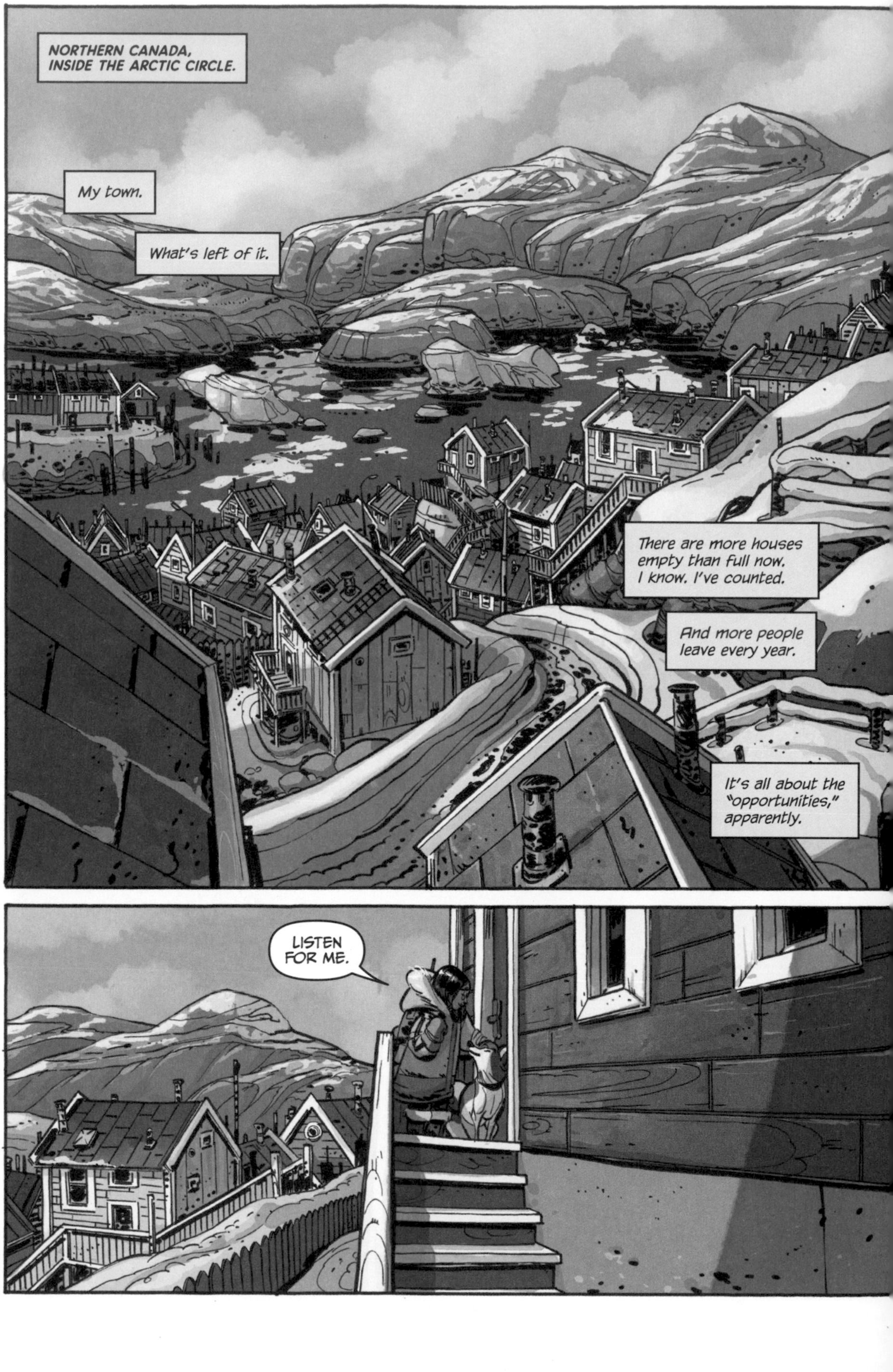

NORTHERN CANADA, INSIDE THE ARCTIC CIRCLE.
My town.
What's left of it.
There are more houses empty than full now. I know. I've counted.
And more people leave every year.
It's all about the "opportunities," apparently.
LISTEN FOR ME.

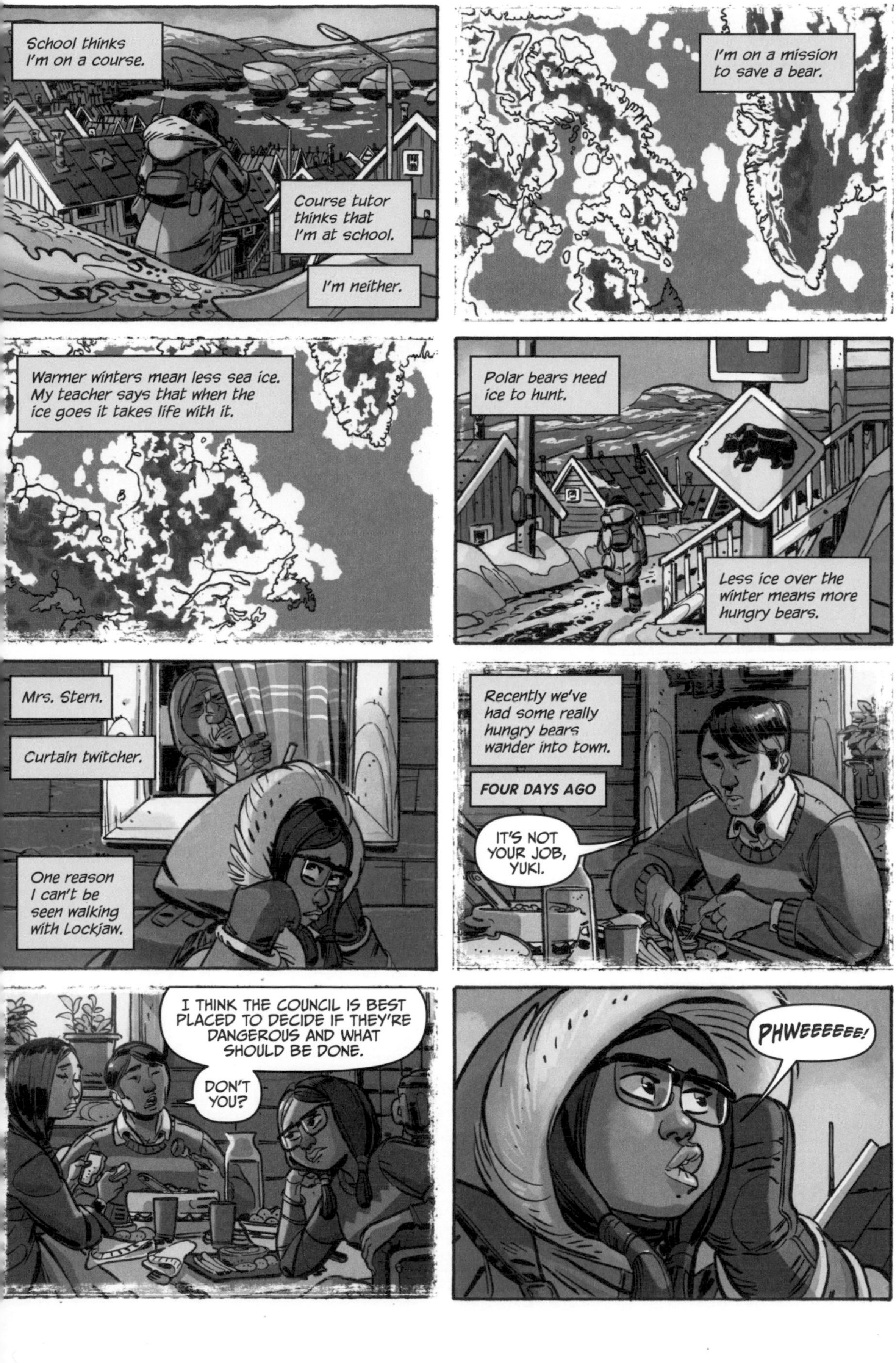

School thinks I'm on a course.
Course tutor thinks that I'm at school.
I'm neither.
I'm on a mission to save a bear.
Warmer winters mean less sea ice. My teacher says that when the ice goes it takes life with it.
Polar bears need ice to hunt.
Less ice over the winter means more hungry bears.
Mrs. Stern.
Curtain twitcher.
One reason I can't be seen walking with Lockjaw.
Recently we've had some really hungry bears wander into town.
FOUR DAYS AGO
IT'S NOT YOUR JOB, YUKI.
I THINK THE COUNCIL IS BEST PLACED TO DECIDE IF THEY'RE DANGEROUS AND WHAT SHOULD BE DONE.
DON'T YOU?
PHWEEEEEEE!

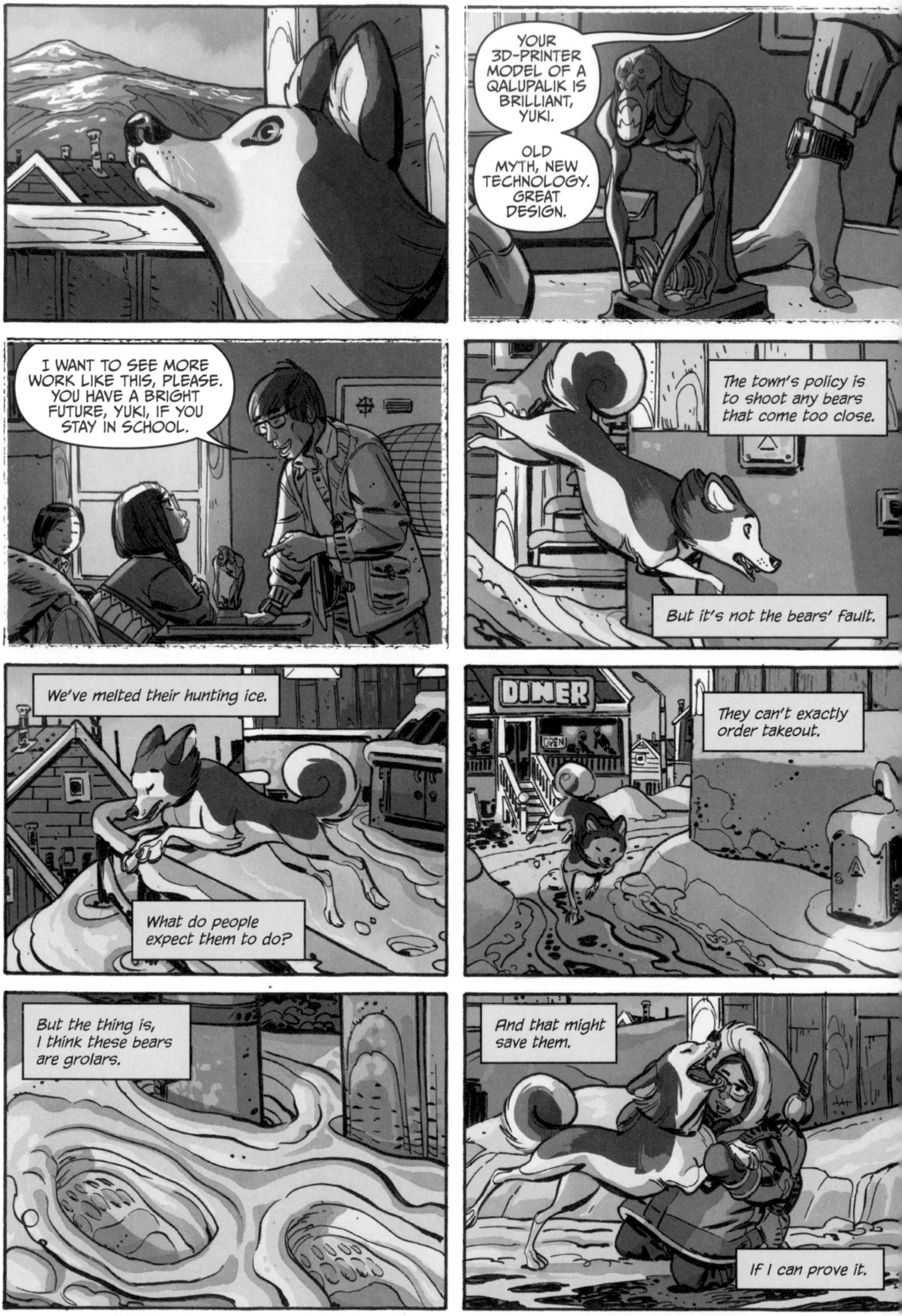
YOUR 3D-PRINTER MODEL OF A QALUPALIK IS BRILLIANT, YUKI.
OLD MYTH, NEW TECHNOLOGY. GREAT DESIGN.
I WANT TO SEE MORE WORK LIKE THIS, PLEASE. YOU HAVE A BRIGHT FUTURE, YUKI, IF YOU STAY IN SCHOOL.
The town's policy is to shoot any bears that come too close.
But it's not the bears' fault.
We've melted their hunting ice.
What do people expect them to do?
DINER
OPEN
They can't exactly order takeout.
But the thing is, I think these bears are grolars.
And that might save them.
If I can prove it.

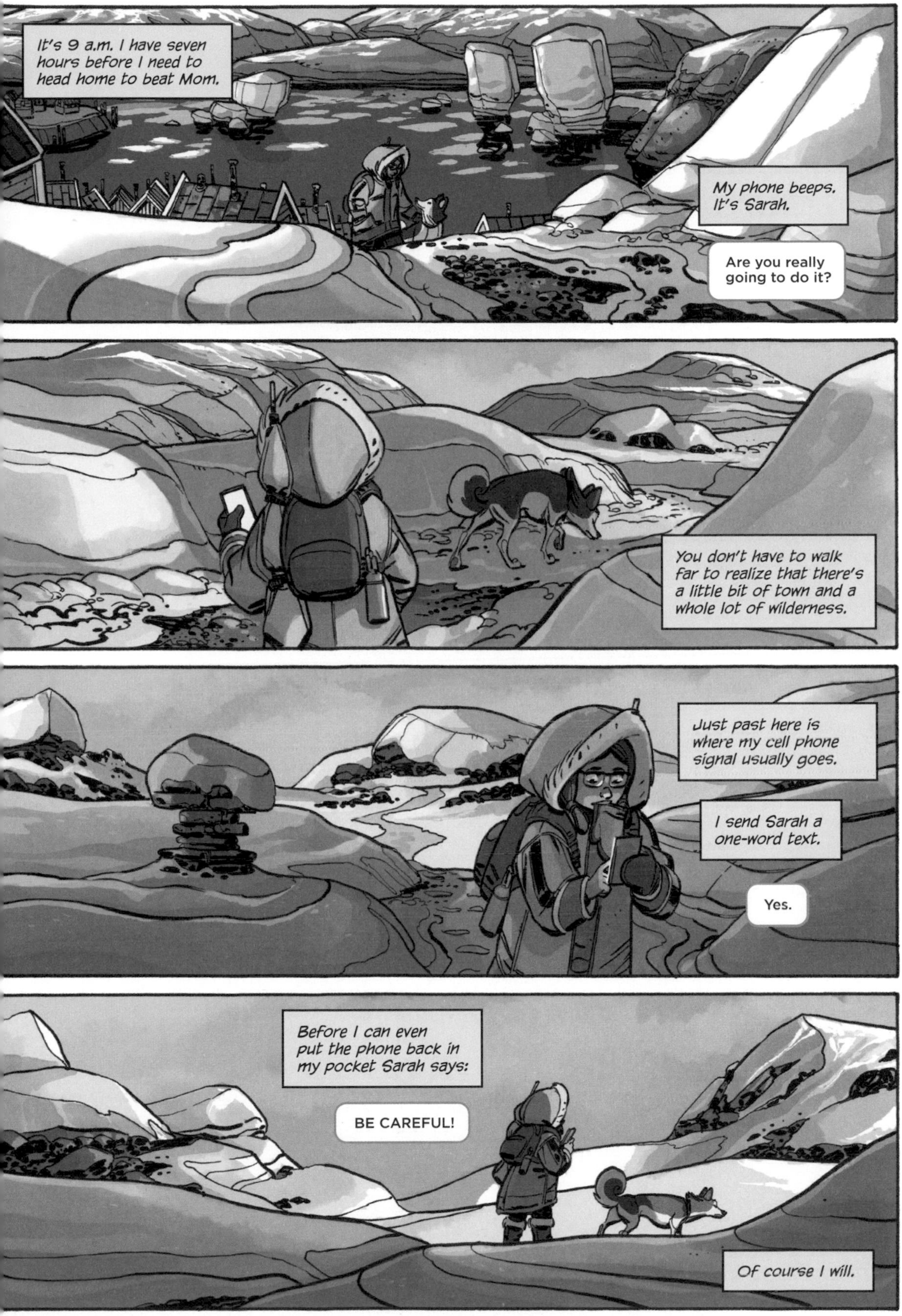
It's 9 a.m. I have seven hours before I need to head home to beat Mom.
My phone beeps. It's Sarah.
Are you really going to do it?
You don't have to walk far to realize that there's a little bit of town and a whole lot of wilderness.
Just past here is where my cell phone signal usually goes.
I send Sarah a one-word text.
Yes.
Before I can even put the phone back in my pocket Sarah says:
BE CAREFUL!
Of course I will.

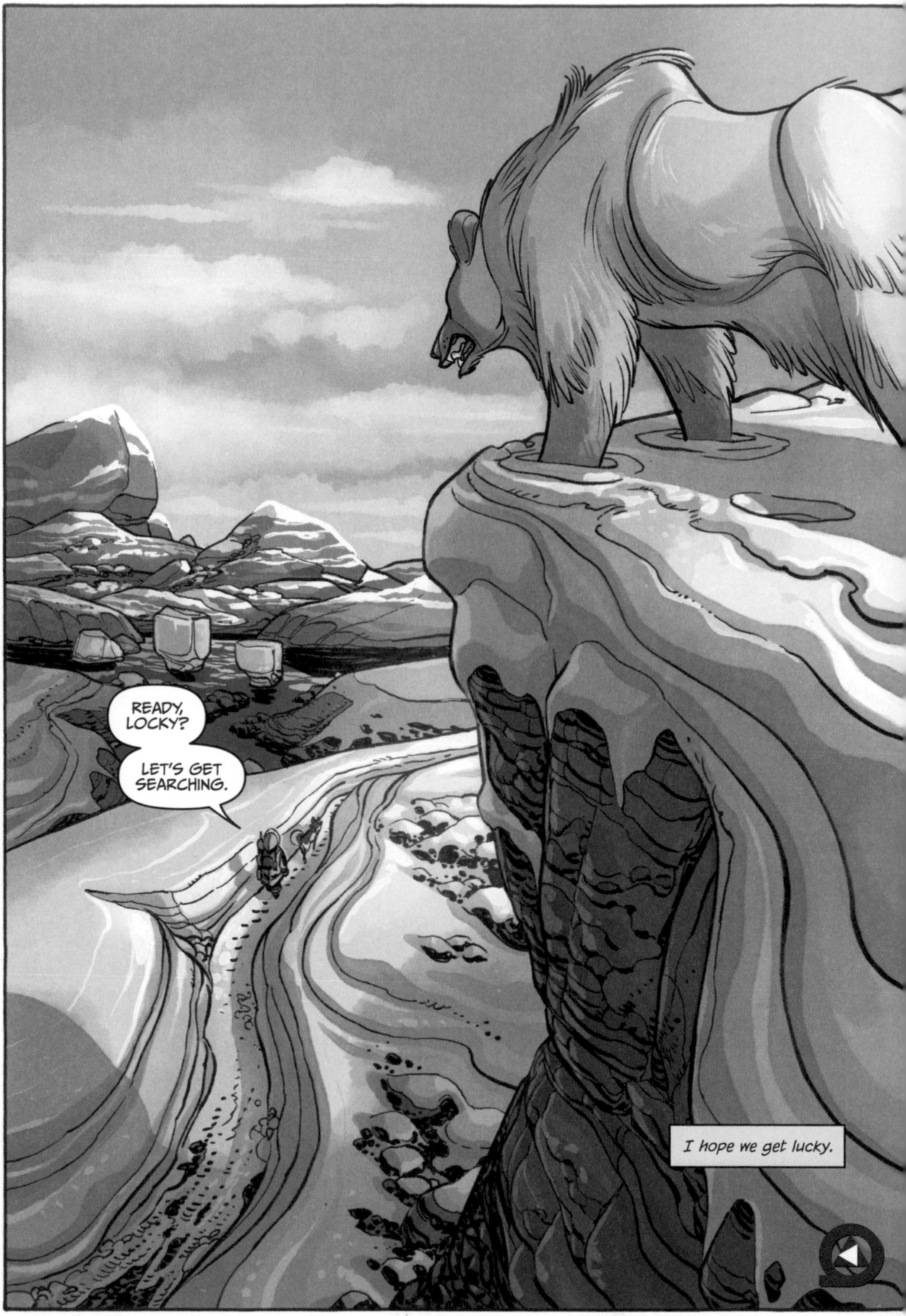
READY, LOCKY?
LET'S GET SEARCHING.
I hope we get lucky.

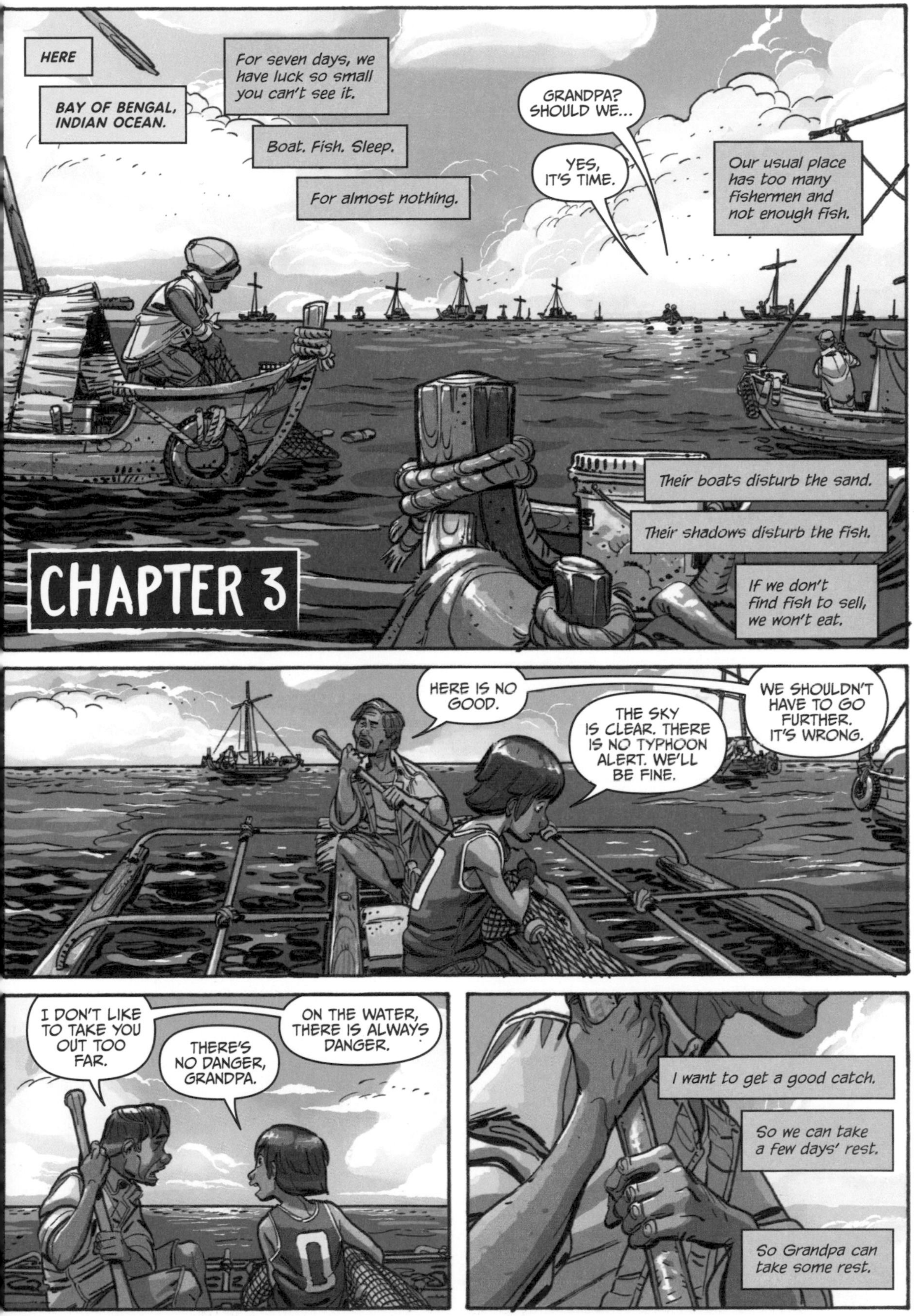
HERE
BAY OF BENGAL, INDIAN OCEAN.
For seven days, we have luck so small you can't see it.
Boat. Fish. Sleep.
For almost nothing.
GRANDPA? SHOULD WE...
YES, IT'S TIME.
Our usual place has too many fishermen and not enough fish.
Their boats disturb the sand.
Their shadows disturb the fish.
If we don't find fish to sell, we won't eat.
CHAPTER 3
HERE IS NO GOOD.
WE SHOULDN'T HAVE TO GO FURTHER. IT'S WRONG.
THE SKY IS CLEAR. THERE IS NO TYPHOON ALERT. WE'LL BE FINE.
I DON'T LIKE TO TAKE YOU OUT TOO FAR.
ON THE WATER, THERE IS ALWAYS DANGER.
THERE'S NO DANGER, GRANDPA.
I want to get a good catch.
So we can take a few days' rest.
So Grandpa can take some rest.

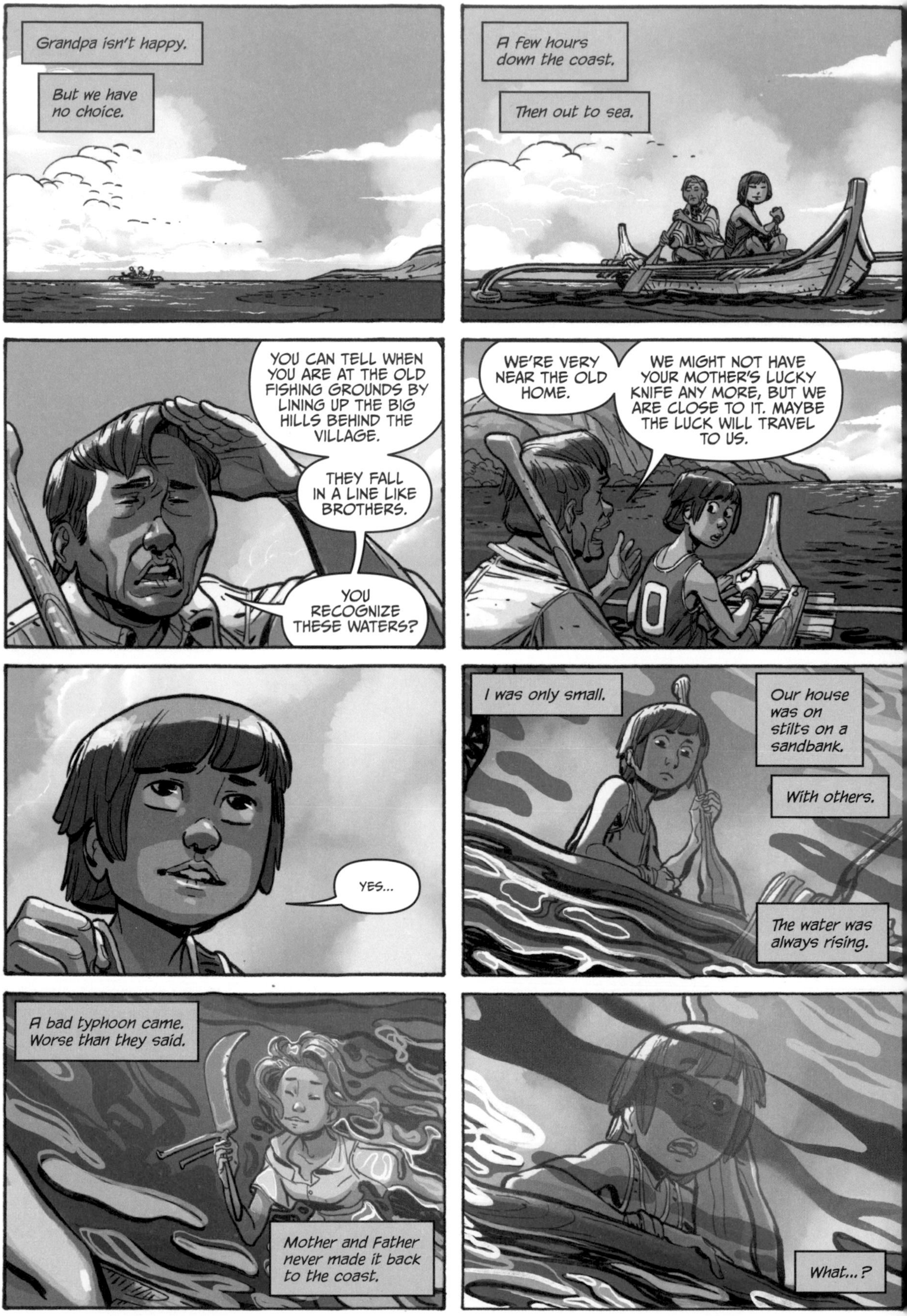
Grandpa isn't happy.
But we have no choice.
A few hours down the coast.
Then out to sea.
YOU CAN TELL WHEN YOU ARE AT THE OLD FISHING GROUNDS BY LINING UP THE BIG HILLS BEHIND THE VILLAGE.
THEY FALL IN A LINE LIKE BROTHERS.
YOU RECOGNIZE THESE WATERS?
WE'RE VERY NEAR THE OLD HOME.
WE MIGHT NOT HAVE YOUR MOTHER'S LUCKY KNIFE ANY MORE, BUT WE ARE CLOSE TO IT. MAYBE THE LUCK WILL TRAVEL TO US.
YES...
I was only small.
Our house was on stilts on a sandbank.
With others.
The water was always rising.
A bad typhoon came. Worse than they said.
Mother and Father never made it back to the coast.
What...?

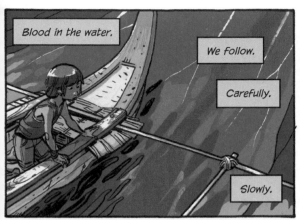

Blood in the water.

We follow.

Carefully.

Slowly.

It could be something big, maybe a good catch for us.

If we can find it before it is eaten or sinks.

A shark!

Caught in some plastic netting. Keeping it afloat.

It's not moving.

Either dead, or exhausted.

GRANDPA, IS IT DEAD?

I DON'T KNOW. IT'S STILL, BUT WE NEED TO MAKE SURE.

MAMA'S LUCK HAS REACHED US. WE CAN SELL IT AND EAT FOR A WEEK. MAYBE TWO.

PERHAPS. FIRST WE NEED TO GET IT ON BOARD.

IT'S BIG AND OUR BOAT IS NOT.

We prepare.

We balance out the prow and the stern.

Secure anything that could be dislodged.

Grandpa puts on the gloves.

They are full of holes but when we get the shark back, we can buy new ones.

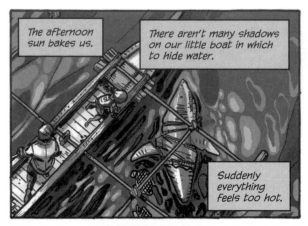

The afternoon sun bakes us.

There aren't many shadows on our little boat in which to hide water.

Suddenly everything feels too hot.

IT WILL BE HARD TO LIFT IN.

WE NEED ANOTHER ANSWER.

We both know we need to get it out of the water before it attracts other things.

Sharks can smell blood in an ocean from five thousand miles away.

Okay, maybe not that far. I don't know *exactly* how far, but I know it's a long way.

IF WE CAN GET THIS BACK, THEN OUR LUCK WILL BE CHANGED FOR GOOD.

WE'RE GOING TO HAVE TO ROLL IT IN, AND YOU NEED TO LEAN WITH ME EXACTLY.

ARE YOU SURE, GRANDPA? WE COULD LIFT IT.

IT'S TOO HEAVY AND TANGLED, AND WE NEED TO GET IT OUT OF THE WATER BEFORE ANYTHING BIGGER COMES.

We lean on the shark side of the boat until the stabilizers are underwater.

Grandpa carefully weaves the shark in between the wooden struts, getting it into the right position.

Then we lean the other way, the stabilizer rises, and flips the shark into our boat.

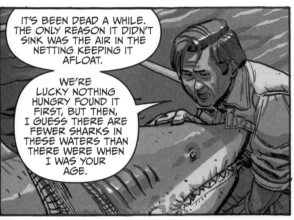

IT'S BEEN DEAD A WHILE. THE ONLY REASON IT DIDN'T SINK WAS THE AIR IN THE NETTING KEEPING IT AFLOAT.

WE'RE LUCKY NOTHING HUNGRY FOUND IT FIRST, BUT THEN, I GUESS THERE ARE FEWER SHARKS IN THESE WATERS THAN THERE WERE WHEN I WAS YOUR AGE.

One of the ships that carry giant metal boxes slowly follows the horizon, ignoring us like always.

WHAT SHALL WE DO WITH THE MONEY? WE CAN GET YOU NEW GLOVES? AND PROPERLY REPAIR THE HULL? OR MOVE OUR HOUSE TO A RENTED AREA AWAY FROM THE SHORE? WE'RE LUCKY NOW. LET'S MAKE SURE WE STAY LUCKY.

WE ALREADY HAVE SOMEWHERE NEW FOR OUR HOUSE. RENTING IS A WASTE OF MONEY. WE SHOULD REPAIR OUR FISHING EQUIPMENT SO IT IS READY FOR MANY TOMORROWS. AND MAYBE BUY SOME MORE BOOKS FOR YOUR SCHOOLING?

OR A NEW HUNTING SPEAR. YOU KNOW I DON'T LIKE THE WEIGHT OF THAT REPLACEMENT.

SAMI.

WITH A NEW FISHING SPEAR I WOULD BE REALLY LUCKY, I KNOW IT.

SAMI!

We row.

Darkness falls.

Waves lap the boat.

HEY, IT'S A SHIP!

DON'T WAVE, SAMI. WE NEED TO GO!

WHAT'S WRONG?

JUST ROW, SAMI. PLEASE.

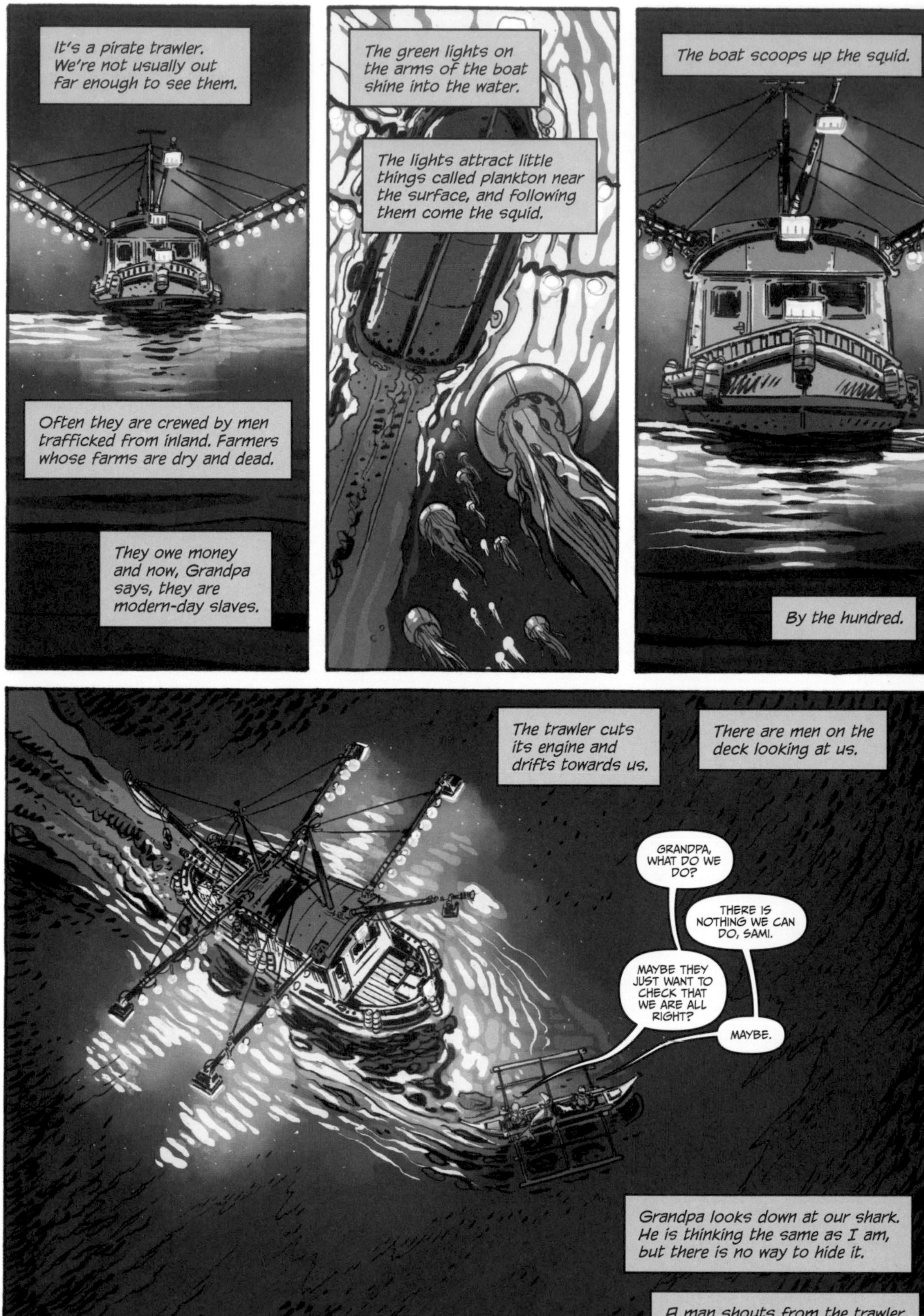
It's a pirate trawler. We're not usually out far enough to see them.
Often they are crewed by men trafficked from inland. Farmers whose farms are dry and dead.
They owe money and now, Grandpa says, they are modern-day slaves.
The green lights on the arms of the boat shine into the water.
The lights attract little things called plankton near the surface, and following them come the squid.
The boat scoops up the squid.
By the hundred.
The trawler cuts its engine and drifts towards us.
There are men on the deck looking at us.
GRANDPA, WHAT DO WE DO?
THERE IS NOTHING WE CAN DO, SAMI.
MAYBE THEY JUST WANT TO CHECK THAT WE ARE ALL RIGHT?
MAYBE.
Grandpa looks down at our shark. He is thinking the same as I am, but there is no way to hide it.
A man shouts from the trawler.

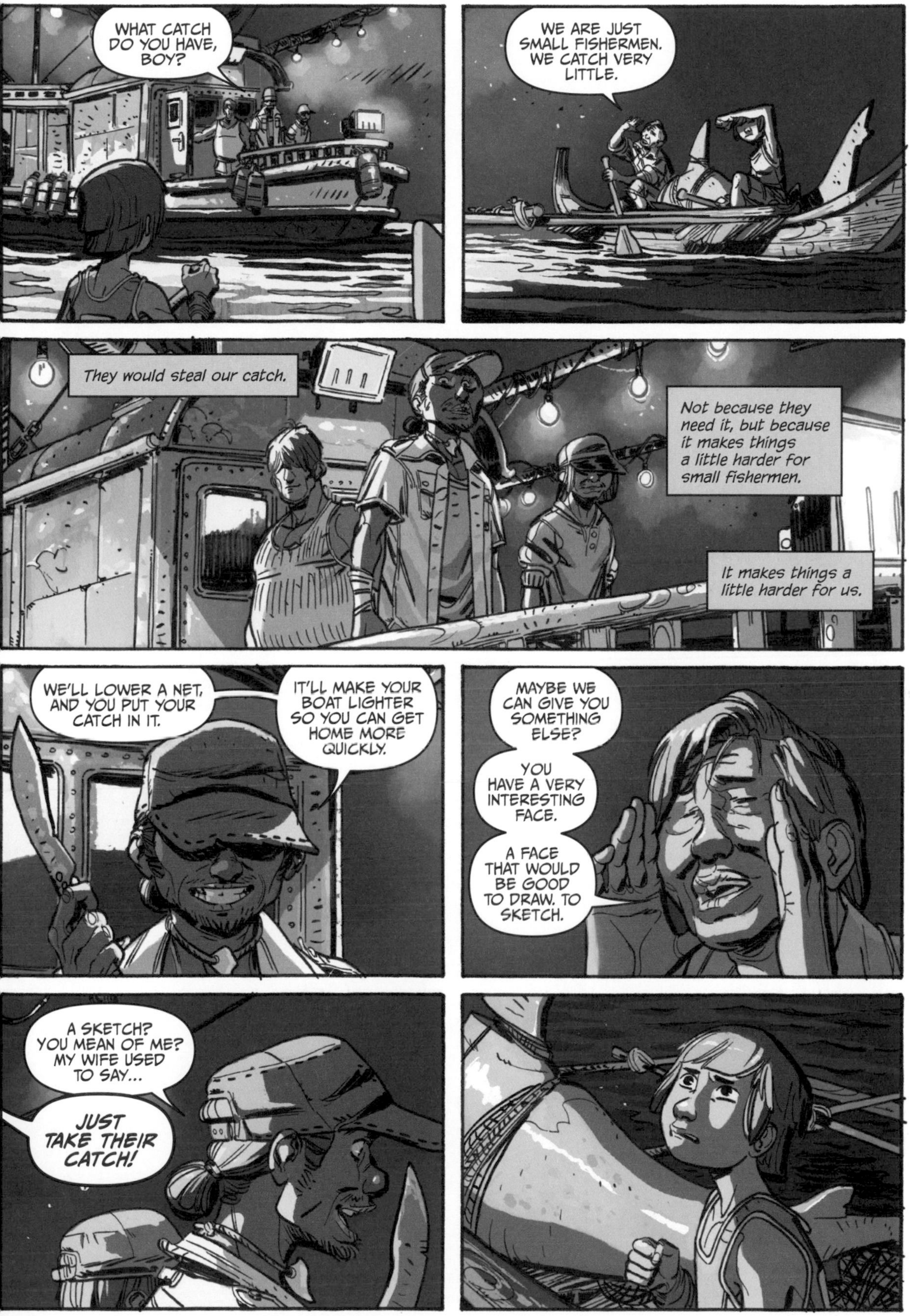
WHAT CATCH DO YOU HAVE, BOY?
WE ARE JUST SMALL FISHERMEN. WE CATCH VERY LITTLE.
They would steal our catch.
Not because they need it, but because it makes things a little harder for small fishermen.
It makes things a little harder for us.
WE'LL LOWER A NET, AND YOU PUT YOUR CATCH IN IT.
IT'LL MAKE YOUR BOAT LIGHTER SO YOU CAN GET HOME MORE QUICKLY.
MAYBE WE CAN GIVE YOU SOMETHING ELSE?
YOU HAVE A VERY INTERESTING FACE.
A FACE THAT WOULD BE GOOD TO DRAW. TO SKETCH.
A SKETCH? YOU MEAN OF ME? MY WIFE USED TO SAY...
JUST TAKE THEIR CATCH!

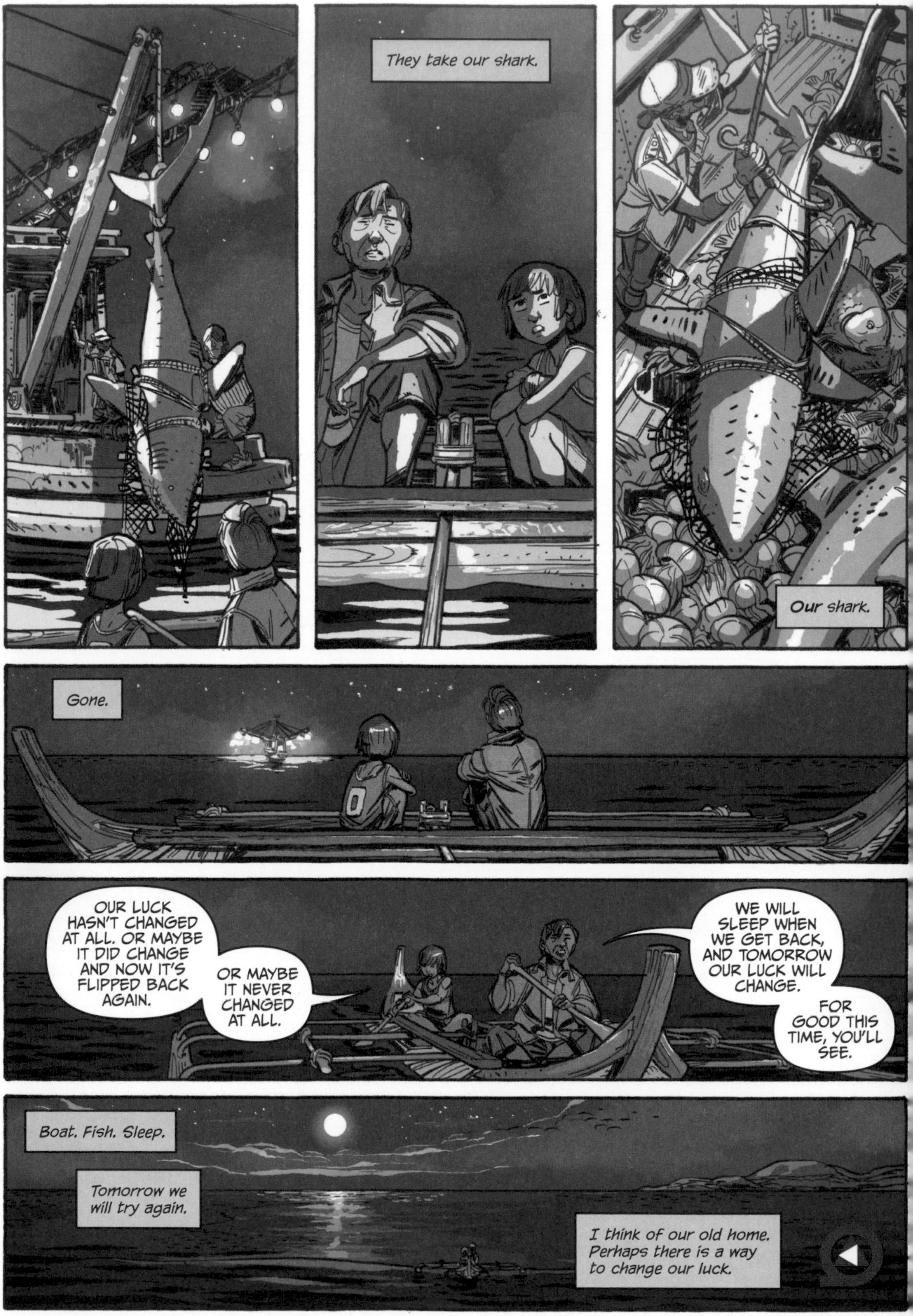
They take our shark.
Our shark.
Gone.
OUR LUCK HASN'T CHANGED AT ALL. OR MAYBE IT DID CHANGE AND NOW IT'S FLIPPED BACK AGAIN.
OR MAYBE IT NEVER CHANGED AT ALL.
WE WILL SLEEP WHEN WE GET BACK, AND TOMORROW OUR LUCK WILL CHANGE.
FOR GOOD THIS TIME, YOU'LL SEE.
Boat. Fish. Sleep.
Tomorrow we will try again.
I think of our old home. Perhaps there is a way to change our luck.

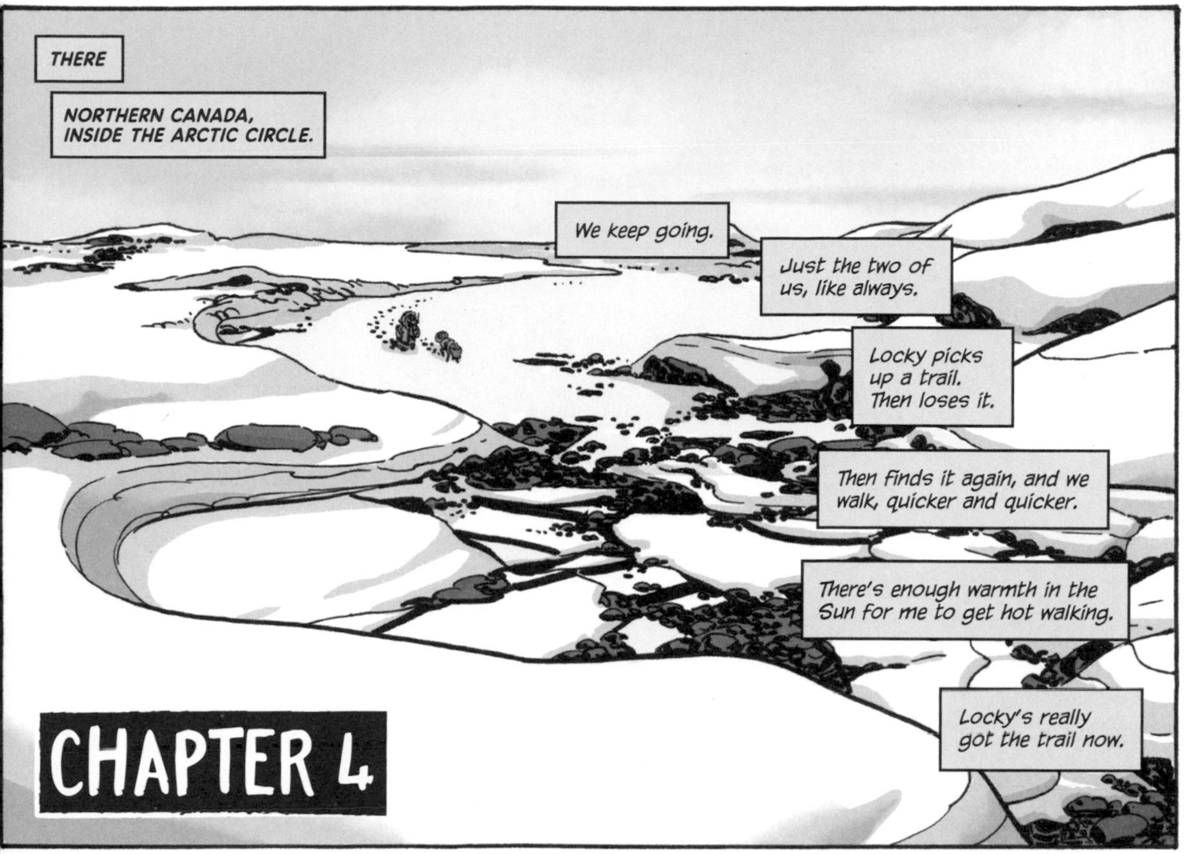
THERE
NORTHERN CANADA, INSIDE THE ARCTIC CIRCLE.
We keep going.
Just the two of us, like always.
Locky picks up a trail. Then loses it.
Then finds it again, and we walk, quicker and quicker.
There's enough warmth in the Sun for me to get hot walking.
Locky's really got the trail now.

CHAPTER 4

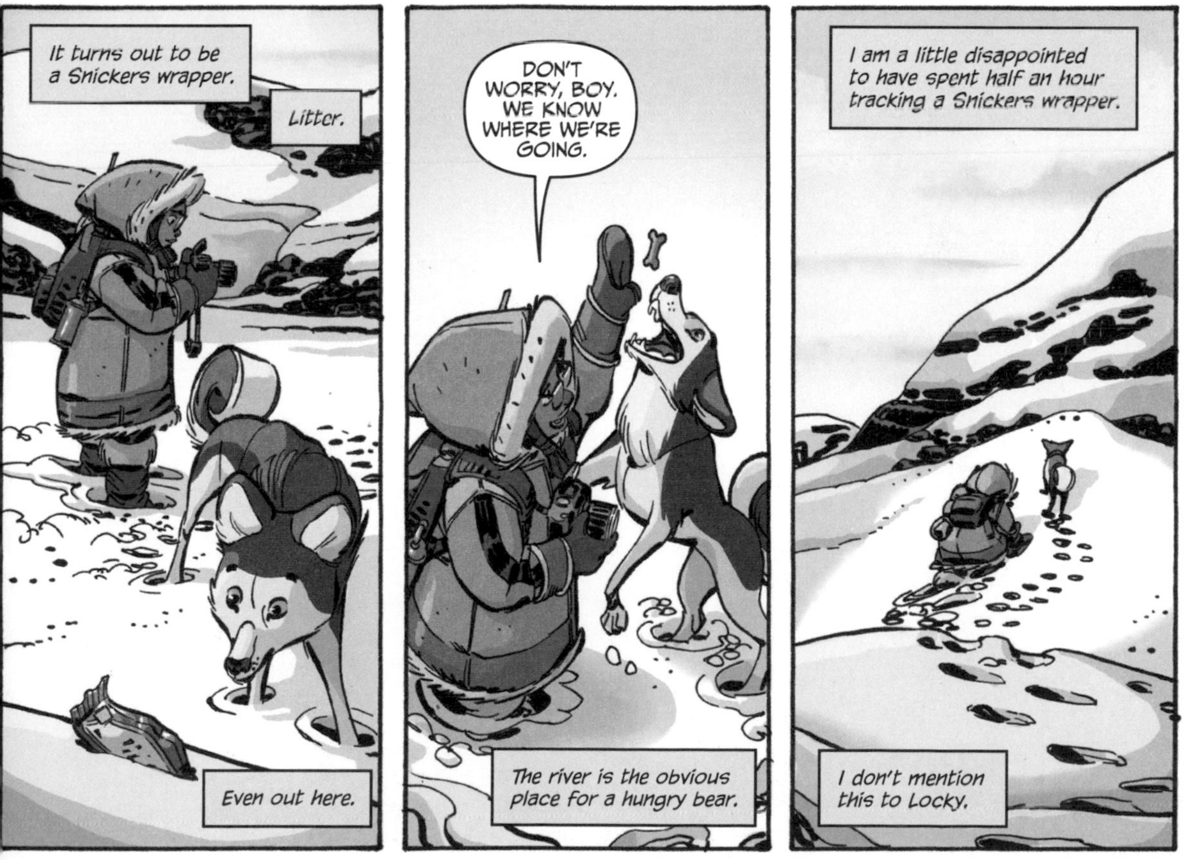
It turns out to be a Snickers wrapper.
Litter.
Even out here.
DON'T WORRY, BOY. WE KNOW WHERE WE'RE GOING.
The river is the obvious place for a hungry bear.
I am a little disappointed to have spent half an hour tracking a Snickers wrapper.
I don't mention this to Locky.

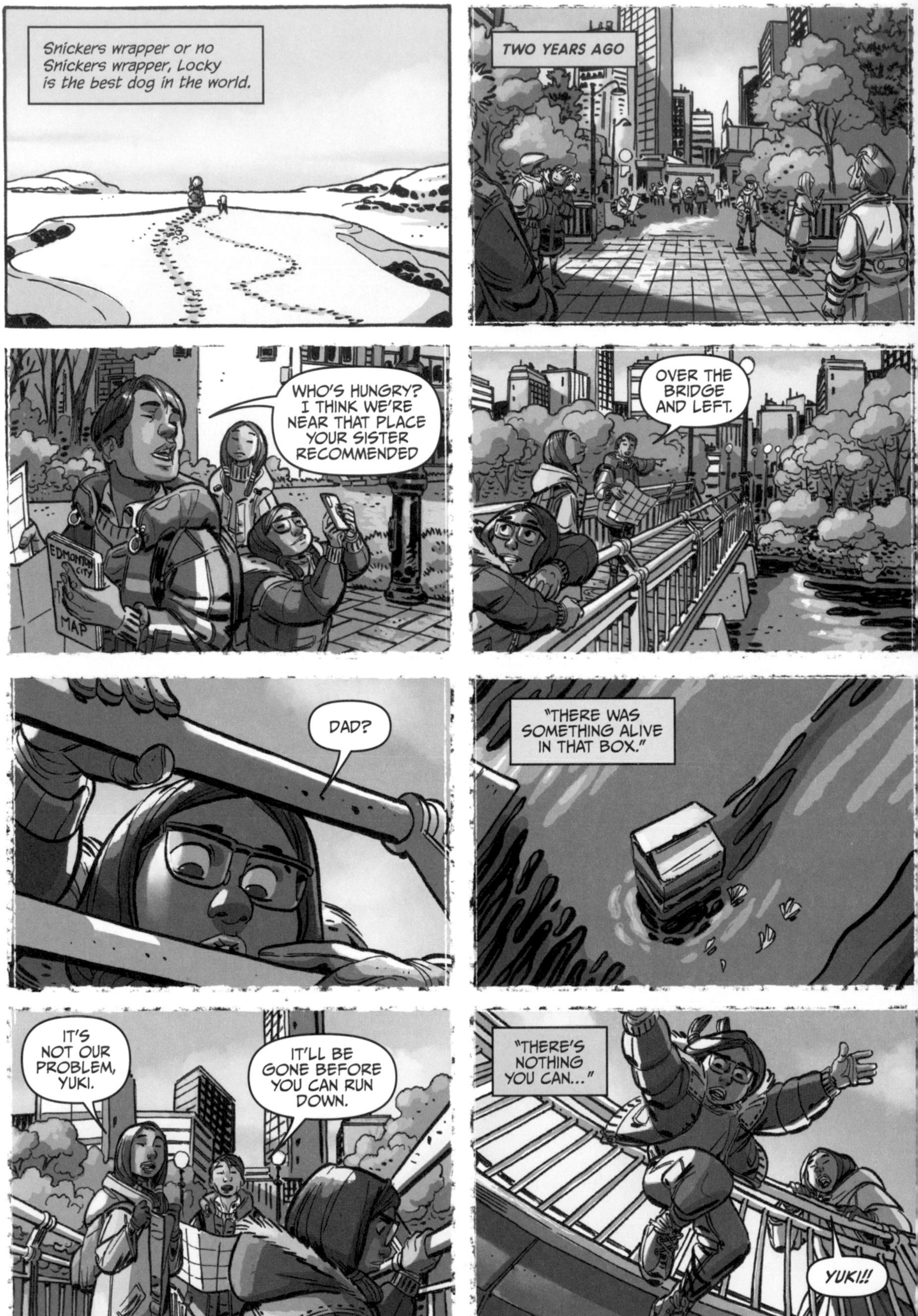
Snickers wrapper or no Snickers wrapper, Locky is the best dog in the world.
TWO YEARS AGO
WHO'S HUNGRY? I THINK WE'RE NEAR THAT PLACE YOUR SISTER RECOMMENDED
EDMONTON CITY MAP
OVER THE BRIDGE AND LEFT.
DAD?
"THERE WAS SOMETHING ALIVE IN THAT BOX."
IT'S NOT OUR PROBLEM, YUKI.
IT'LL BE GONE BEFORE YOU CAN RUN DOWN.
"THERE'S NOTHING YOU CAN..."
YUKI!!

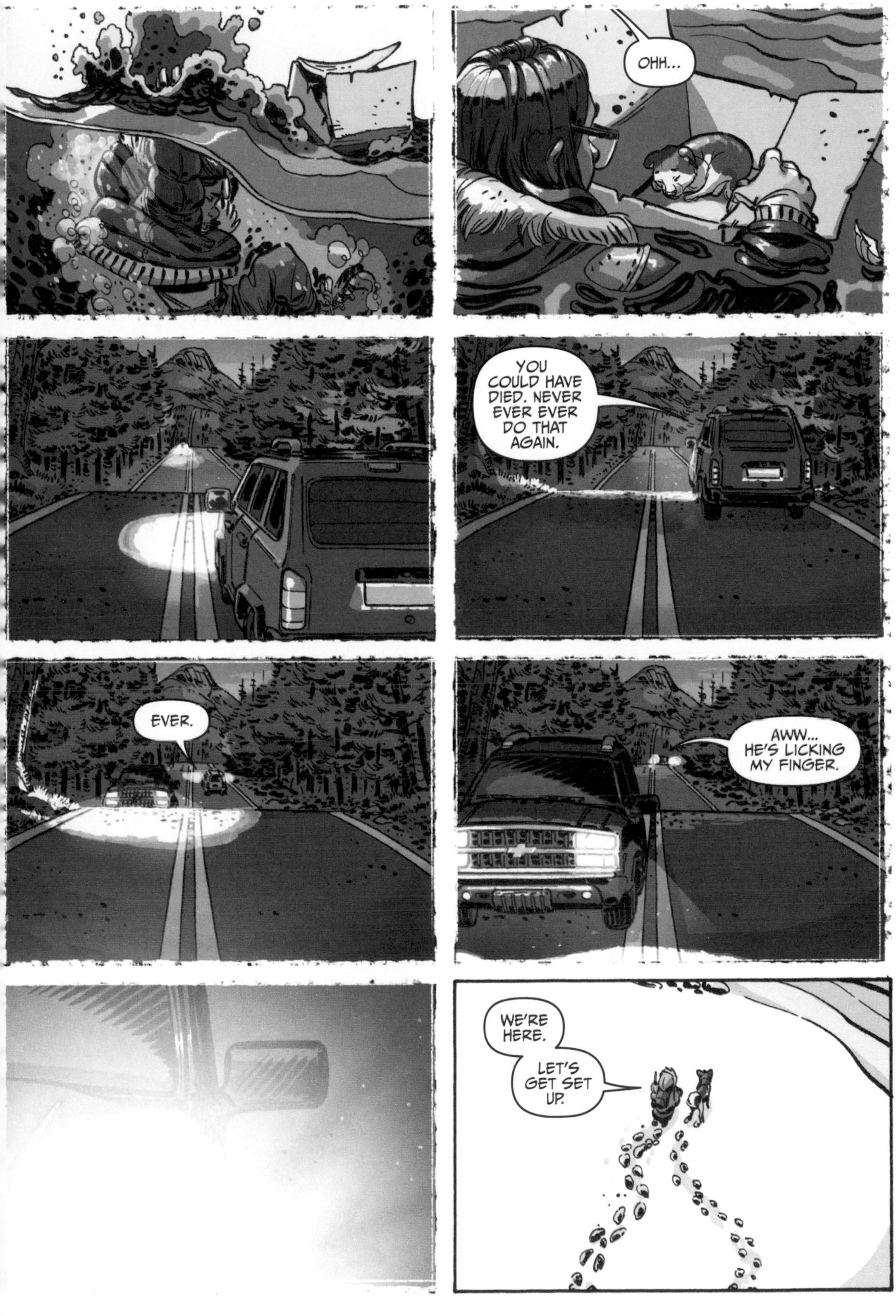
OHH...
YOU COULD HAVE DIED. NEVER EVER EVER DO THAT AGAIN.
EVER.
AWW... HE'S LICKING MY FINGER.
WE'RE HERE.
LET'S GET SET UP.

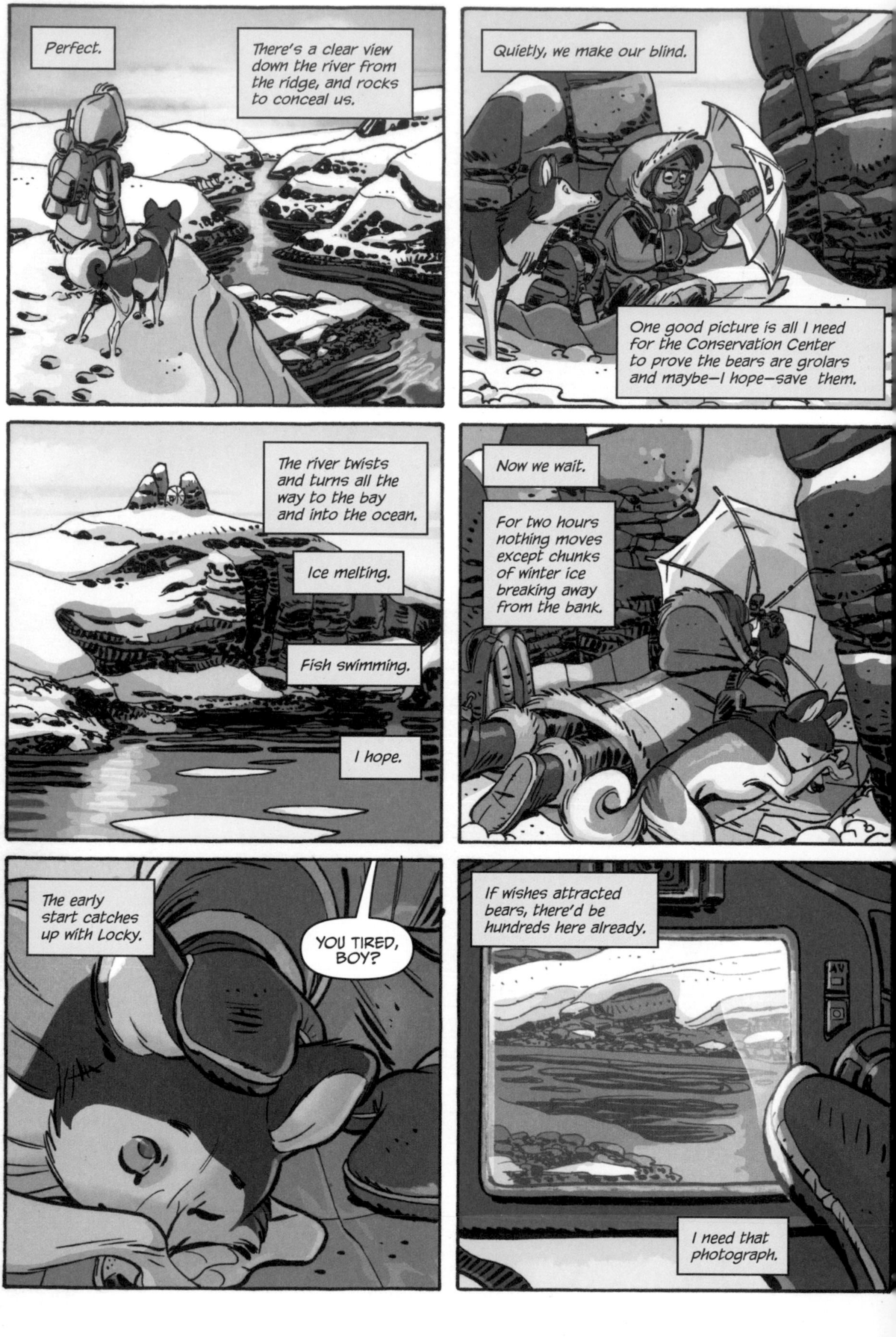
Perfect.
There's a clear view down the river from the ridge, and rocks to conceal us.
Quietly, we make our blind.
One good picture is all I need for the Conservation Center to prove the bears are grolars and maybe—I hope—save them.
The river twists and turns all the way to the bay and into the ocean.
Ice melting.
Fish swimming.
I hope.
Now we wait.
For two hours nothing moves except chunks of winter ice breaking away from the bank.
The early start catches up with Locky.
YOU TIRED, BOY?
If wishes attracted bears, there'd be hundreds here already.
I need that photograph.

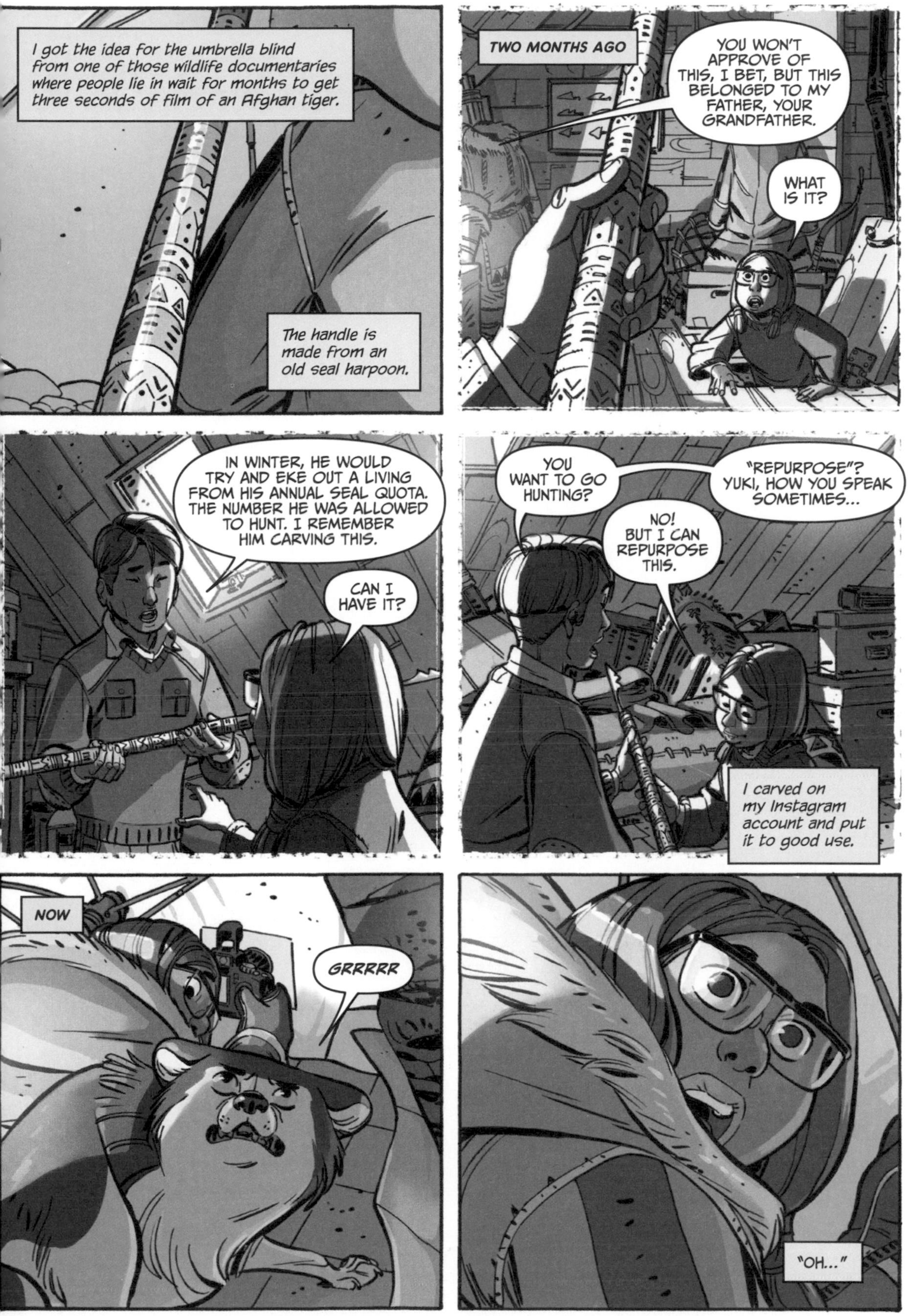
I got the idea for the umbrella blind from one of those wildlife documentaries where people lie in wait for months to get three seconds of film of an Afghan tiger.
The handle is made from an old seal harpoon.
TWO MONTHS AGO
YOU WON'T APPROVE OF THIS, I BET, BUT THIS BELONGED TO MY FATHER, YOUR GRANDFATHER.
WHAT IS IT?
IN WINTER, HE WOULD TRY AND EKE OUT A LIVING FROM HIS ANNUAL SEAL QUOTA. THE NUMBER HE WAS ALLOWED TO HUNT. I REMEMBER HIM CARVING THIS.
CAN I HAVE IT?
YOU WANT TO GO HUNTING?
NO! BUT I CAN REPURPOSE THIS.
"REPURPOSE"? YUKI, HOW YOU SPEAK SOMETIMES...
I carved on my Instagram account and put it to good use.
NOW
GRRRRR
"OH..."

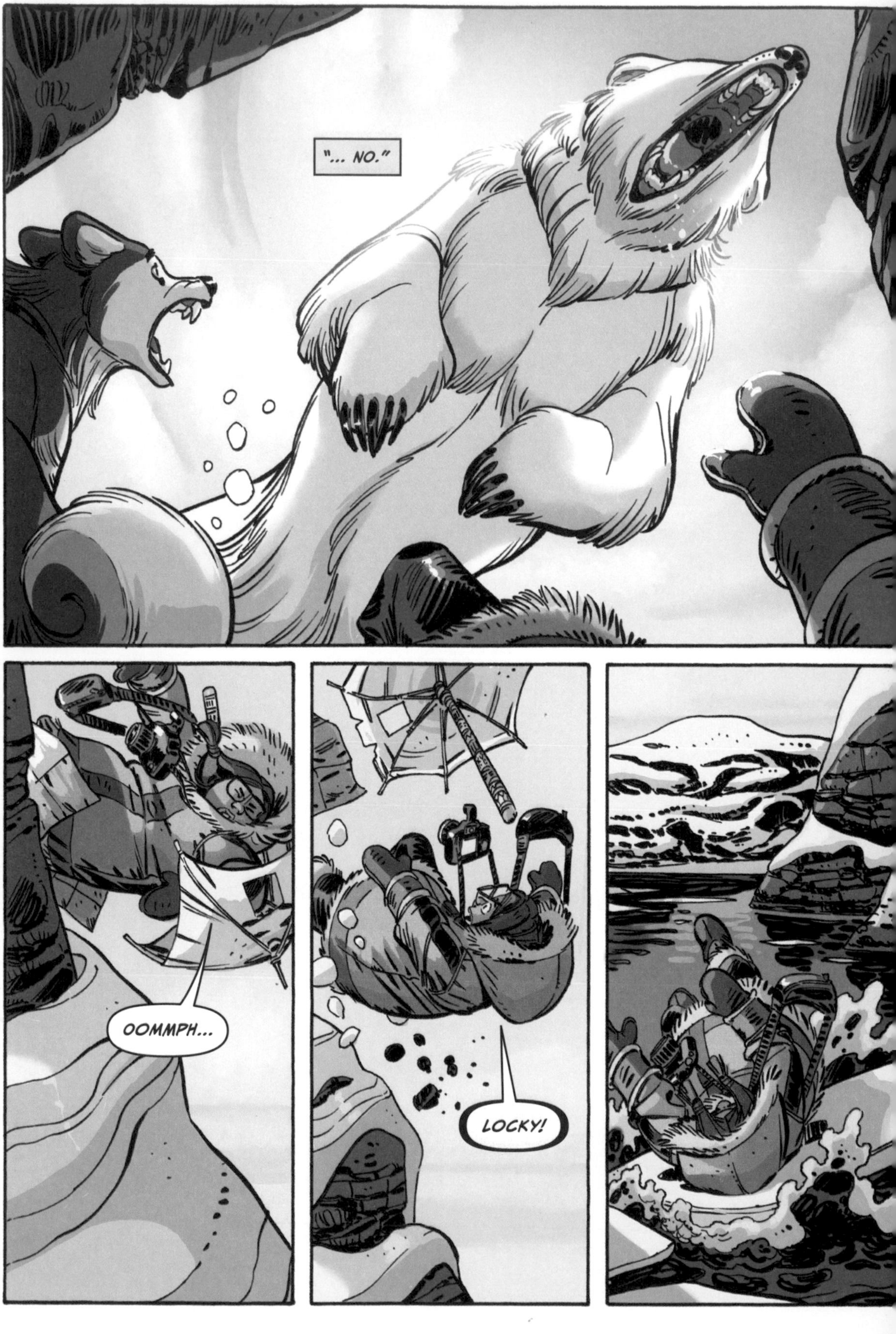
"... NO."
OOMMPH...
LOCKY!

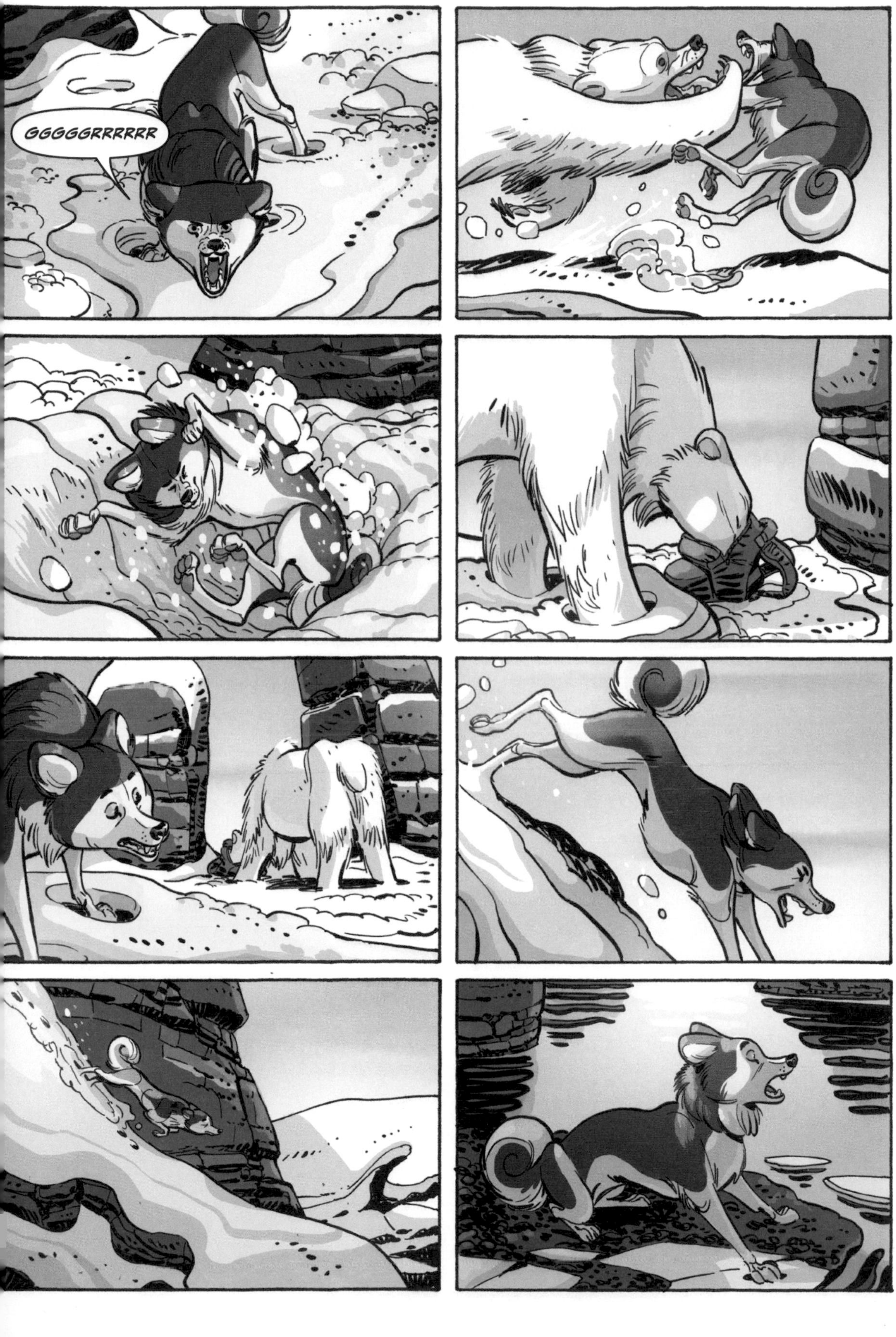
GGGGGRRRRRR

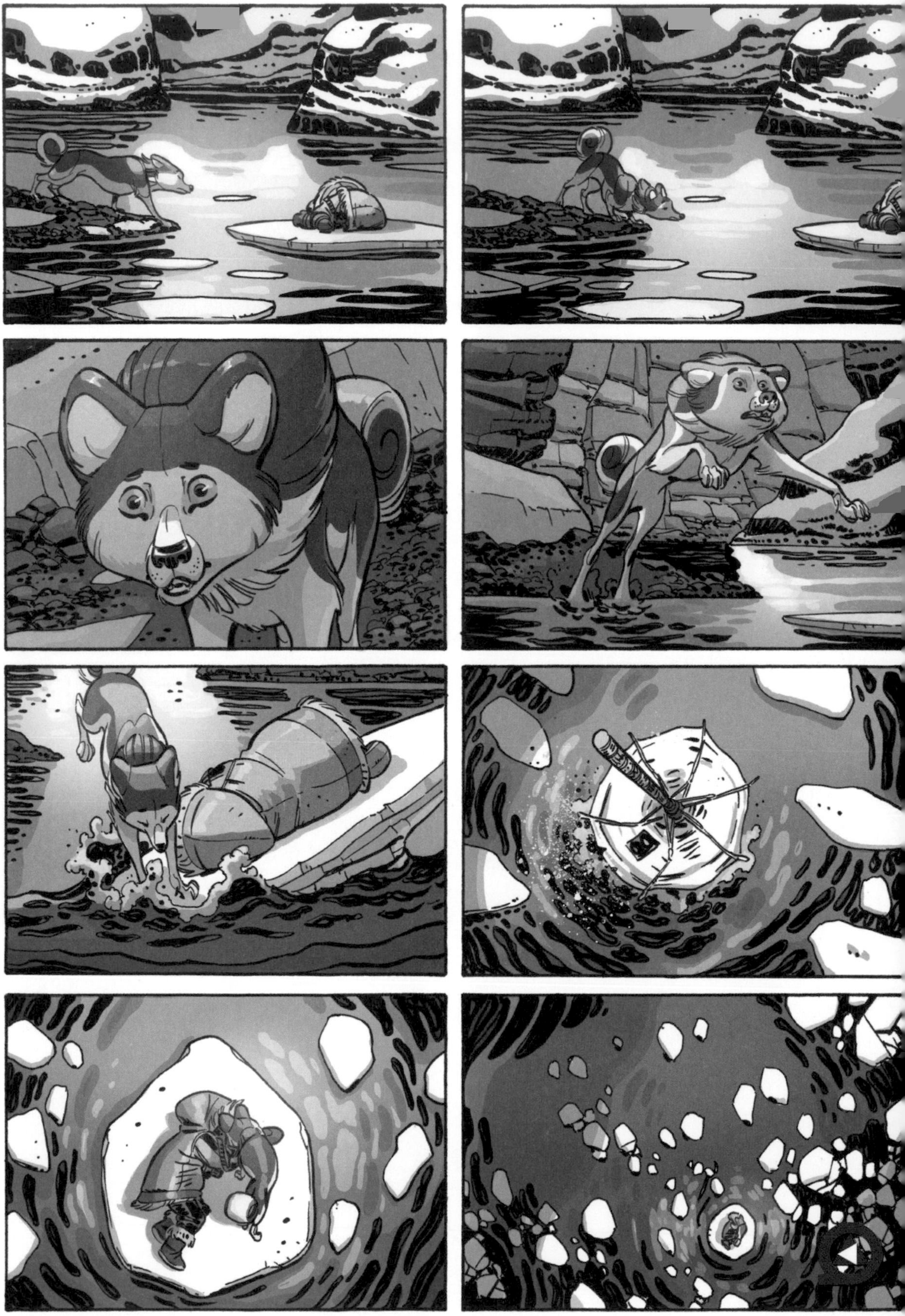

HERE

BAY OF BENGAL, INDIAN OCEAN.

CHAPTER 5

"WAKE UP."

It's the dream again.

"SAMI, WAKE UP."

The same dream.

"SAMI?"

That night. The storm.

We were rowing out and I fell asleep.

Fish.

They are much closer to the shore than normal.

Grandpa looks at the clouds on the horizon.

Maybe the fish know something?

Either way, it's good for us.

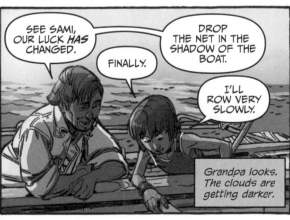

SEE SAMI, OUR LUCK *HAS* CHANGED.

FINALLY.

DROP THE NET IN THE SHADOW OF THE BOAT.

I'LL ROW VERY SLOWLY.

Grandpa looks. The clouds are getting darker.

"WAKE UP."

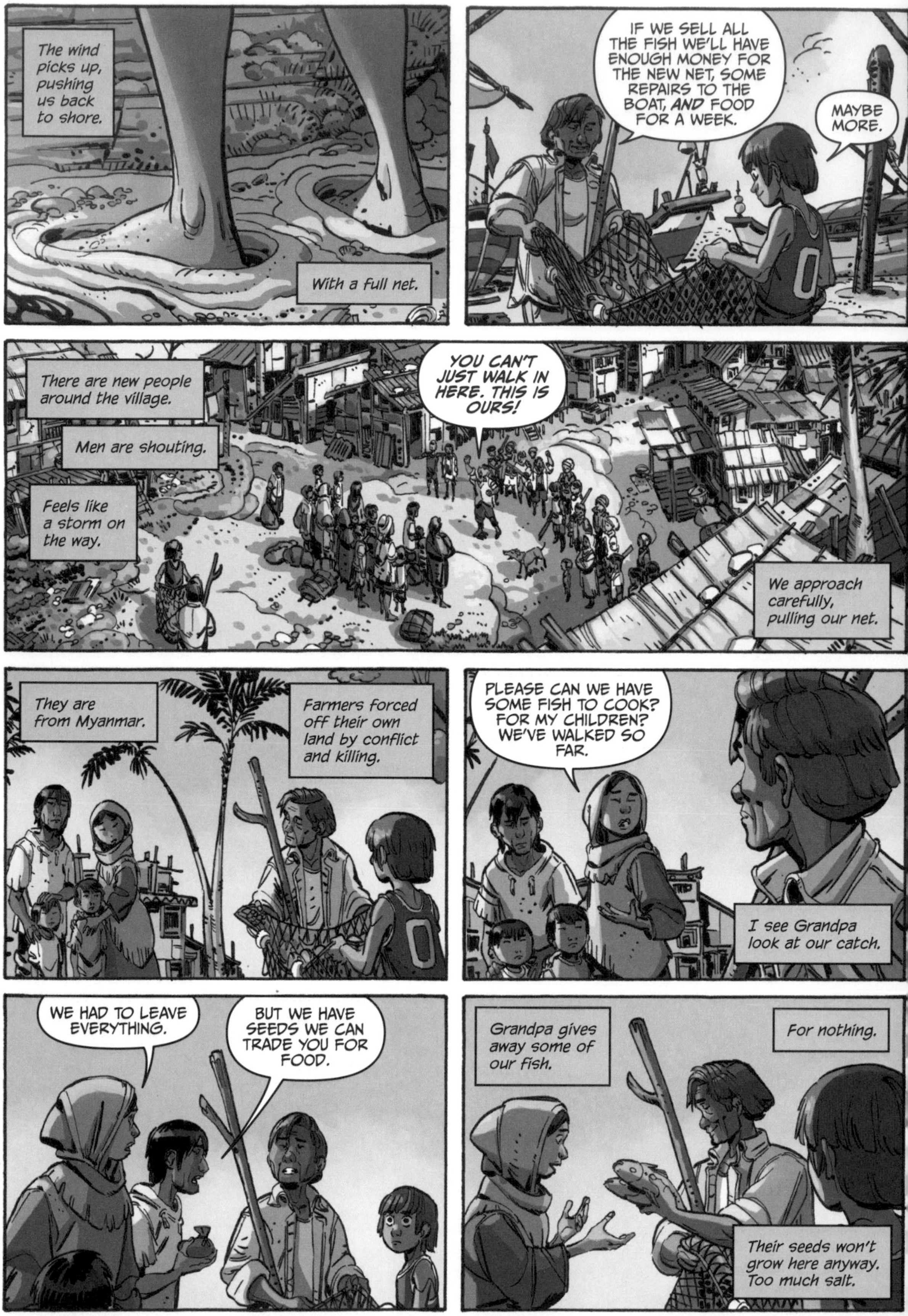
The wind picks up, pushing us back to shore.
With a full net.
IF WE SELL ALL THE FISH WE'LL HAVE ENOUGH MONEY FOR THE NEW NET, SOME REPAIRS TO THE BOAT, AND FOOD FOR A WEEK.
MAYBE MORE.
There are new people around the village.
Men are shouting.
Feels like a storm on the way.
YOU CAN'T JUST WALK IN HERE. THIS IS OURS!
We approach carefully, pulling our net.
They are from Myanmar.
Farmers forced off their own land by conflict and killing.
PLEASE CAN WE HAVE SOME FISH TO COOK? FOR MY CHILDREN? WE'VE WALKED SO FAR.
I see Grandpa look at our catch.
WE HAD TO LEAVE EVERYTHING.
BUT WE HAVE SEEDS WE CAN TRADE YOU FOR FOOD.
Grandpa gives away some of our fish.
For nothing.
Their seeds won't grow here anyway. Too much salt.

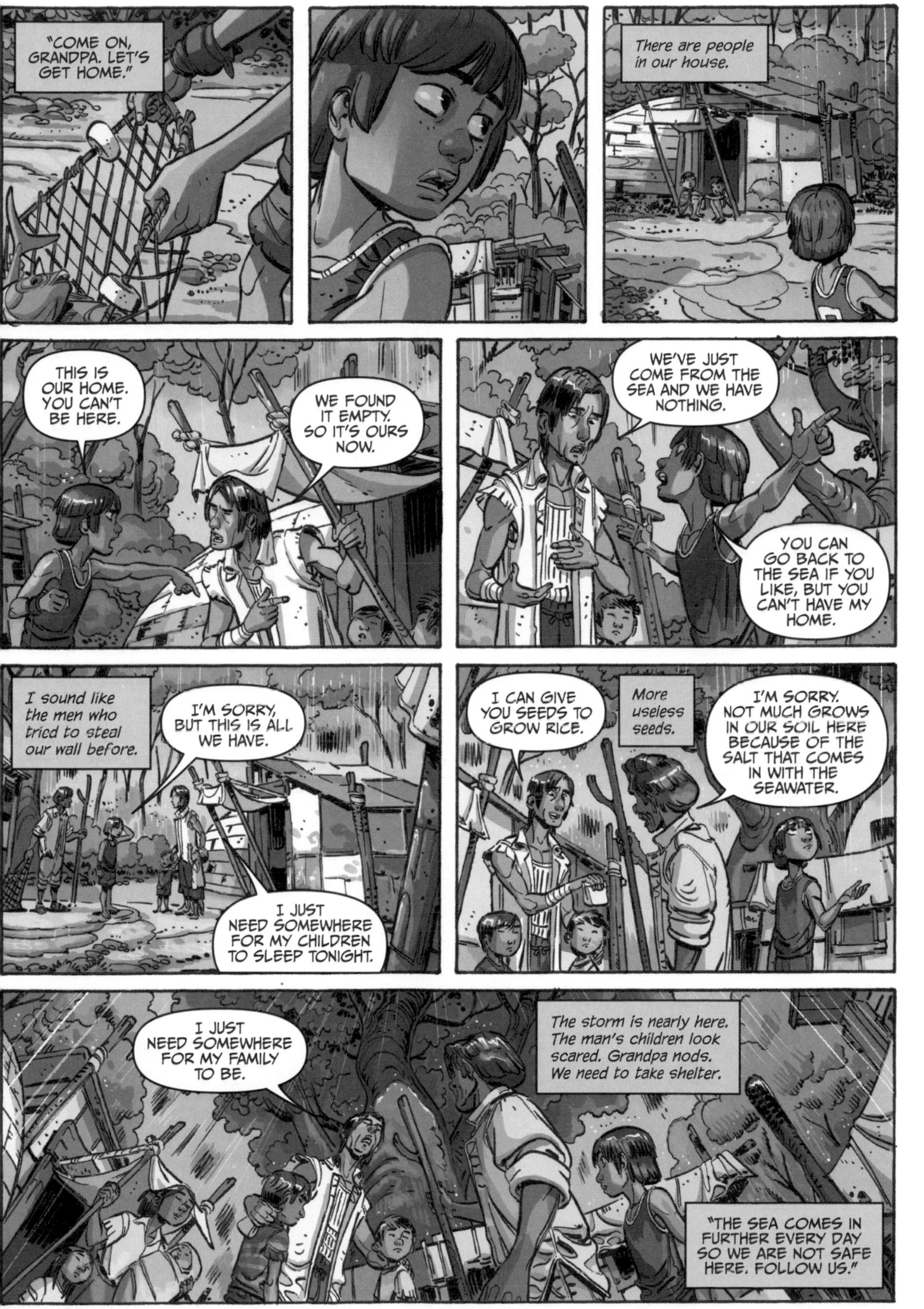
"COME ON, GRANDPA. LET'S GET HOME."
There are people in our house.
THIS IS OUR HOME. YOU CAN'T BE HERE.
WE FOUND IT EMPTY. SO IT'S OURS NOW.
WE'VE JUST COME FROM THE SEA AND WE HAVE NOTHING.
YOU CAN GO BACK TO THE SEA IF YOU LIKE, BUT YOU CAN'T HAVE MY HOME.
I sound like the men who tried to steal our wall before.
I'M SORRY, BUT THIS IS ALL WE HAVE.
I JUST NEED SOMEWHERE FOR MY CHILDREN TO SLEEP TONIGHT.
I CAN GIVE YOU SEEDS TO GROW RICE.
More useless seeds.
I'M SORRY. NOT MUCH GROWS IN OUR SOIL HERE BECAUSE OF THE SALT THAT COMES IN WITH THE SEAWATER.
I JUST NEED SOMEWHERE FOR MY FAMILY TO BE.
The storm is nearly here. The man's children look scared. Grandpa nods. We need to take shelter.
"THE SEA COMES IN FURTHER EVERY DAY SO WE ARE NOT SAFE HERE. FOLLOW US."

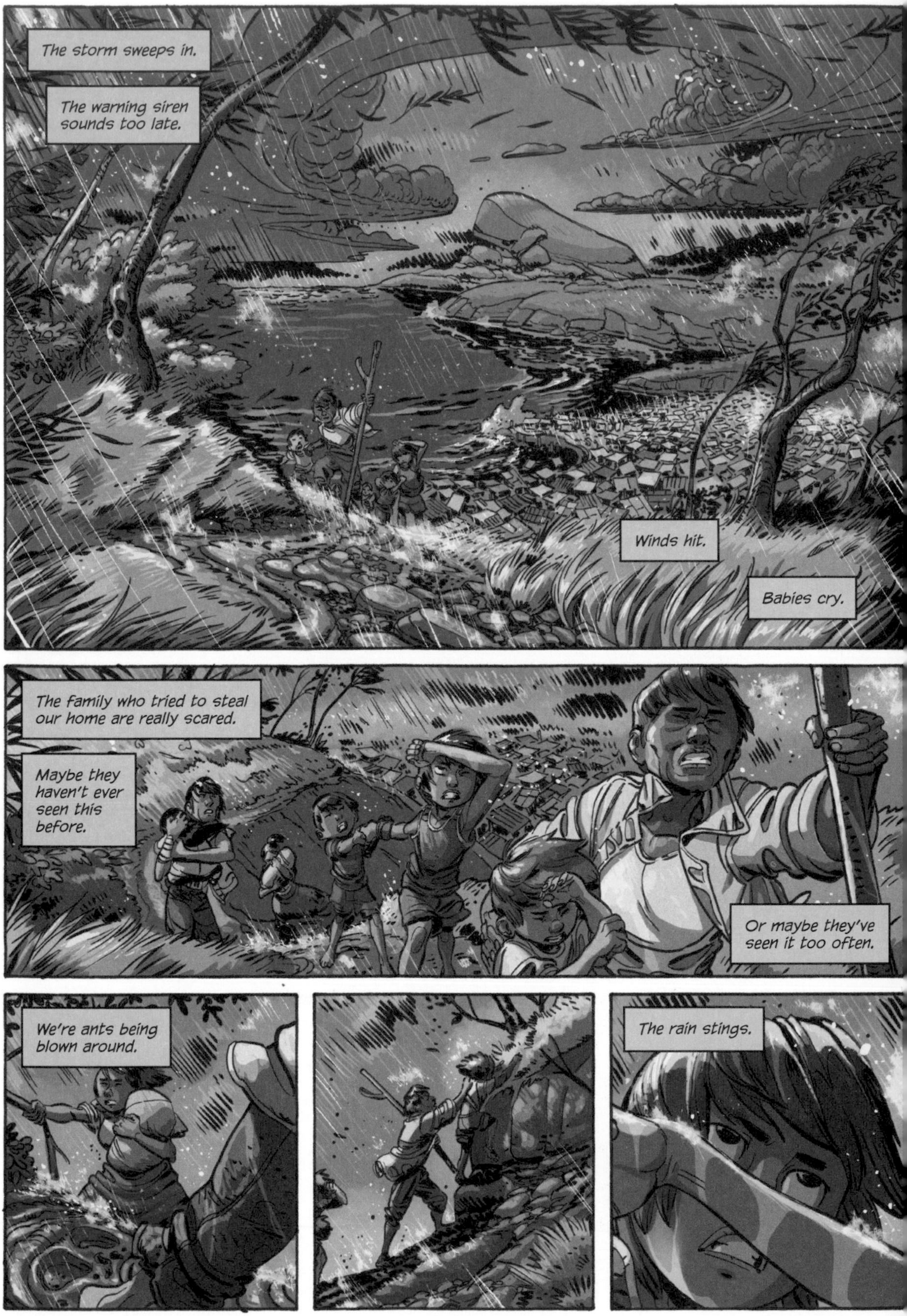
The storm sweeps in.
The warning siren sounds too late.
Winds hit.
Babies cry.
The family who tried to steal our home are really scared.
Maybe they haven't ever seen this before.
Or maybe they've seen it too often.
We're ants being blown around.
The rain stings.

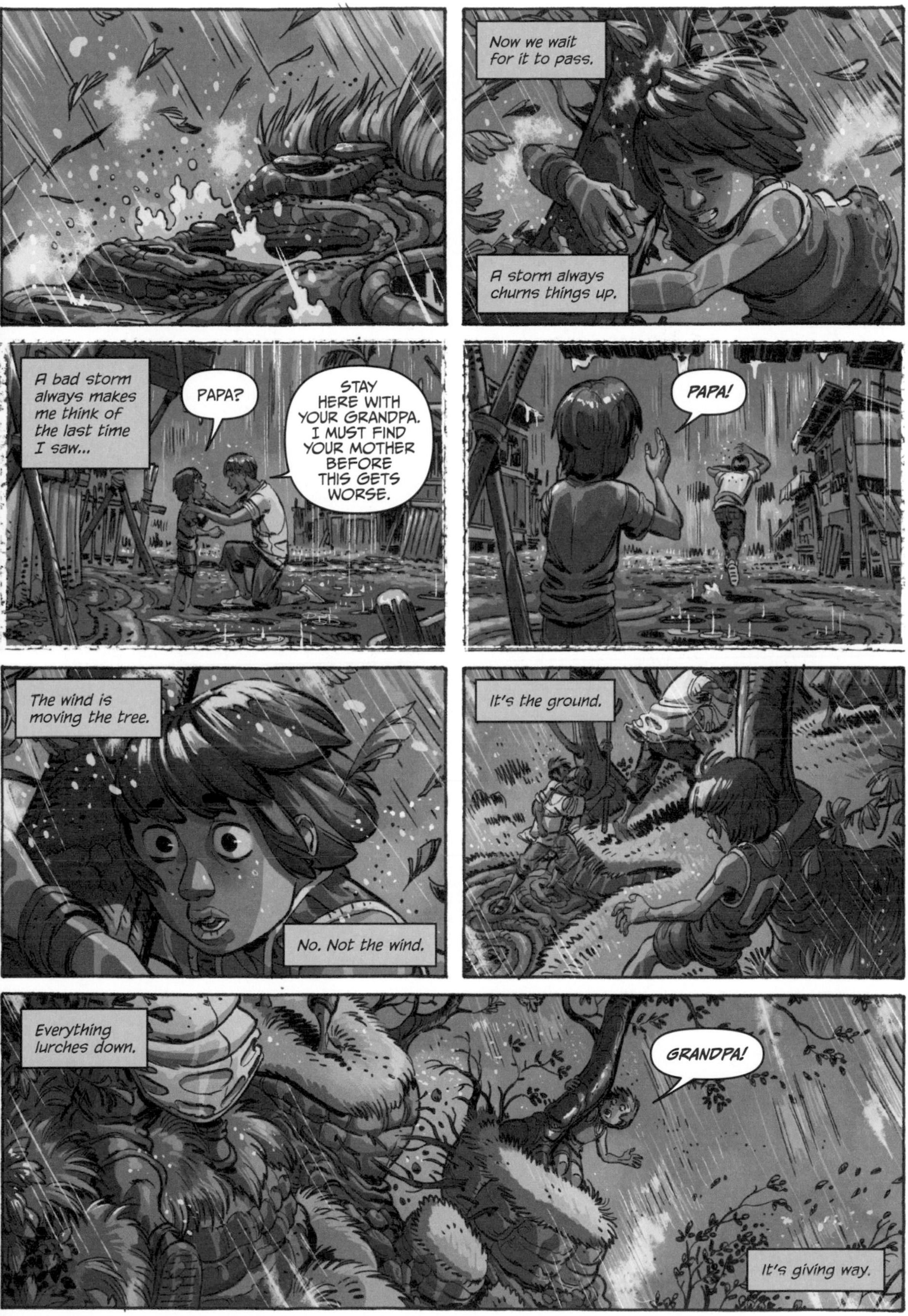

Now we wait for it to pass.
A storm always churns things up.
A bad storm always makes me think of the last time I saw...
PAPA?
STAY HERE WITH YOUR GRANDPA. I MUST FIND YOUR MOTHER BEFORE THIS GETS WORSE.
PAPA!
The wind is moving the tree.
No. Not the wind.
It's the ground.
Everything lurches down.
GRANDPA!
It's giving way.

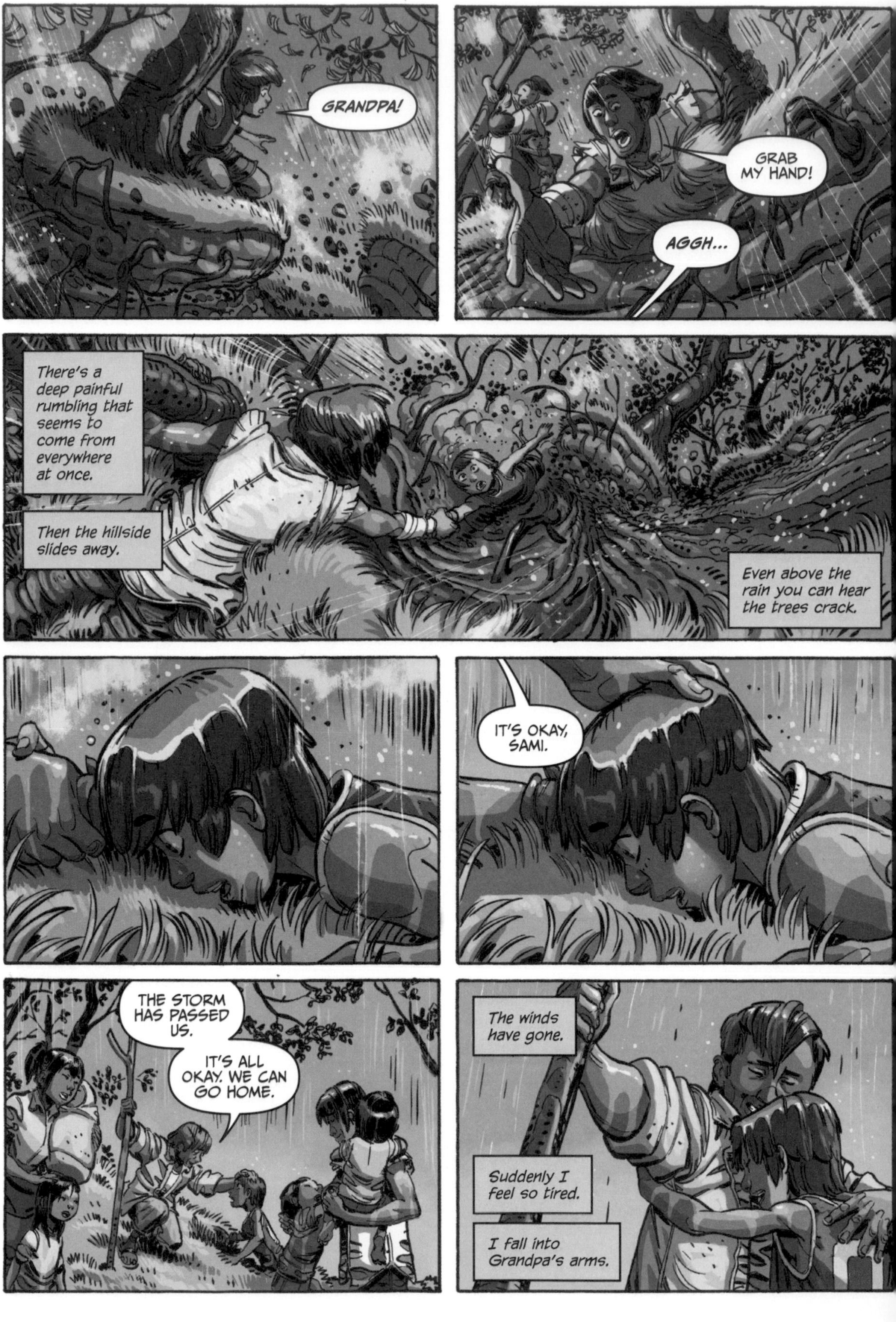
GRANDPA!
GRAB MY HAND!
AGGH...
There's a deep painful rumbling that seems to come from everywhere at once.
Then the hillside slides away.
Even above the rain you can hear the trees crack.
IT'S OKAY, SAMI.
THE STORM HAS PASSED US.
IT'S ALL OKAY. WE CAN GO HOME.
The winds have gone.
Suddenly I feel so tired.
I fall into Grandpa's arms.

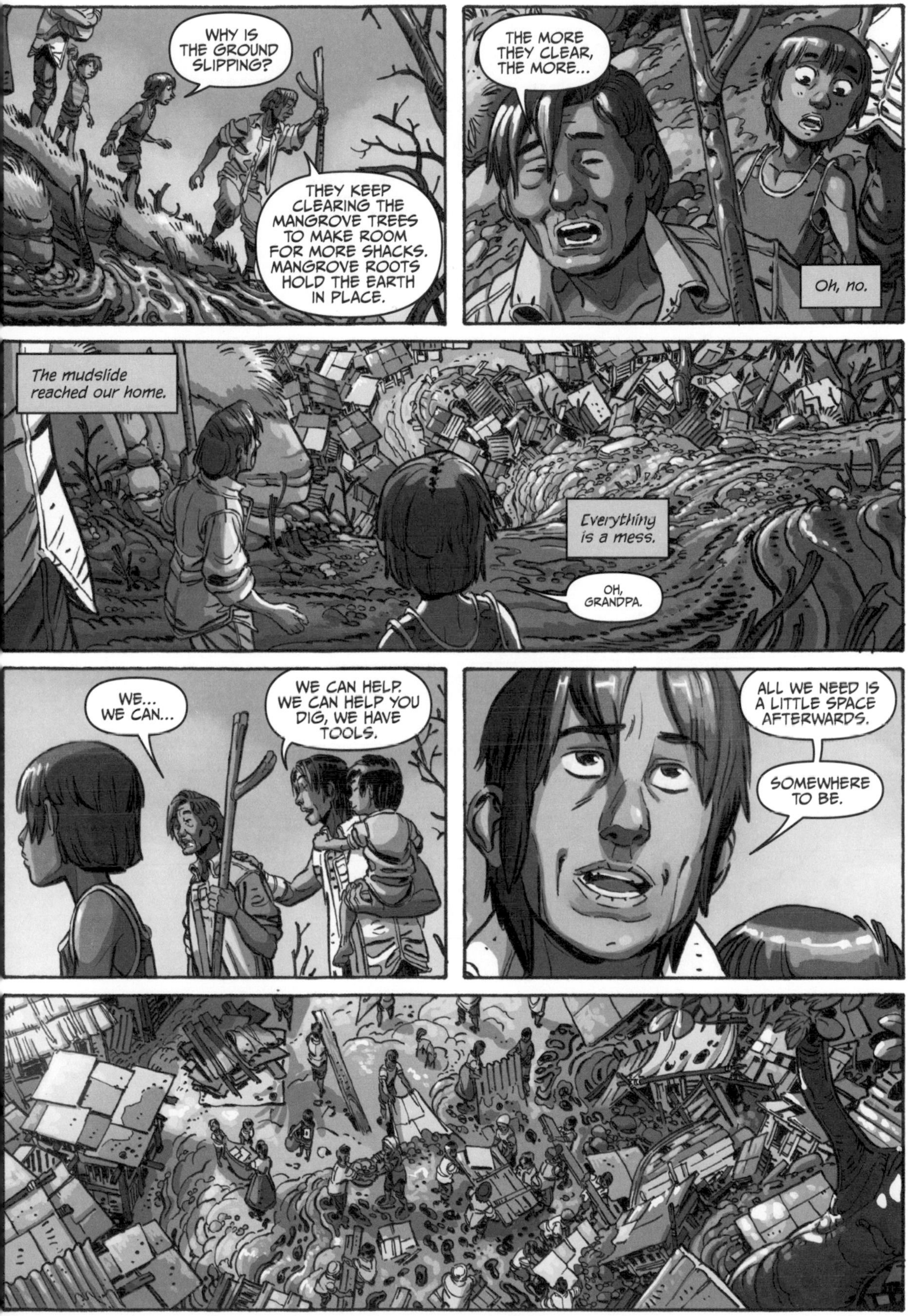
WHY IS THE GROUND SLIPPING?
THEY KEEP CLEARING THE MANGROVE TREES TO MAKE ROOM FOR MORE SHACKS. MANGROVE ROOTS HOLD THE EARTH IN PLACE.
THE MORE THEY CLEAR, THE MORE...
Oh, no.
The mudslide reached our home.
Everything is a mess.
OH, GRANDPA.
WE... WE CAN...
WE CAN HELP. WE CAN HELP YOU DIG, WE HAVE TOOLS.
ALL WE NEED IS A LITTLE SPACE AFTERWARDS.
SOMEWHERE TO BE.

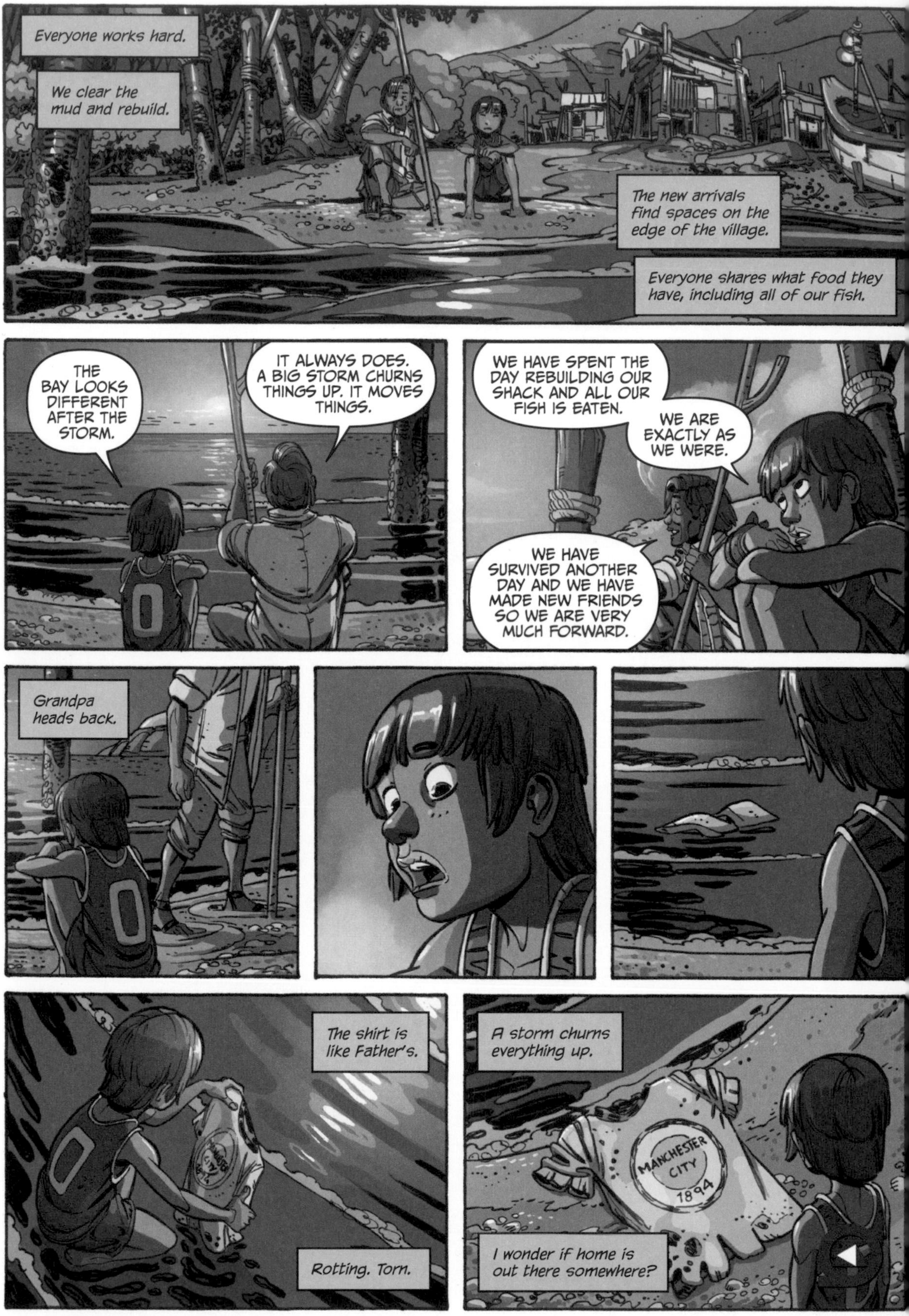
Everyone works hard.
We clear the mud and rebuild.
The new arrivals find spaces on the edge of the village.
Everyone shares what food they have, including all of our fish.
THE BAY LOOKS DIFFERENT AFTER THE STORM.
IT ALWAYS DOES. A BIG STORM CHURNS THINGS UP. IT MOVES THINGS.
WE HAVE SPENT THE DAY REBUILDING OUR SHACK AND ALL OUR FISH IS EATEN.
WE ARE EXACTLY AS WE WERE.
WE HAVE SURVIVED ANOTHER DAY AND WE HAVE MADE NEW FRIENDS SO WE ARE VERY MUCH FORWARD.
Grandpa heads back.
The shirt is like Father's.
Rotting. Torn.
A storm churns everything up.
MANCHESTER CITY 1894
I wonder if home is out there somewhere?

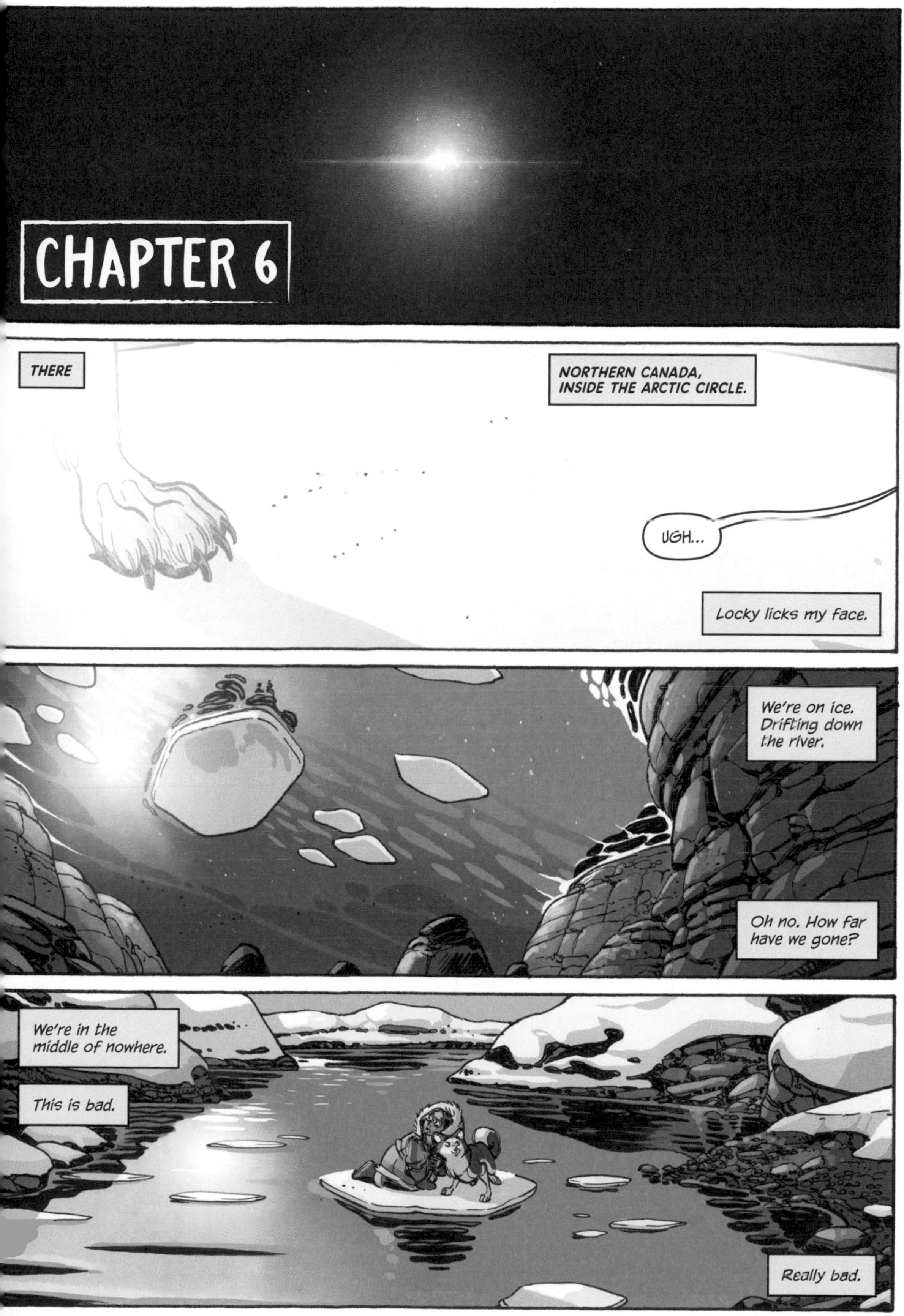
CHAPTER 6
THERE
NORTHERN CANADA, INSIDE THE ARCTIC CIRCLE.
UGH...
Locky licks my face.
We're on ice. Drifting down the river.
Oh no. How far have we gone?
We're in the middle of nowhere.
This is bad.
Really bad.

At least we've moved away from the bear.

For now.

So cold.

...

Locky is whining. He's anxious.

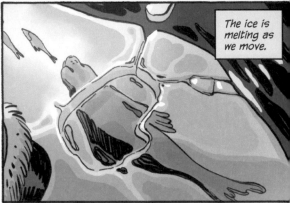

The ice is melting as we move.

IF EITHER OF US FALLS IN THE WATER, WE WON'T LIVE LONG IN THIS COLD.

WE HAVE TO GET OFF THIS MELTING ICE, LOCKY.

NOW.

YOU GOTTA JUMP WITH ME, BOY. OK?

READY?

JUMP!

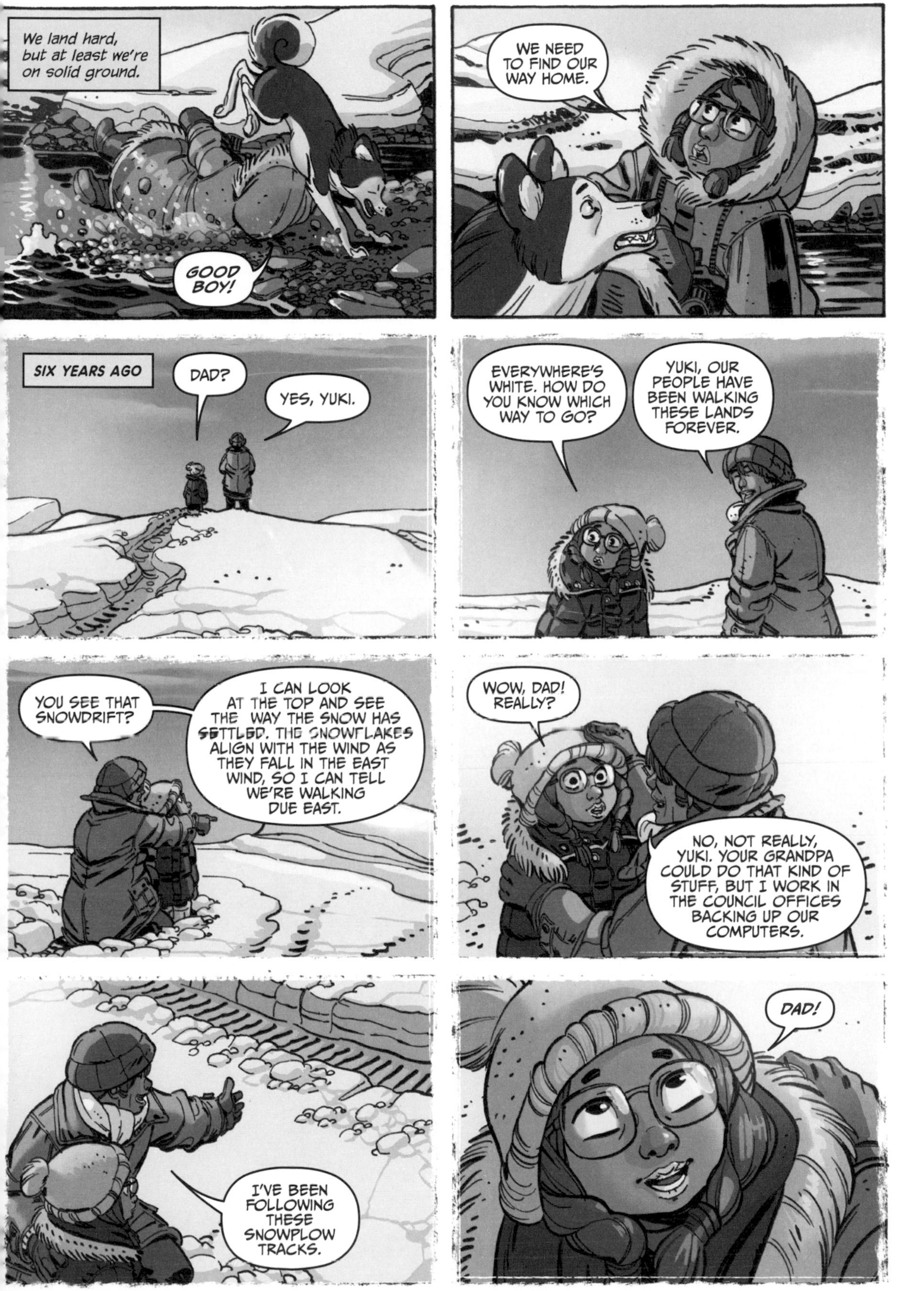
We land hard, but at least we're on solid ground.
GOOD BOY!
WE NEED TO FIND OUR WAY HOME.
SIX YEARS AGO
DAD?
YES, YUKI.
EVERYWHERE'S WHITE. HOW DO YOU KNOW WHICH WAY TO GO?
YUKI, OUR PEOPLE HAVE BEEN WALKING THESE LANDS FOREVER.
YOU SEE THAT SNOWDRIFT?
I CAN LOOK AT THE TOP AND SEE THE WAY THE SNOW HAS SETTLED. THE SNOWFLAKES ALIGN WITH THE WIND AS THEY FALL IN THE EAST WIND, SO I CAN TELL WE'RE WALKING DUE EAST.
WOW, DAD! REALLY?
NO, NOT REALLY, YUKI. YOUR GRANDPA COULD DO THAT KIND OF STUFF, BUT I WORK IN THE COUNCIL OFFICES BACKING UP OUR COMPUTERS.
I'VE BEEN FOLLOWING THESE SNOWPLOW TRACKS.
DAD!

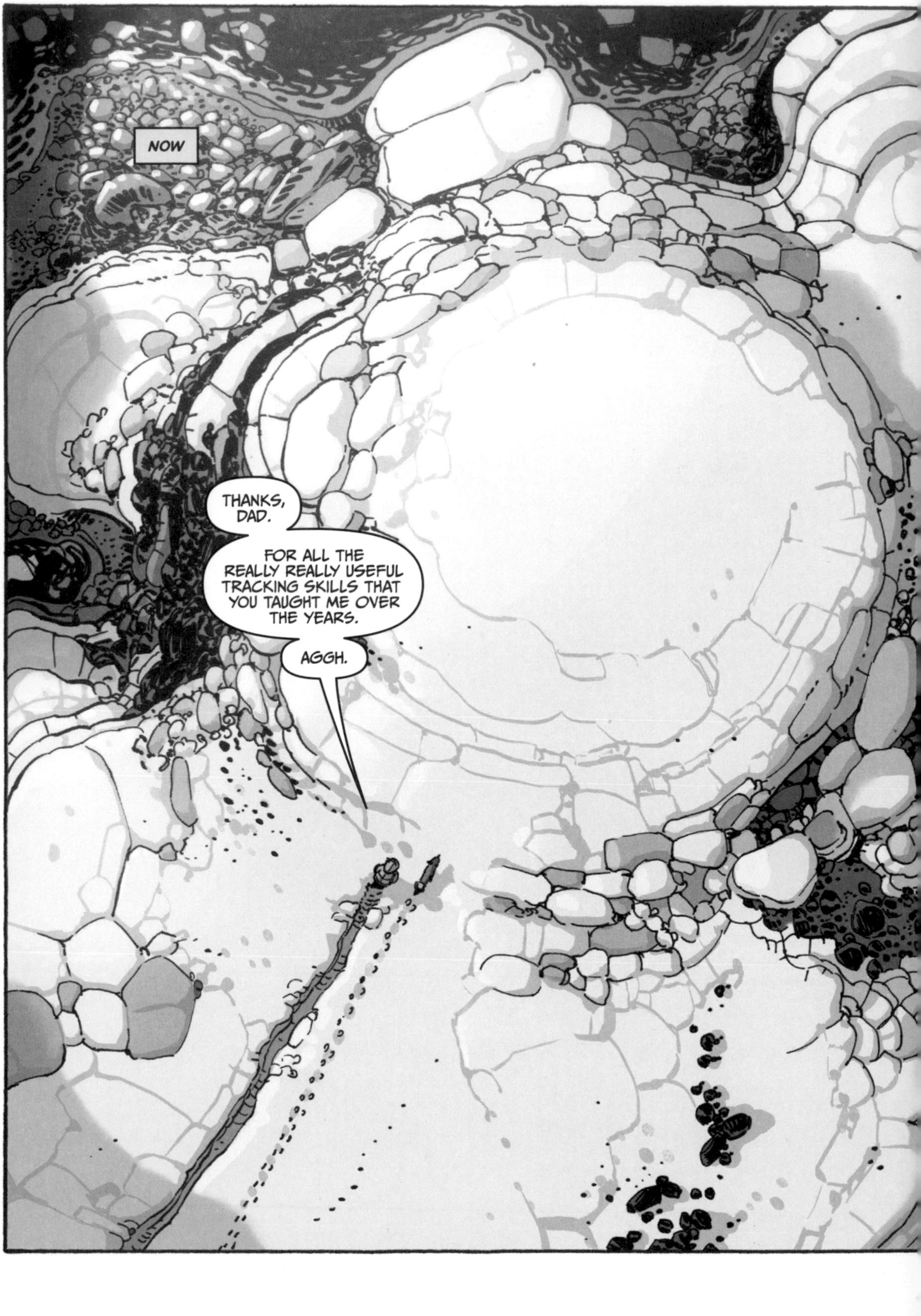
NOW
THANKS, DAD.
FOR ALL THE REALLY REALLY USEFUL TRACKING SKILLS THAT YOU TAUGHT ME OVER THE YEARS.
AGGH.

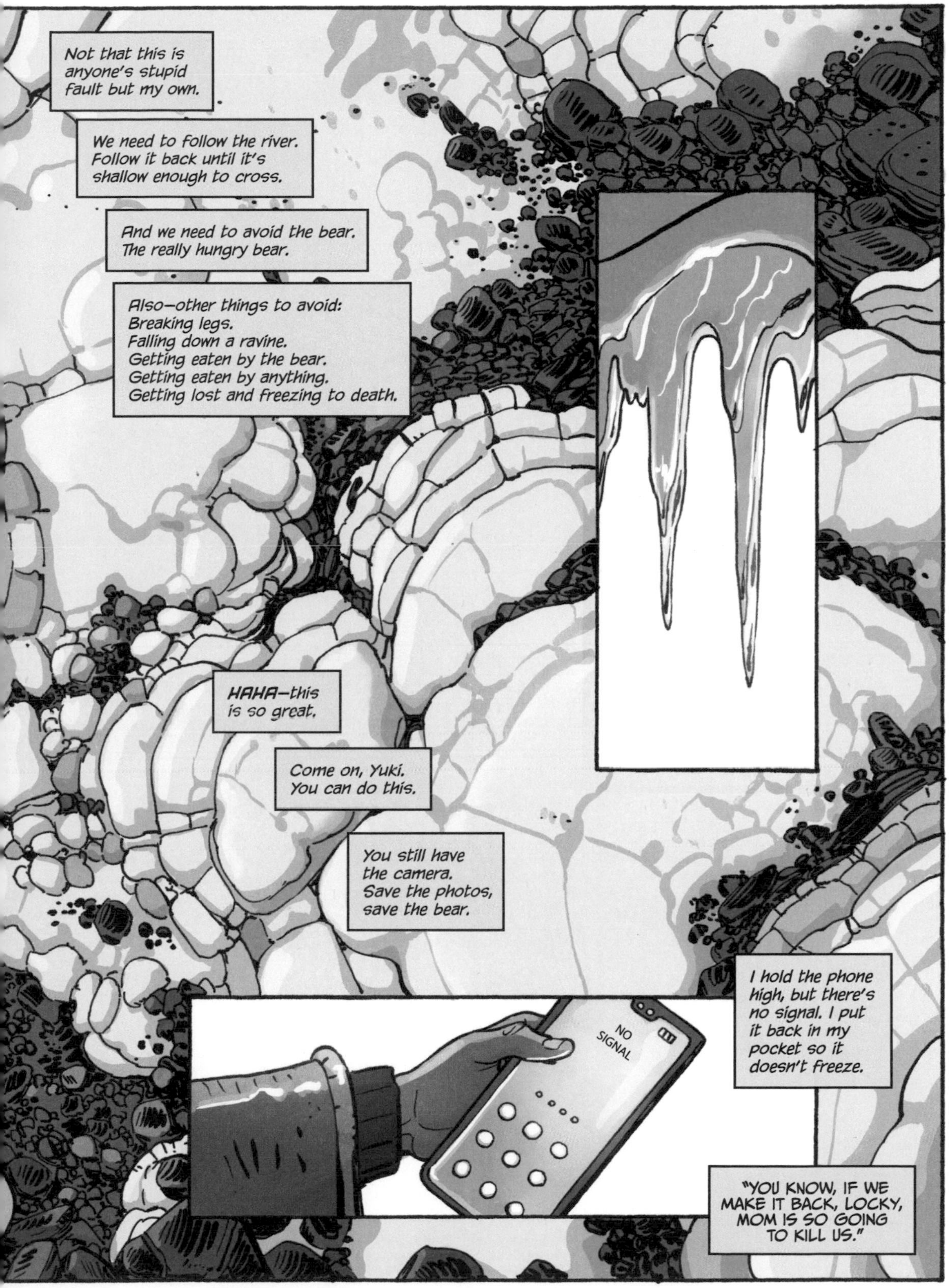
Not that this is anyone's stupid fault but my own.
We need to follow the river. Follow it back until it's shallow enough to cross.
And we need to avoid the bear. The really hungry bear.
Also—other things to avoid: Breaking legs. Falling down a ravine. Getting eaten by the bear. Getting eaten by anything. Getting lost and freezing to death.
HAHA—this is so great.
Come on, Yuki. You can do this.
You still have the camera. Save the photos, save the bear.
I hold the phone high, but there's no signal. I put it back in my pocket so it doesn't freeze.
NO SIGNAL
"YOU KNOW, IF WE MAKE IT BACK, LOCKY, MOM IS SO GOING TO KILL US."

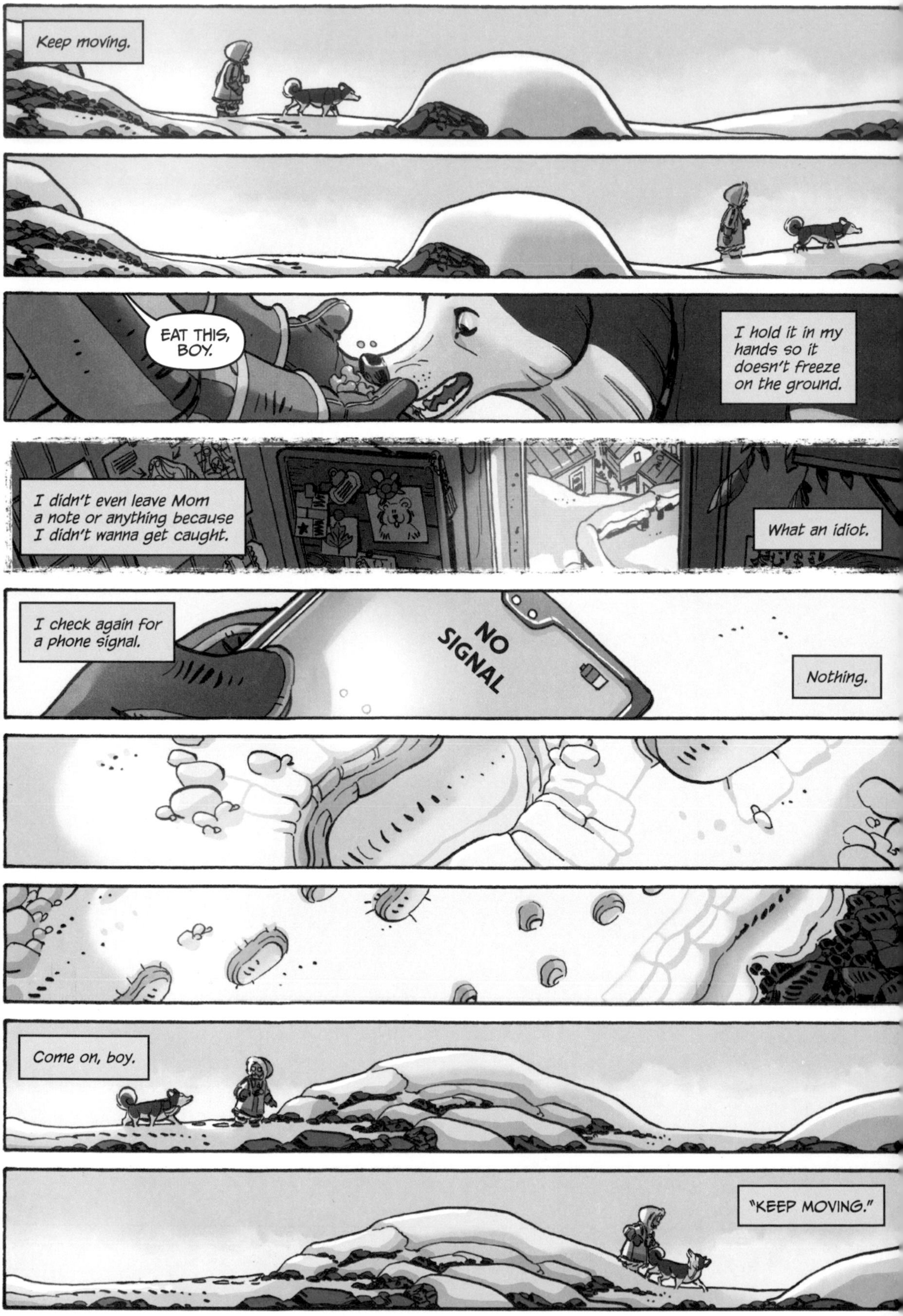

Keep moving.
EAT THIS, BOY.
I hold it in my hands so it doesn't freeze on the ground.
I didn't even leave Mom a note or anything because I didn't wanna get caught.
What an idiot.
I check again for a phone signal.
NO SIGNAL
Nothing.
Come on, boy.
"KEEP MOVING."

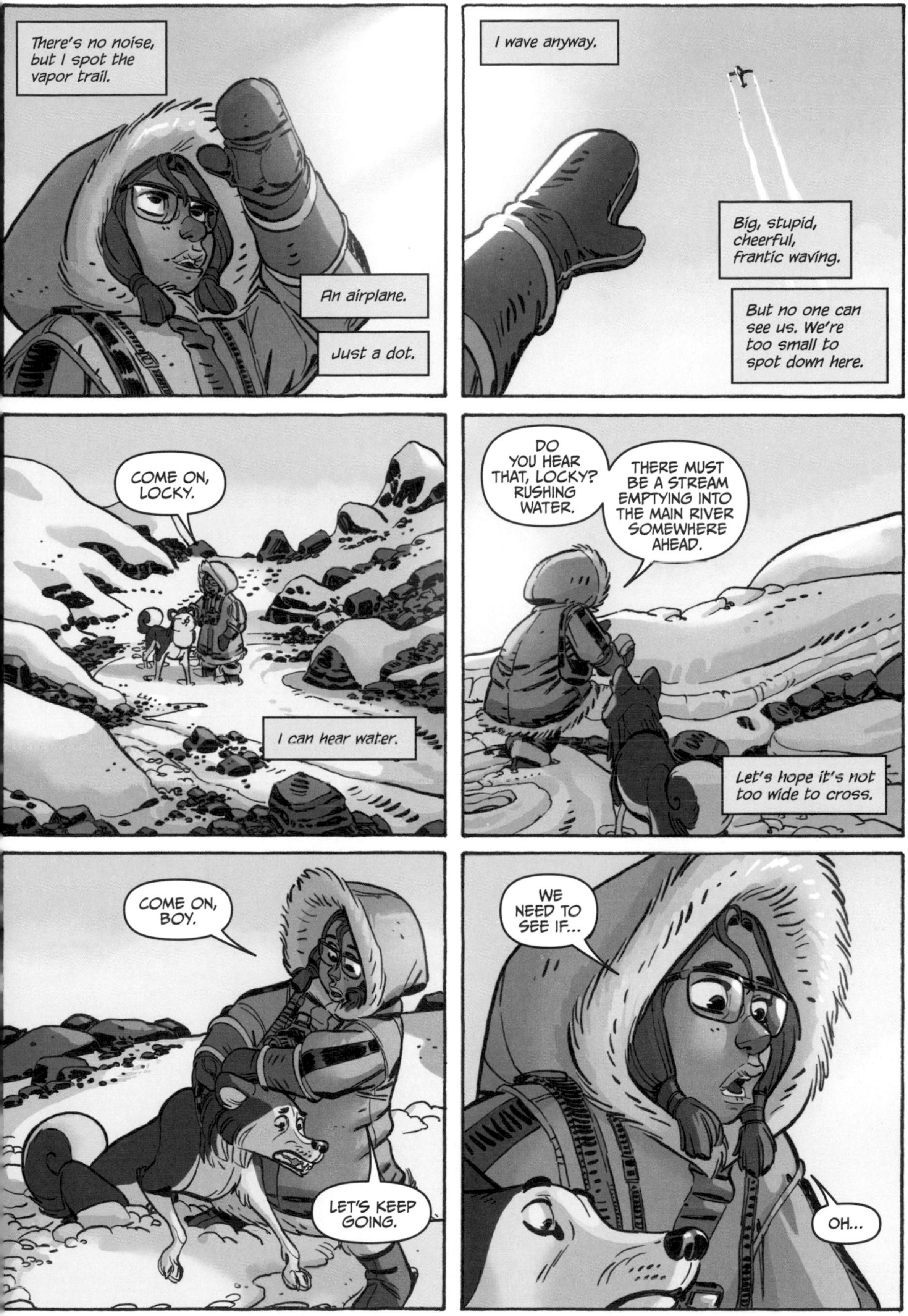
There's no noise, but I spot the vapor trail.
An airplane.
Just a dot.
I wave anyway.
Big, stupid, cheerful, frantic waving.
But no one can see us. We're too small to spot down here.
COME ON, LOCKY.
I can hear water.
DO YOU HEAR THAT, LOCKY? RUSHING WATER.
THERE MUST BE A STREAM EMPTYING INTO THE MAIN RIVER SOMEWHERE AHEAD.
Let's hope it's not too wide to cross.
COME ON, BOY.
LET'S KEEP GOING.
WE NEED TO SEE IF...
OH...

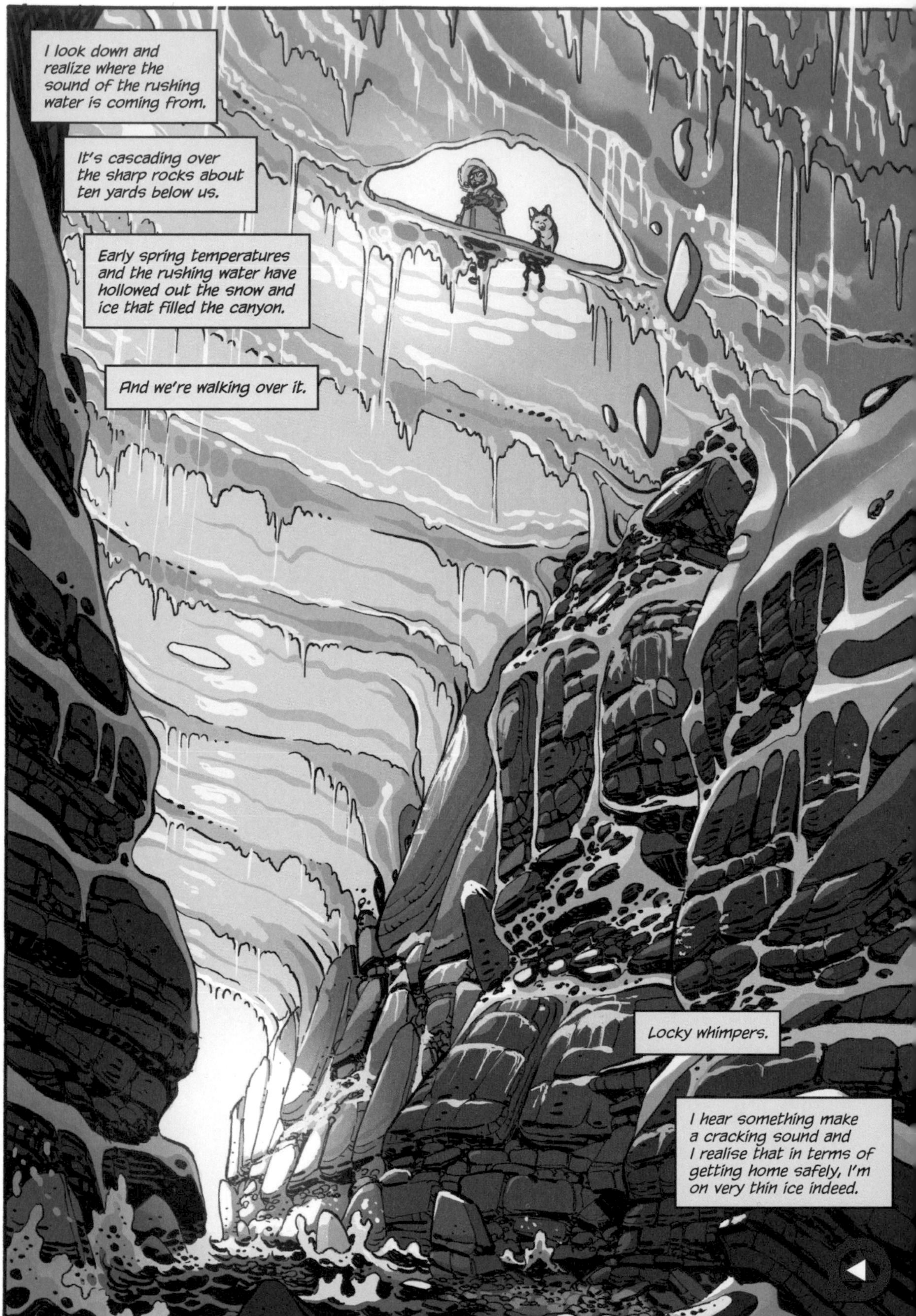
I look down and realize where the sound of the rushing water is coming from.
It's cascading over the sharp rocks about ten yards below us.
Early spring temperatures and the rushing water have hollowed out the snow and ice that filled the canyon.
And we're walking over it.
Locky whimpers.
I hear something make a cracking sound and I realise that in terms of getting home safely, I'm on very thin ice indeed.

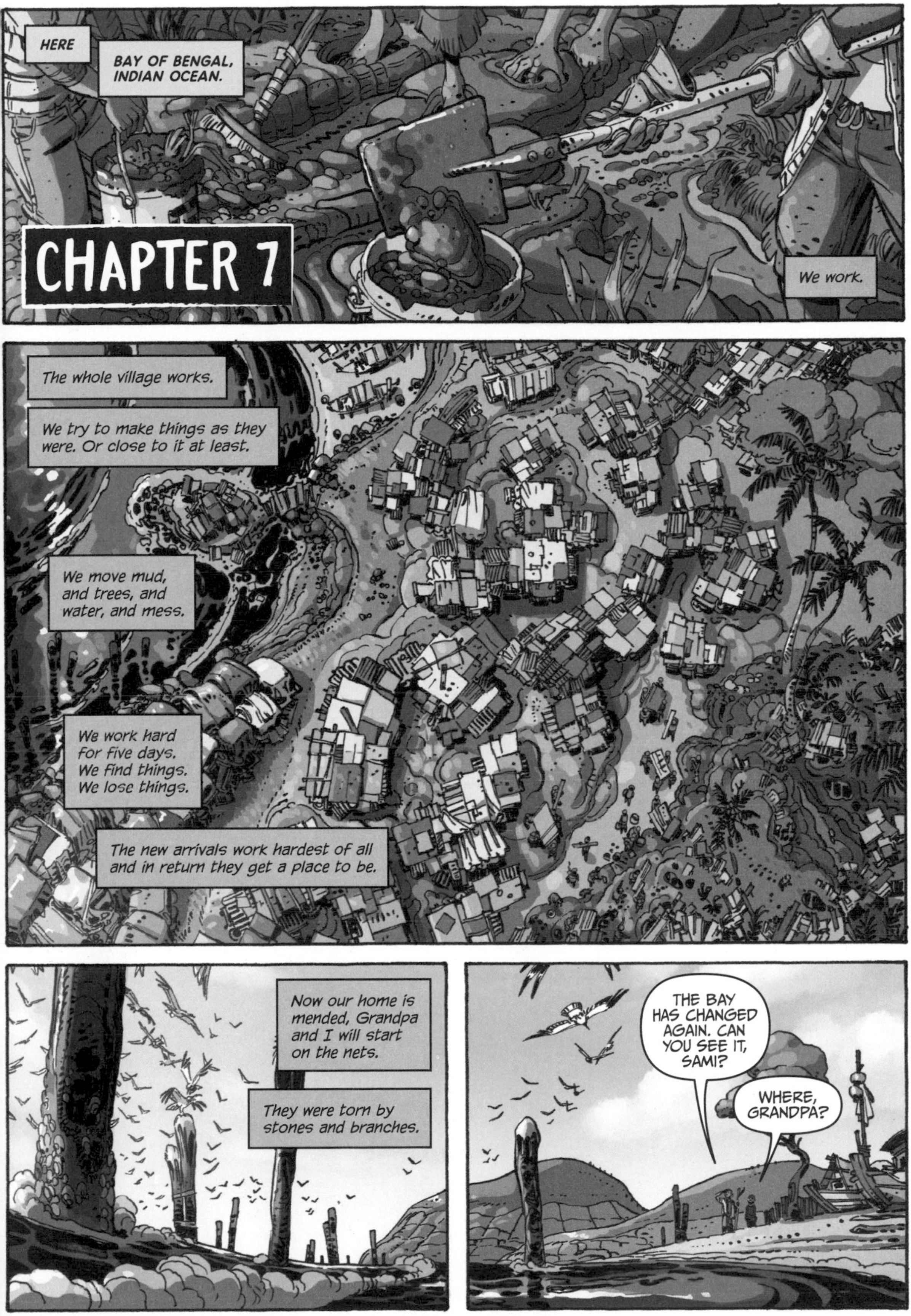
HERE
BAY OF BENGAL, INDIAN OCEAN.
CHAPTER 7
We work.
The whole village works.
We try to make things as they were. Or close to it at least.
We move mud, and trees, and water, and mess.
We work hard for five days. We find things. We lose things.
The new arrivals work hardest of all and in return they get a place to be.
Now our home is mended, Grandpa and I will start on the nets.
They were torn by stones and branches.
THE BAY HAS CHANGED AGAIN. CAN YOU SEE IT, SAMI?
WHERE, GRANDPA?

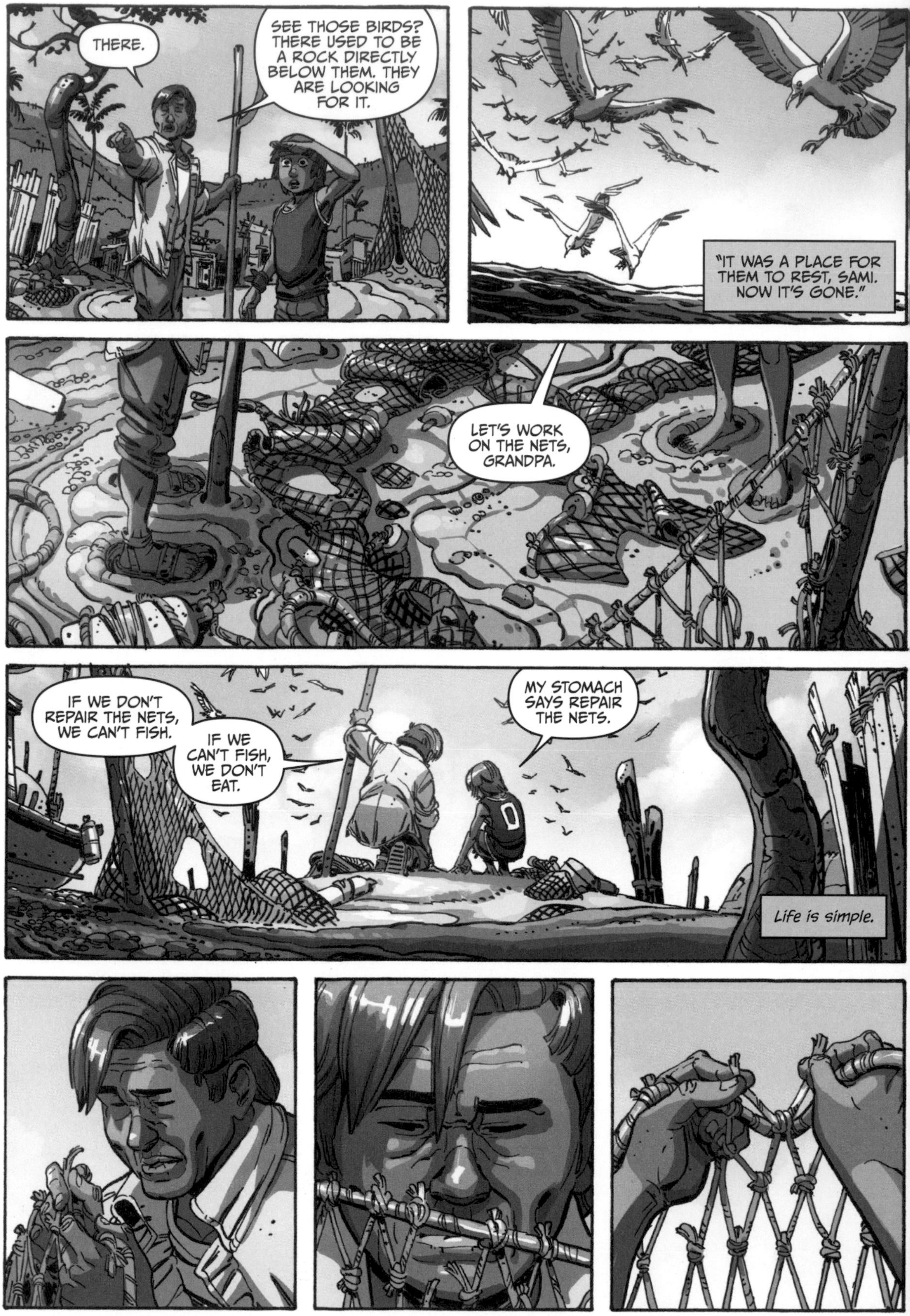
THERE.
SEE THOSE BIRDS? THERE USED TO BE A ROCK DIRECTLY BELOW THEM. THEY ARE LOOKING FOR IT.
"IT WAS A PLACE FOR THEM TO REST, SAMI. NOW IT'S GONE."
LET'S WORK ON THE NETS, GRANDPA.
IF WE DON'T REPAIR THE NETS, WE CAN'T FISH.
IF WE CAN'T FISH, WE DON'T EAT.
MY STOMACH SAYS REPAIR THE NETS.
Life is simple.

WHAT?

NOTHING, GRANDPA.

IT'S NOT THAT MY EYES ARE GETTING WORSE, SAMI.

THE THREADS ON THIS NET ARE GETTING SMALLER!

HA!

"WE'RE NEARLY DONE, SAMI. ONCE WE HAVE OUR NETS BACK WE CAN FISH AGAIN."

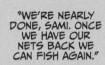

"WE NEED MORE THAN NETS, WE WILL NEED LUCK AS WELL."

"WE ALWAYS FIND LUCK, SAMI."

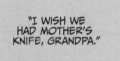

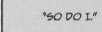

"I WISH WE HAD MOTHER'S KNIFE, GRANDPA."

"SO DO I."

"IT WAS HER FATHER'S BEFORE HER AND SHE ALWAYS SAID IT CARRIED LUCK INSIDE THE BLADE."

"I KNOW."

"I REMEMBER YOU AND FATHER WORKING WITH IT. BEFORE... BEFORE THEY WEREN'T HERE."

"FORGET THE KNIFE, SAMI."

"BUT GRANDPA..."

"THE KNIFE IS LOST."

So much is lost.

Mother is gone.

YOUR FATHER SAID YOU WERE SO GOOD AT FISHING TODAY. I'M SO PROUD OF YOU.

Father, too.

WHEN WE'VE FINISHED THIS, WE'LL HAVE A BIGGER BOAT AND WE CAN CATCH MORE FISH.

BUY SOME BETTER NETS AND SOON BUILD *ANOTHER* BOAT.

Even the knife...

THIS WAS MY FATHER'S BEFORE ME, AND ONE DAY, SAMI, IT WILL BE YOURS TO BRING LUCK TO YOUR OWN FAMILY.

"IN TIME OF COURSE, WHEN YOU'RE GROWN. I'M NOT READY TO PASS IT ON YET."

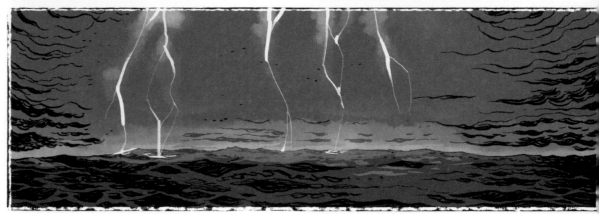

PAPA?

STAY HERE WITH YOUR GRANDPA. I MUST FIND YOUR MOTHER BEFORE THIS GETS WORSE.

PAPA!

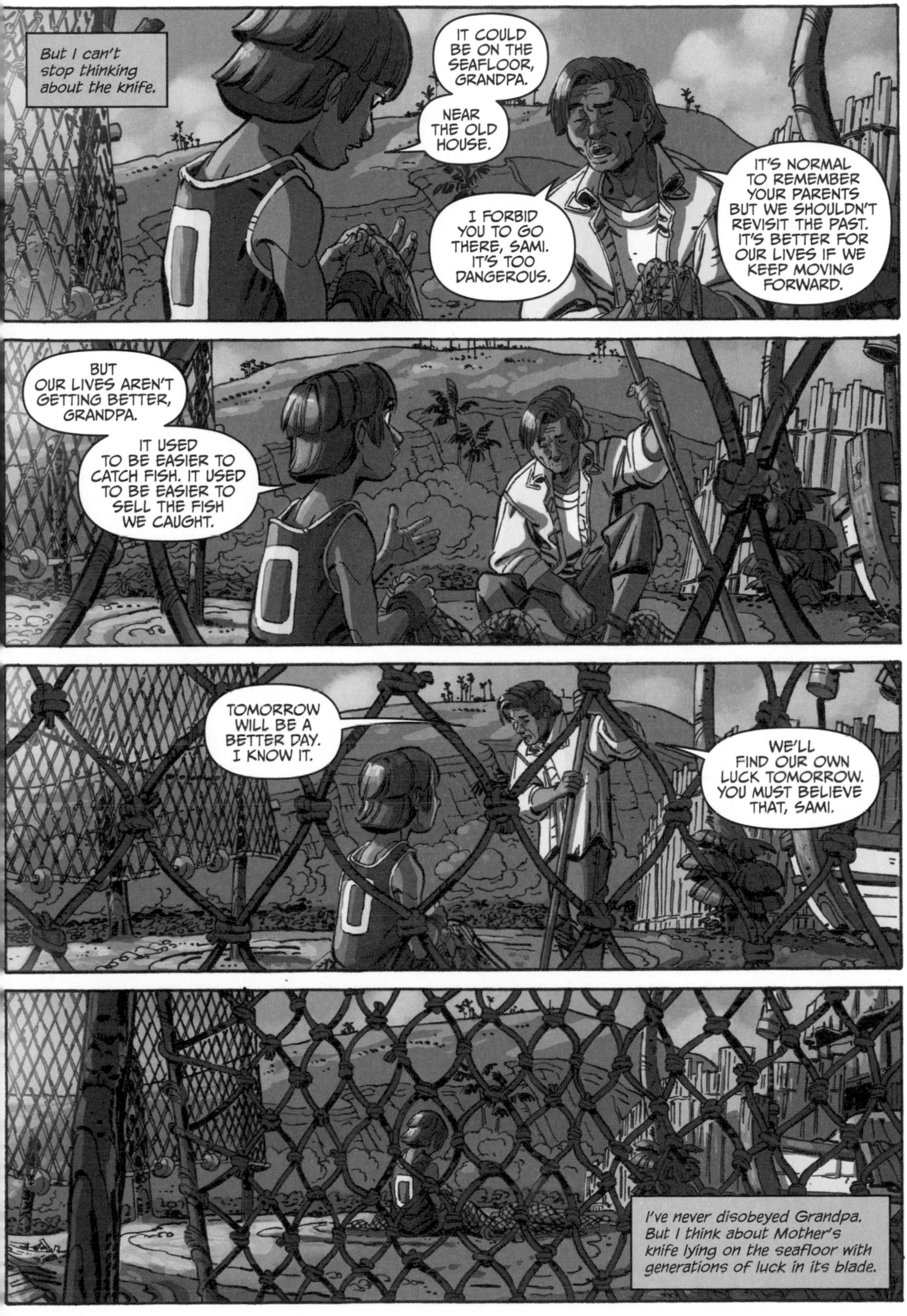
But I can't stop thinking about the knife.
IT COULD BE ON THE SEAFLOOR, GRANDPA.
NEAR THE OLD HOUSE.
I FORBID YOU TO GO THERE, SAMI. IT'S TOO DANGEROUS.
IT'S NORMAL TO REMEMBER YOUR PARENTS BUT WE SHOULDN'T REVISIT THE PAST. IT'S BETTER FOR OUR LIVES IF WE KEEP MOVING FORWARD.
BUT OUR LIVES AREN'T GETTING BETTER, GRANDPA.
IT USED TO BE EASIER TO CATCH FISH. IT USED TO BE EASIER TO SELL THE FISH WE CAUGHT.
TOMORROW WILL BE A BETTER DAY. I KNOW IT.
WE'LL FIND OUR OWN LUCK TOMORROW. YOU MUST BELIEVE THAT, SAMI.
I've never disobeyed Grandpa. But I think about Mother's knife lying on the seafloor with generations of luck in its blade.

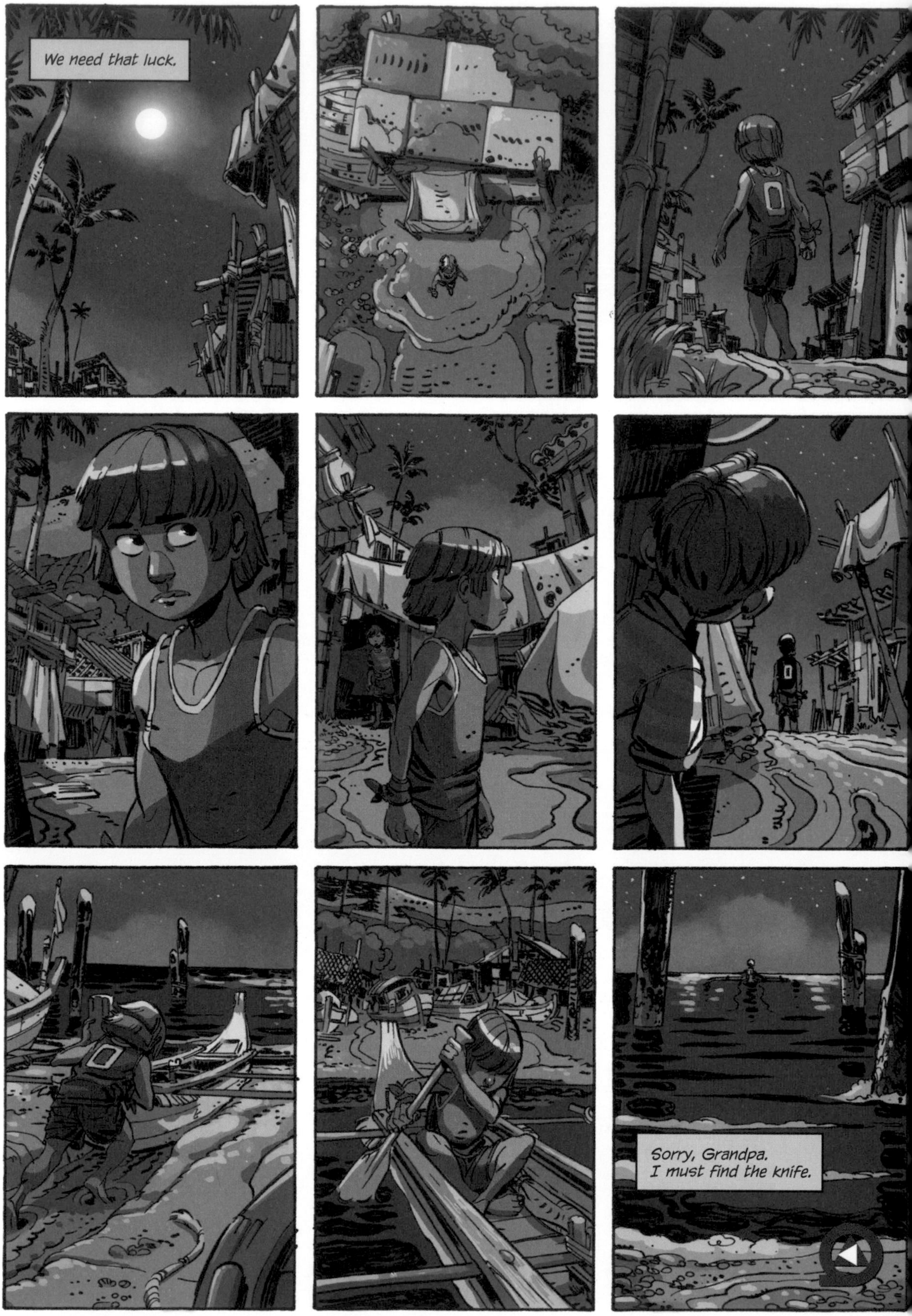
We need that luck.
Sorry, Grandpa. I must find the knife.

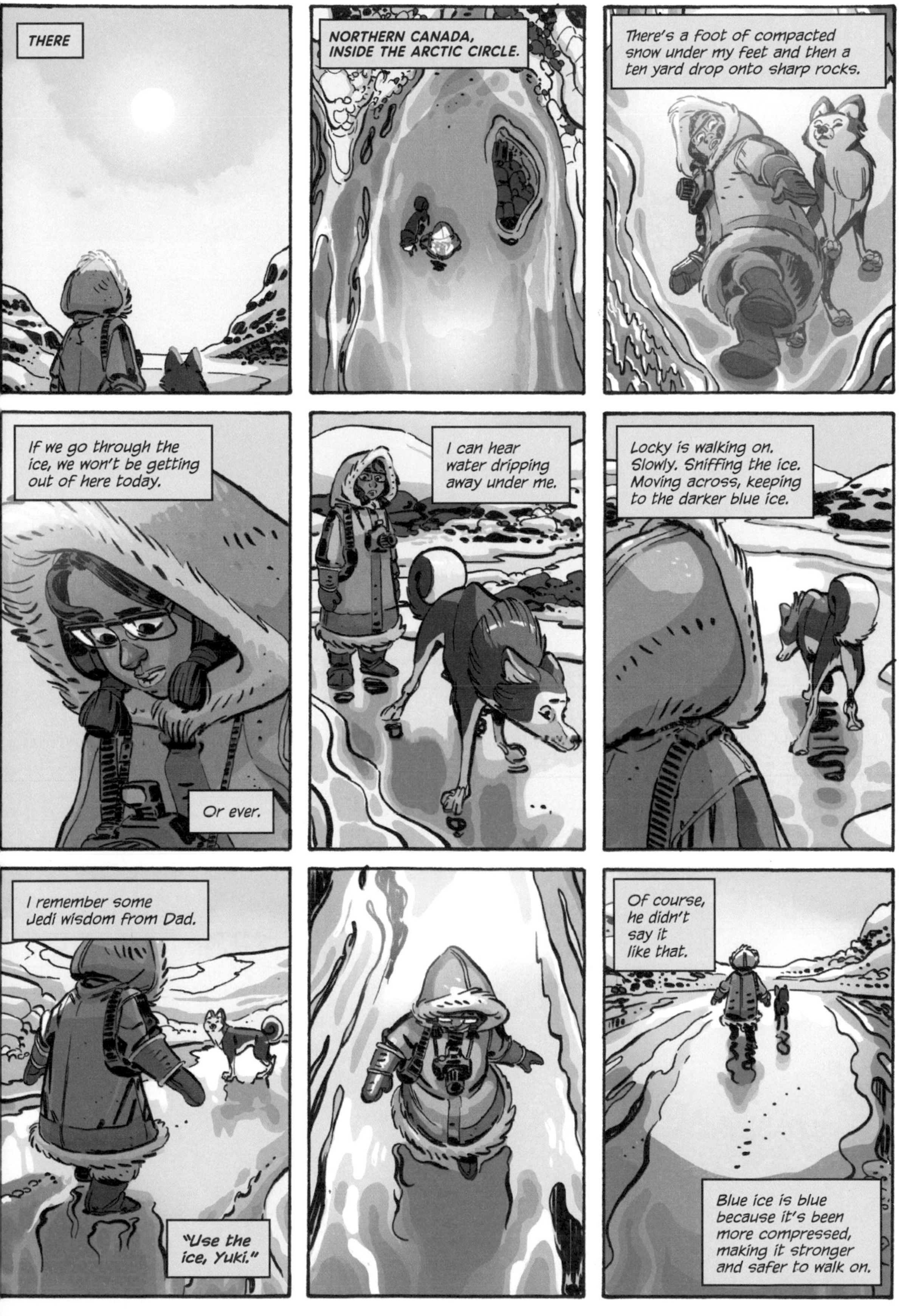
THERE
NORTHERN CANADA, INSIDE THE ARCTIC CIRCLE.
There's a foot of compacted snow under my feet and then a ten yard drop onto sharp rocks.
If we go through the ice, we won't be getting out of here today.
Or ever.
I can hear water dripping away under me.
Locky is walking on. Slowly. Sniffing the ice. Moving across, keeping to the darker blue ice.
I remember some Jedi wisdom from Dad.
"Use the ice, Yuki."
Of course, he didn't say it like that.
Blue ice is blue because it's been more compressed, making it stronger and safer to walk on.

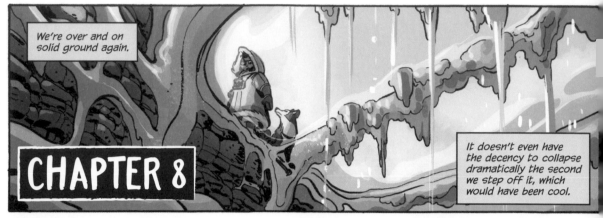

We're over and on solid ground again.

CHAPTER 8

It doesn't even have the decency to collapse dramatically the second we step off it, which would have been cool.

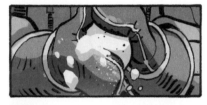

FUPP!

FUPP!

FUPP!

Nothing. Not even a crack.

I'm brushing the snow off my fingers when I think of Locky.

COME HERE, BOY.

Locky's been walking in the cold for hours.

THESE LENS CASES COST ME ALL THE MONEY I HAD ONCE.

"LET'S KEEP MOVING."

Yes, I hear it shatter.

It's not cool like I thought it would be.

We were on that bridge.

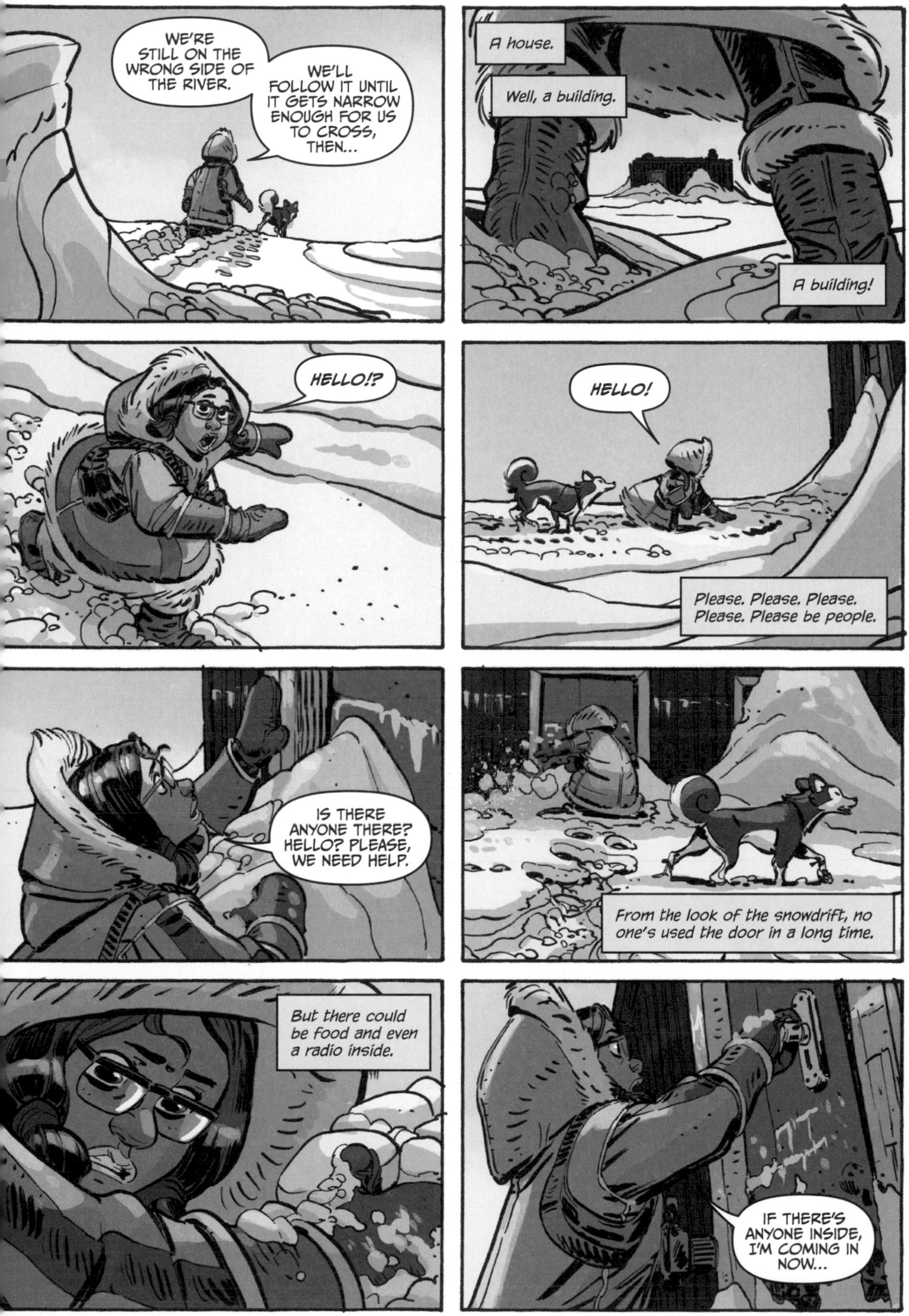
WE'RE STILL ON THE WRONG SIDE OF THE RIVER.
WE'LL FOLLOW IT UNTIL IT GETS NARROW ENOUGH FOR US TO CROSS, THEN...
A house.
Well, a building.
A building!
HELLO!?
HELLO!
Please. Please. Please. Please. Please be people.
IS THERE ANYONE THERE? HELLO? PLEASE, WE NEED HELP.
From the look of the snowdrift, no one's used the door in a long time.
But there could be food and even a radio inside.
IF THERE'S ANYONE INSIDE, I'M COMING IN NOW...

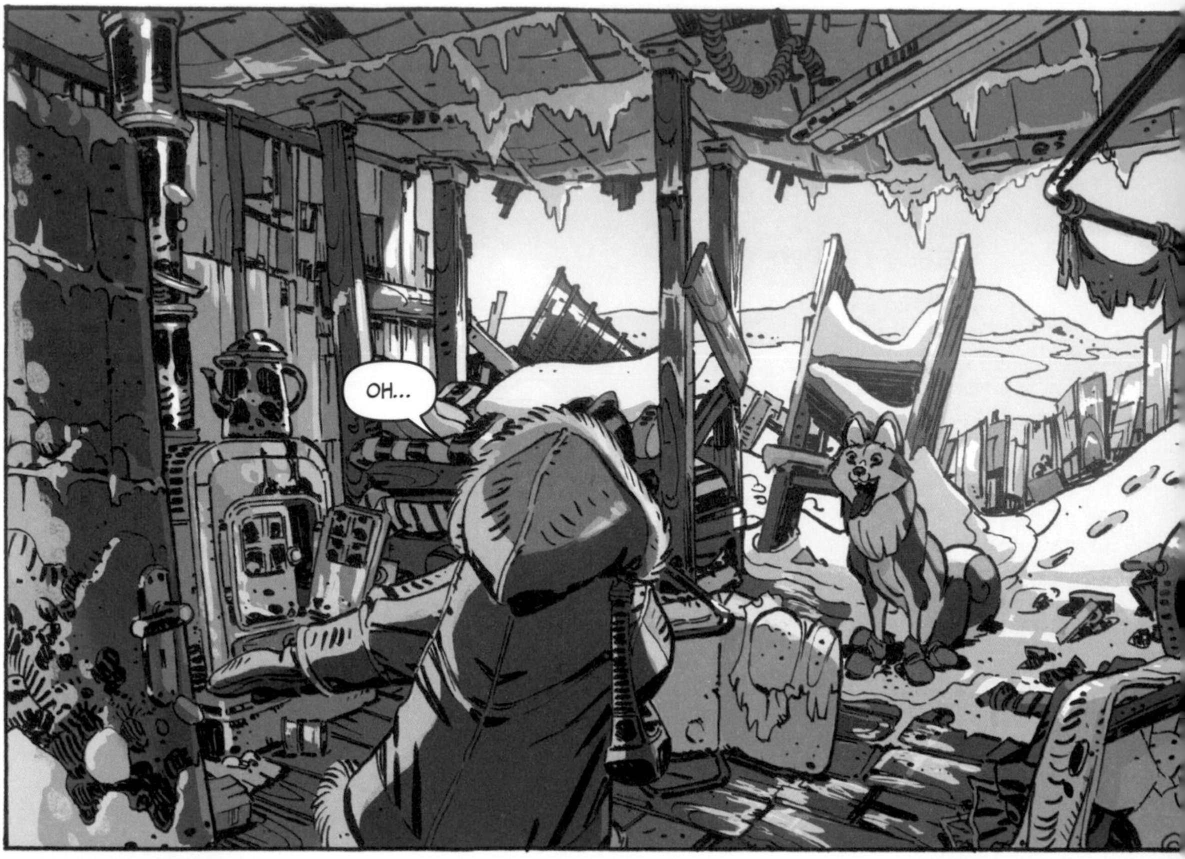
OH...

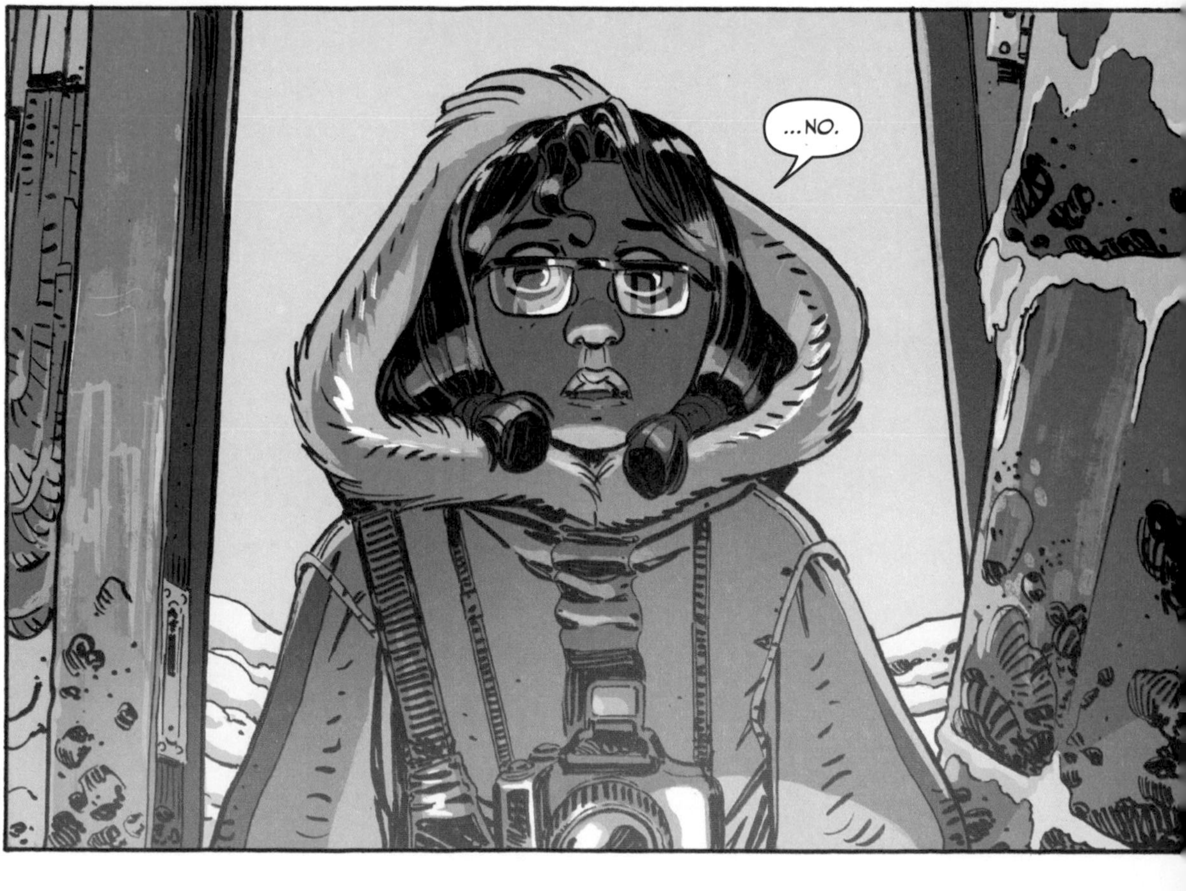
...NO.

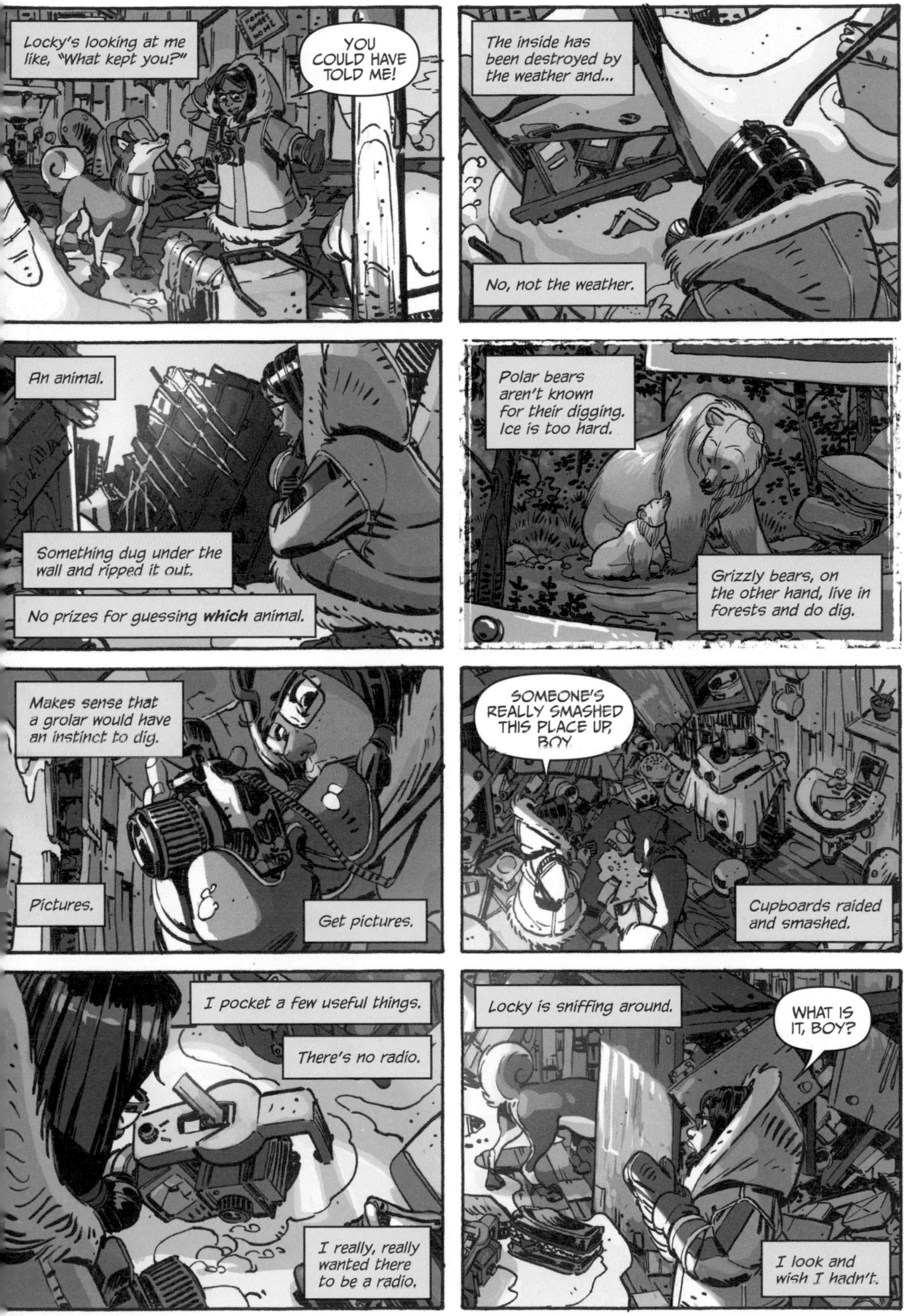

Locky's looking at me like, "What kept you?"
YOU COULD HAVE TOLD ME!
The inside has been destroyed by the weather and...
No, not the weather.
An animal.
Something dug under the wall and ripped it out.
No prizes for guessing **which** animal.
Polar bears aren't known for their digging. Ice is too hard.
Grizzly bears, on the other hand, live in forests and do dig.
Makes sense that a grolar would have an instinct to dig.
Pictures.
Get pictures.
SOMEONE'S REALLY SMASHED THIS PLACE UP, BOY.
Cupboards raided and smashed.
I pocket a few useful things.
There's no radio.
I really, really wanted there to be a radio.
Locky is sniffing around.
WHAT IS IT, BOY?
I look and wish I hadn't.

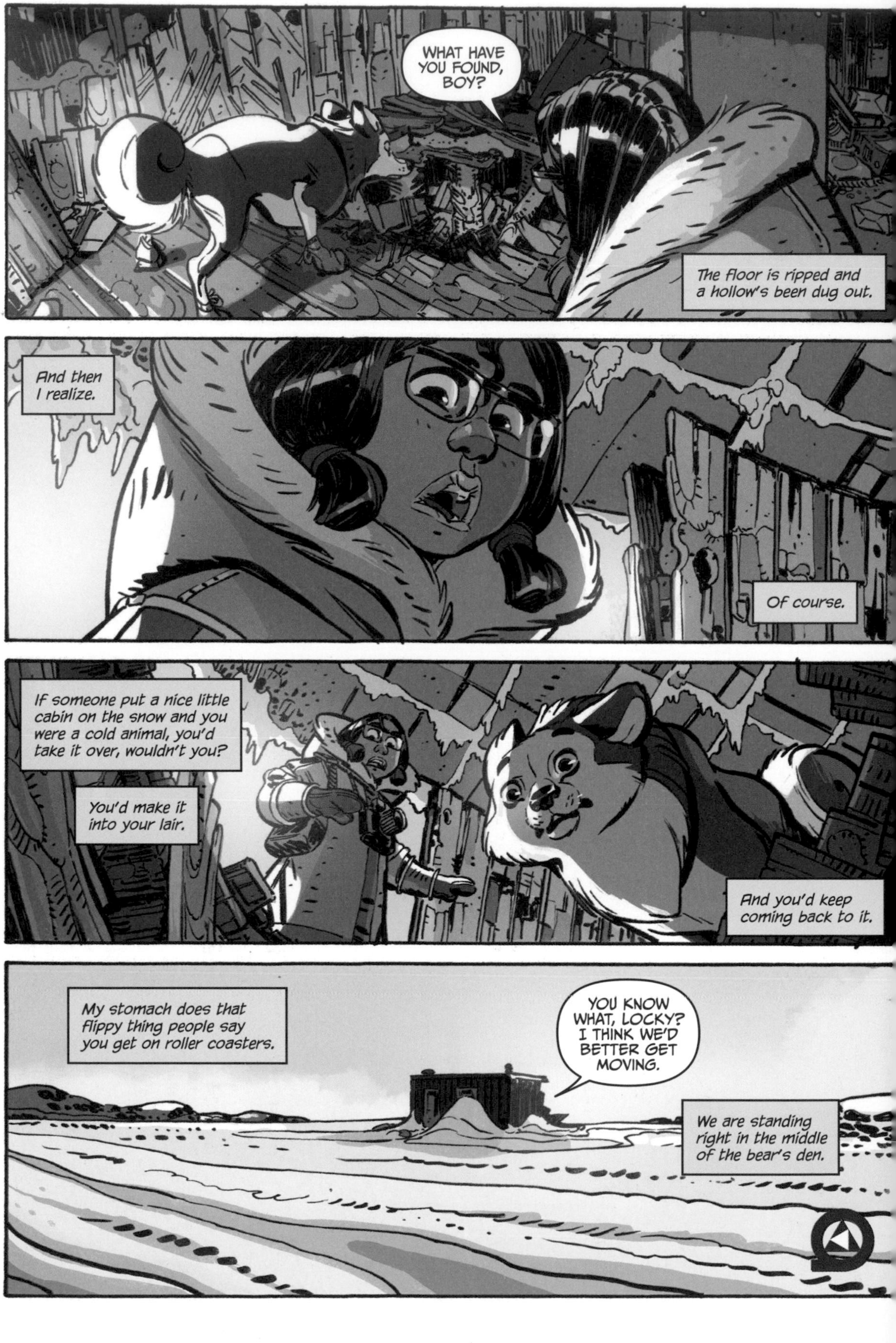
WHAT HAVE YOU FOUND, BOY?
The floor is ripped and a hollow's been dug out.
And then I realize.
Of course.
If someone put a nice little cabin on the snow and you were a cold animal, you'd take it over, wouldn't you?
You'd make it into your lair.
And you'd keep coming back to it.
My stomach does that flippy thing people say you get on roller coasters.
YOU KNOW WHAT, LOCKY? I THINK WE'D BETTER GET MOVING.
We are standing right in the middle of the bear's den.

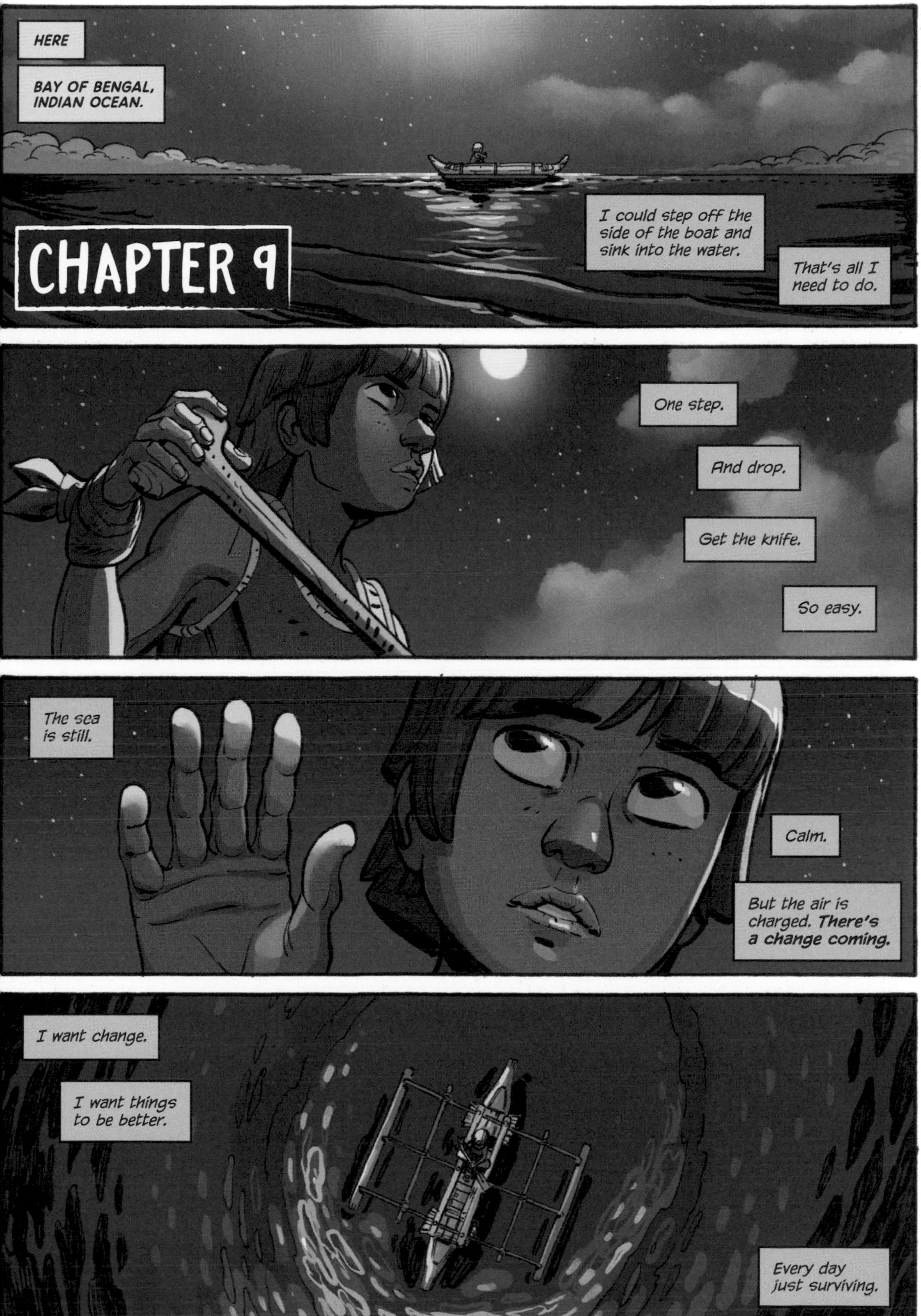
HERE
BAY OF BENGAL, INDIAN OCEAN.
CHAPTER 9
I could step off the side of the boat and sink into the water.
That's all I need to do.
One step.
And drop.
Get the knife.
So easy.
The sea is still.
Calm.
But the air is charged. There's a change coming.
I want change.
I want things to be better.
Every day just surviving.

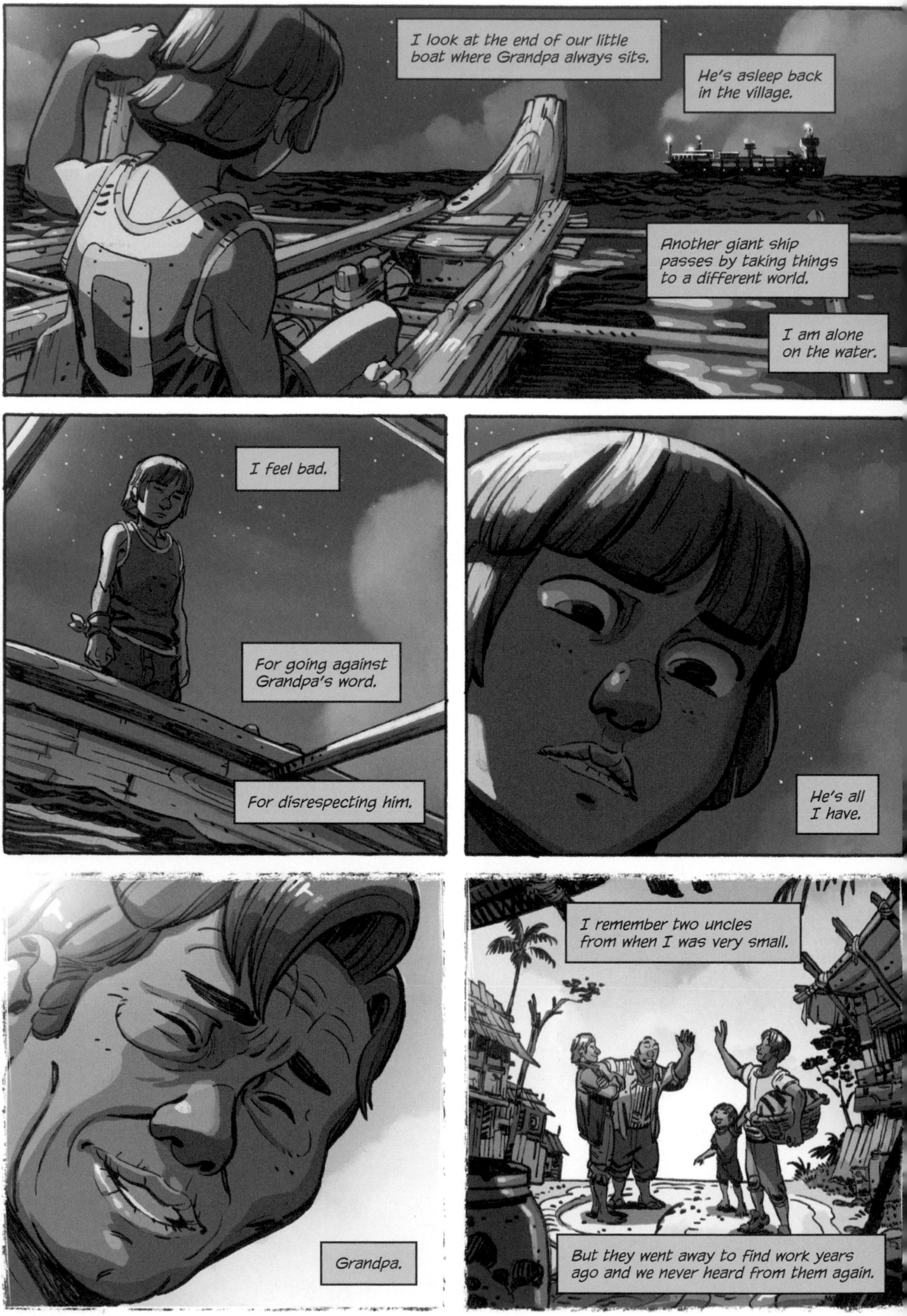
I look at the end of our little boat where Grandpa always sits.
He's asleep back in the village.
Another giant ship passes by taking things to a different world.
I am alone on the water.
I feel bad.
For going against Grandpa's word.
For disrespecting him.
He's all I have.
Grandpa.
I remember two uncles from when I was very small.
But they went away to find work years ago and we never heard from them again.

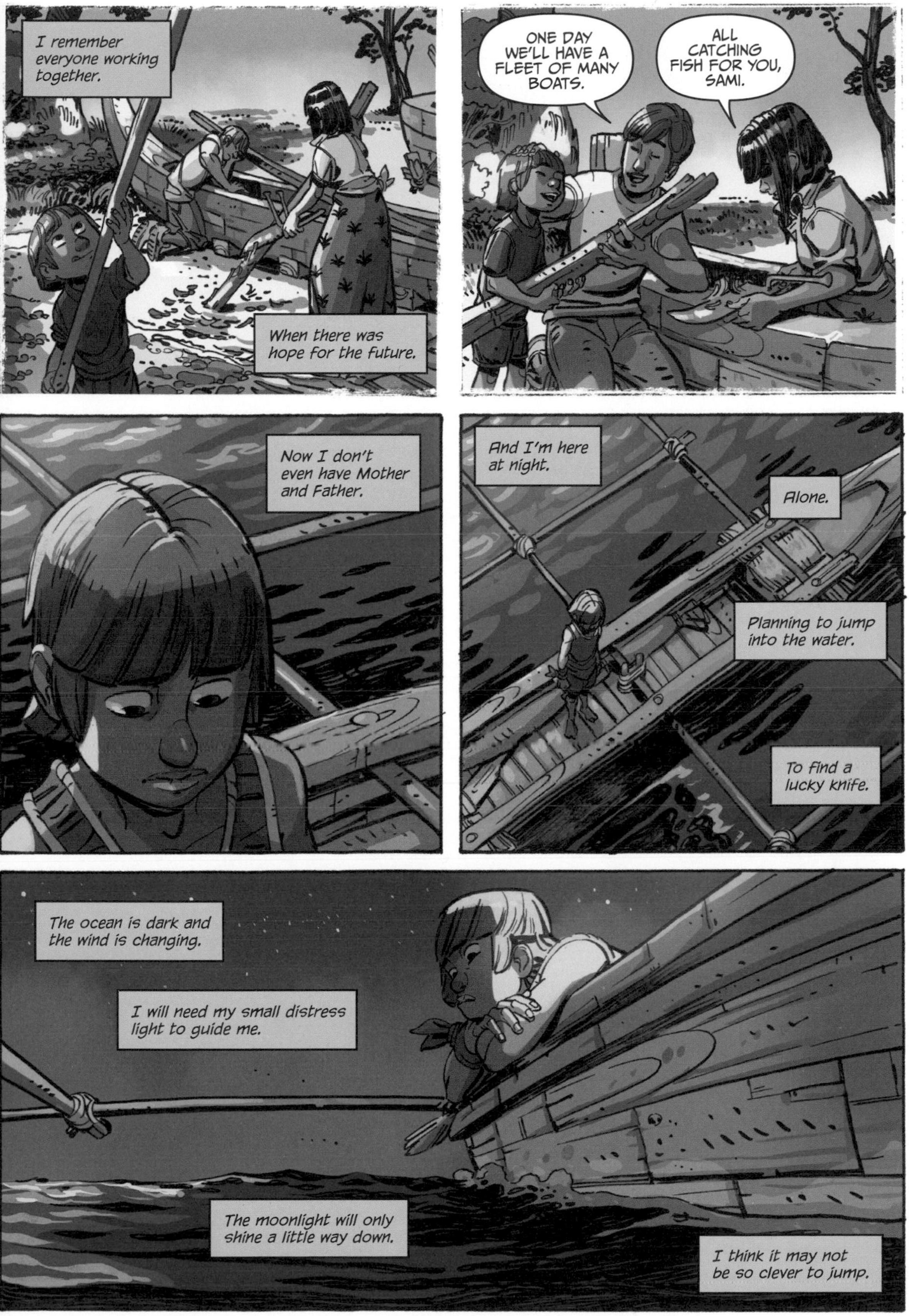
I remember everyone working together.
When there was hope for the future.
ONE DAY WE'LL HAVE A FLEET OF MANY BOATS.
ALL CATCHING FISH FOR YOU, SAMI.
Now I don't even have Mother and Father.
And I'm here at night.
Alone.
Planning to jump into the water.
To find a lucky knife.
The ocean is dark and the wind is changing.
I will need my small distress light to guide me.
The moonlight will only shine a little way down.
I think it may not be so clever to jump.

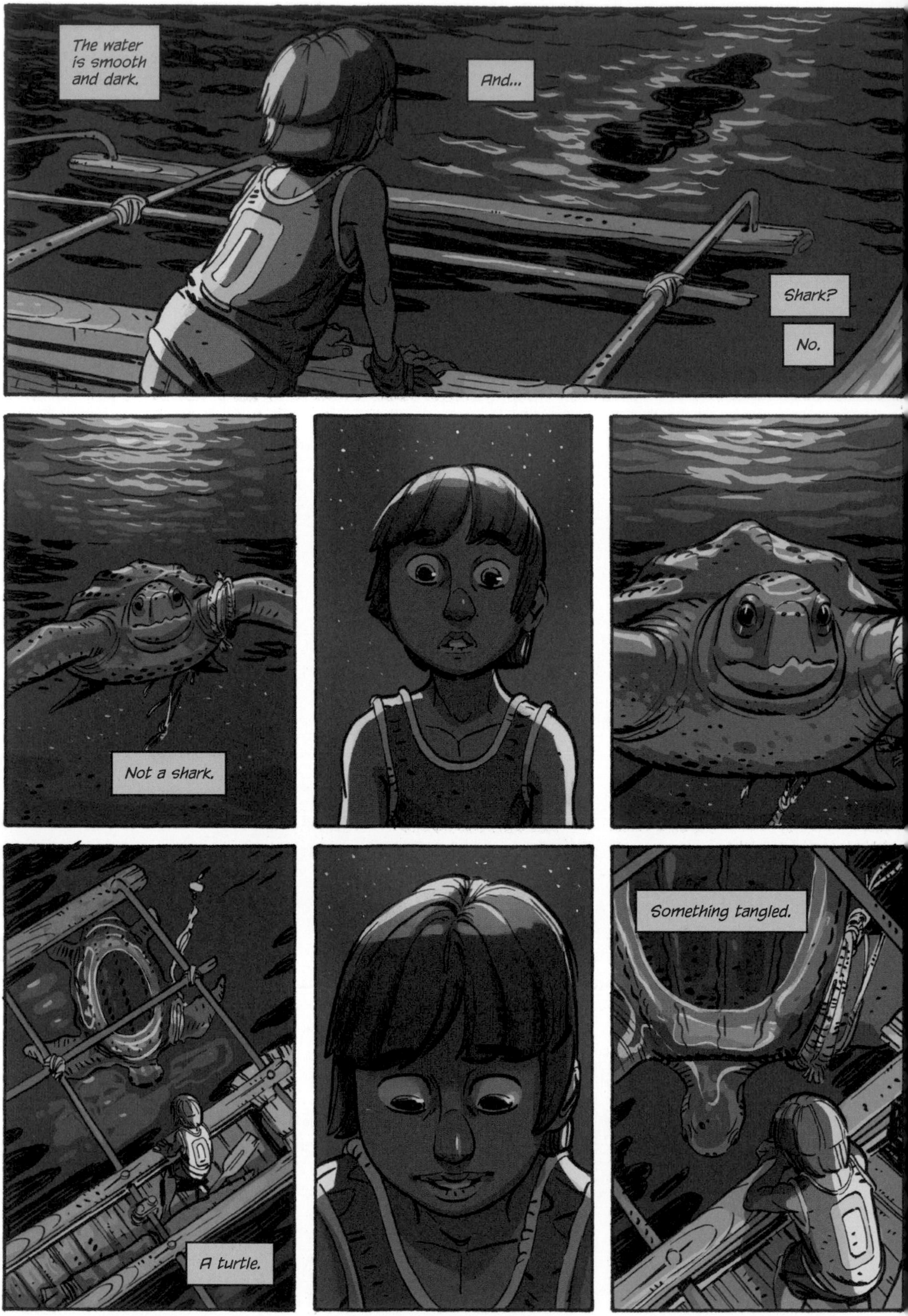
The water is smooth and dark.
And...
Shark?
No.
Not a shark.
A turtle.
Something tangled.

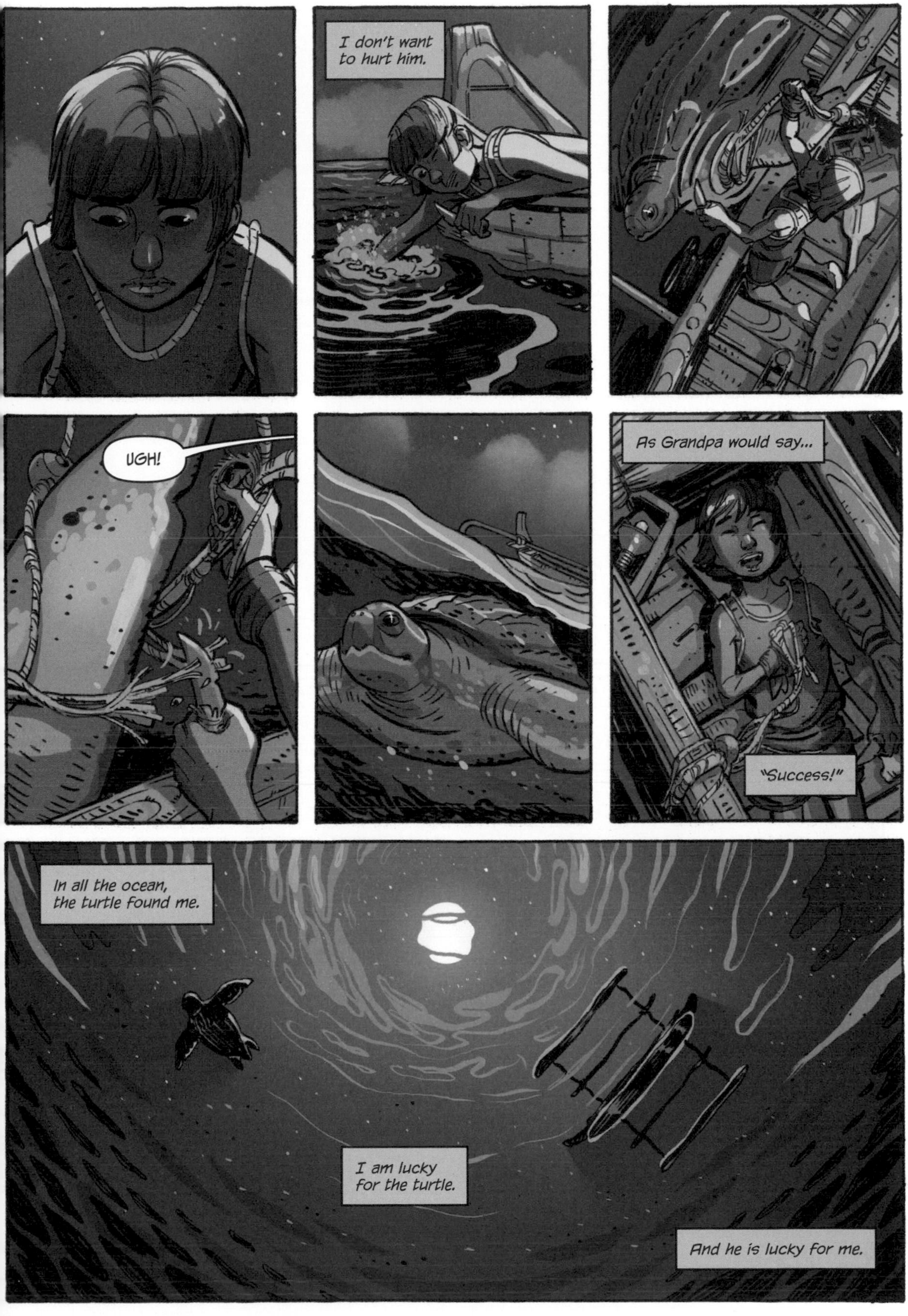
I don't want to hurt him.
UGH!
As Grandpa would say...
"Success!"
In all the ocean, the turtle found me.
I am lucky for the turtle.
And he is lucky for me.

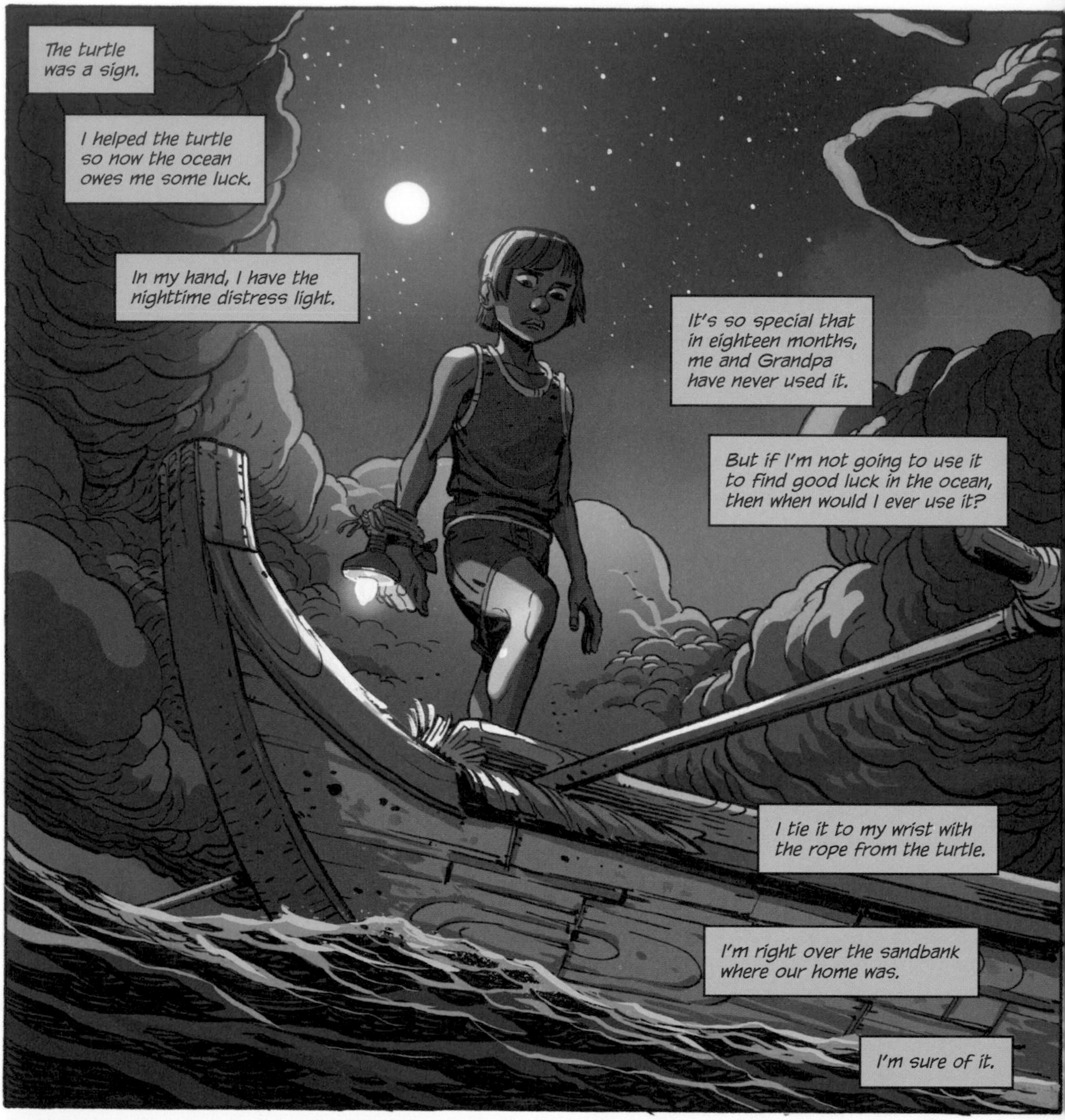
The turtle was a sign.
I helped the turtle so now the ocean owes me some luck.
In my hand, I have the nighttime distress light.
It's so special that in eighteen months, me and Grandpa have never used it.
But if I'm not going to use it to find good luck in the ocean, then when would I ever use it?
I tie it to my wrist with the rope from the turtle.
I'm right over the sandbank where our home was.
I'm sure of it.

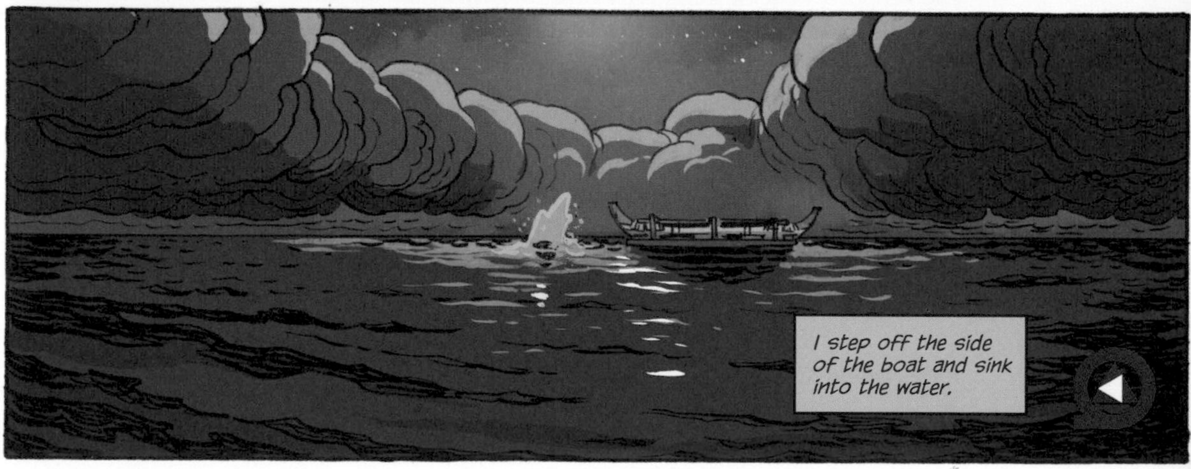
I step off the side of the boat and sink into the water.

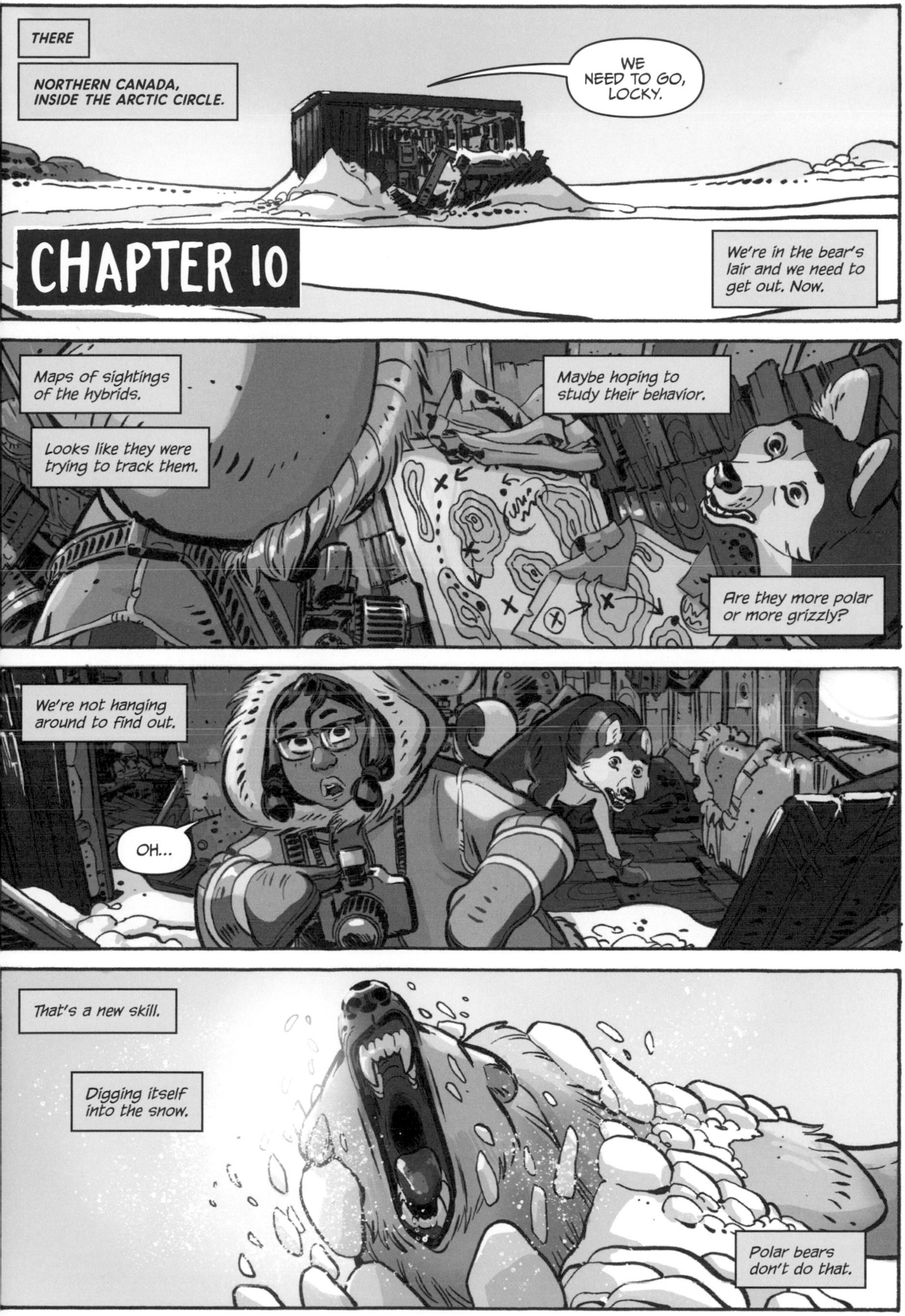
THERE
NORTHERN CANADA, INSIDE THE ARCTIC CIRCLE.
WE NEED TO GO, LOCKY.
CHAPTER 10
We're in the bear's lair and we need to get out. Now.
Maps of sightings of the hybrids.
Looks like they were trying to track them.
Maybe hoping to study their behavior.
Are they more polar or more grizzly?
We're not hanging around to find out.
OH...
That's a new skill.
Digging itself into the snow.
Polar bears don't do that.

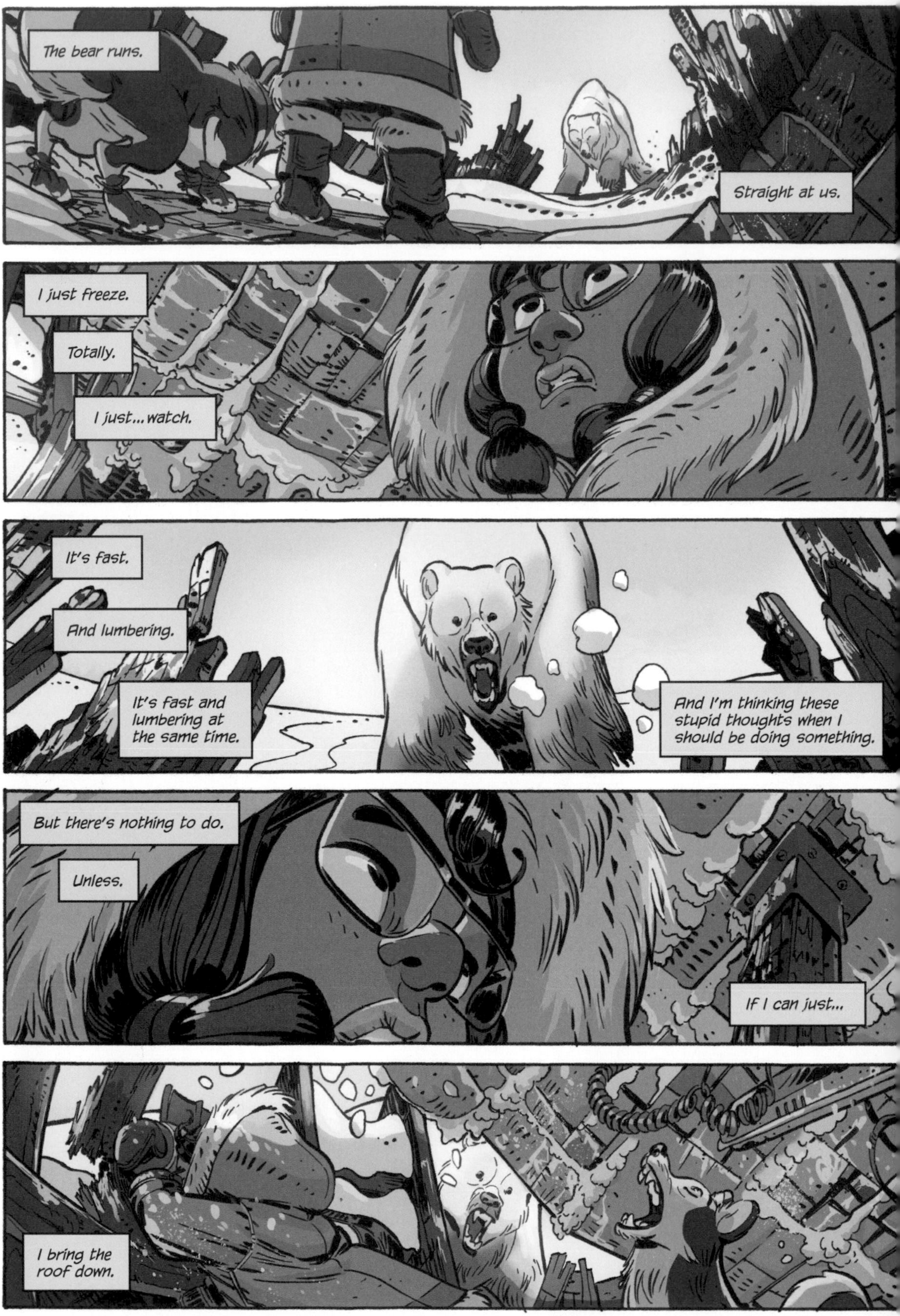
The bear runs.
Straight at us.
I just freeze.
Totally.
I just...watch.
It's fast.
And lumbering.
It's fast and lumbering at the same time.
And I'm thinking these stupid thoughts when I should be doing something.
But there's nothing to do.
Unless.
If I can just...
I bring the roof down.

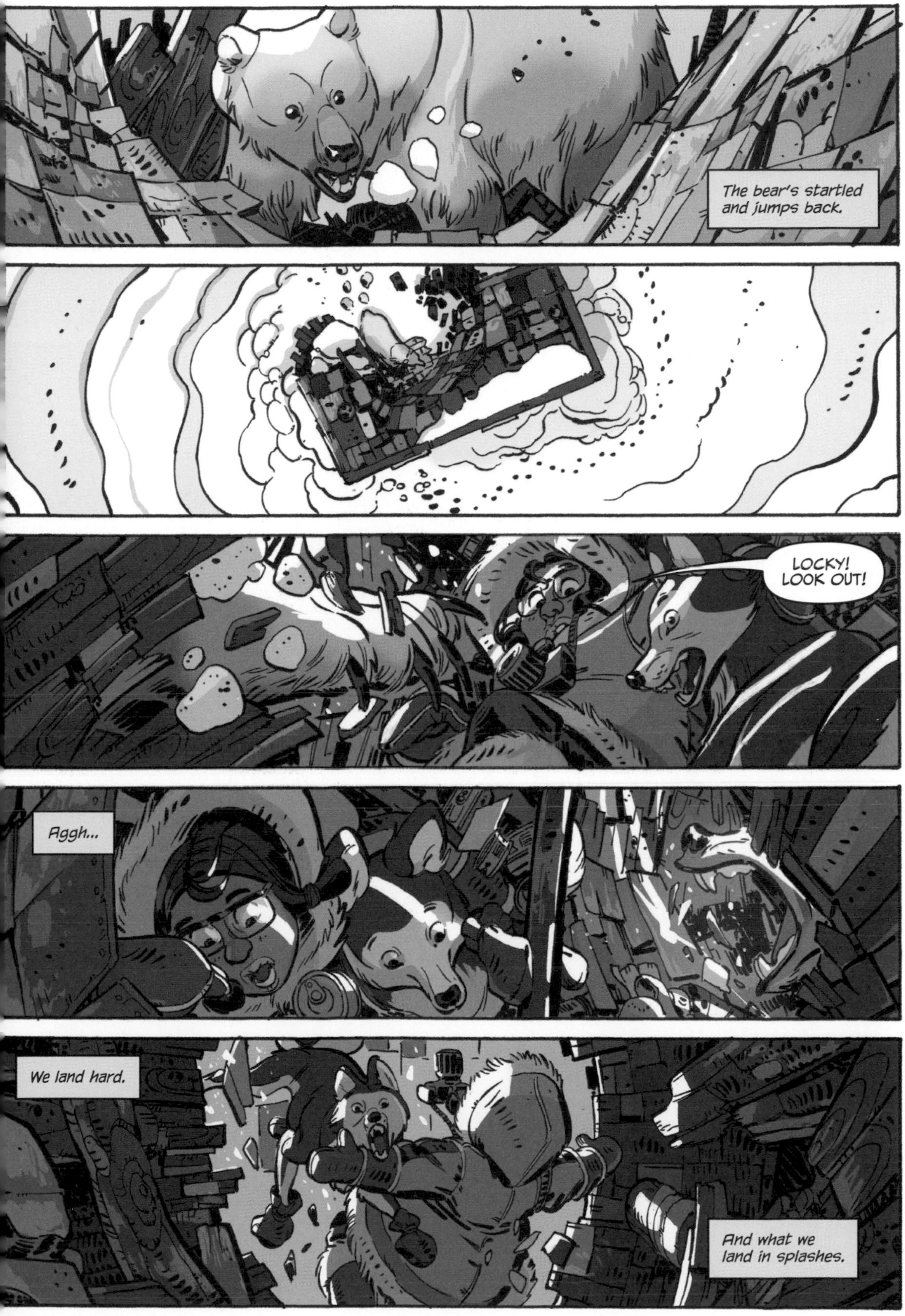
The bear's startled and jumps back.
LOCKY! LOOK OUT!
Aggh...
We land hard.
And what we land in splashes.

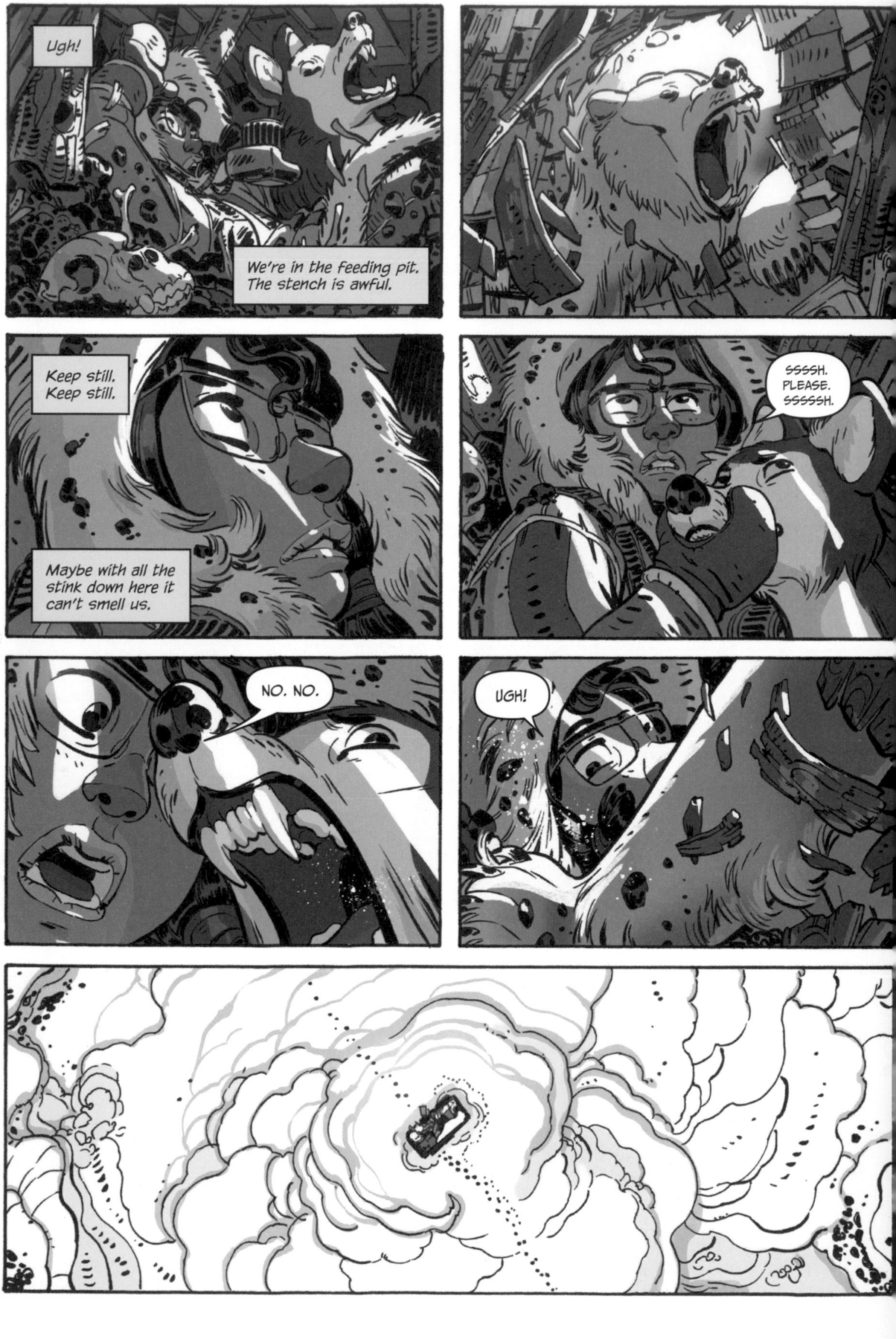
Ugh!
We're in the feeding pit. The stench is awful.
Keep still. Keep still.
Maybe with all the stink down here it can't smell us.
SSSSH. PLEASE. SSSSSH.
NO. NO.
UGH!

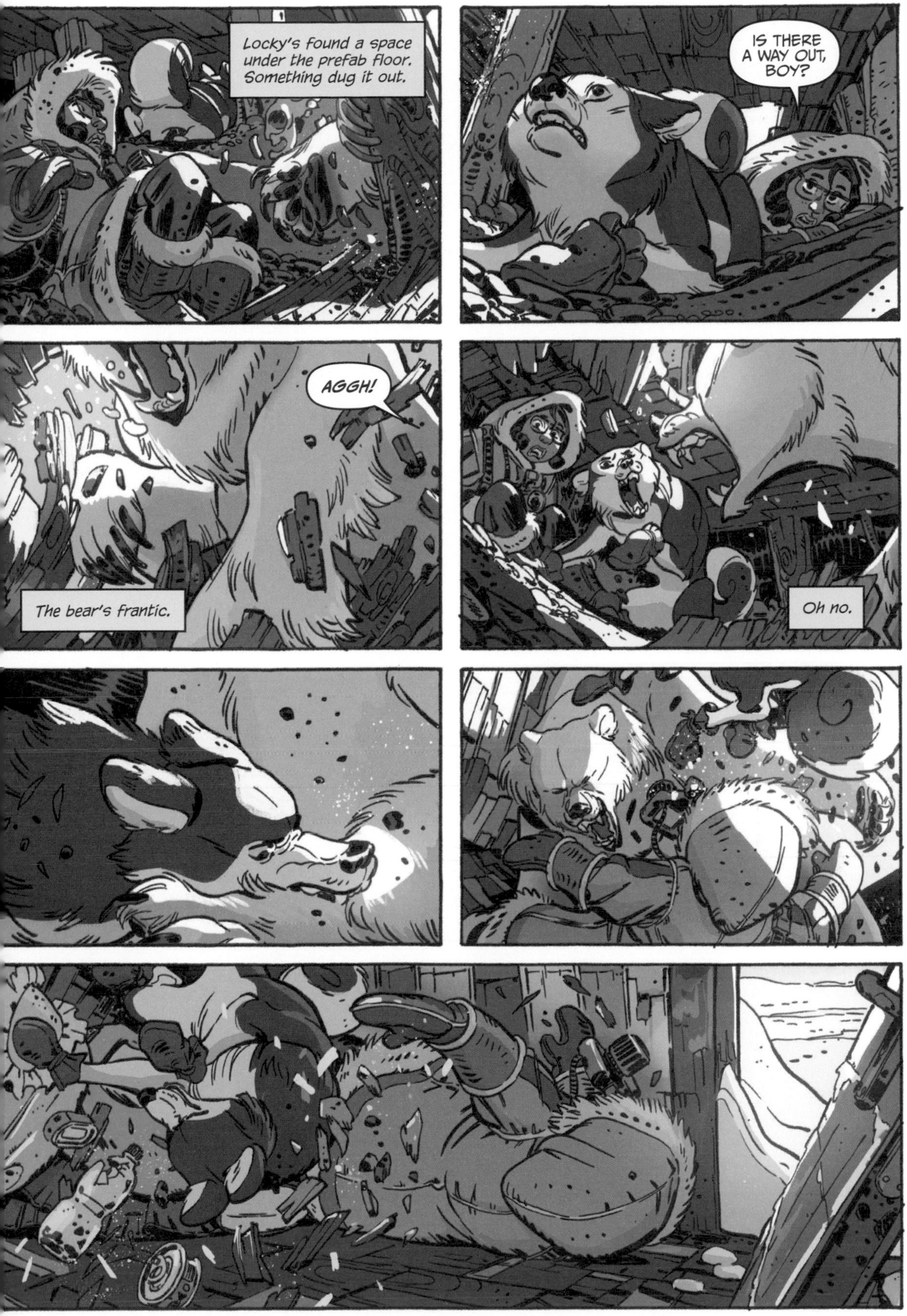
Locky's found a space under the prefab floor. Something dug it out.
IS THERE A WAY OUT, BOY?
AGGH!
The bear's frantic.
Oh no.

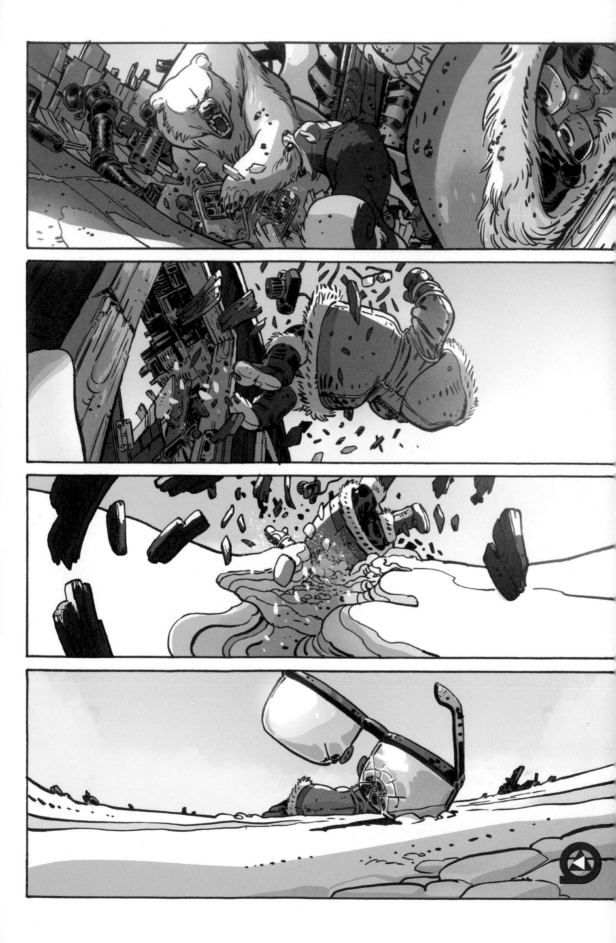

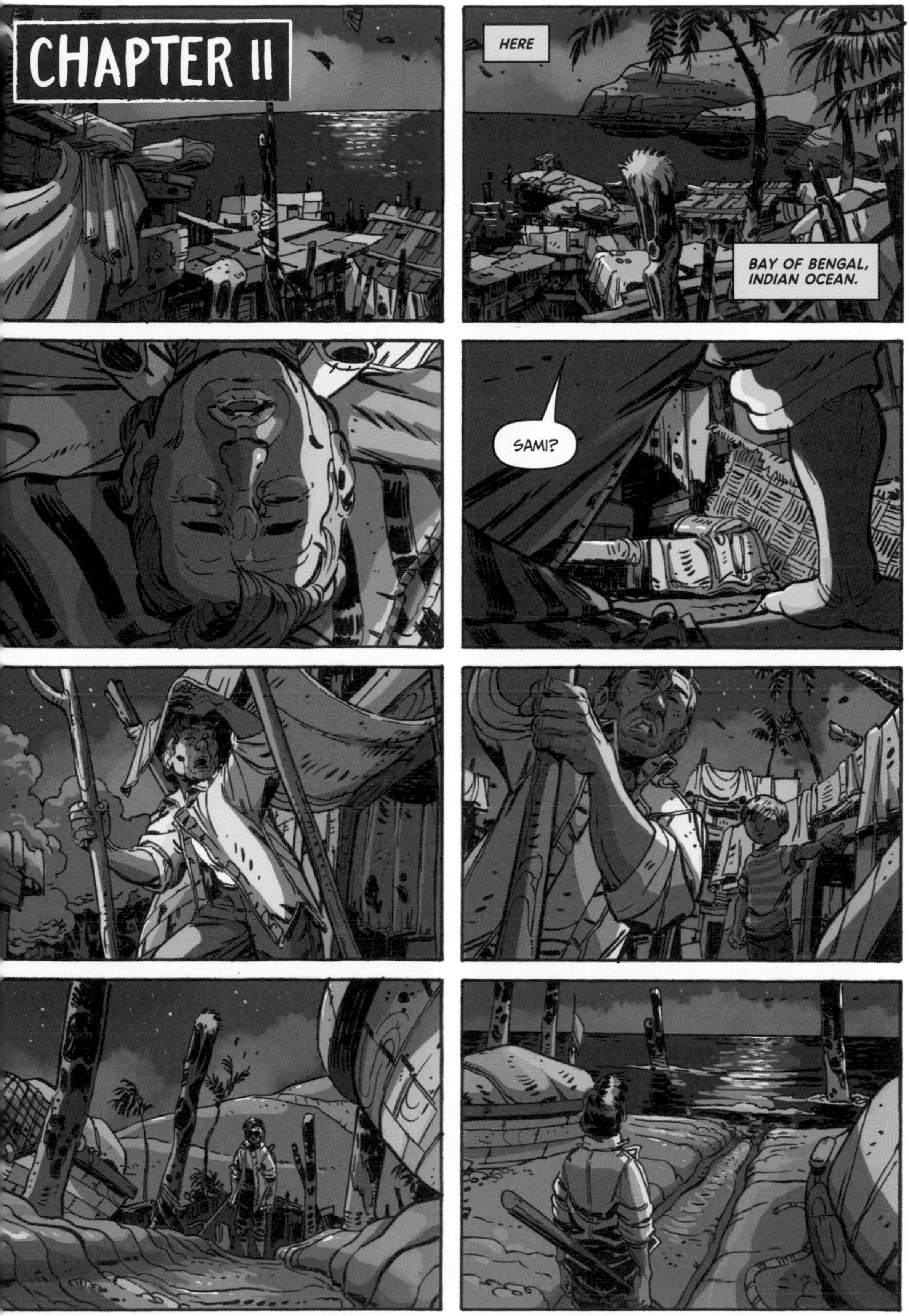
CHAPTER II
HERE
BAY OF BENGAL, INDIAN OCEAN.
SAMI?

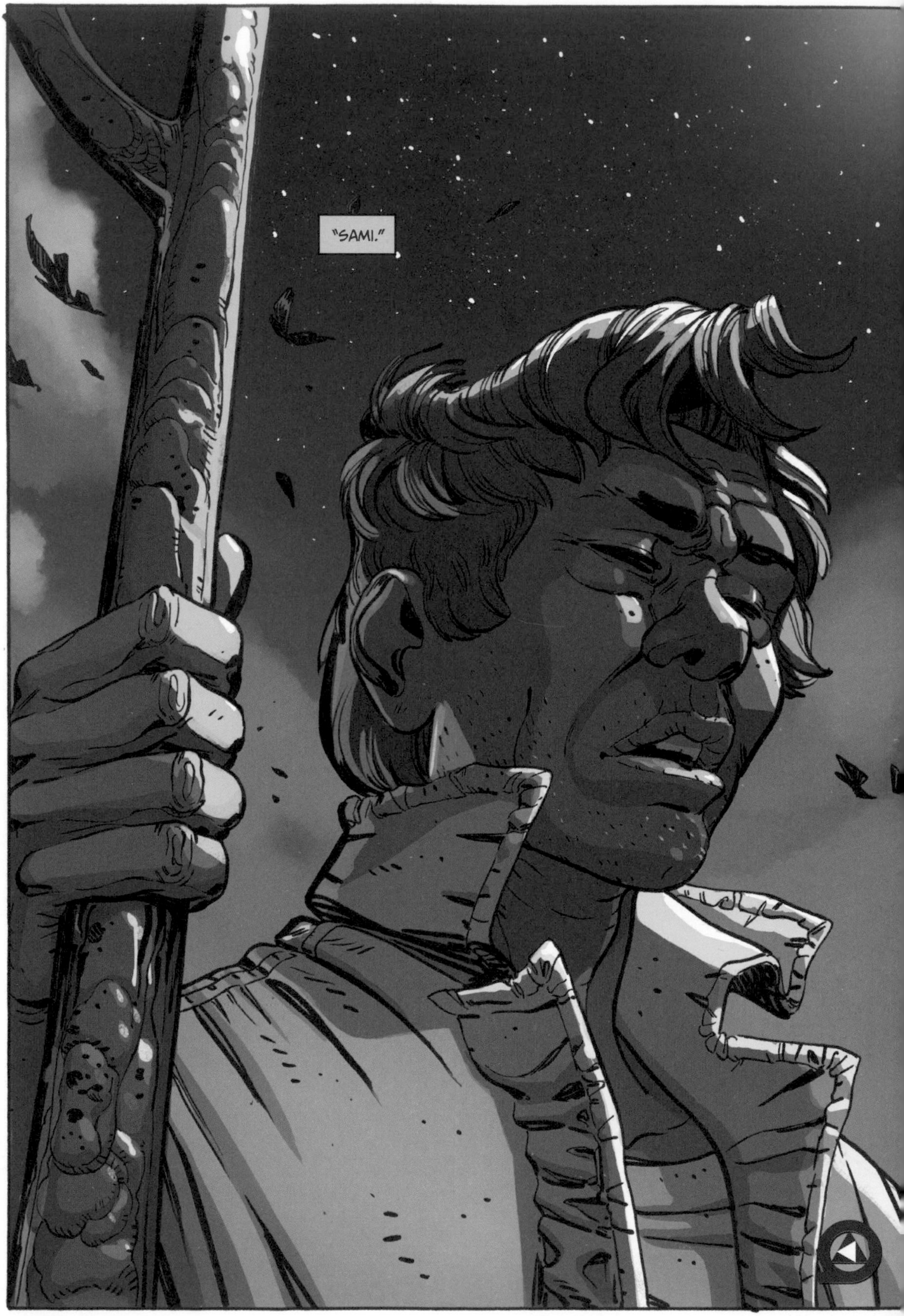
"SAMI."

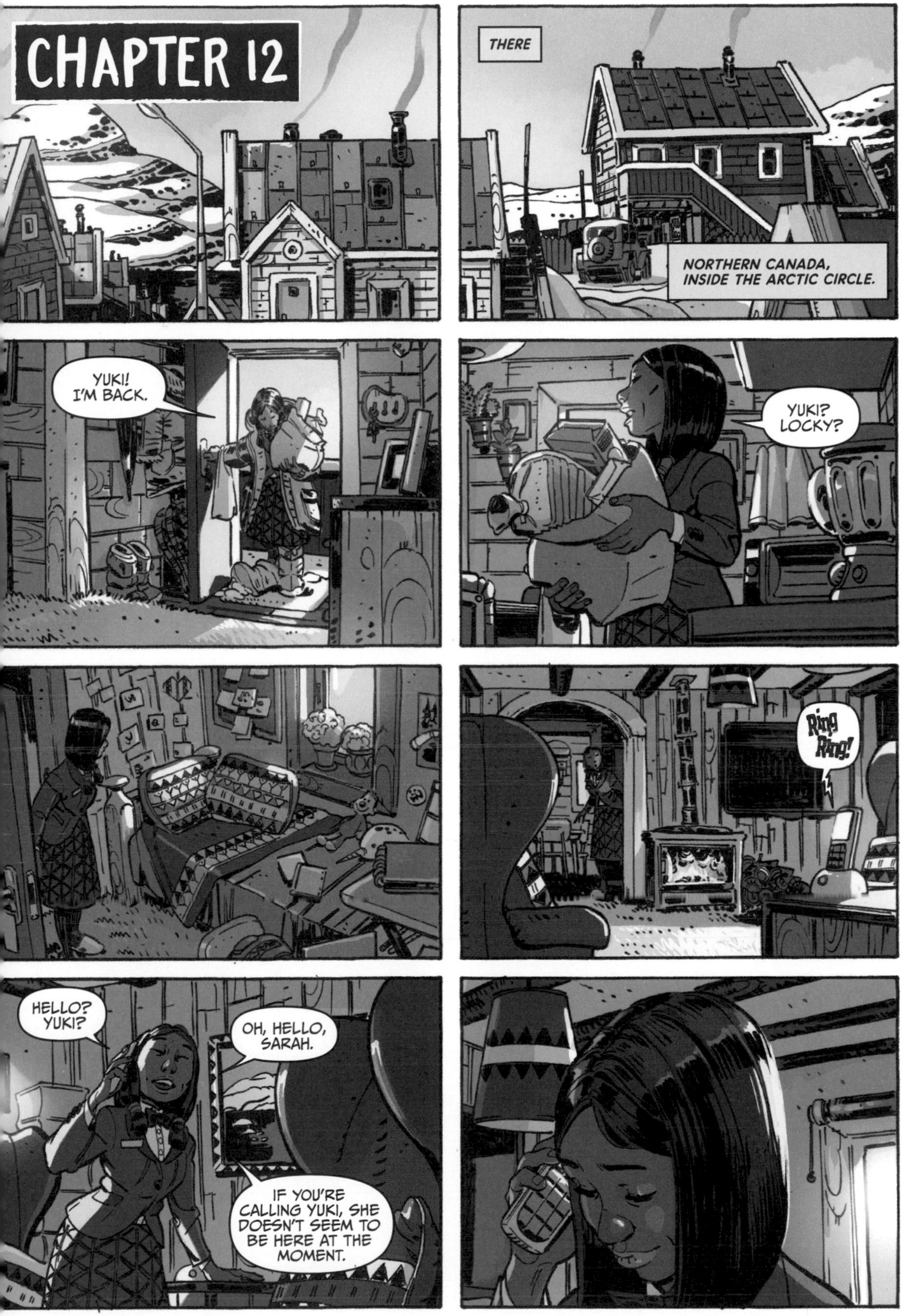
CHAPTER 12
THERE
NORTHERN CANADA, INSIDE THE ARCTIC CIRCLE.
YUKI! I'M BACK.
YUKI? LOCKY?
Ring Ring!
HELLO? YUKI?
OH, HELLO, SARAH.
IF YOU'RE CALLING YUKI, SHE DOESN'T SEEM TO BE HERE AT THE MOMENT.

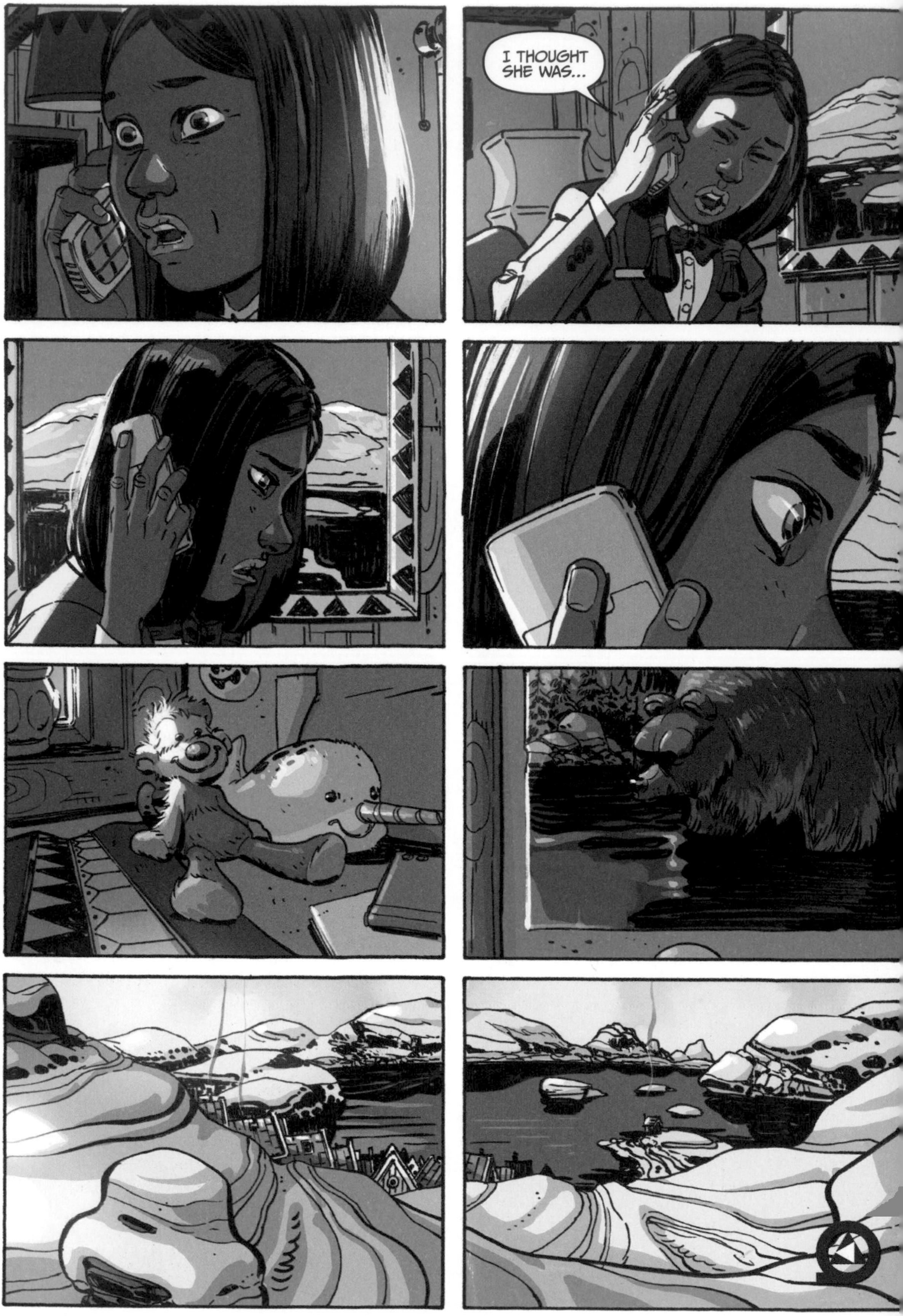
I THOUGHT SHE WAS...

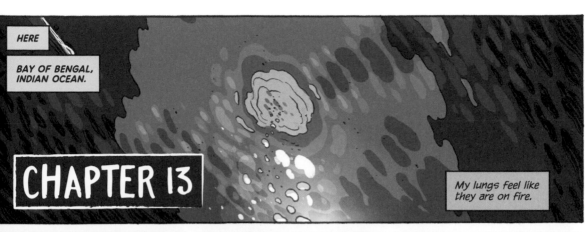

HERE

BAY OF BENGAL, INDIAN OCEAN.

CHAPTER 13

My lungs feel like they are on fire.

≥GASP≥

Each dive, I stay down a bit longer.

Each dive, it hurts a bit more.

But I'm not going back without that knife.

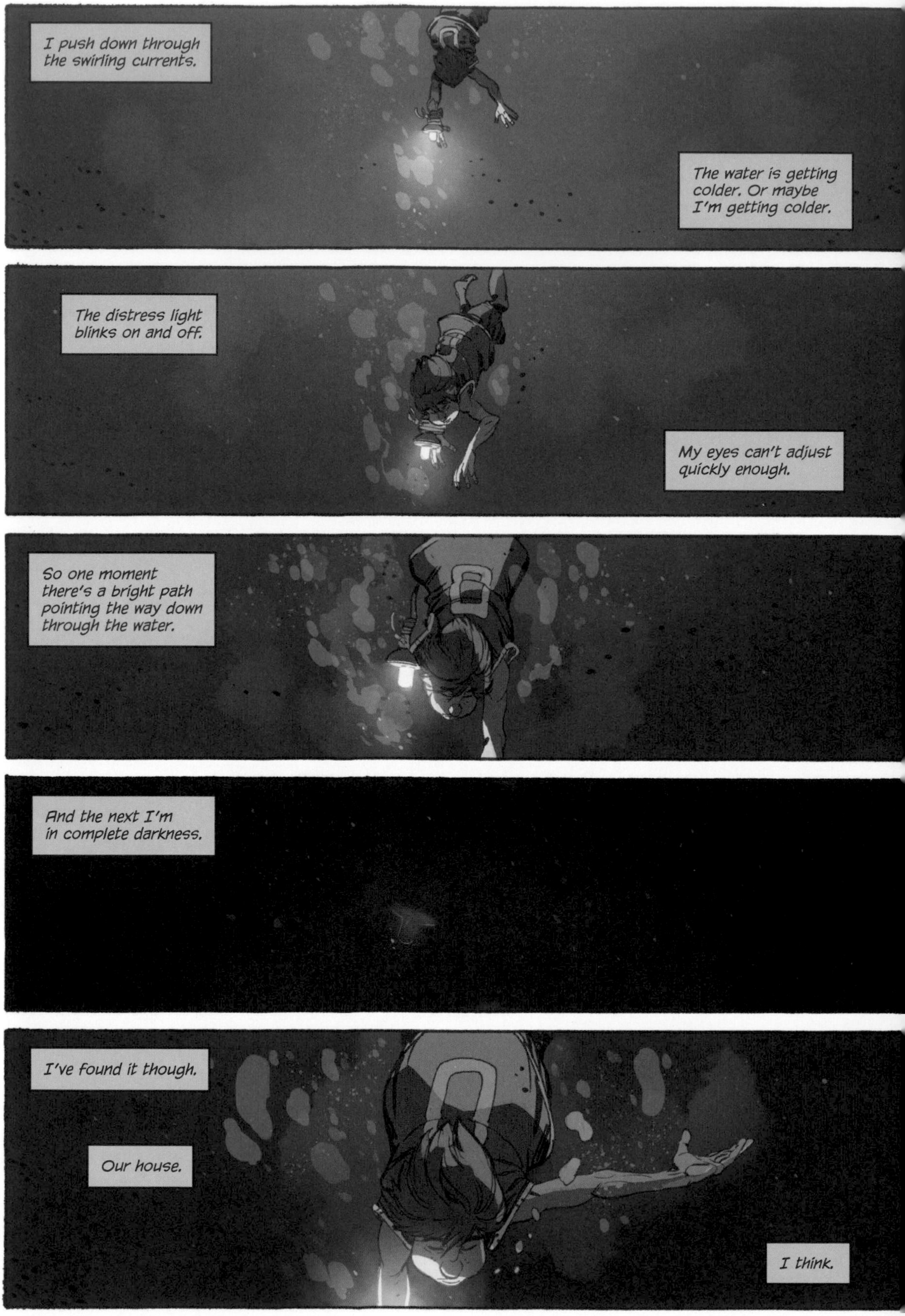
I push down through the swirling currents.
The water is getting colder. Or maybe I'm getting colder.
The distress light blinks on and off.
My eyes can't adjust quickly enough.
So one moment there's a bright path pointing the way down through the water.
And the next I'm in complete darkness.
I've found it though.
Our house.
I think.

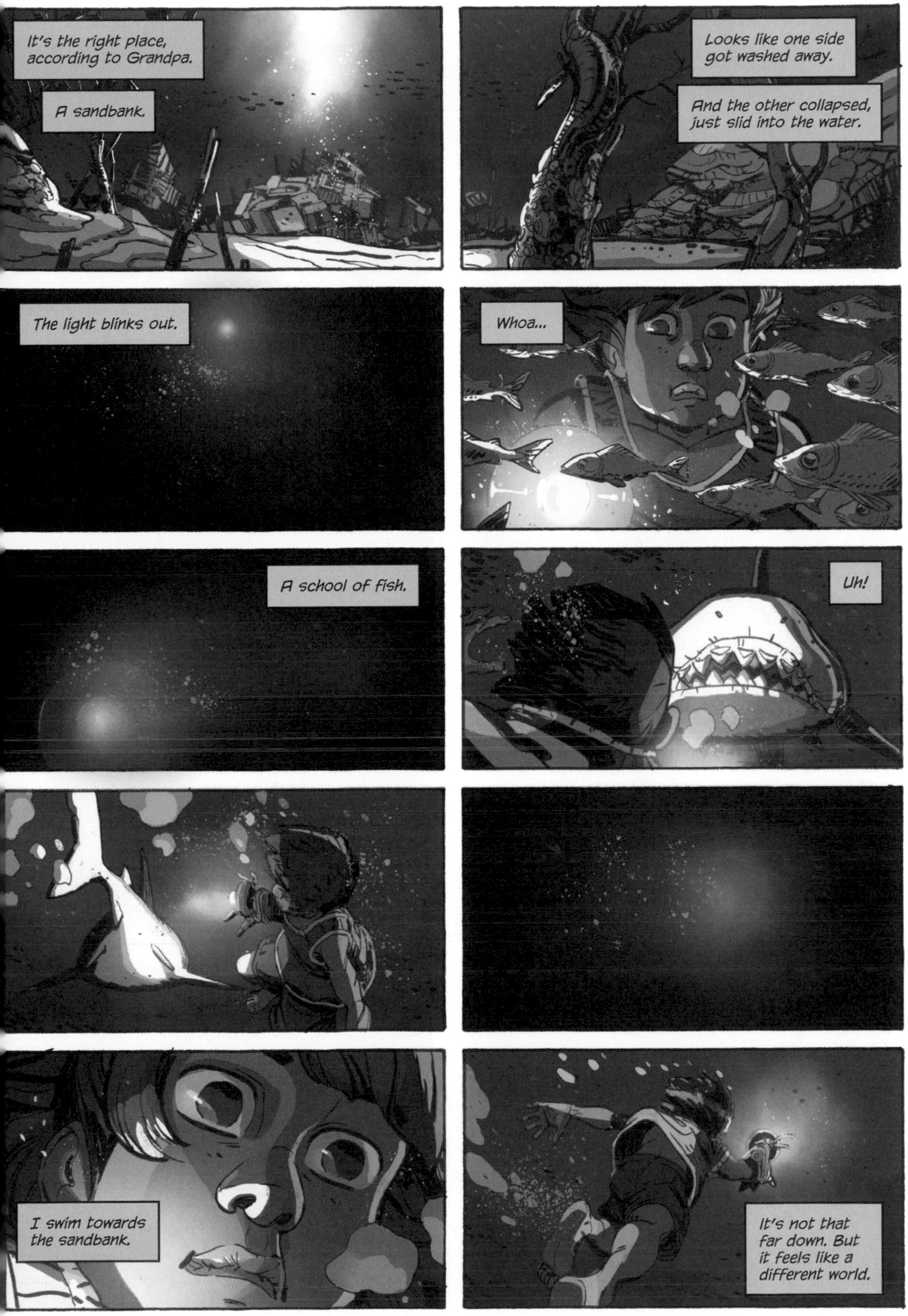
It's the right place, according to Grandpa.
A sandbank.
Looks like one side got washed away.
And the other collapsed, just slid into the water.
The light blinks out.
Whoa...
A school of fish.
Uh!
I swim towards the sandbank.
It's not that far down. But it feels like a different world.

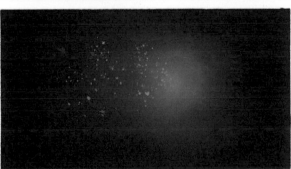

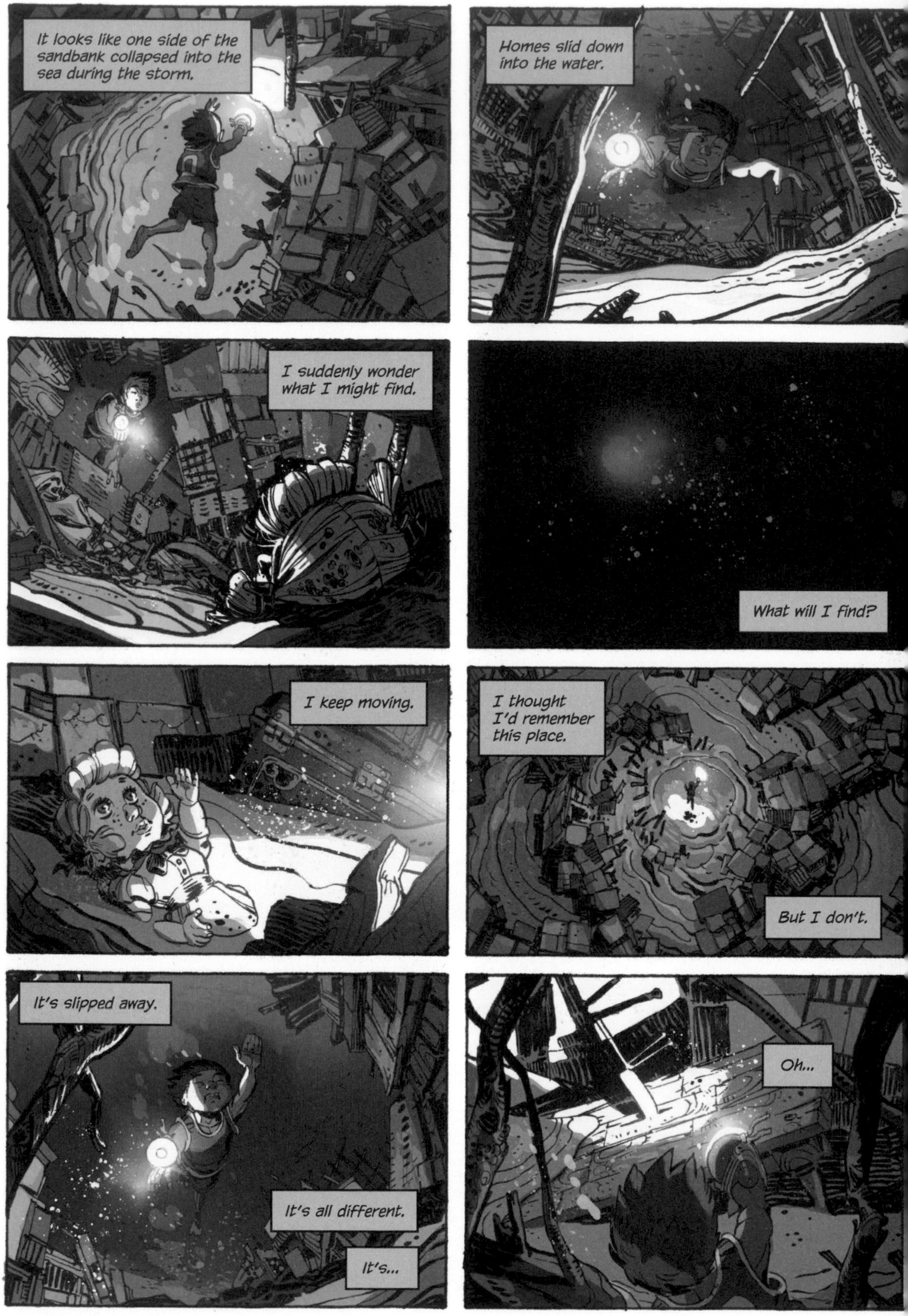
It looks like one side of the sandbank collapsed into the sea during the storm.
Homes slid down into the water.
I suddenly wonder what I might find.
What will I find?
I keep moving.
I thought I'd remember this place.
But I don't.
It's slipped away.
It's all different.
It's...
Oh...

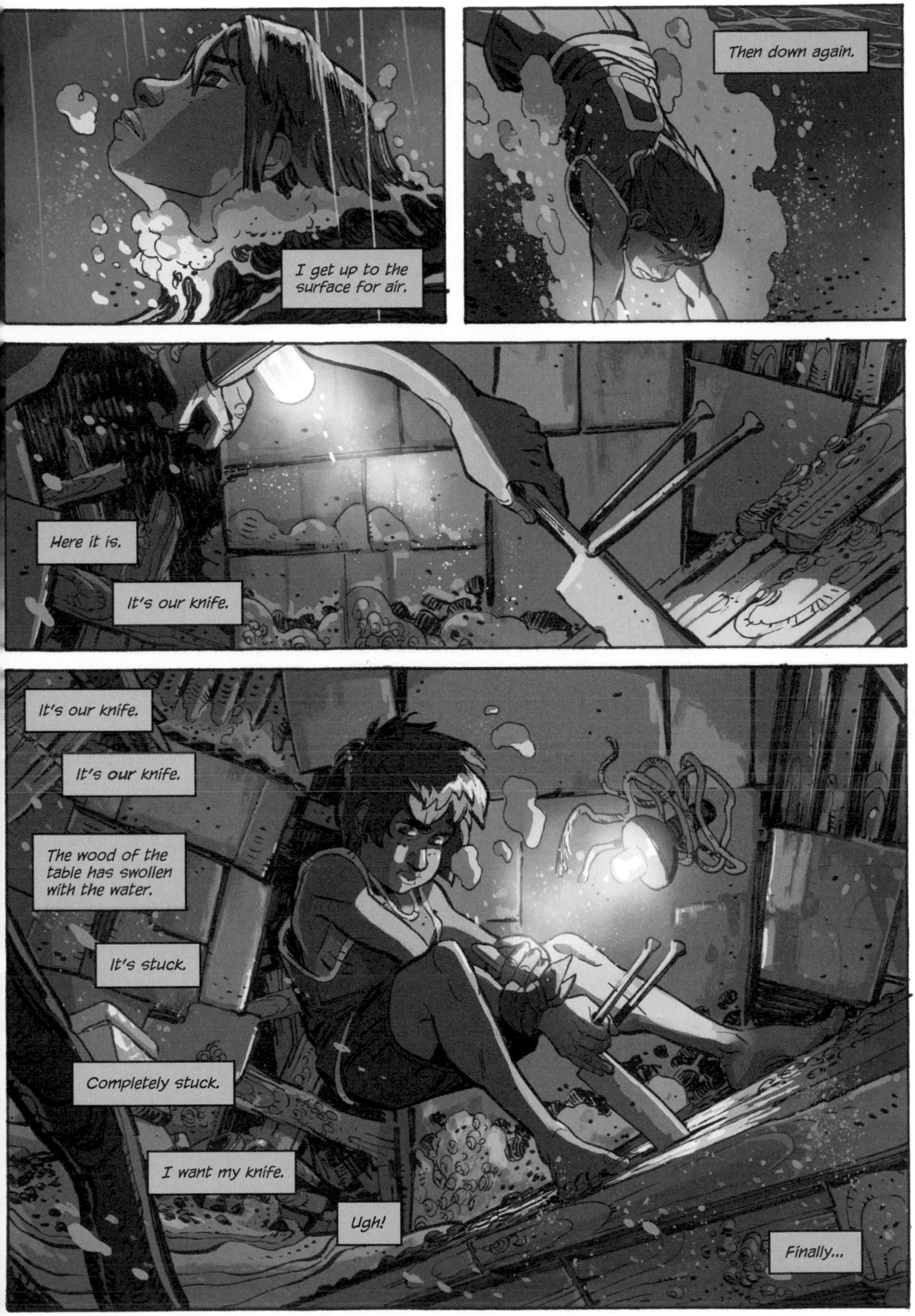

I get up to the surface for air.
Then down again.
Here it is.
It's our knife.
It's our knife.
It's our knife.
The wood of the table has swollen with the water.
It's stuck.
Completely stuck.
I want my knife.
Ugh!
Finally...

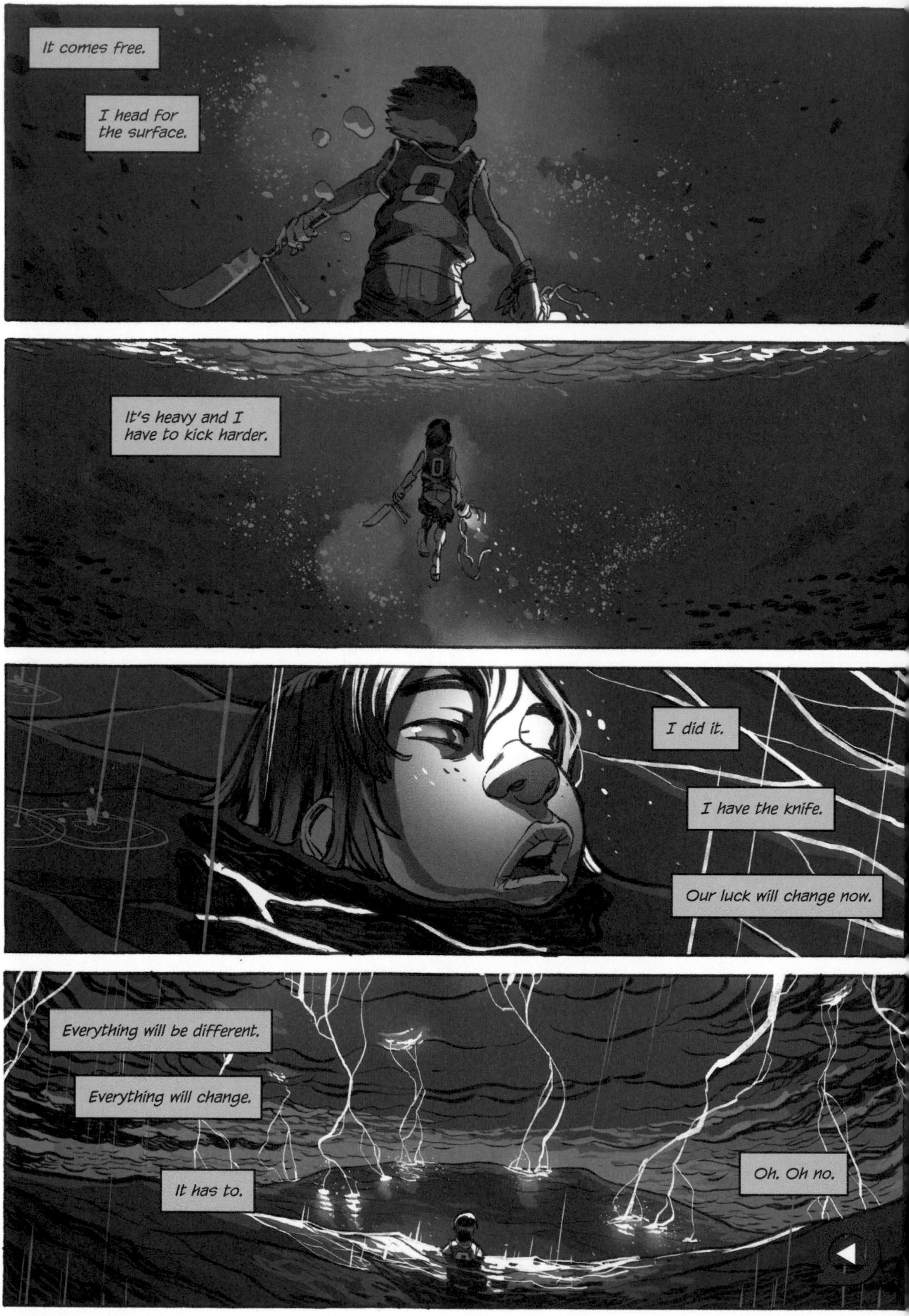
It comes free.
I head for the surface.
It's heavy and I have to kick harder.
I did it.
I have the knife.
Our luck will change now.
Everything will be different.
Everything will change.
It has to.
Oh. Oh no.

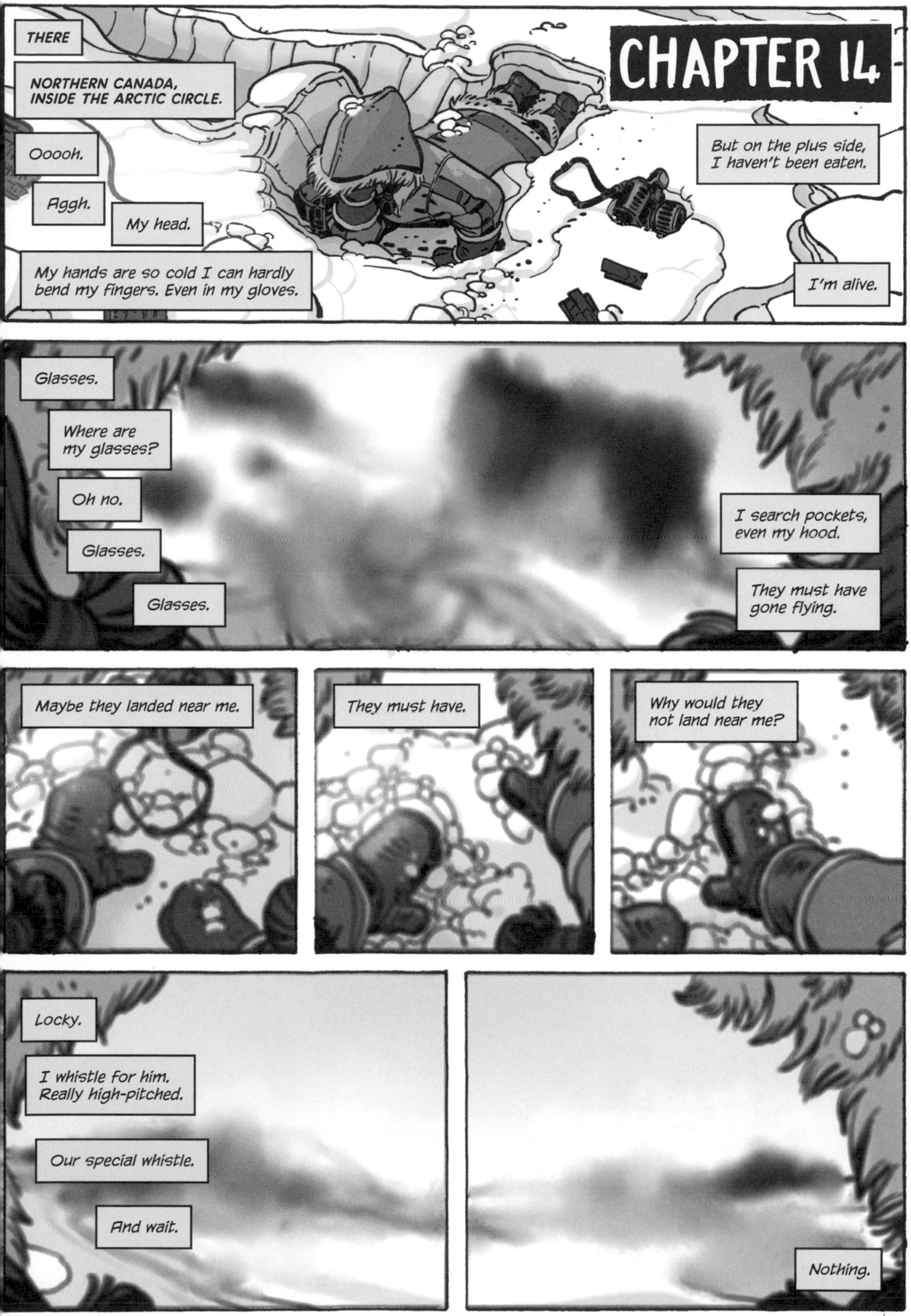

THERE
NORTHERN CANADA, INSIDE THE ARCTIC CIRCLE.
CHAPTER 14
Ooooh.
Aggh.
My head.
My hands are so cold I can hardly bend my fingers. Even in my gloves.
But on the plus side, I haven't been eaten.
I'm alive.
Glasses.
Where are my glasses?
Oh no.
Glasses.
Glasses.
I search pockets, even my hood.
They must have gone flying.
Maybe they landed near me.
They must have.
Why would they not land near me?
Locky.
I whistle for him. Really high-pitched.
Our special whistle.
And wait.
Nothing.

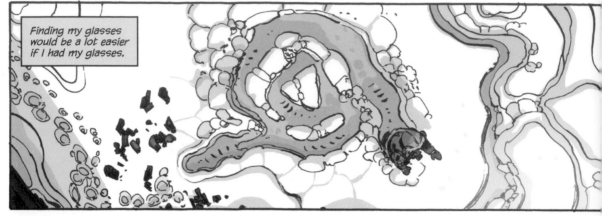

Finding my glasses would be a lot easier if I had my glasses.

I can see shapes.

The shapes could be snowdrifts. Or Locky, injured.

Or the bear.

I can't find my glasses and if I keep looking I'm going to freeze to death right here.

LOCKY? WHERE ARE YOU, BOY? ♪

I keep walking, staying low.

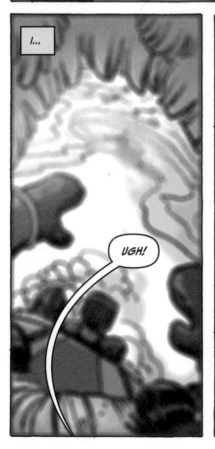

I....

UGH!

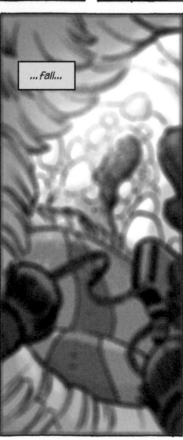

...fall...

OMFFF!

...like a baby.

I slide straight down into soft snow.

How will I ever get home without my glasses?

But then I see something and I know I'm not going home.

I see the bear.

Just sitting there.

Right in front of me.

Oh no.

The bear must be asleep.

How long before it hears me? Smells me?

Oh no.

Don't turn around.

Don't turn around.

Don't...

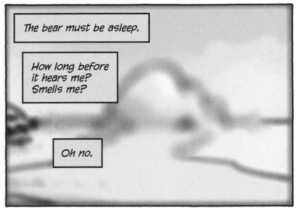

I have a penknife in my bag.

Maybe I should attack it. Scare it.

With a penknife? Against a hungry bear? Maybe not.

I don't think it knows I'm here.

Maybe I can scare it. With a really loud noise.

A really sudden, really loud noise.

If I move, it's going to hear me.

I've got almost nothing to lose.

If I can scare it, maybe I have a chance.

I have to do it.

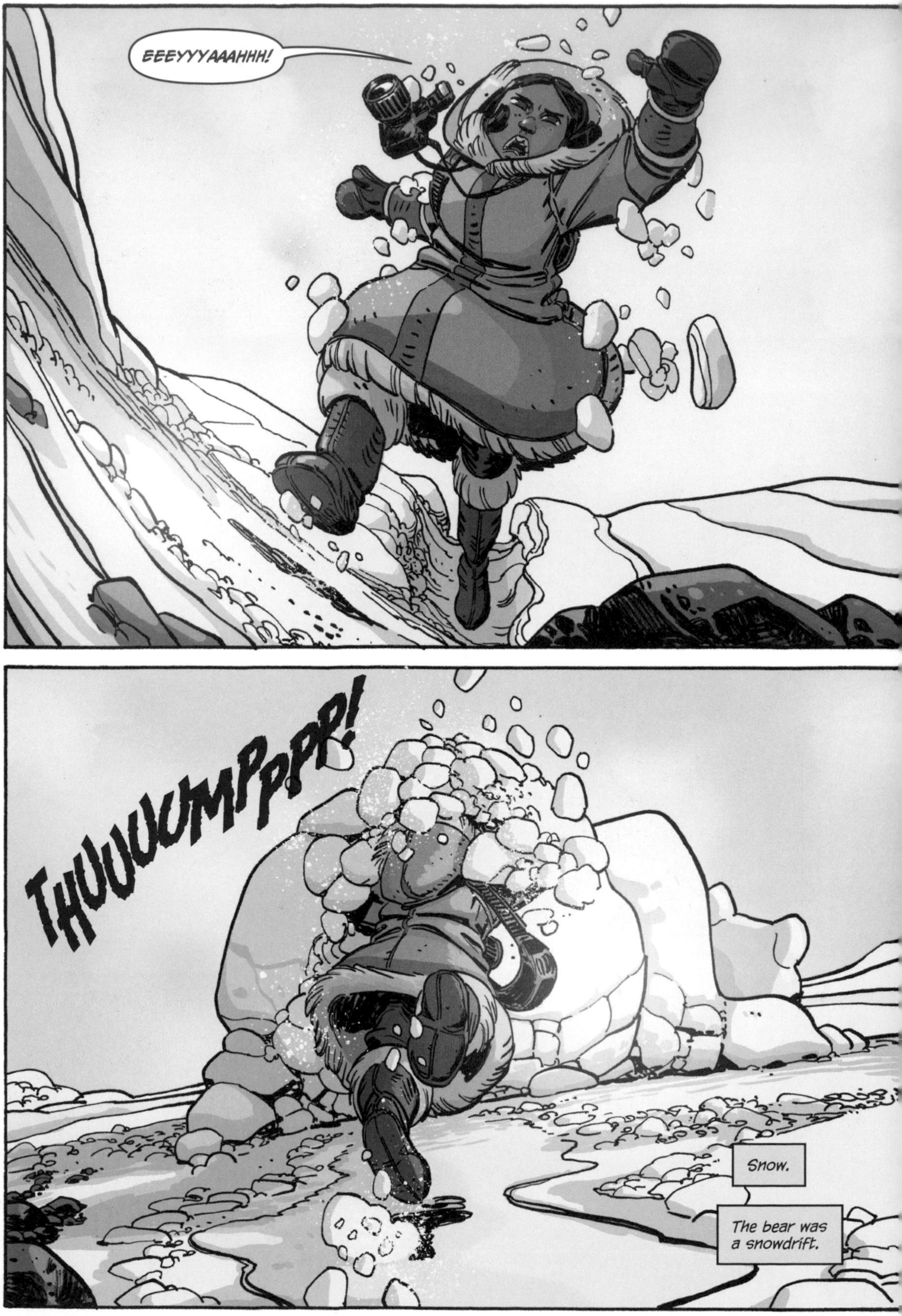
EEEYYYAAAHHH!
THUUUUMPPPP!
Snow.
The bear was a snowdrift.

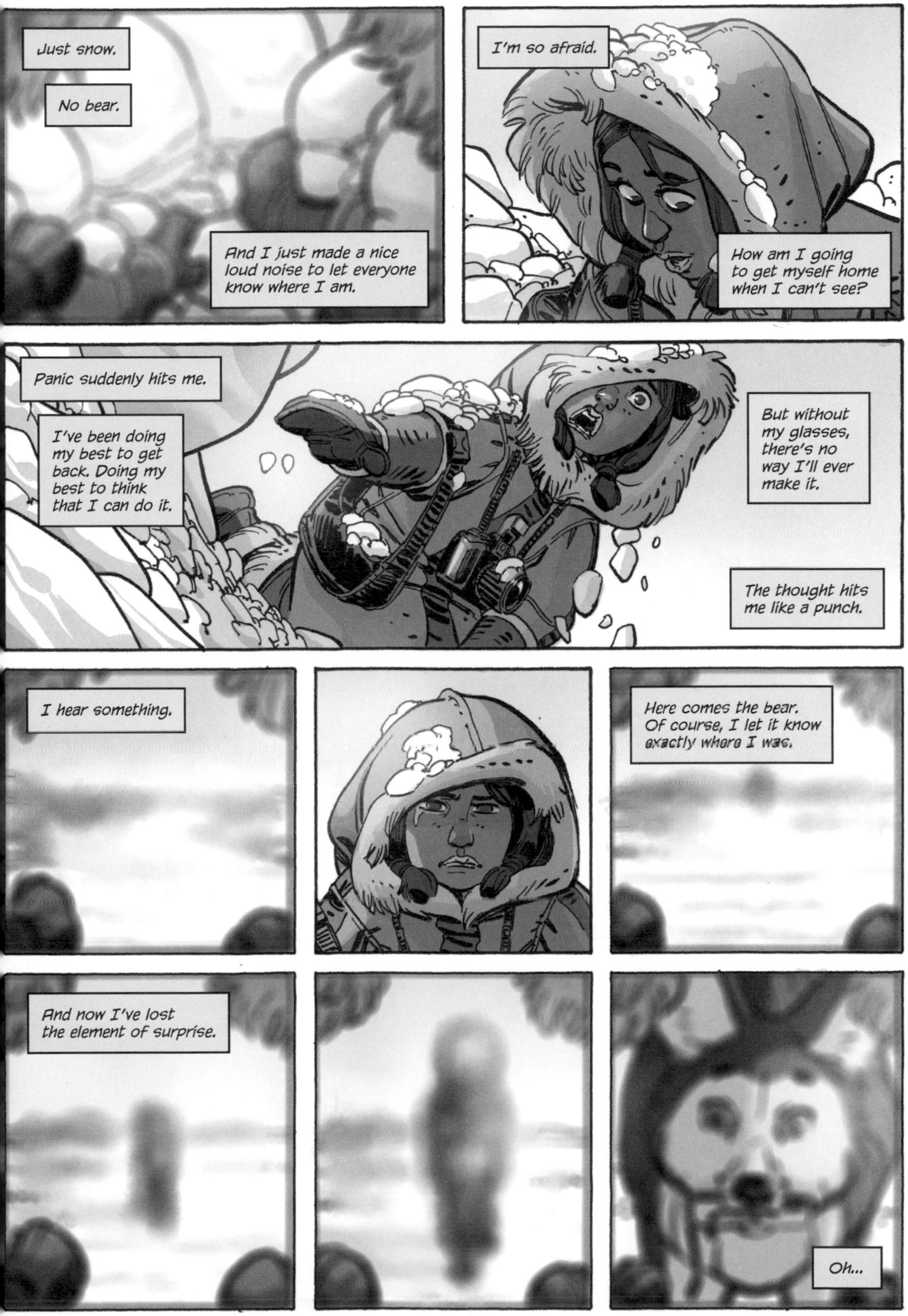
Just snow.
No bear.
And I just made a nice loud noise to let everyone know where I am.
I'm so afraid.
How am I going to get myself home when I can't see?
Panic suddenly hits me.
I've been doing my best to get back. Doing my best to think that I can do it.
But without my glasses, there's no way I'll ever make it.
The thought hits me like a punch.
I hear something.
Here comes the bear. Of course, I let it know exactly where I was.
And now I've lost the element of surprise.
Oh...

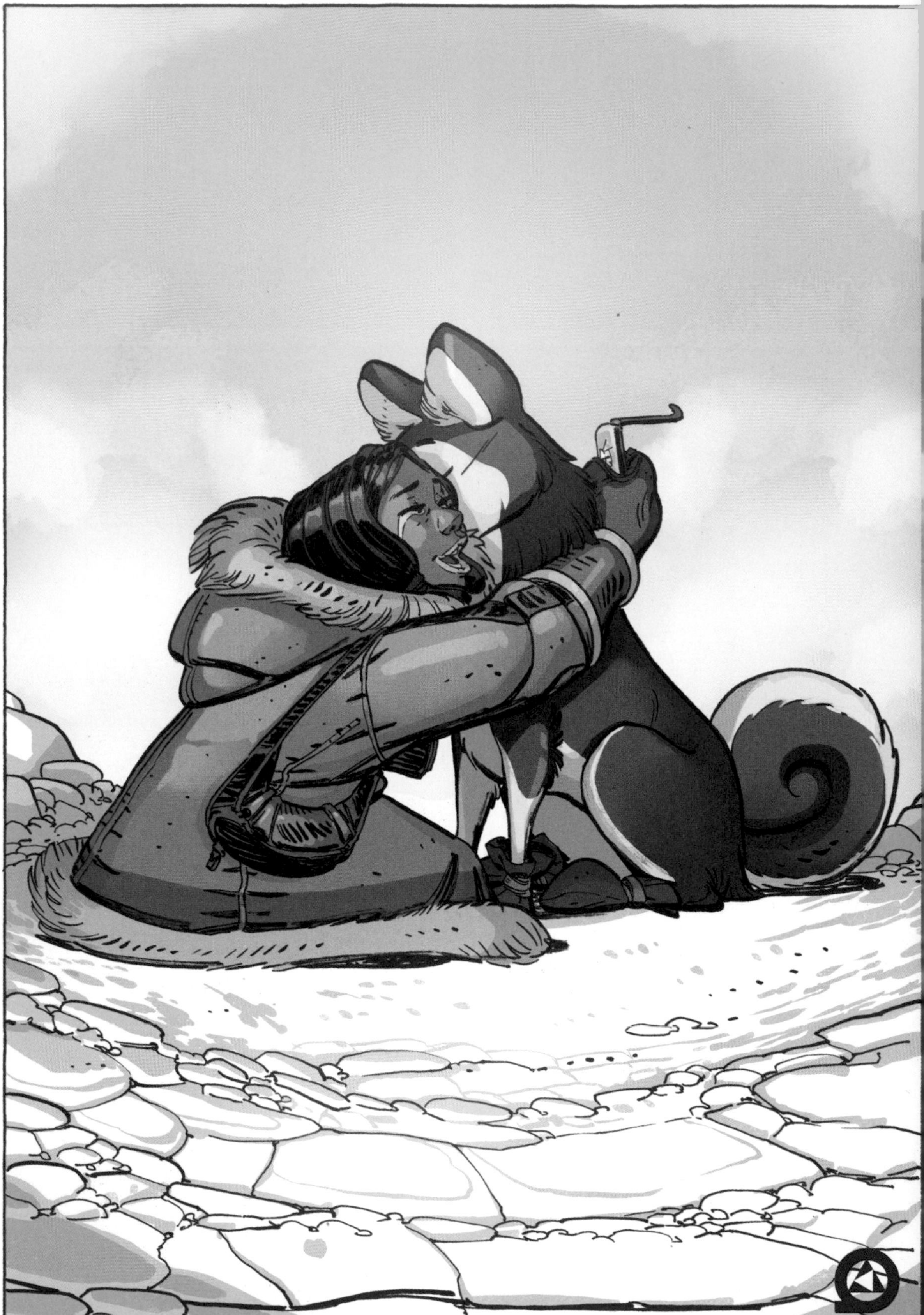

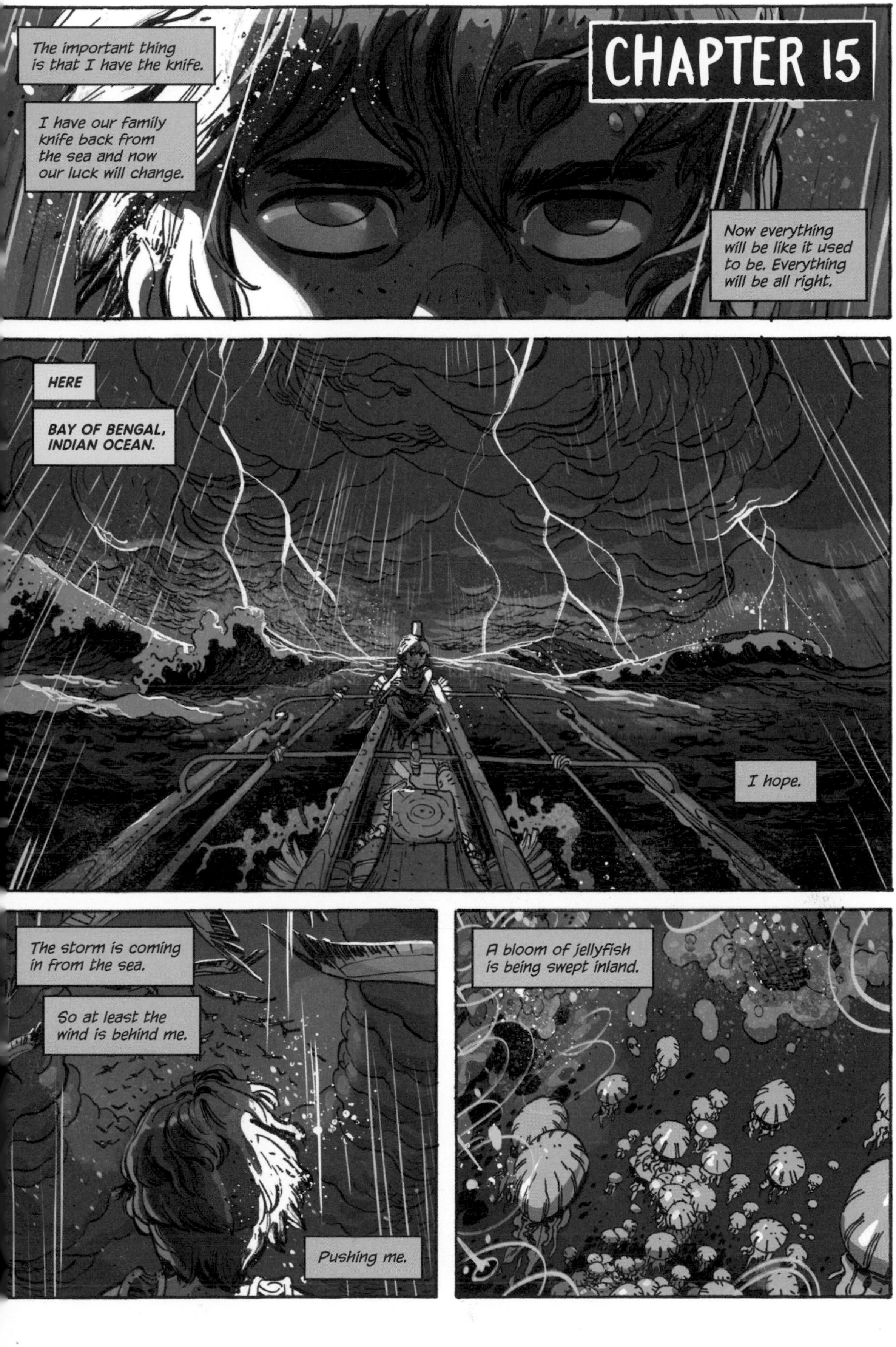
CHAPTER 15
The important thing is that I have the knife.
I have our family knife back from the sea and now our luck will change.
Now everything will be like it used to be. Everything will be all right.
HERE
BAY OF BENGAL, INDIAN OCEAN.
I hope.
The storm is coming in from the sea.
So at least the wind is behind me.
Pushing me.
A bloom of jellyfish is being swept inland.

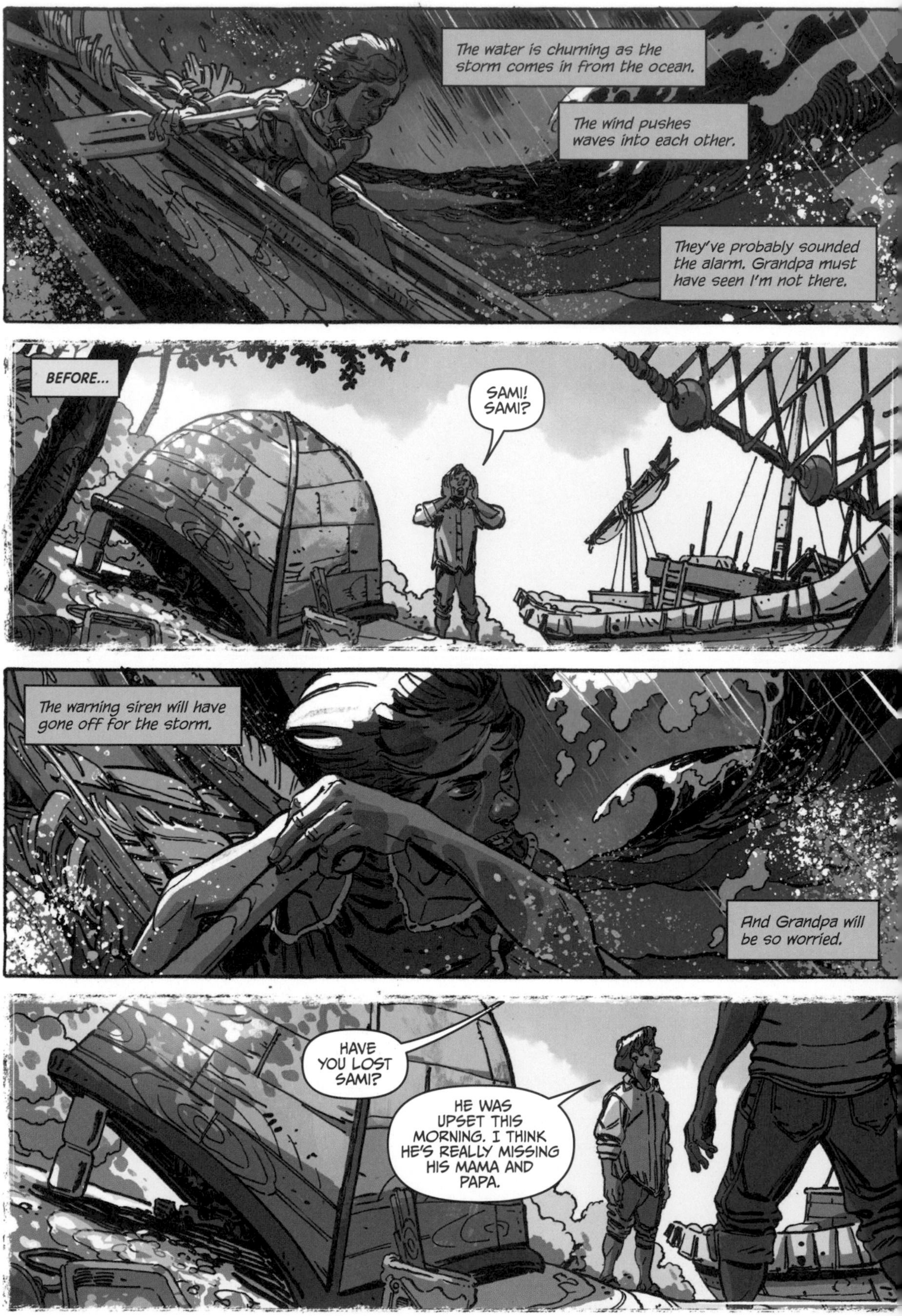
The water is churning as the storm comes in from the ocean.
The wind pushes waves into each other.
They've probably sounded the alarm. Grandpa must have seen I'm not there.
BEFORE...
SAMI! SAMI?
The warning siren will have gone off for the storm.
And Grandpa will be so worried.
HAVE YOU LOST SAMI?
HE WAS UPSET THIS MORNING. I THINK HE'S REALLY MISSING HIS MAMA AND PAPA.

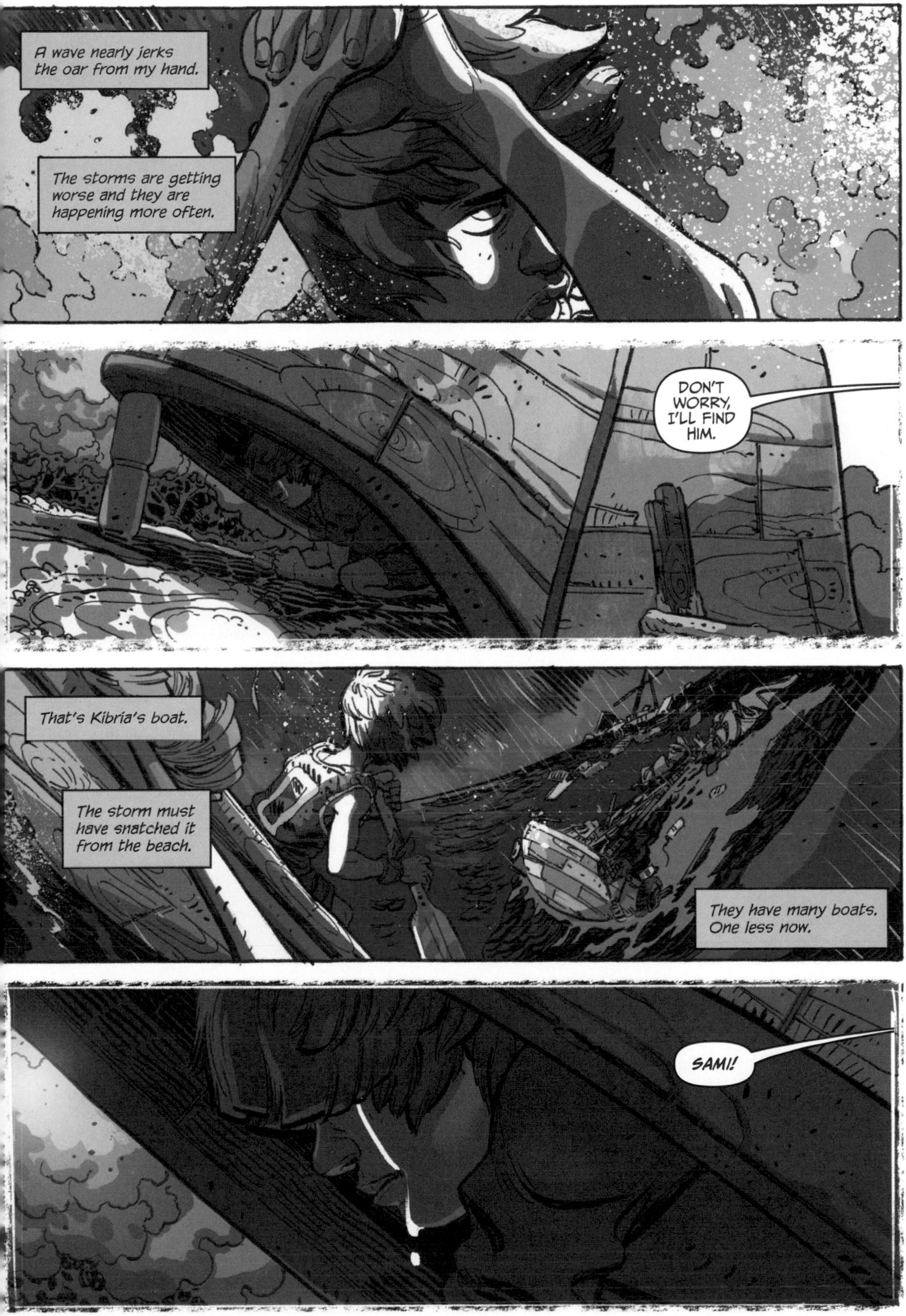
A wave nearly jerks the oar from my hand.
The storms are getting worse and they are happening more often.
DON'T WORRY, I'LL FIND HIM.
That's Kibria's boat.
The storm must have snatched it from the beach.
They have many boats. One less now.
SAMI!

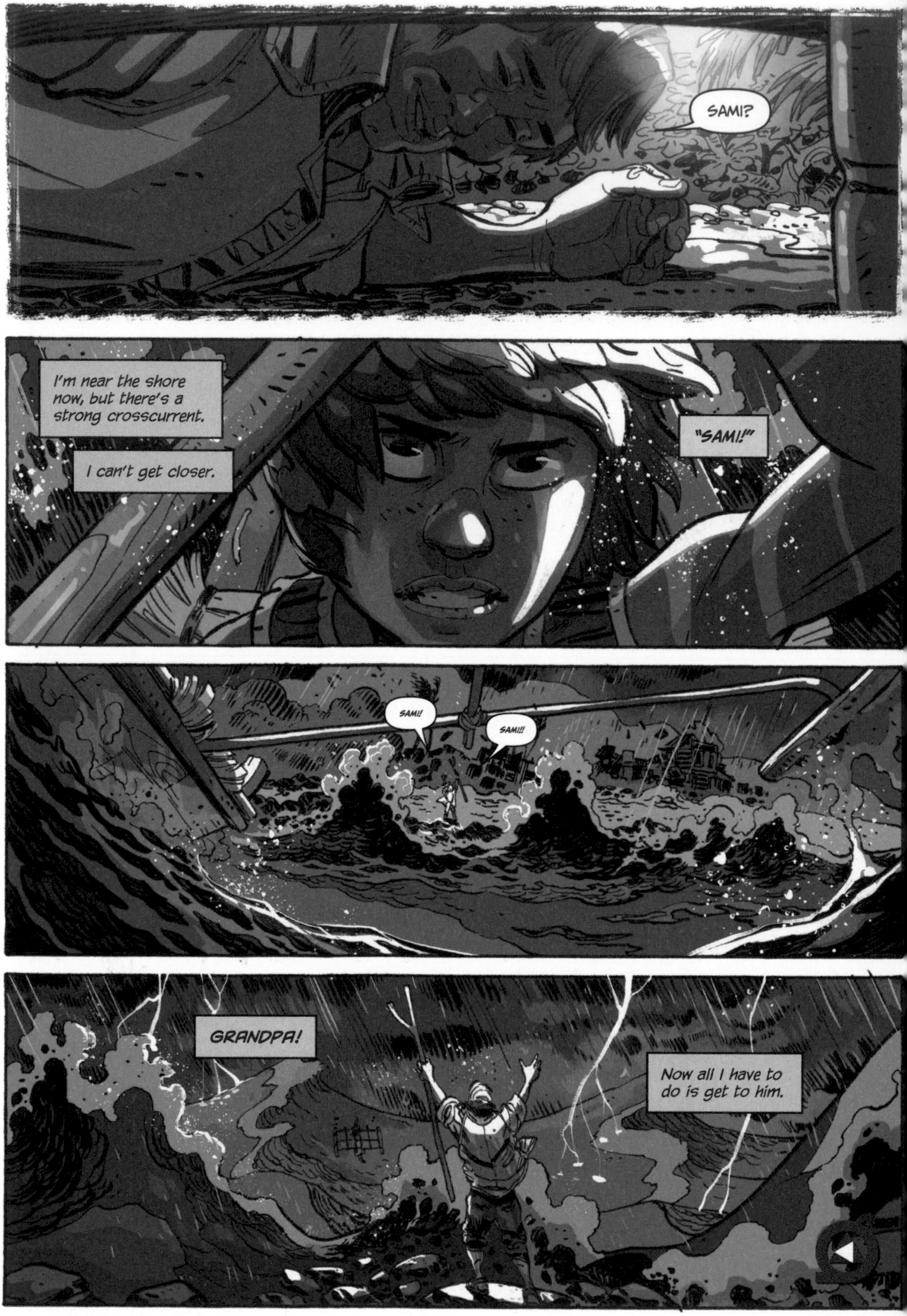
SAMI?
I'm near the shore now, but there's a strong crosscurrent.
I can't get closer.
"SAMI!"
SAMI!
SAMI!!
GRANDPA!
Now all I have to do is get to him.

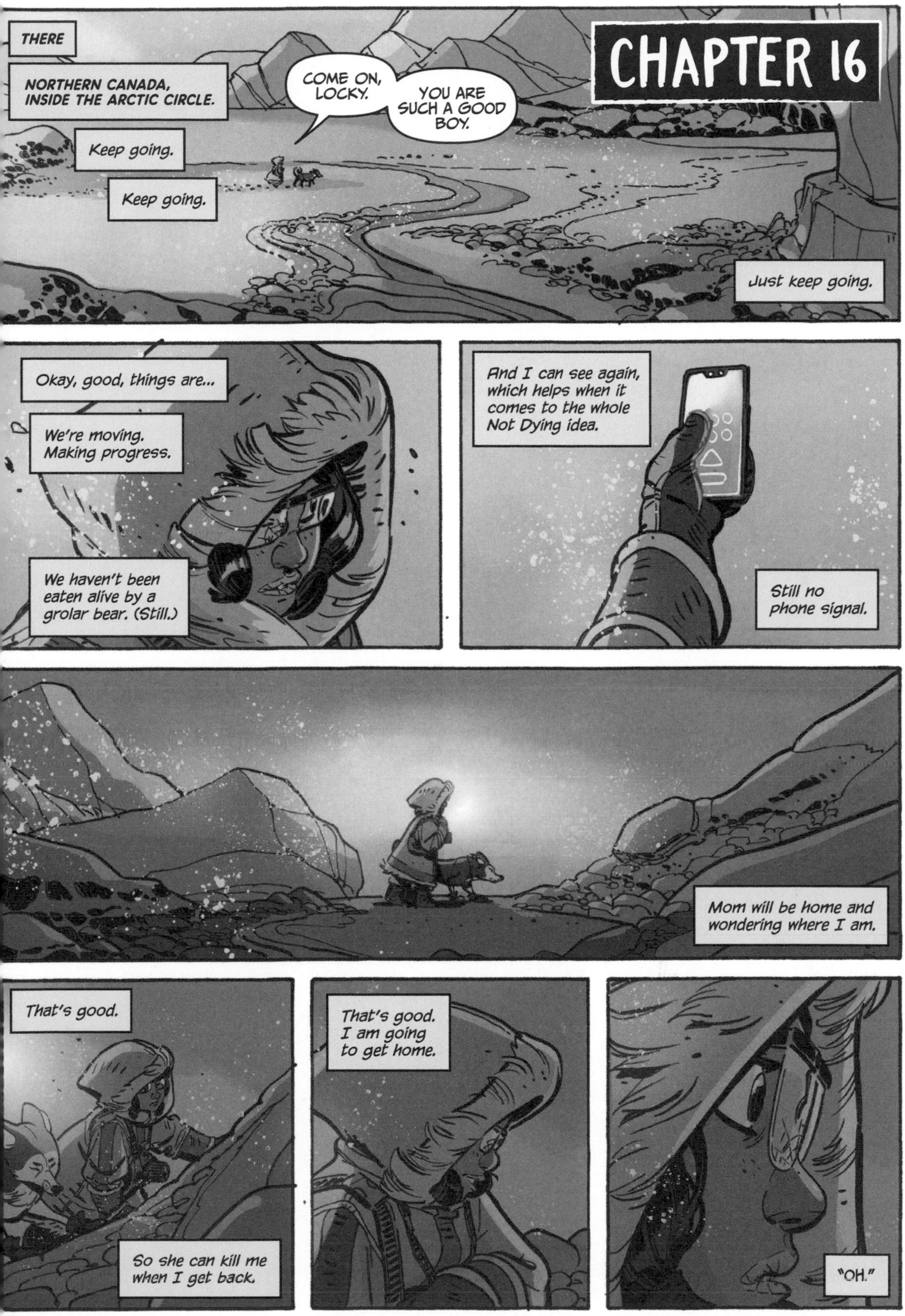
THERE
NORTHERN CANADA, INSIDE THE ARCTIC CIRCLE.
Keep going.
Keep going.
COME ON, LOCKY.
YOU ARE SUCH A GOOD BOY.
CHAPTER 16
Just keep going.
Okay, good, things are...
We're moving. Making progress.
We haven't been eaten alive by a grolar bear. (Still.)
And I can see again, which helps when it comes to the whole Not Dying idea.
Still no phone signal.
Mom will be home and wondering where I am.
That's good.
So she can kill me when I get back.
That's good. I am going to get home.
"OH."

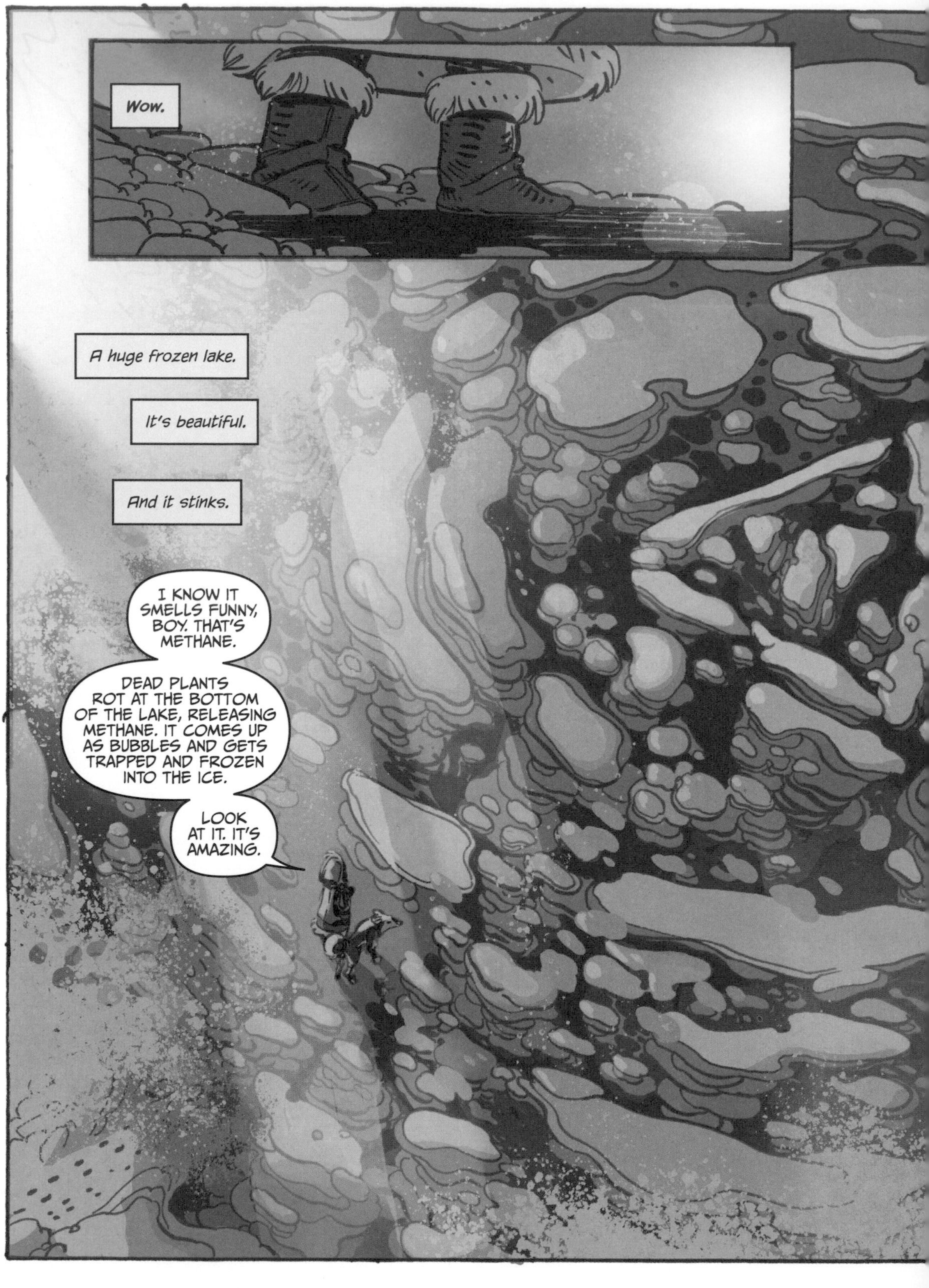
Wow.
A huge frozen lake.
It's beautiful.
And it stinks.
I KNOW IT SMELLS FUNNY, BOY. THAT'S METHANE.
DEAD PLANTS ROT AT THE BOTTOM OF THE LAKE, RELEASING METHANE. IT COMES UP AS BUBBLES AND GETS TRAPPED AND FROZEN INTO THE ICE.
LOOK AT IT. IT'S AMAZING.

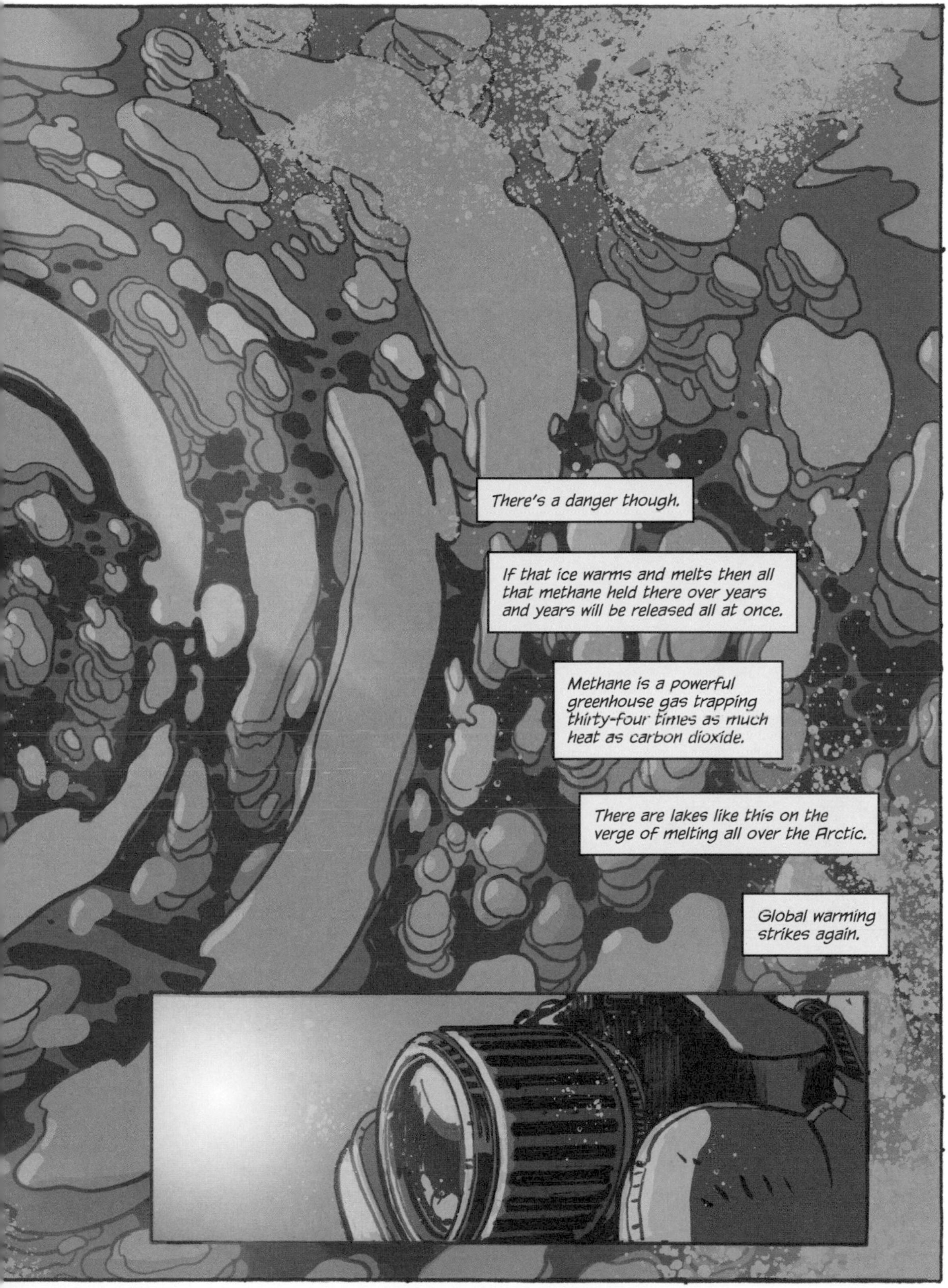
There's a danger though.
If that ice warms and melts then all that methane held there over years and years will be released all at once.
Methane is a powerful greenhouse gas trapping thirty-four times as much heat as carbon dioxide.
There are lakes like this on the verge of melting all over the Arctic.
Global warming strikes again.

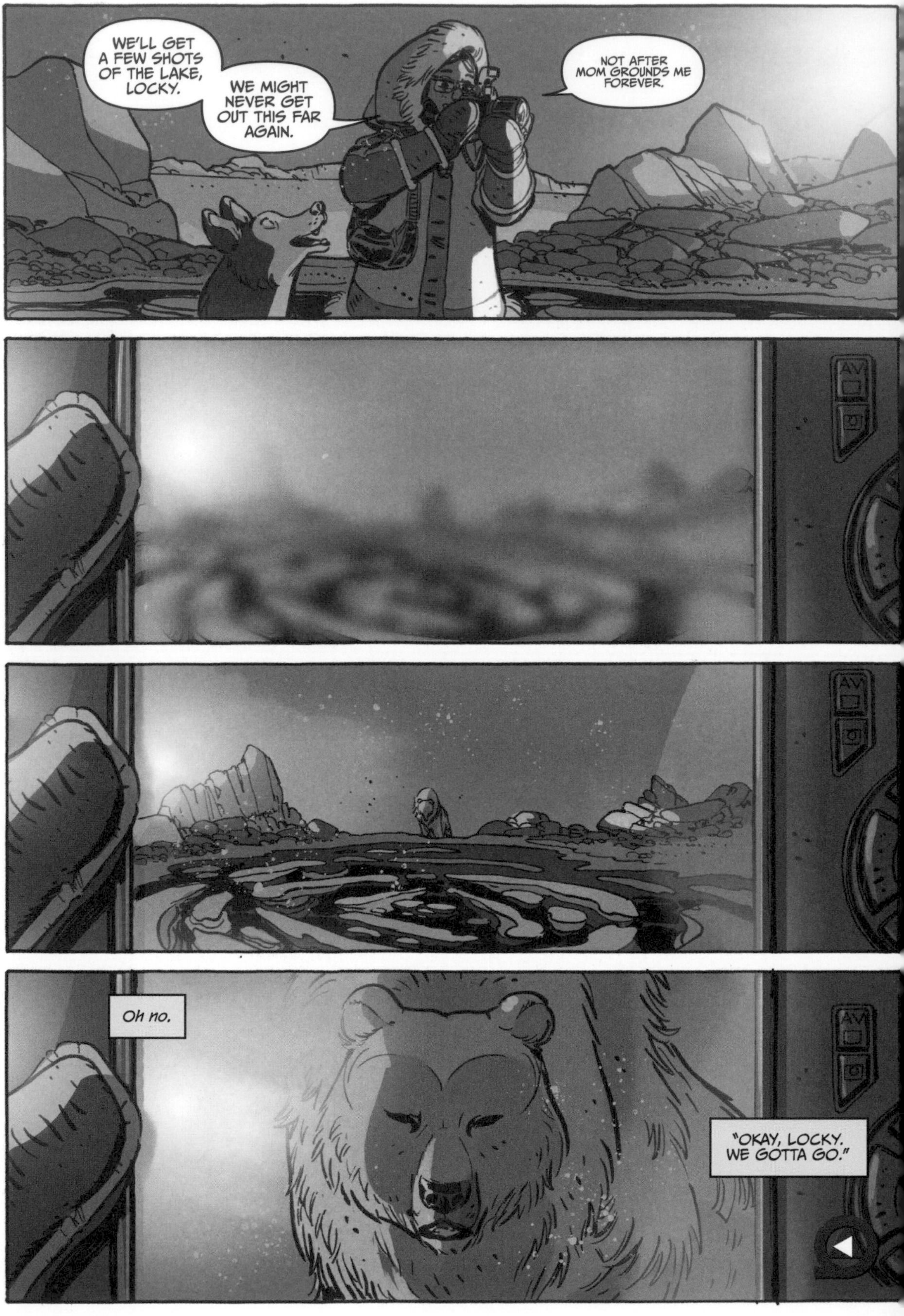
WE'LL GET A FEW SHOTS OF THE LAKE, LOCKY.
WE MIGHT NEVER GET OUT THIS FAR AGAIN.
NOT AFTER MOM GROUNDS ME FOREVER.
AV
AV
Oh no.
AV
"OKAY, LOCKY. WE GOTTA GO."

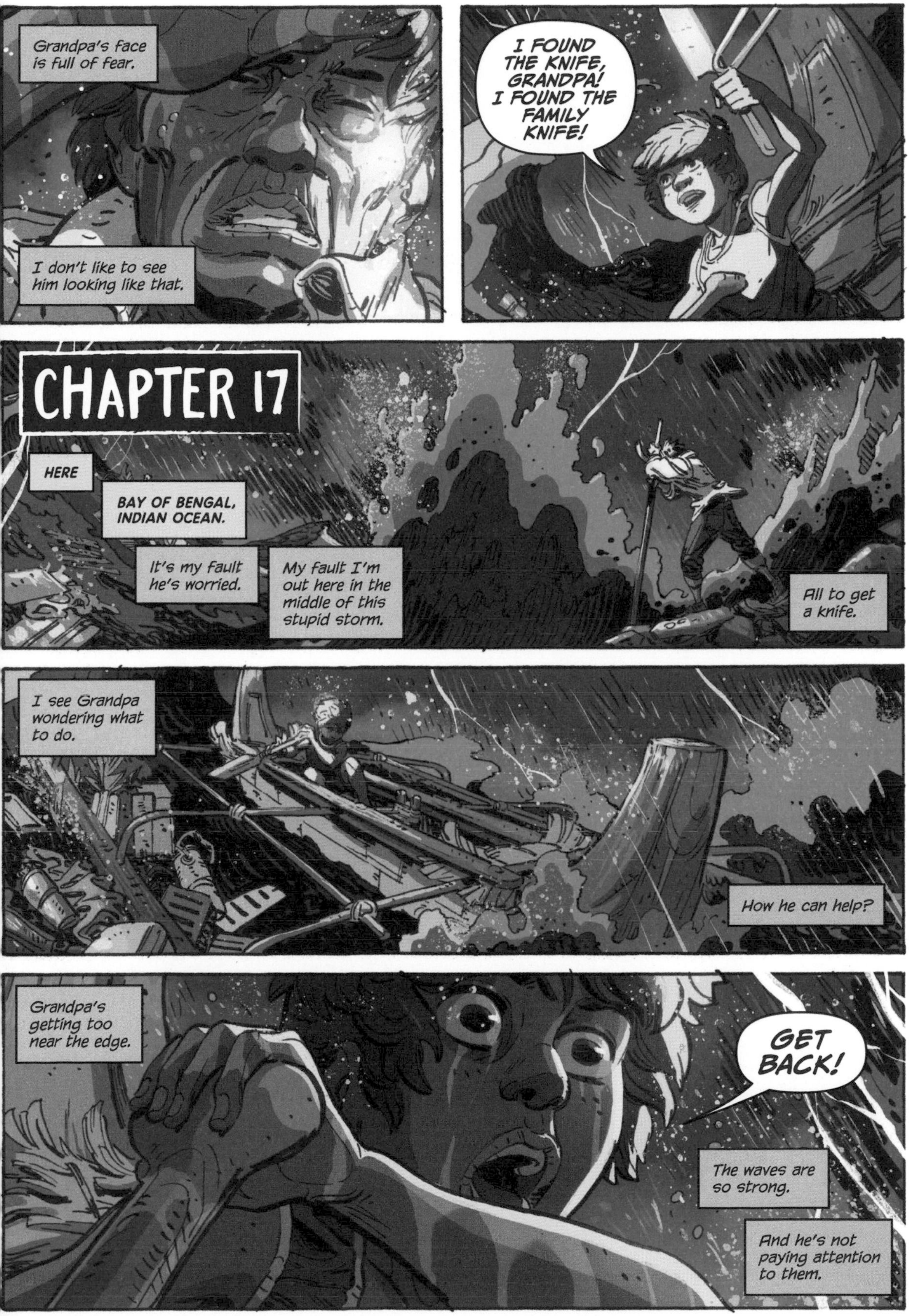
Grandpa's face is full of fear.
I don't like to see him looking like that.
I FOUND THE KNIFE, GRANDPA! I FOUND THE FAMILY KNIFE!
CHAPTER 17
HERE
BAY OF BENGAL, INDIAN OCEAN.
It's my fault he's worried.
My fault I'm out here in the middle of this stupid storm.
All to get a knife.
I see Grandpa wondering what to do.
How he can help?
Grandpa's getting too near the edge.
GET BACK!
The waves are so strong.
And he's not paying attention to them.

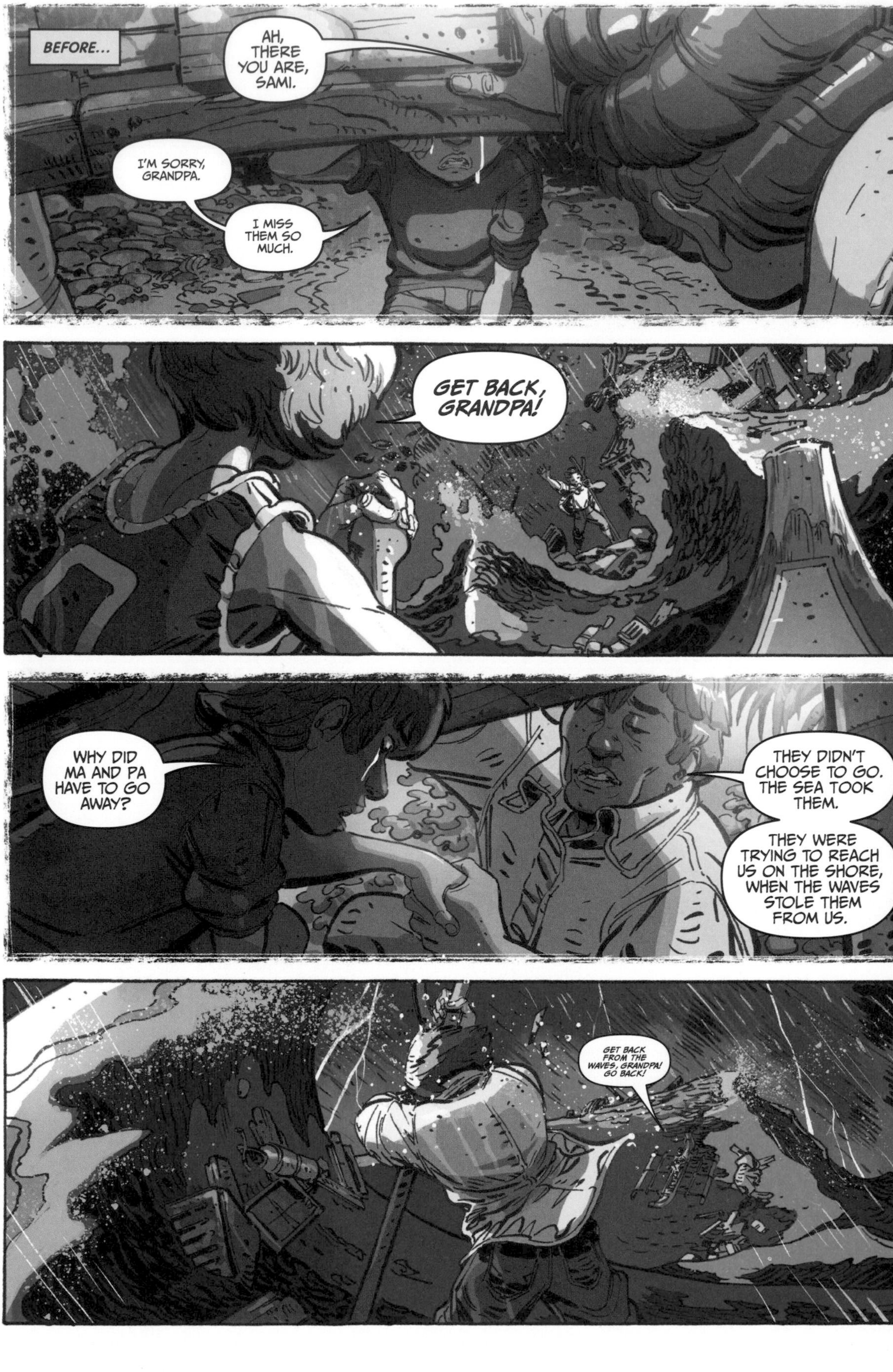
BEFORE...
AH, THERE YOU ARE, SAMI.
I'M SORRY, GRANDPA.
I MISS THEM SO MUCH.
GET BACK, GRANDPA!
WHY DID MA AND PA HAVE TO GO AWAY?
THEY DIDN'T CHOOSE TO GO. THE SEA TOOK THEM.
THEY WERE TRYING TO REACH US ON THE SHORE, WHEN THE WAVES STOLE THEM FROM US.
GET BACK FROM THE WAVES, GRANDPA! GO BACK!

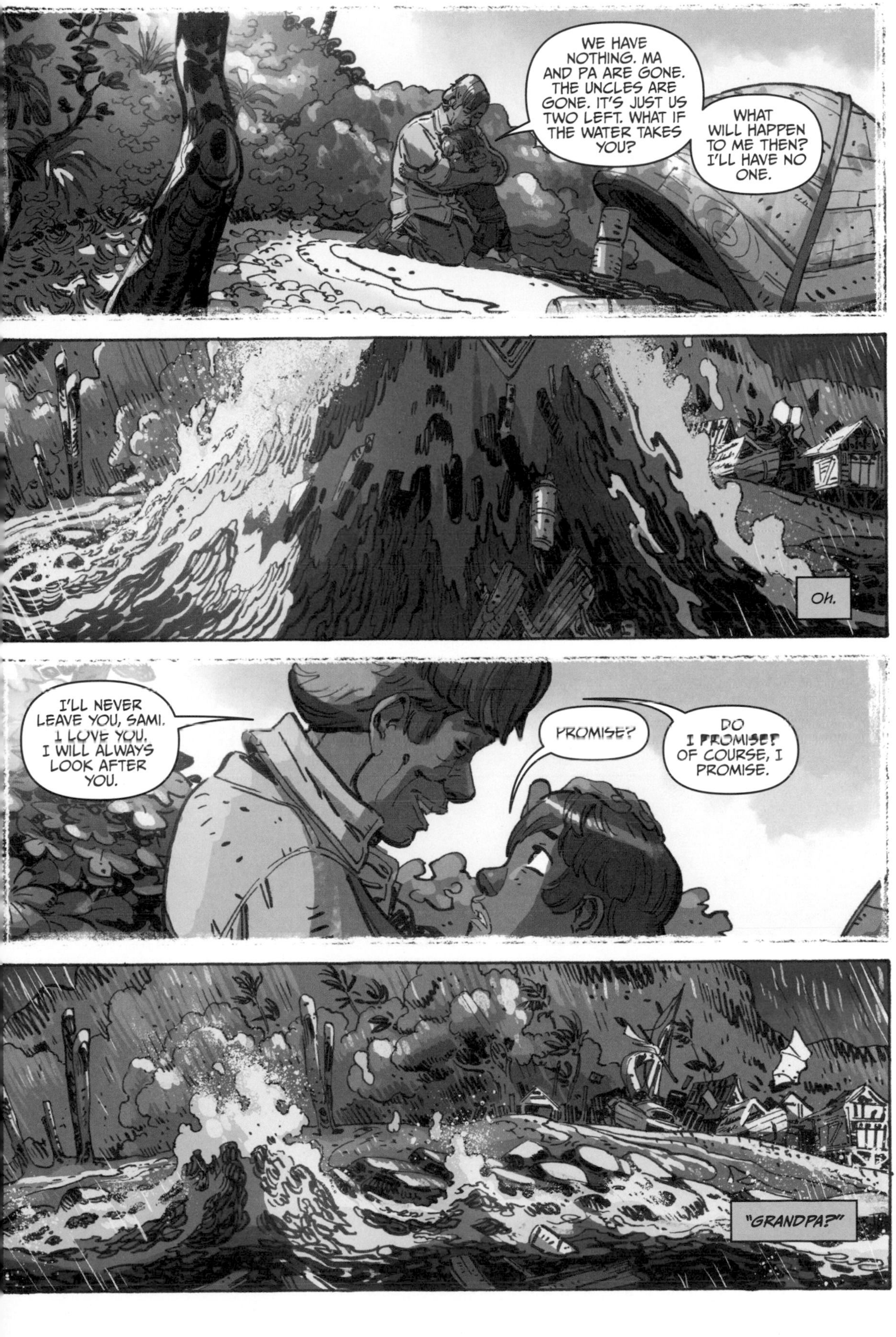
WE HAVE NOTHING. MA AND PA ARE GONE. THE UNCLES ARE GONE. IT'S JUST US TWO LEFT. WHAT IF THE WATER TAKES YOU?
WHAT WILL HAPPEN TO ME THEN? I'LL HAVE NO ONE.
Oh.
I'LL NEVER LEAVE YOU, SAMI. I LOVE YOU. I WILL ALWAYS LOOK AFTER YOU.
PROMISE?
DO I PROMISE? OF COURSE, I PROMISE.
"GRANDPA?"

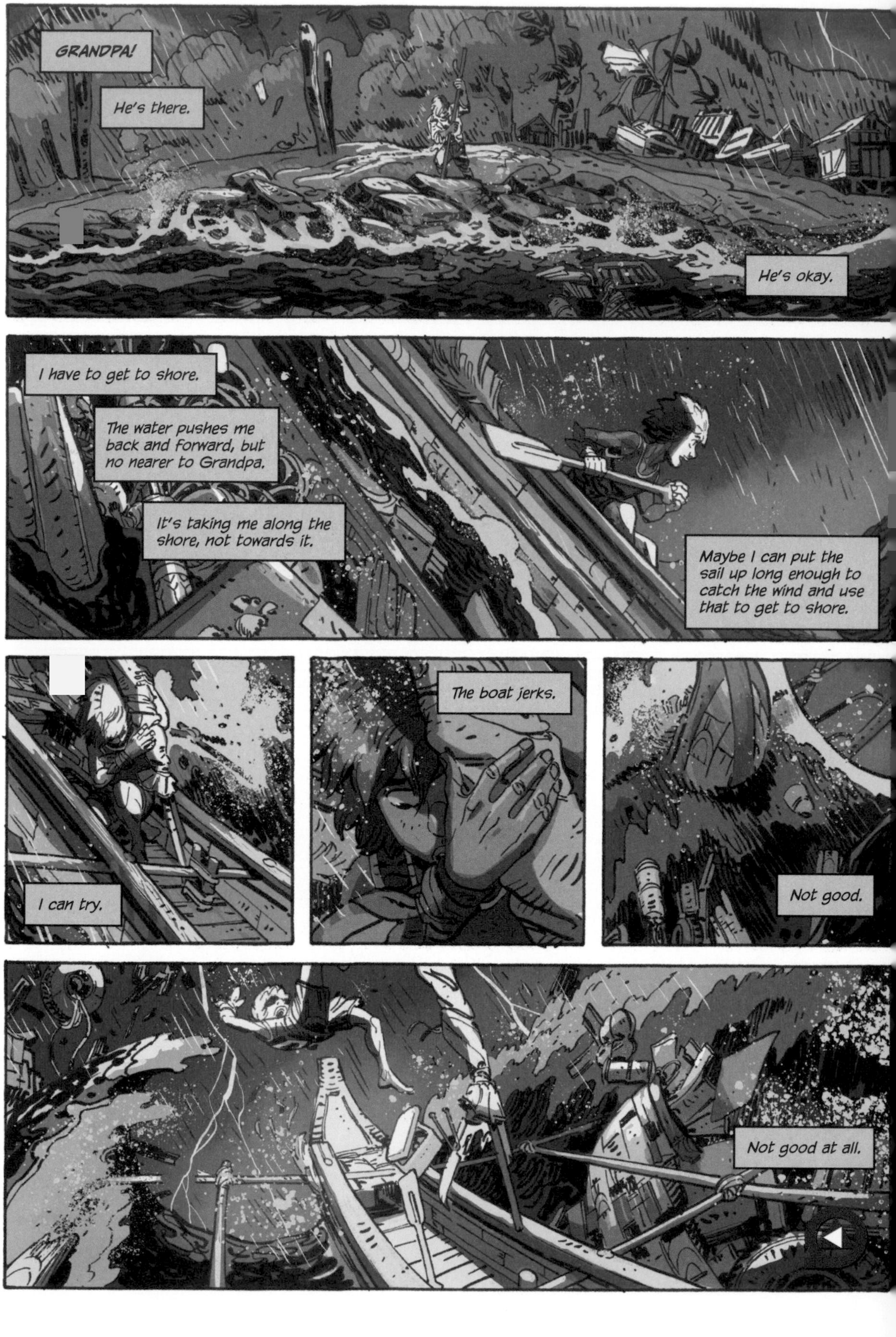
GRANDPA!
He's there.
He's okay.
I have to get to shore.
The water pushes me back and forward, but no nearer to Grandpa.
It's taking me along the shore, not towards it.
Maybe I can put the sail up long enough to catch the wind and use that to get to shore.
I can try.
The boat jerks.
Not good.
Not good at all.

THERE

NORTHERN CANADA, INSIDE THE ARCTIC CIRCLE.

CHAPTER 18

We run.

It's behind us.

That slow, fast, lumbering movement.

On the horizon, I see two sharp mountains with a third one—smaller—exactly in the middle. A transit—something that lines up with something else in the landscape to show you the way.

I know home is in line with that.

Dad would be proud.

We run.

We need to cross the river, Locky.

if we follow the transit it will lead us to a rope bridge.

I hear it before I see it.

Rushing water.

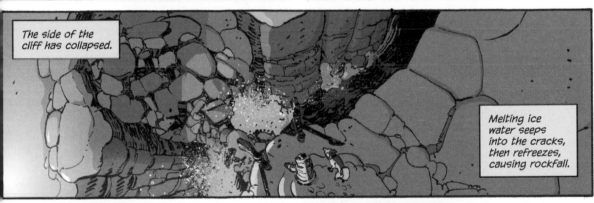

The side of the cliff has collapsed.

Melting ice water seeps into the cracks, then refreezes, causing rockfall.

We can scramble across and then jump.

I think.

I hope.

We don't have much time.

Should I put Locky in his harness?

I don't want to pull him in if I fall, but he might not cross otherwise.

I guess I can always let go if I do fall.

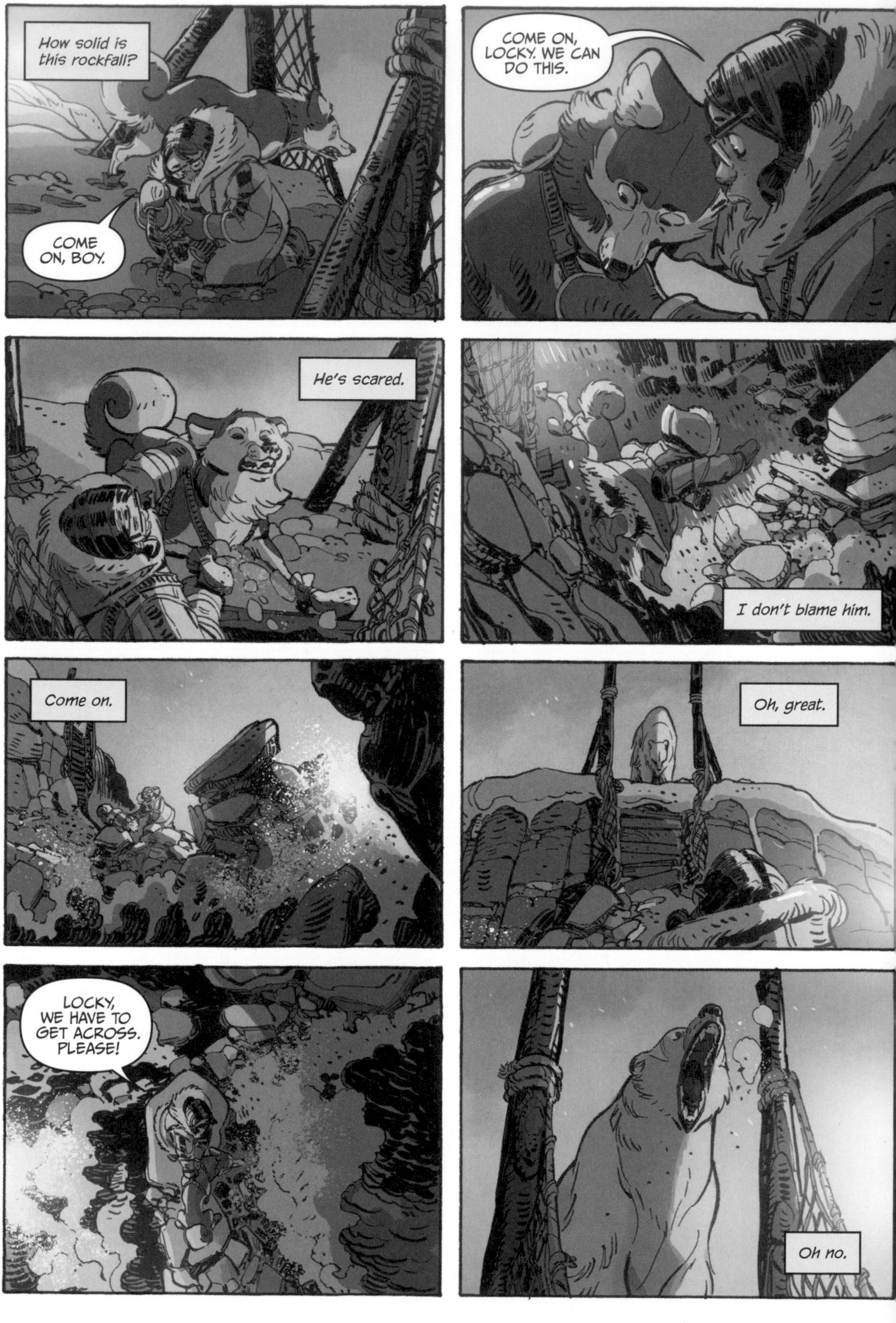
How solid is this rockfall?
COME ON, BOY.
COME ON, LOCKY. WE CAN DO THIS.
He's scared.
I don't blame him.
Come on.
Oh, great.
LOCKY, WE HAVE TO GET ACROSS. PLEASE!
Oh no.

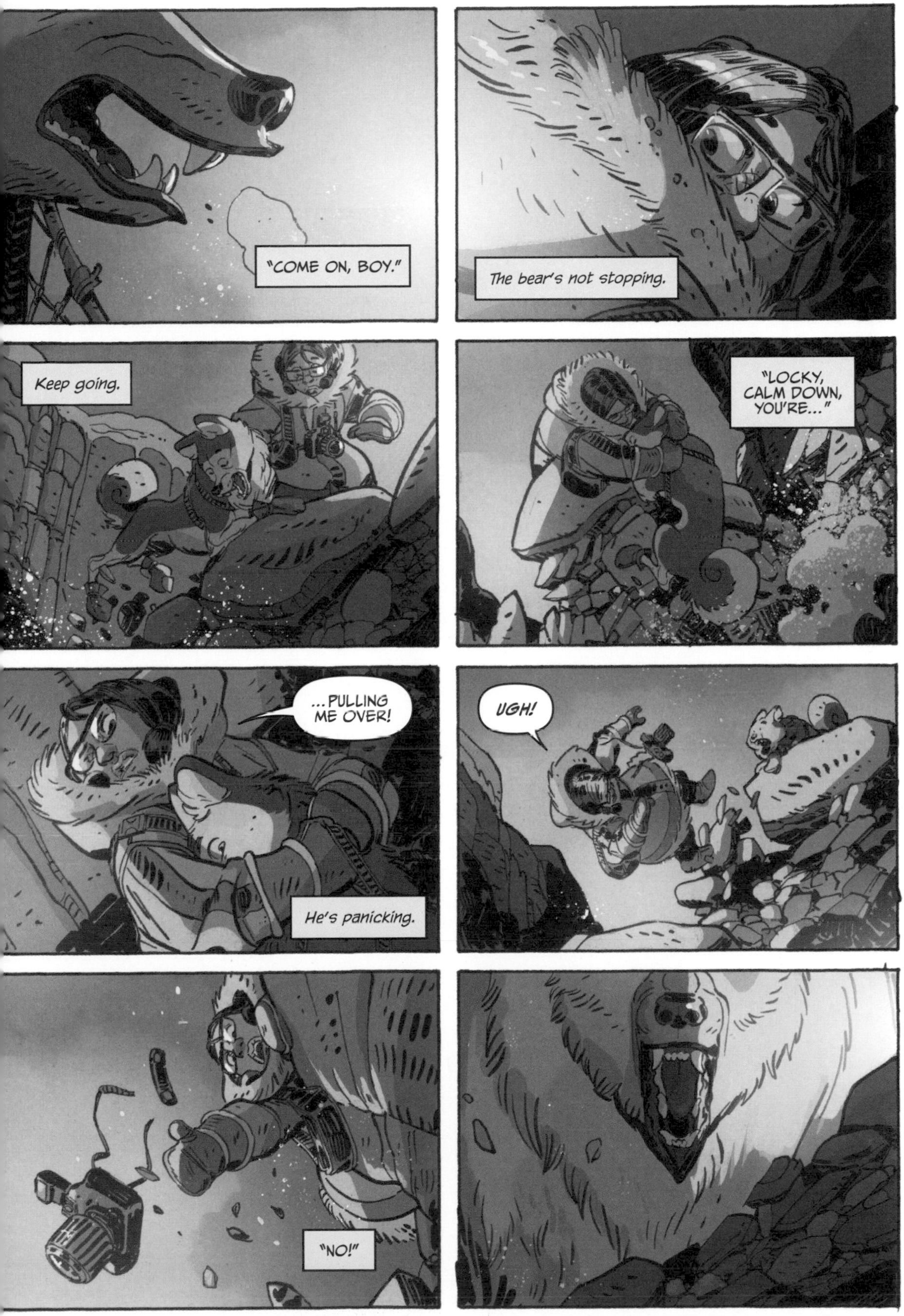
"COME ON, BOY."
The bear's not stopping.
Keep going.
"LOCKY, CALM DOWN, YOU'RE..."
...PULLING ME OVER!
He's panicking.
UGH!
"NO!"

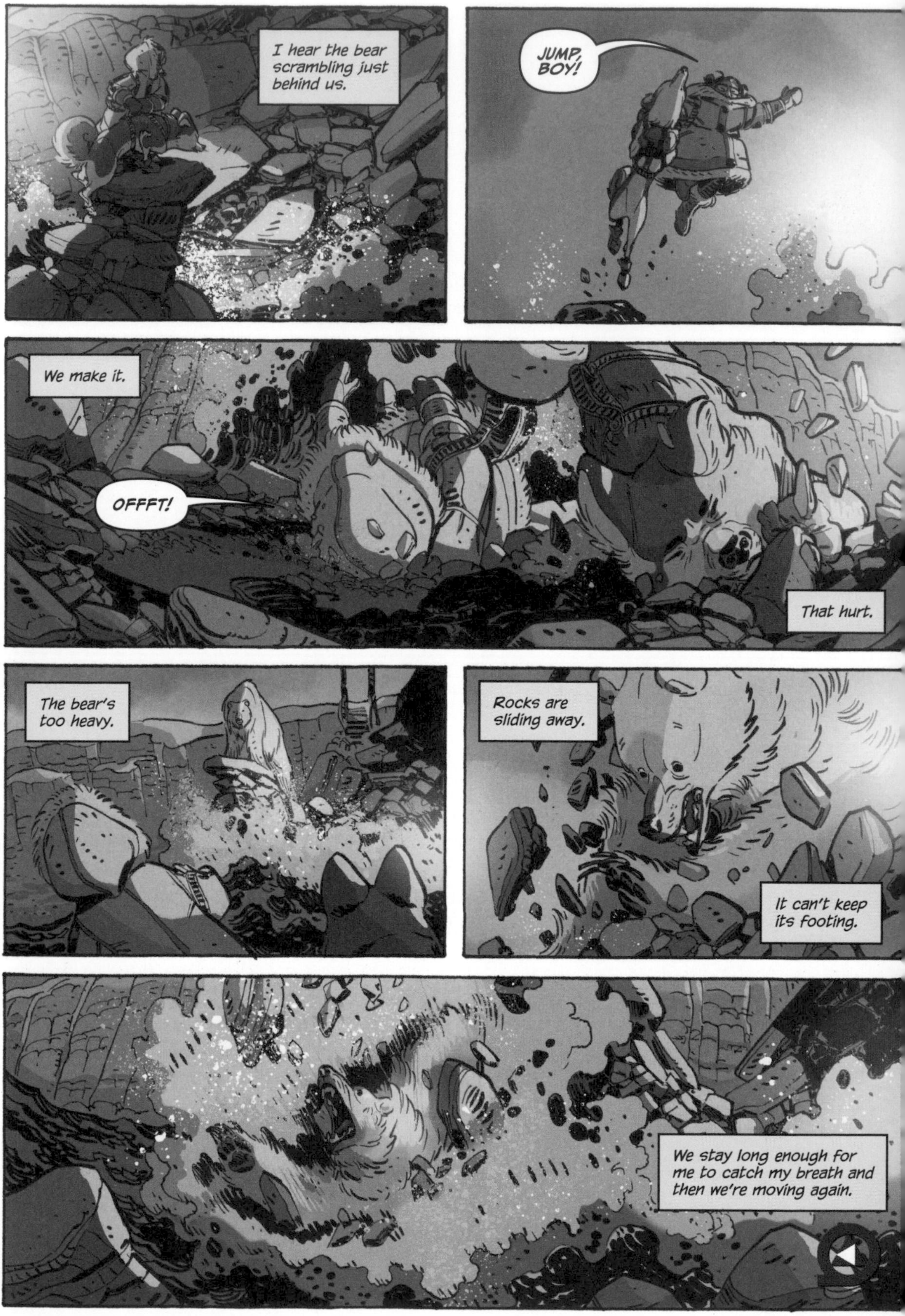
I hear the bear scrambling just behind us.
JUMP, BOY!
We make it.
OFFFT!
That hurt.
The bear's too heavy.
Rocks are sliding away.
It can't keep its footing.
We stay long enough for me to catch my breath and then we're moving again.

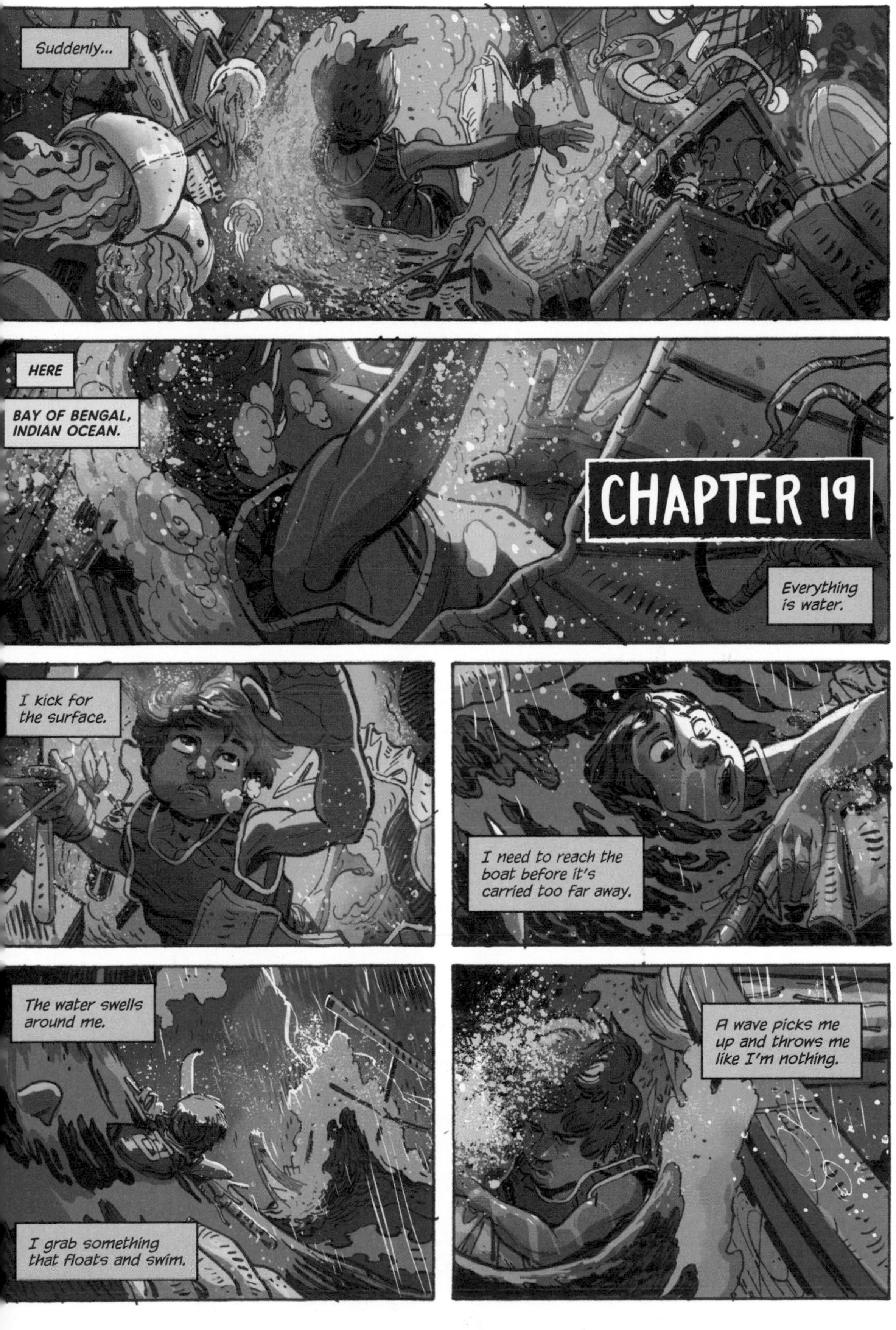
Suddenly...
HERE
BAY OF BENGAL, INDIAN OCEAN.
CHAPTER 19
Everything is water.
I kick for the surface.
I need to reach the boat before it's carried too far away.
The water swells around me.
I grab something that floats and swim.
A wave picks me up and throws me like I'm nothing.

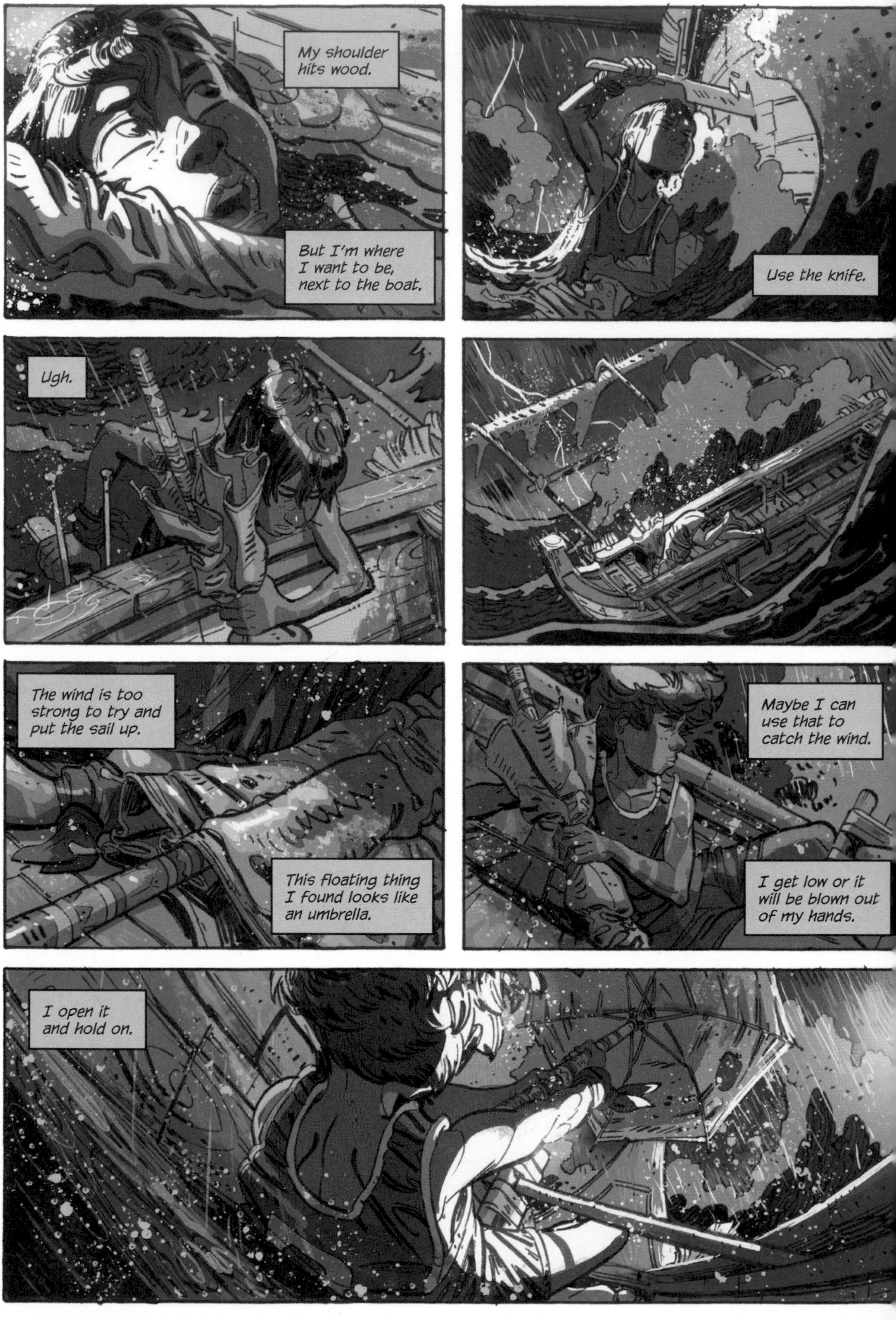
My shoulder hits wood.
But I'm where I want to be, next to the boat.
Use the knife.
Ugh.
The wind is too strong to try and put the sail up.
This floating thing I found looks like an umbrella.
Maybe I can use that to catch the wind.
I get low or it will be blown out of my hands.
I open it and hold on.

It catches the wind and nearly jerks out of my hands.

I hold the umbrella high enough to catch the wind but low enough to keep it from being pulled apart.

I hold on.

It's working.

The wind is pushing us across the current.

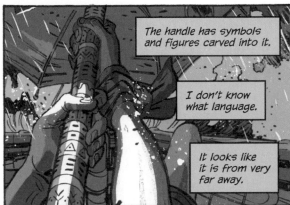

The handle has symbols and figures carved into it.

I don't know what language.

It looks like it is from very far away.

SAMI!

I hold on and hope the shore is getting closer.

It's all I can do.

The waves are so high and there's so much spray that it's hard to see where the sea ends and the shore begins.

What is that?

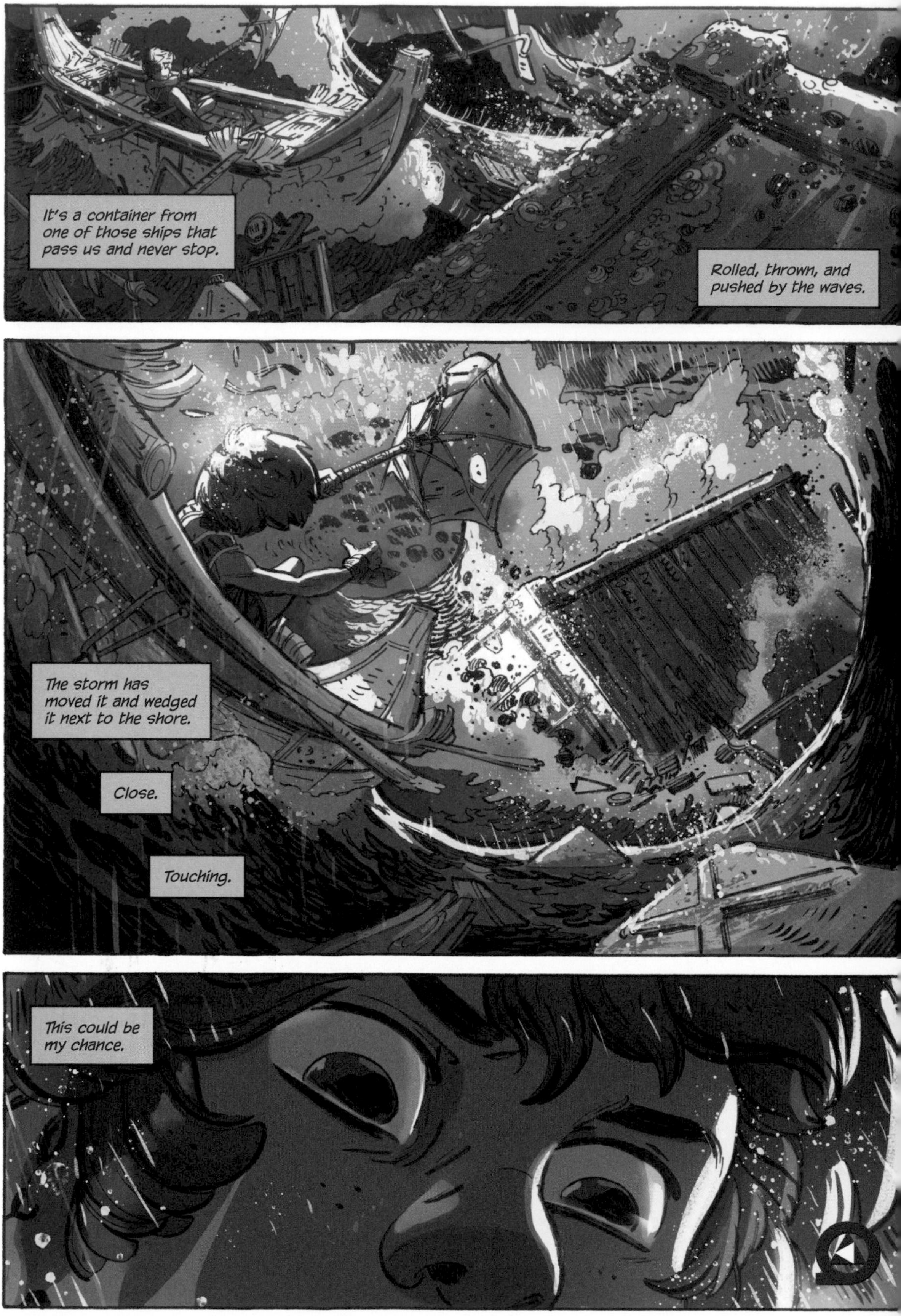
It's a container from one of those ships that pass us and never stop.
Rolled, thrown, and pushed by the waves.
The storm has moved it and wedged it next to the shore.
Close.
Touching.
This could be my chance.

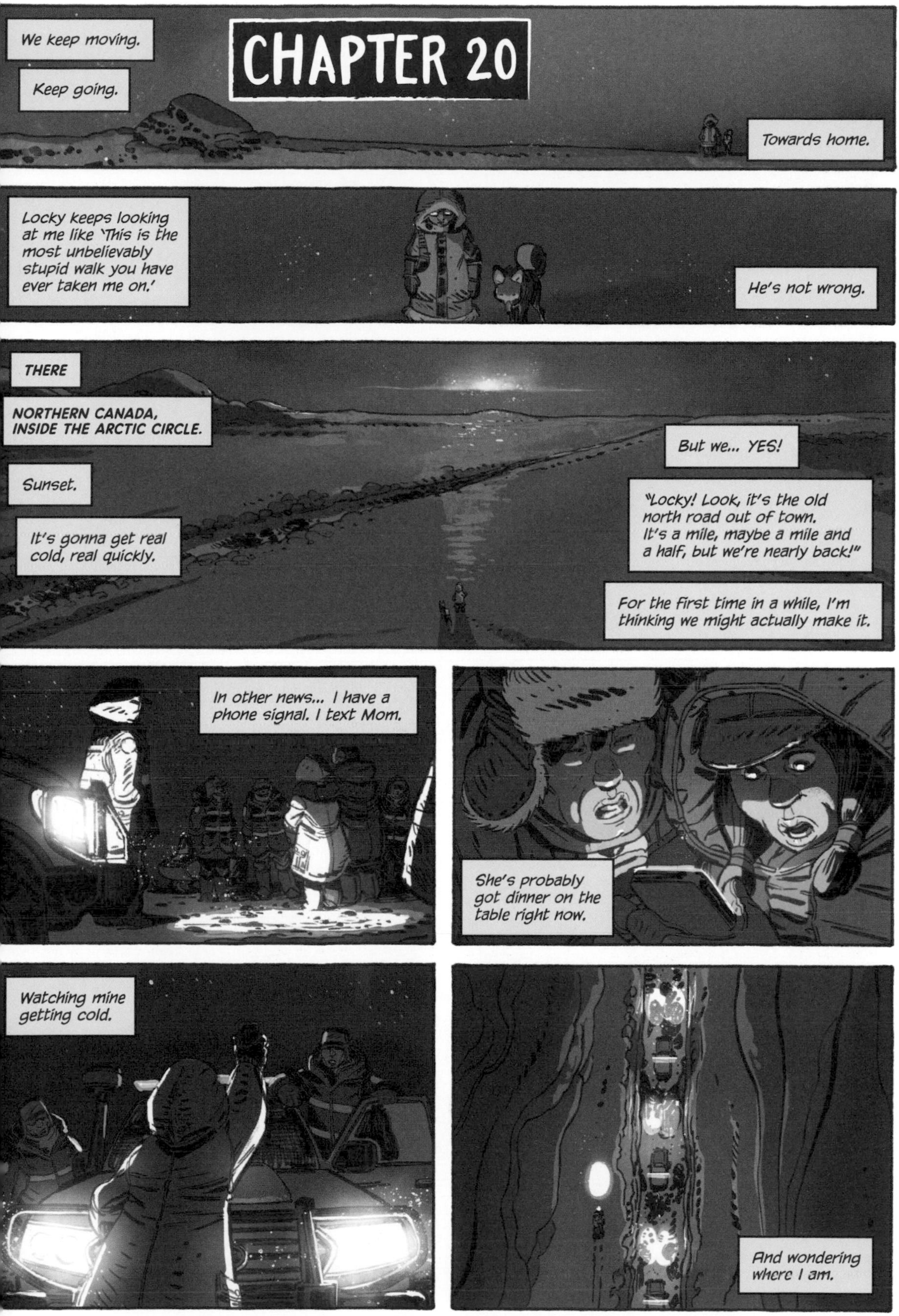
We keep moving.
CHAPTER 20
Keep going.
Towards home.
Locky keeps looking at me like 'This is the most unbelievably stupid walk you have ever taken me on.'
He's not wrong.
THERE
NORTHERN CANADA, INSIDE THE ARCTIC CIRCLE.
Sunset.
It's gonna get real cold, real quickly.
But we... YES!
"Locky! Look, it's the old north road out of town. It's a mile, maybe a mile and a half, but we're nearly back!"
For the first time in a while, I'm thinking we might actually make it.
In other news... I have a phone signal. I text Mom.
She's probably got dinner on the table right now.
Watching mine getting cold.
And wondering where I am.

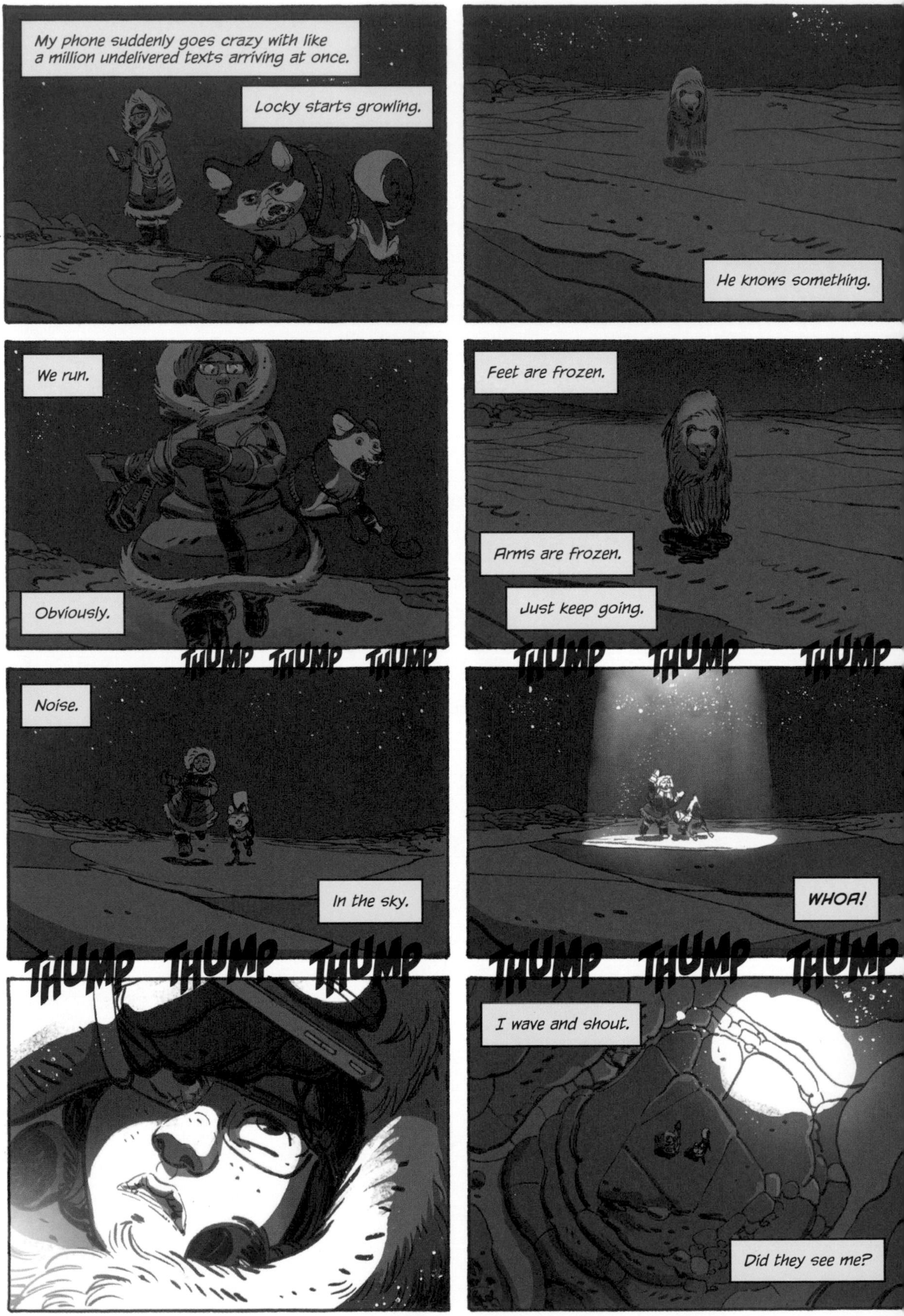
My phone suddenly goes crazy with like a million undelivered texts arriving at once.
Locky starts growling.
He knows something.
We run.
Obviously.
Feet are frozen.
Arms are frozen.
Just keep going.
THUMP THUMP THUMP
THUMP THUMP THUMP
Noise.
In the sky.
WHOA!
THUMP THUMP THUMP
THUMP THUMP THUMP
I wave and shout.
Did they see me?

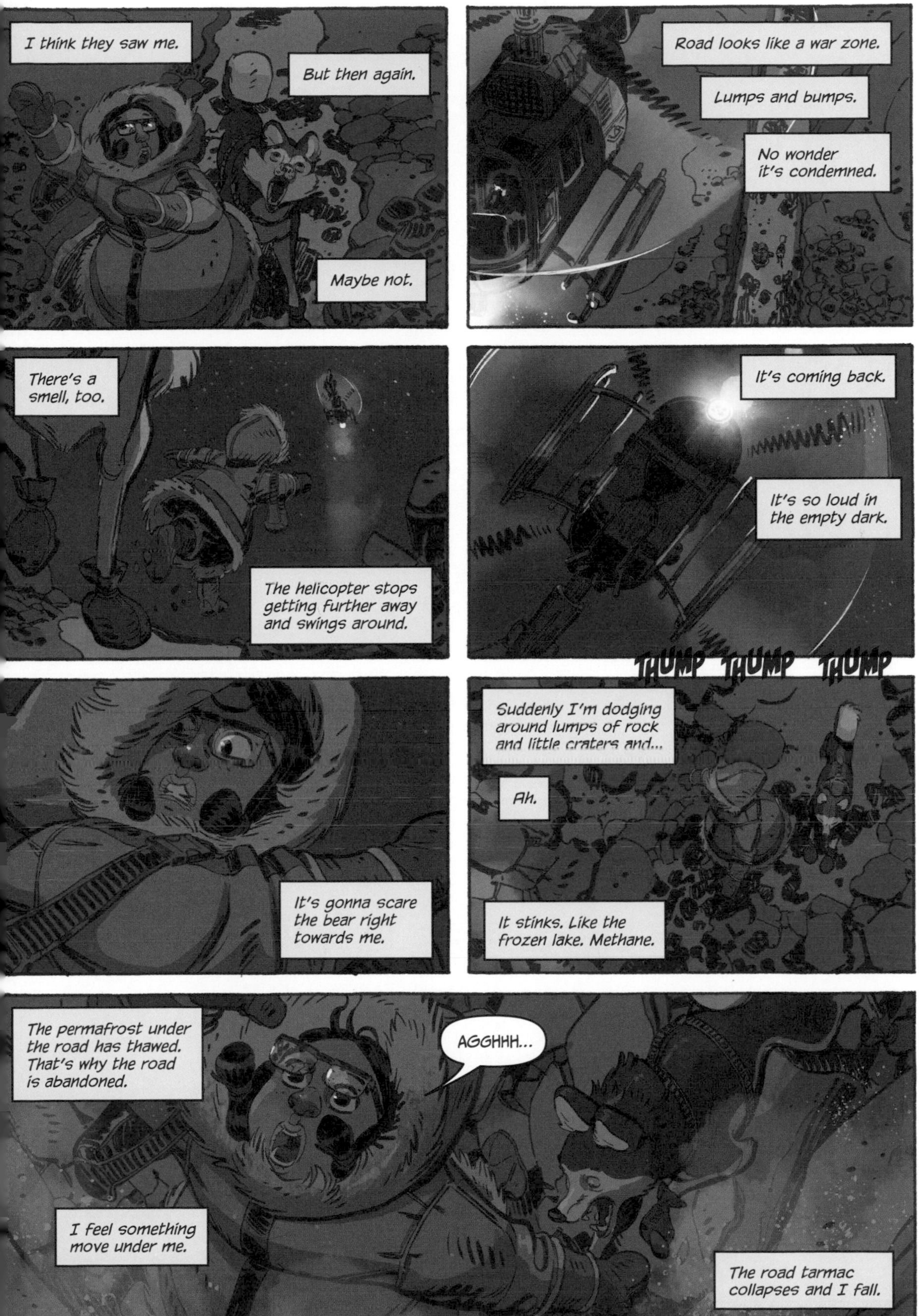
I think they saw me.
But then again.
Maybe not.
Road looks like a war zone.
Lumps and bumps.
No wonder it's condemned.
There's a smell, too.
The helicopter stops getting further away and swings around.
It's coming back.
It's so loud in the empty dark.
THUMP THUMP THUMP
It's gonna scare the bear right towards me.
Suddenly I'm dodging around lumps of rock and little craters and...
Ah.
It stinks. Like the frozen lake. Methane.
The permafrost under the road has thawed. That's why the road is abandoned.
AGGHHH...
I feel something move under me.
The road tarmac collapses and I fall.

I didn't see that coming.

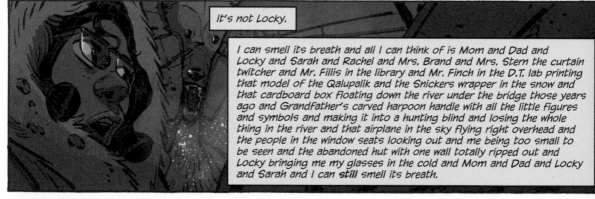

I'm winded and gasp for breath.

I hear Locky moving.

He's down here too.

No.

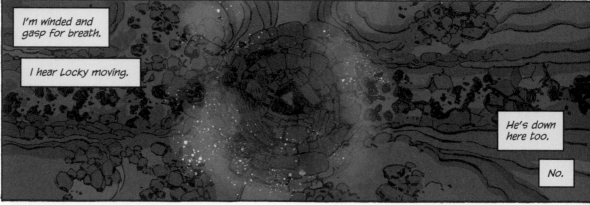

It's not Locky.

I can smell its breath and all I can think of is Mom and Dad and Locky and Sarah and Rachel and Mrs. Brand and Mrs. Stern the curtain twitcher and Mr. Fillis in the library and Mr. Finch in the D.T. lab printing that model of the Qalupalik and the Snickers wrapper in the snow and that cardboard box floating down the river under the bridge those years ago and Grandfather's carved harpoon handle with all the little figures and symbols and making it into a hunting blind and losing the whole thing in the river and that airplane in the sky flying right overhead and the people in the window seats looking out and me being too small to be seen and the abandoned hut with one wall totally ripped out and Locky bringing me my glasses in the cold and Mom and Dad and Locky and Sarah and I can still smell its breath.

Then I hear someone screaming and I'm pretty certain it's probably me.

CHAPTER 21

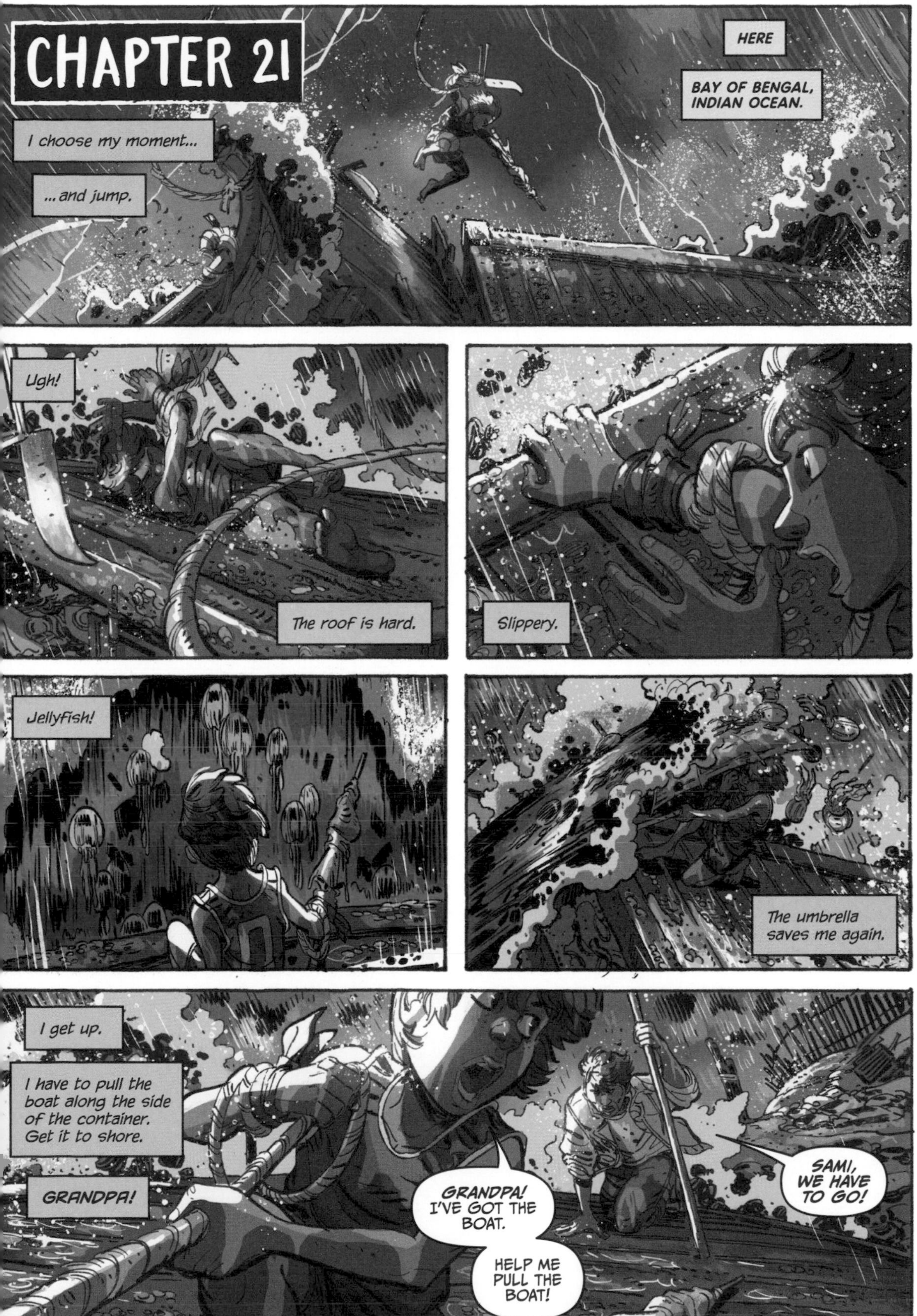
HERE
BAY OF BENGAL, INDIAN OCEAN.
I choose my moment...
...and jump.
Ugh!
The roof is hard.
Slippery.
Jellyfish!
The umbrella saves me again.
I get up.
I have to pull the boat along the side of the container. Get it to shore.
GRANDPA!
GRANDPA! I'VE GOT THE BOAT.
HELP ME PULL THE BOAT!
SAMI, WE HAVE TO GO!

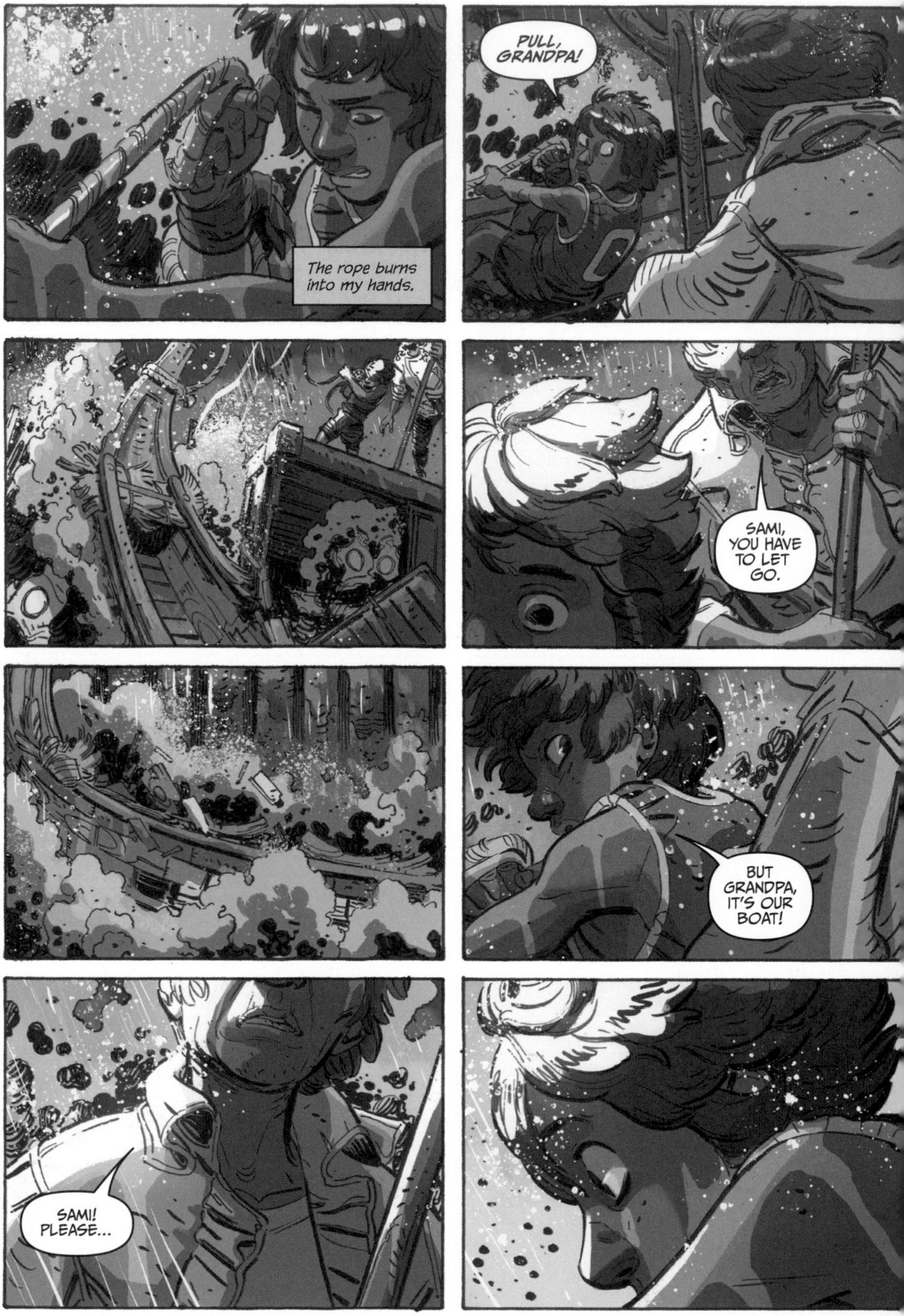
The rope burns into my hands.
PULL, GRANDPA!
SAMI, YOU HAVE TO LET GO.
BUT GRANDPA, IT'S OUR BOAT!
SAMI! PLEASE...

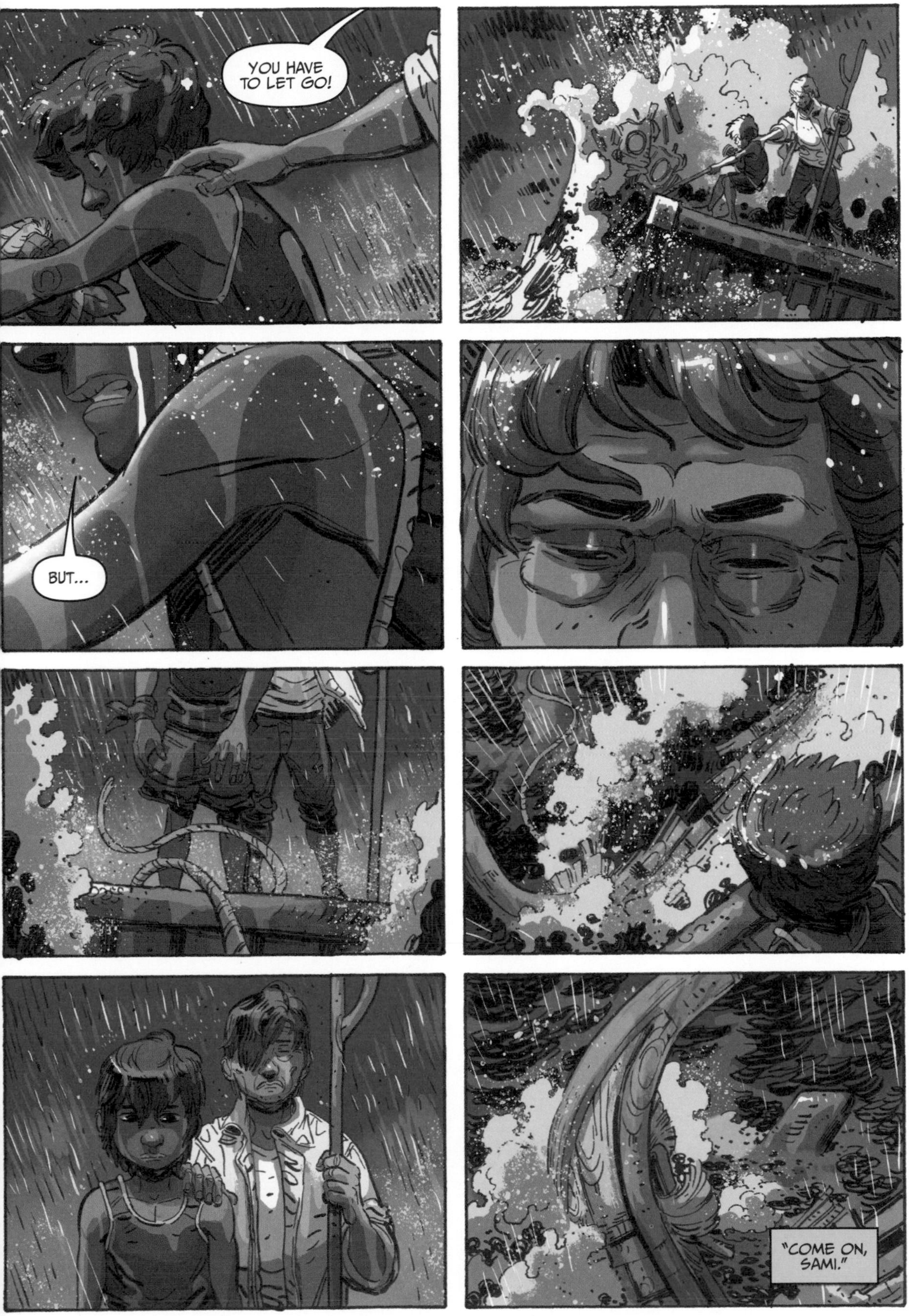
YOU HAVE TO LET GO!
BUT...
"COME ON, SAMI."

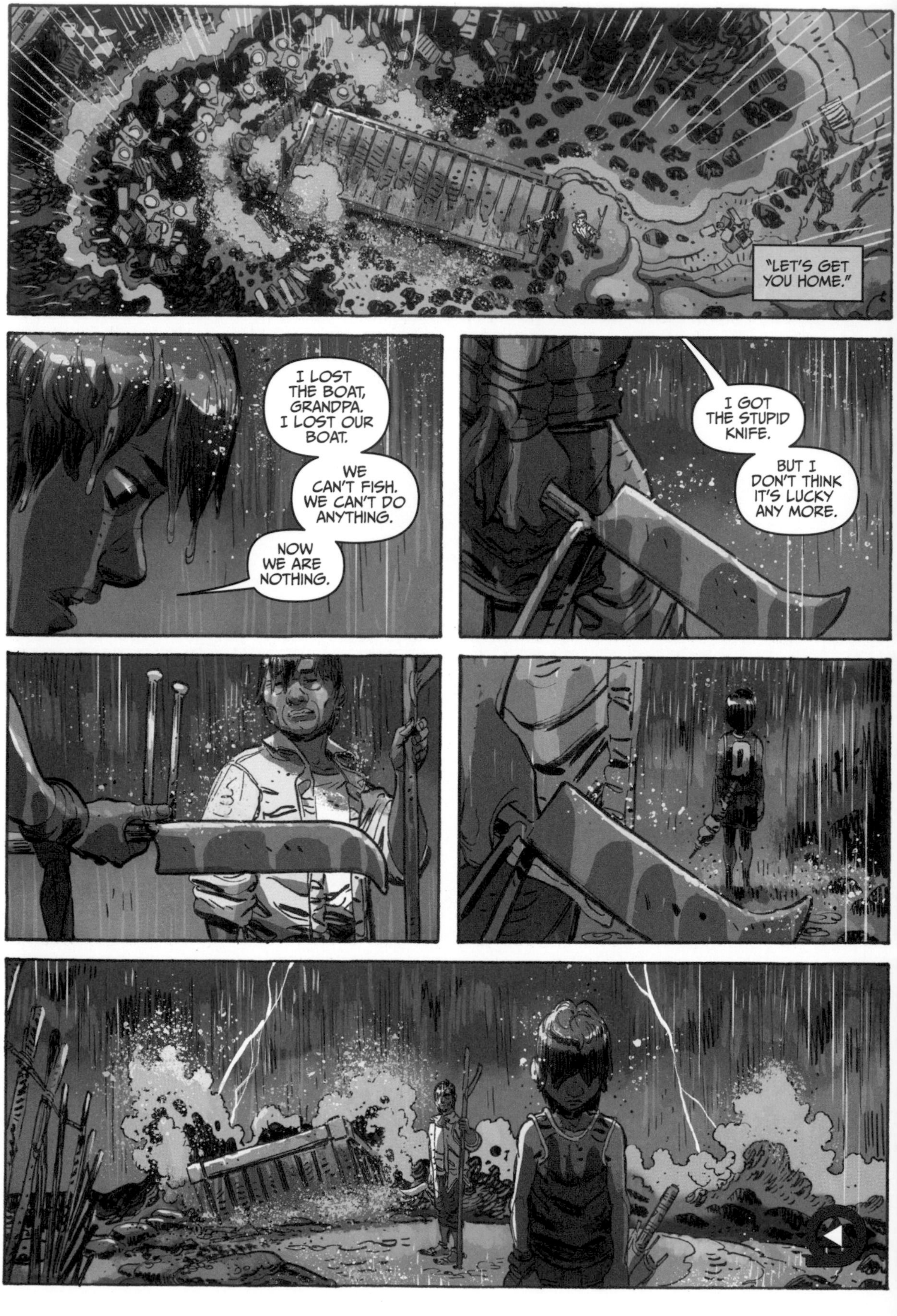
"LET'S GET YOU HOME."
I LOST THE BOAT, GRANDPA. I LOST OUR BOAT.
WE CAN'T FISH. WE CAN'T DO ANYTHING.
NOW WE ARE NOTHING.
I GOT THE STUPID KNIFE.
BUT I DON'T THINK IT'S LUCKY ANY MORE.

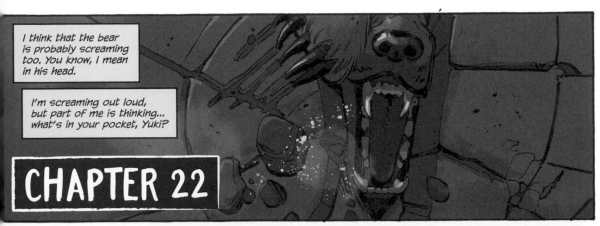

I think that the bear is probably screaming too. You know, I mean in his head.

I'm screaming out loud, but part of me is thinking... what's in your pocket, Yuki?

CHAPTER 22

We've eaten all the food.

Nothing to distract him.

Just... ah... my phone.

I don't freeze.

Not this time.

I just act.

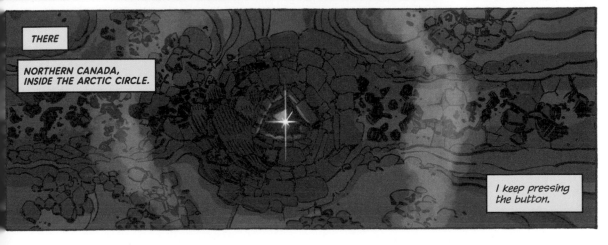

THERE

NORTHERN CANADA, INSIDE THE ARCTIC CIRCLE.

I keep pressing the button.

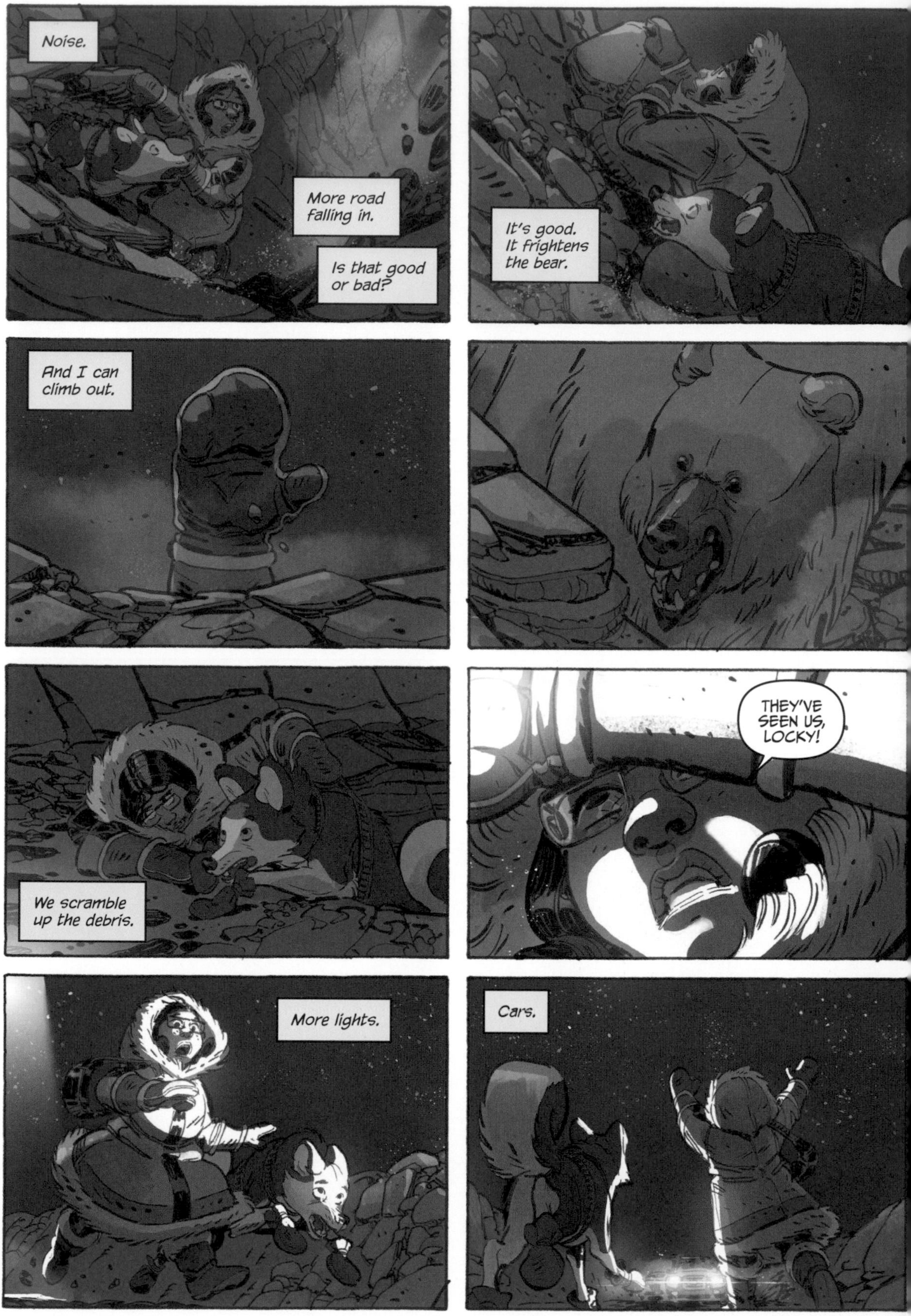
Noise.
More road falling in.
Is that good or bad?
It's good. It frightens the bear.
And I can climb out.
We scramble up the debris.
THEY'VE SEEN US, LOCKY!
More lights.
Cars.

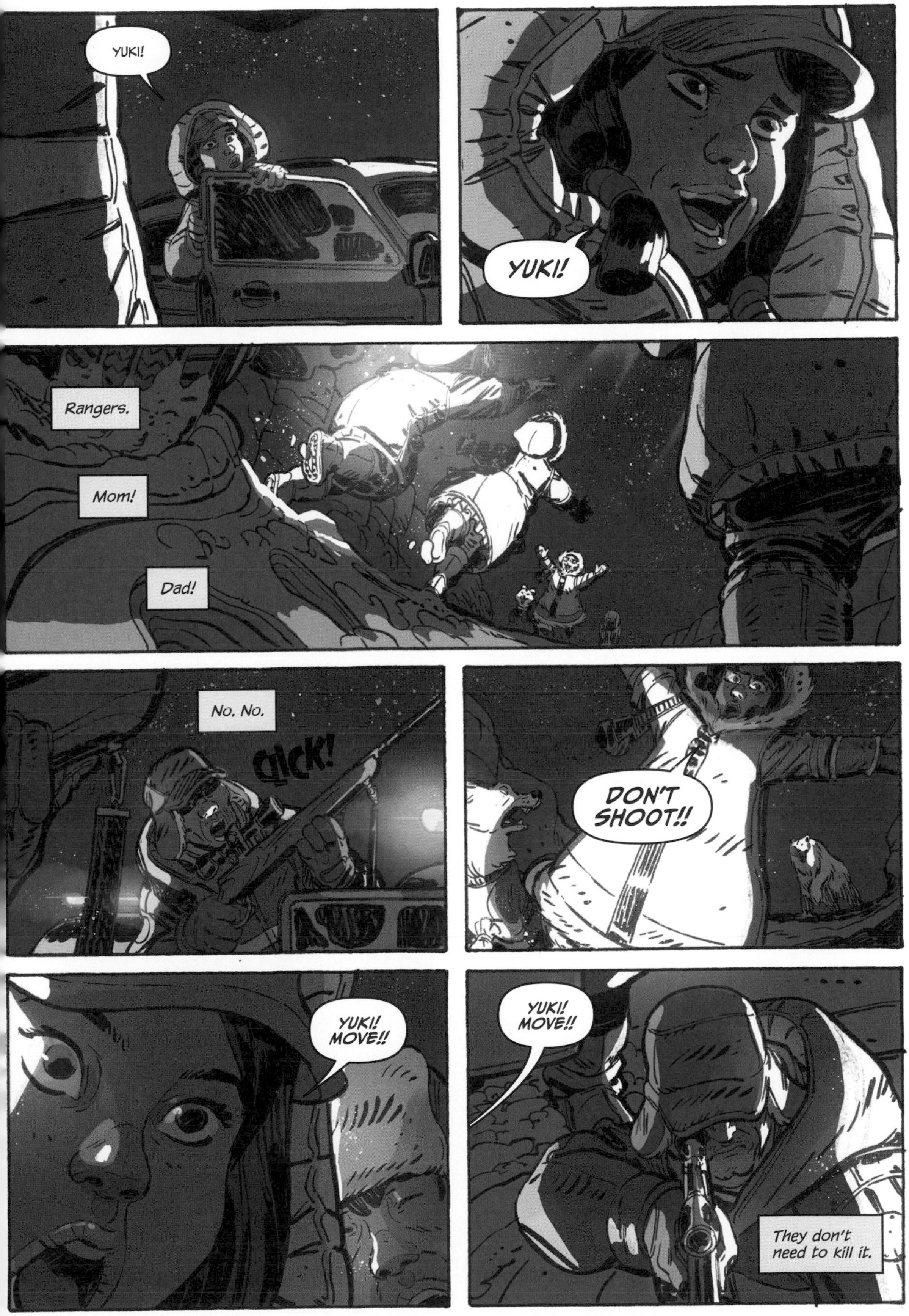

YUKI!
YUKI!
Rangers.
Mom!
Dad!
No. No.
CLICK!
DON'T SHOOT!!
YUKI! MOVE!!
YUKI! MOVE!!
They don't need to kill it.

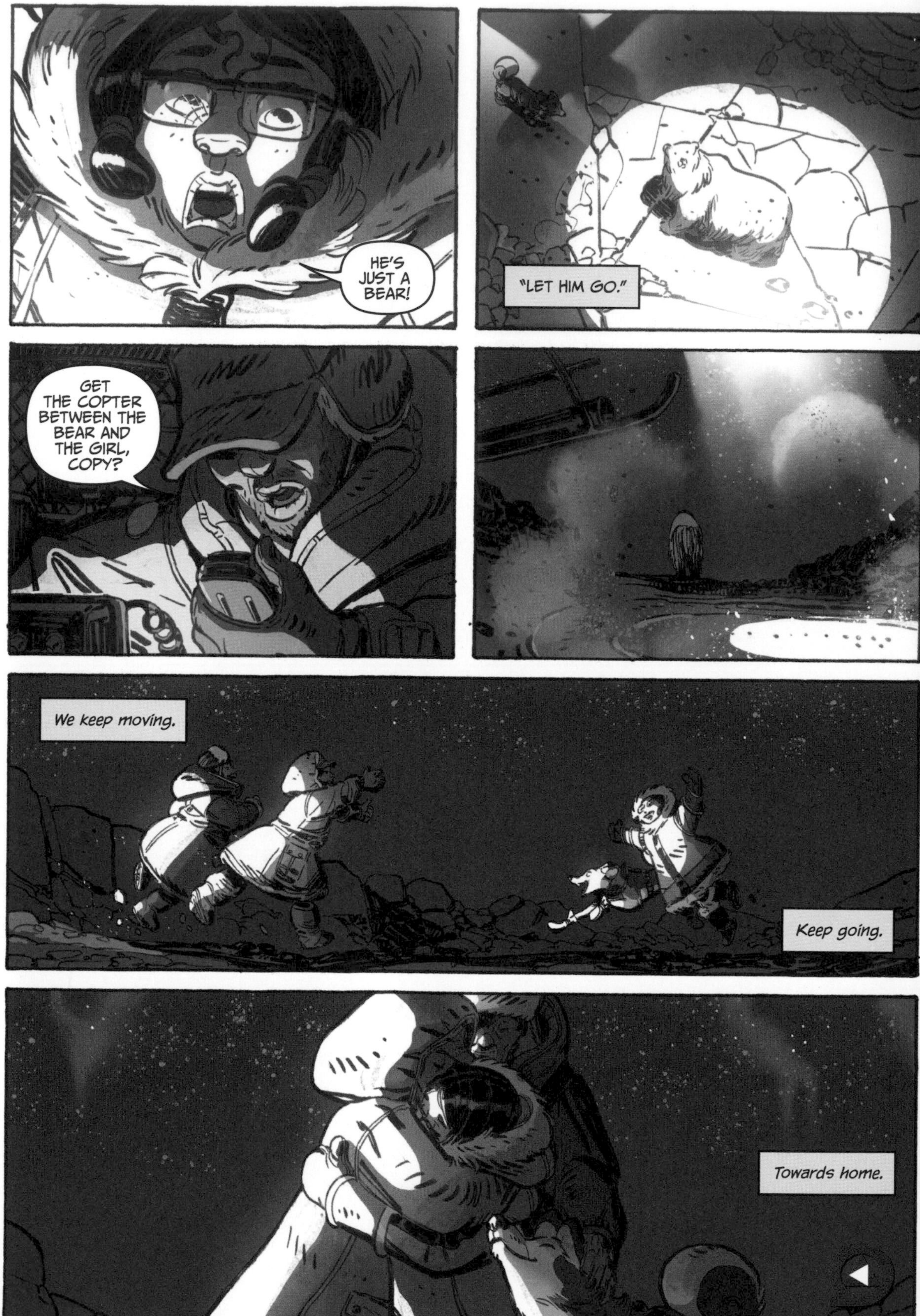
HE'S JUST A BEAR!
"LET HIM GO."
GET THE COPTER BETWEEN THE BEAR AND THE GIRL, COPY?
We keep moving.
Keep going.
Towards home.

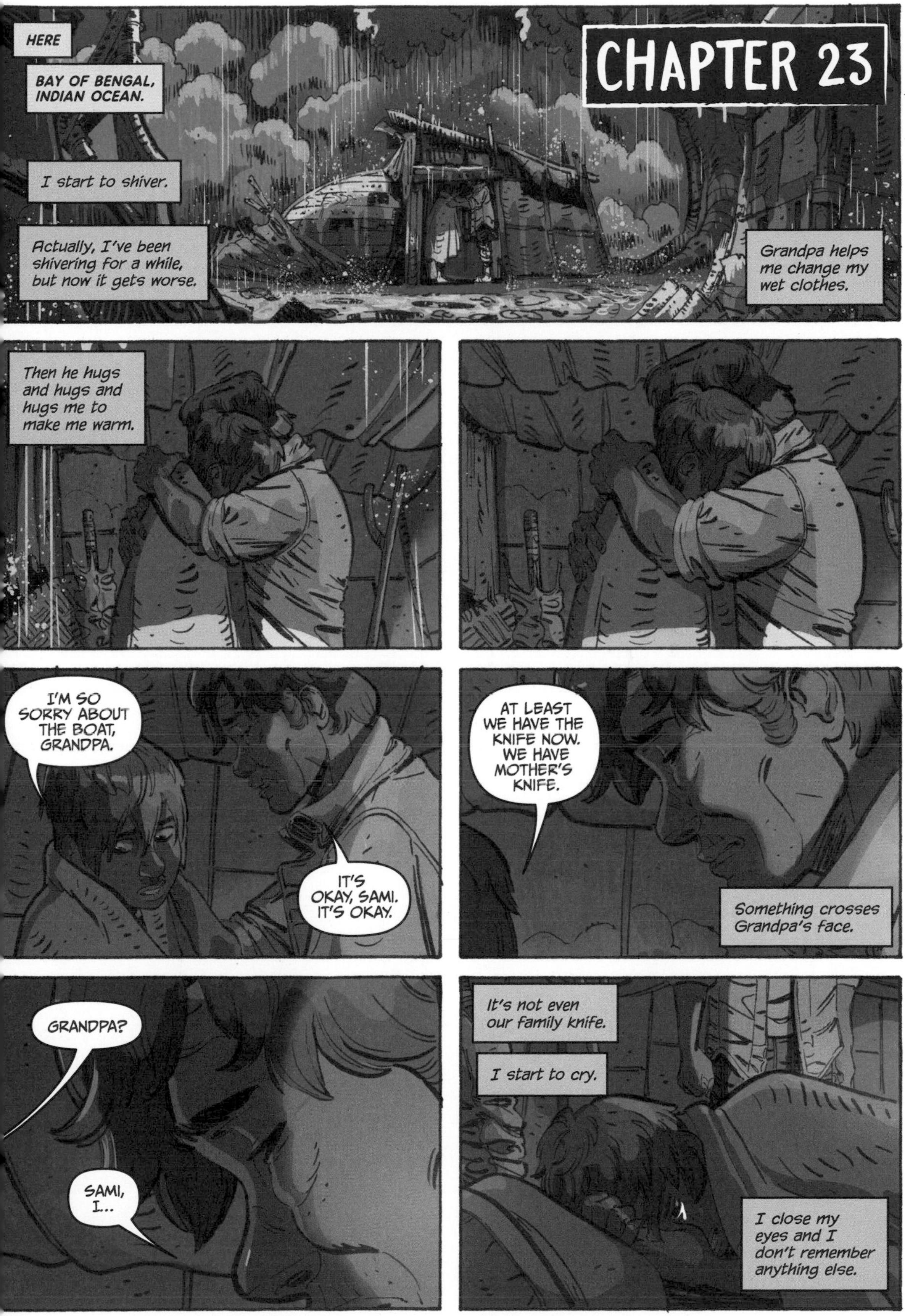
HERE
BAY OF BENGAL, INDIAN OCEAN.
CHAPTER 23
I start to shiver.
Actually, I've been shivering for a while, but now it gets worse.
Grandpa helps me change my wet clothes.
Then he hugs and hugs and hugs me to make me warm.
I'M SO SORRY ABOUT THE BOAT, GRANDPA.
IT'S OKAY, SAMI. IT'S OKAY.
AT LEAST WE HAVE THE KNIFE NOW. WE HAVE MOTHER'S KNIFE.
Something crosses Grandpa's face.
GRANDPA?
SAMI, I...
It's not even our family knife.
I start to cry.
I close my eyes and I don't remember anything else.

Morning.

I look out.

People are clearing up after the storm, and I slept through it all.

AH, SAMI! YOU'RE AWAKE! YOU'VE MISSED MOST OF THE MORNING.

SAMI, THAT KNIFE YOU FOUND...

IT'S NOT REALLY OUR FAMILY'S, IS IT? I FIGURED THAT OUT.

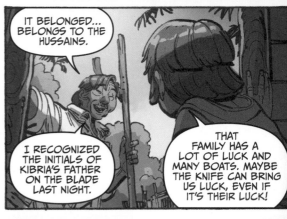

IT BELONGED... BELONGS TO THE HUSSAINS.

I RECOGNIZED THE INITIALS OF KIBRIA'S FATHER ON THE BLADE LAST NIGHT.

THAT FAMILY HAS A LOT OF LUCK AND MANY BOATS. MAYBE THE KNIFE CAN BRING US LUCK, EVEN IF IT'S THEIR LUCK!

SAMI, I WENT TO SEE THEM AND I'VE GIVEN THEM THE KNIFE. IT WAS THE RIGHT THING TO DO.

HE IS AS FOOLISH AS YOU AND WAS SO HAPPY TO HAVE IT BACK.

BUT...

I SPOKE WITH HIM AND IN RETURN THEY ARE GOING TO GIVE US A BOAT.

BUT THEY'RE NOT GOING TO JUST GIVE US A BOAT, GRANDPA.

NO, WE HAVE TO GIVE THEM TWENTY PERCENT OF OUR CATCH UNTIL THE BOAT IS PAID FOR AND IS OURS.

AND?

AND TEACH THEIR YOUNGEST TO DRAW FOR TWO HOURS A WEEK. BUT THAT'S FINE.

SO THE KNIFE *HAS* BROUGHT US LUCK. YOU SAVED US, SAMI.

"NO, GRANDPA, YOU'VE SAVED US."

"LIKE ALWAYS."

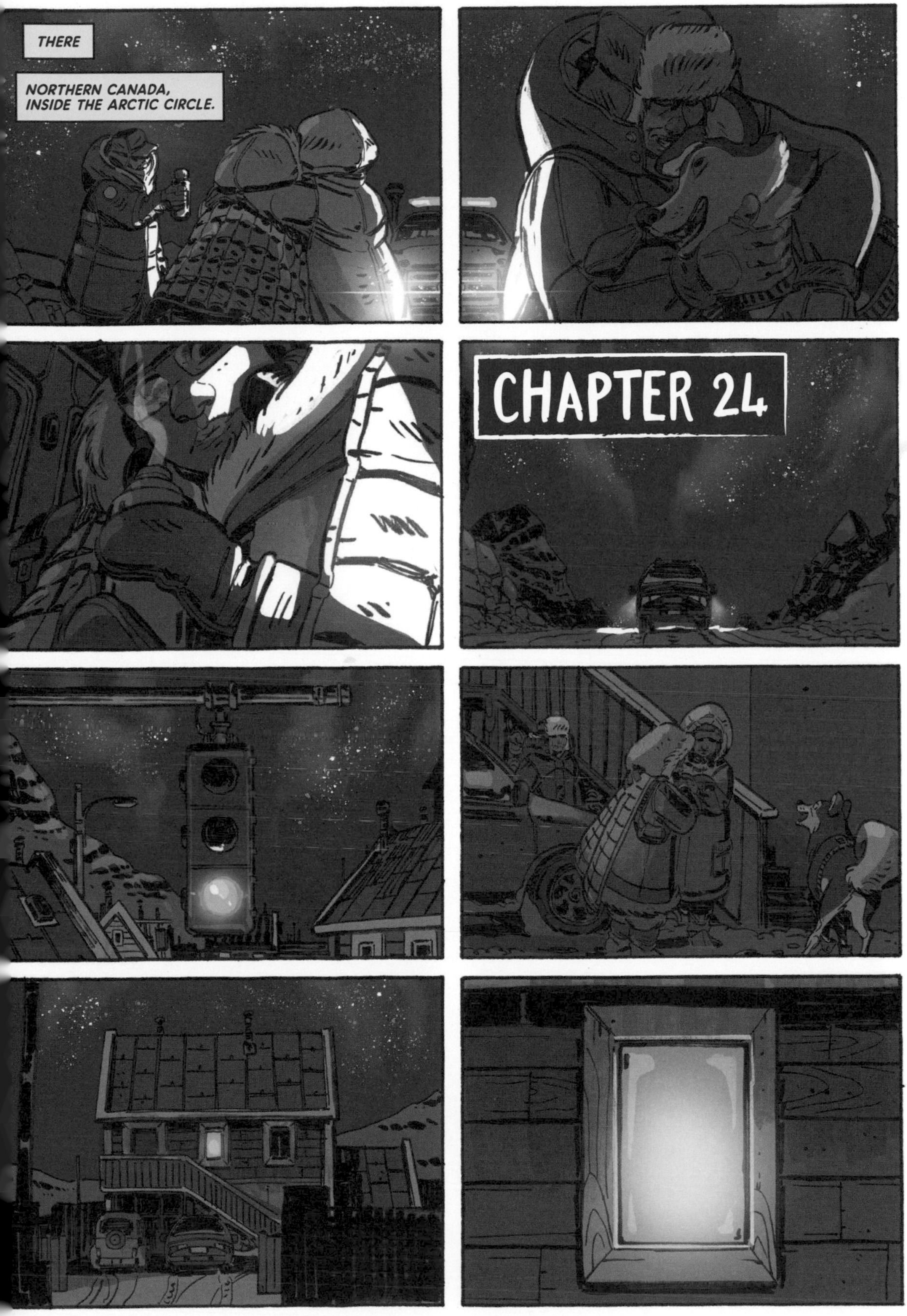
THERE
NORTHERN CANADA, INSIDE THE ARCTIC CIRCLE.
CHAPTER 24

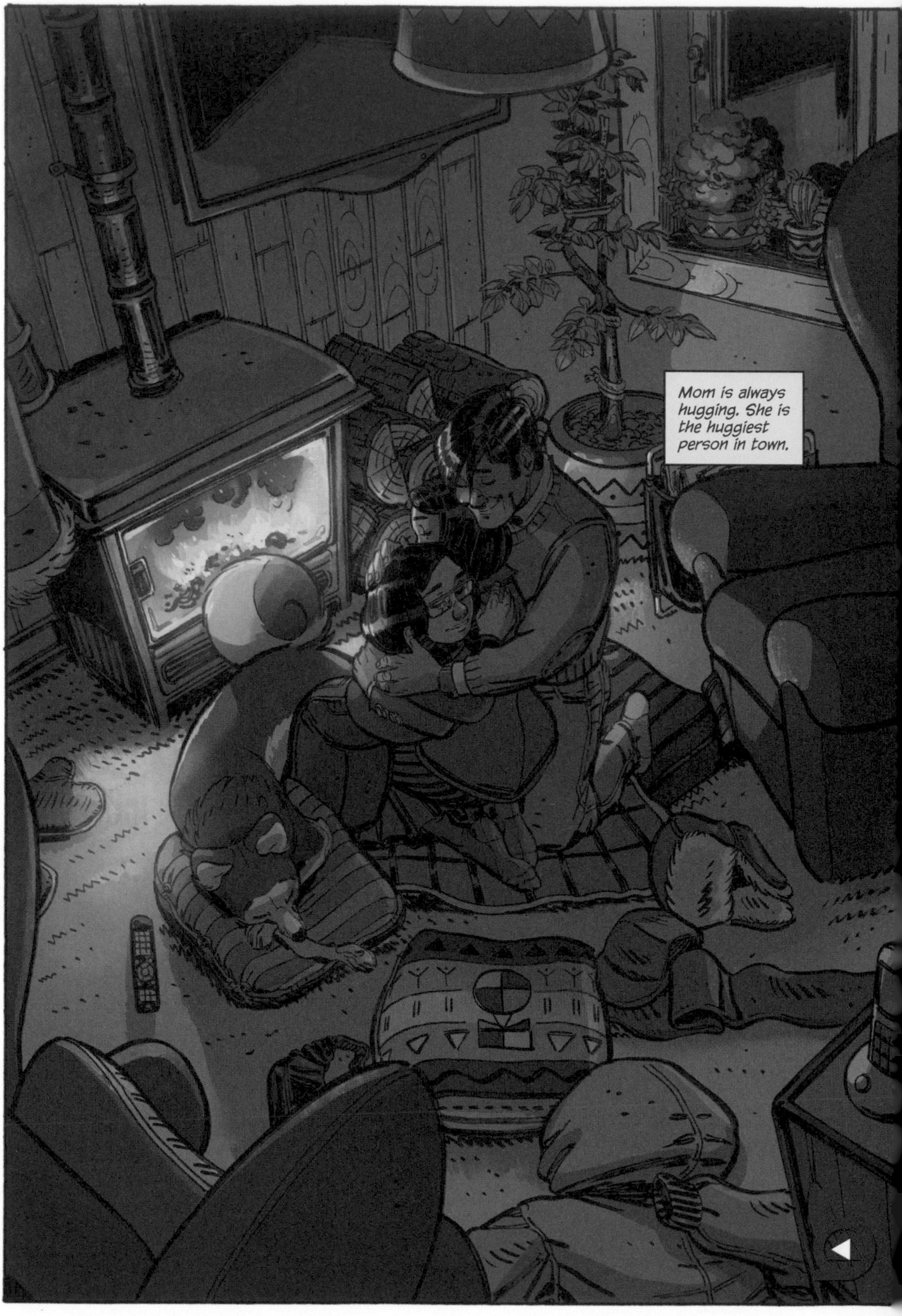
Mom is always hugging. She is the huggiest person in town.

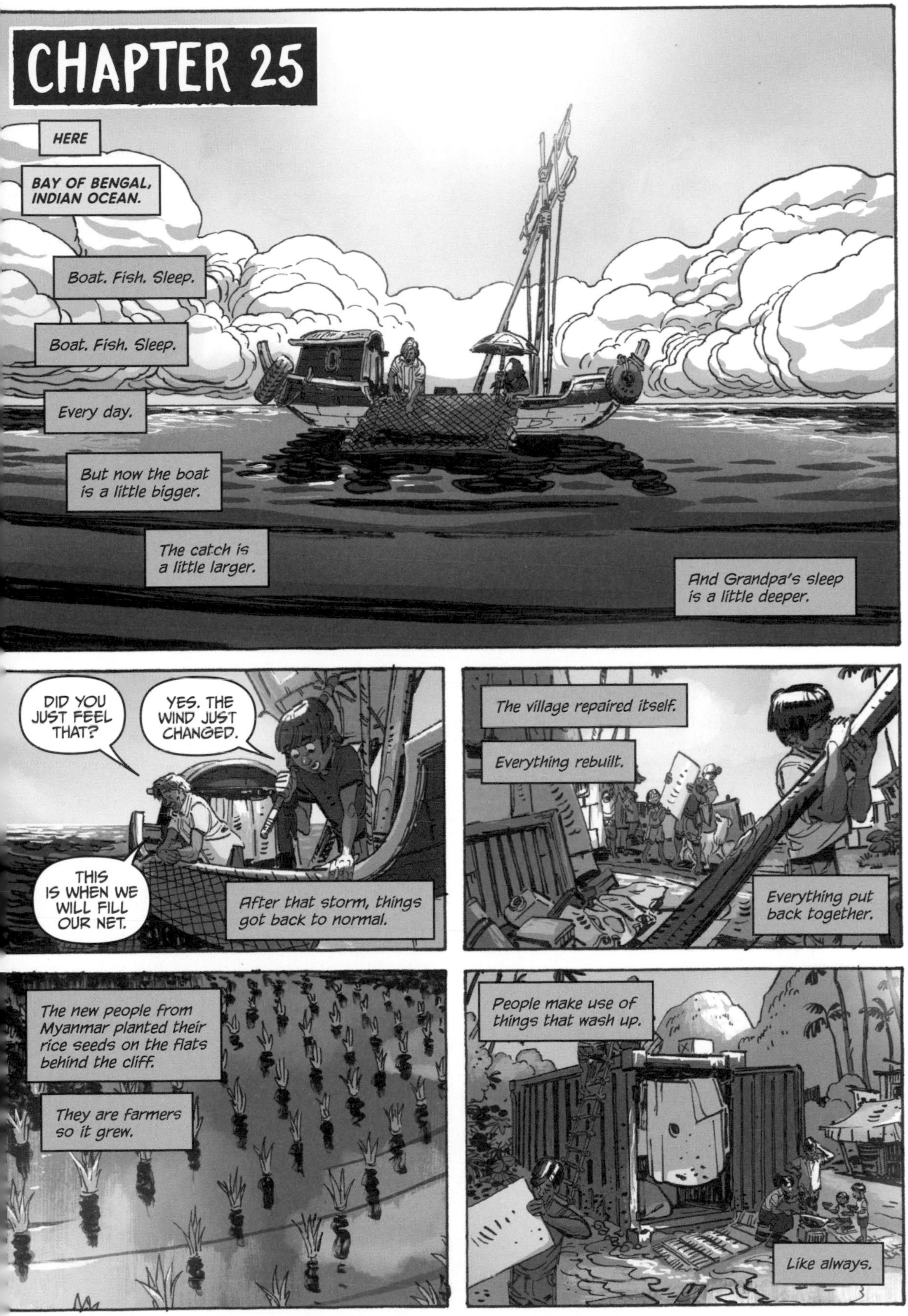
CHAPTER 25
HERE
BAY OF BENGAL, INDIAN OCEAN.
Boat. Fish. Sleep.
Boat. Fish. Sleep.
Every day.
But now the boat is a little bigger.
The catch is a little larger.
And Grandpa's sleep is a little deeper.
DID YOU JUST FEEL THAT?
YES. THE WIND JUST CHANGED.
THIS IS WHEN WE WILL FILL OUR NET.
After that storm, things got back to normal.
The village repaired itself.
Everything rebuilt.
Everything put back together.
The new people from Myanmar planted their rice seeds on the flats behind the cliff.
They are farmers so it grew.
People make use of things that wash up.
Like always.

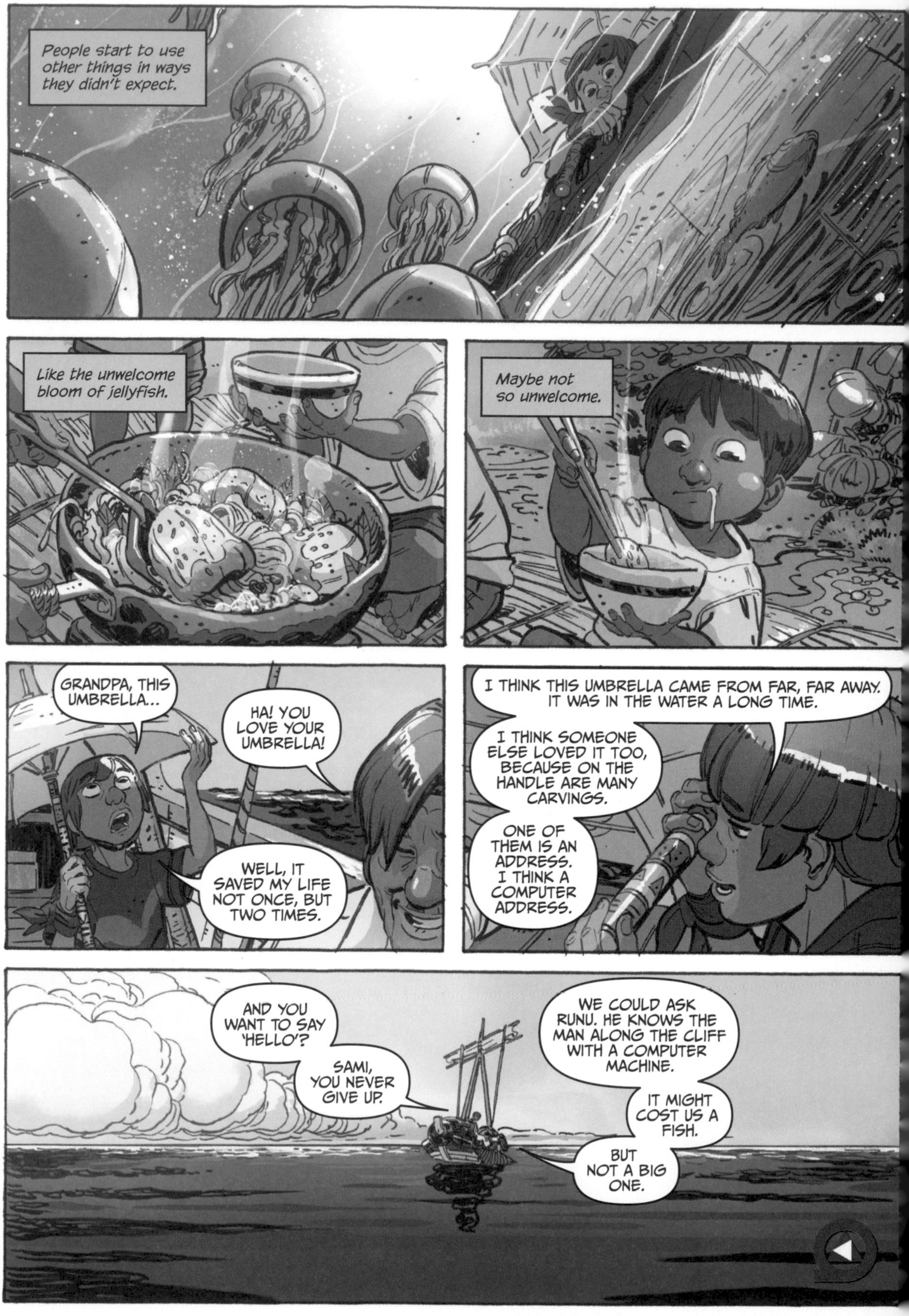

People start to use other things in ways they didn't expect.
Like the unwelcome bloom of jellyfish.
Maybe not so unwelcome.
GRANDPA, THIS UMBRELLA...
HA! YOU LOVE YOUR UMBRELLA!
WELL, IT SAVED MY LIFE NOT ONCE, BUT TWO TIMES.
I THINK THIS UMBRELLA CAME FROM FAR, FAR AWAY. IT WAS IN THE WATER A LONG TIME.
I THINK SOMEONE ELSE LOVED IT TOO, BECAUSE ON THE HANDLE ARE MANY CARVINGS.
ONE OF THEM IS AN ADDRESS. I THINK A COMPUTER ADDRESS.
AND YOU WANT TO SAY 'HELLO'?
SAMI, YOU NEVER GIVE UP.
WE COULD ASK RUNU. HE KNOWS THE MAN ALONG THE CLIFF WITH A COMPUTER MACHINE.
IT MIGHT COST US A FISH.
BUT NOT A BIG ONE.

CHAPTER 26

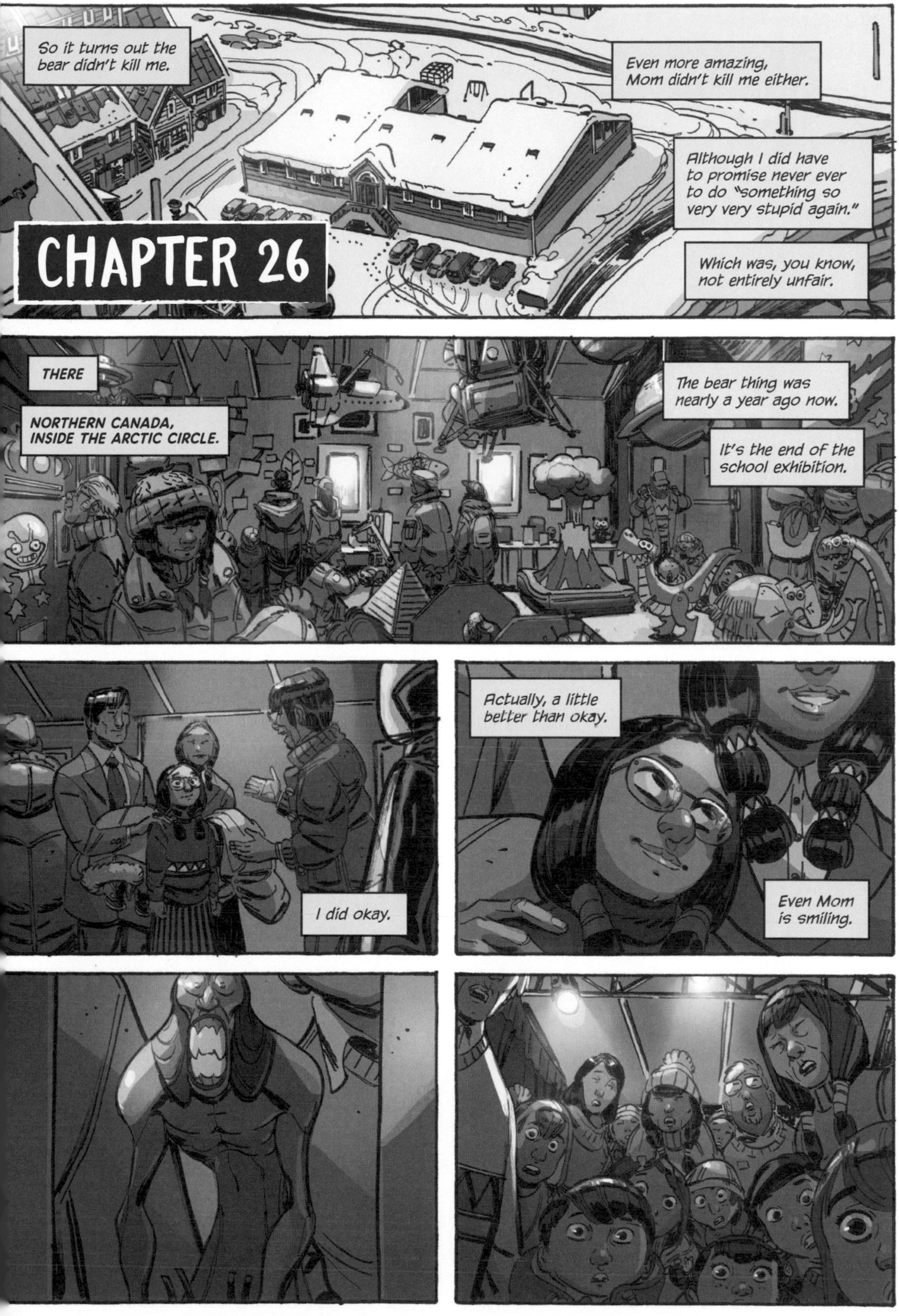
So it turns out the bear didn't kill me.
Even more amazing, Mom didn't kill me either.
Although I did have to promise never ever to do "something so very very stupid again."
Which was, you know, not entirely unfair.
THERE
NORTHERN CANADA, INSIDE THE ARCTIC CIRCLE.
The bear thing was nearly a year ago now.
It's the end of the school exhibition.
I did okay.
Actually, a little better than okay.
Even Mom is smiling.

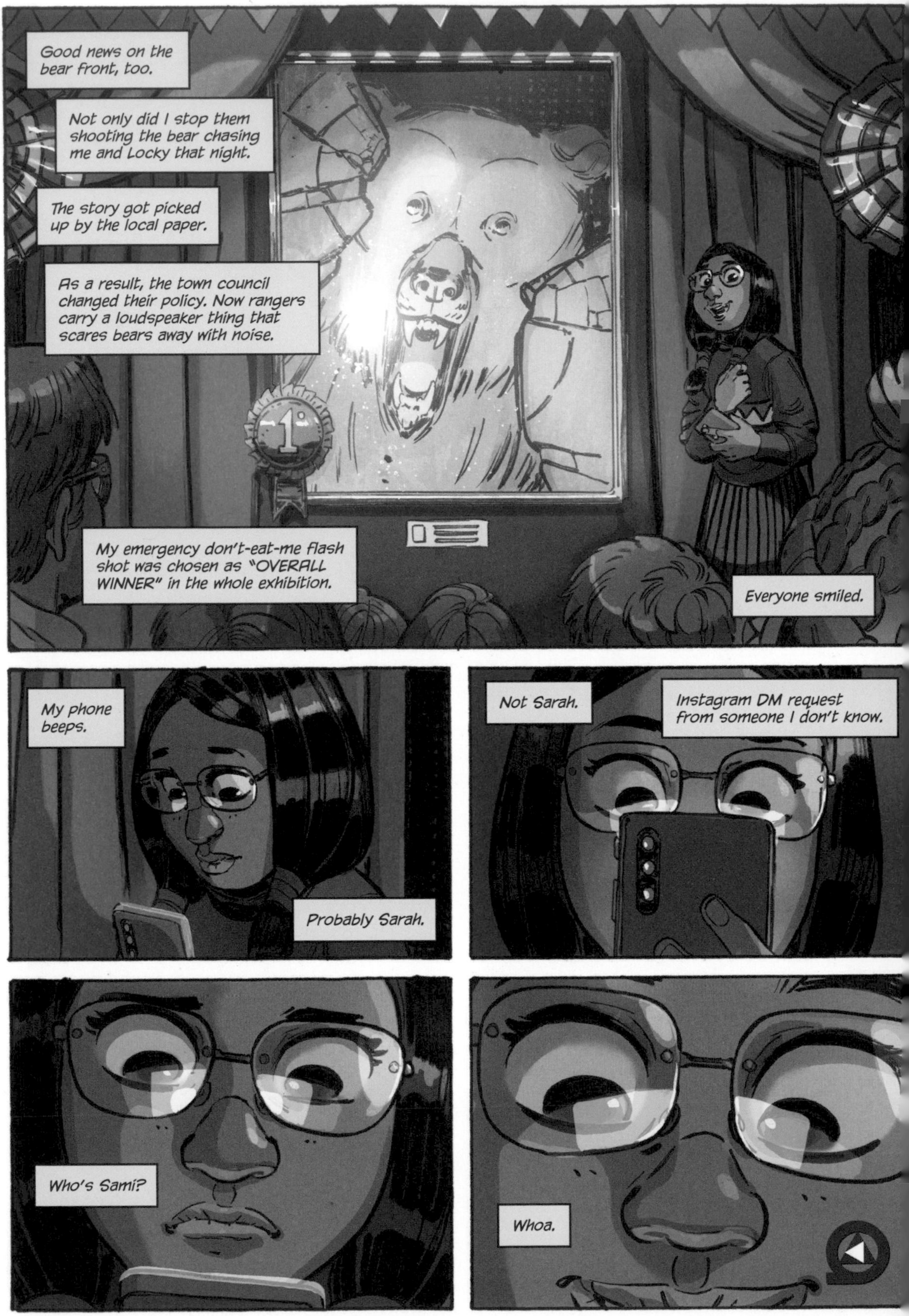
Good news on the bear front, too.
Not only did I stop them shooting the bear chasing me and Locky that night.
The story got picked up by the local paper.
As a result, the town council changed their policy. Now rangers carry a loudspeaker thing that scares bears away with noise.
My emergency don't-eat-me flash shot was chosen as "OVERALL WINNER" in the whole exhibition.
Everyone smiled.
My phone beeps.
Probably Sarah.
Not Sarah.
Instagram DM request from someone I don't know.
Who's Sami?
Whoa.

SAMI & YUKI'S LOCATIONS

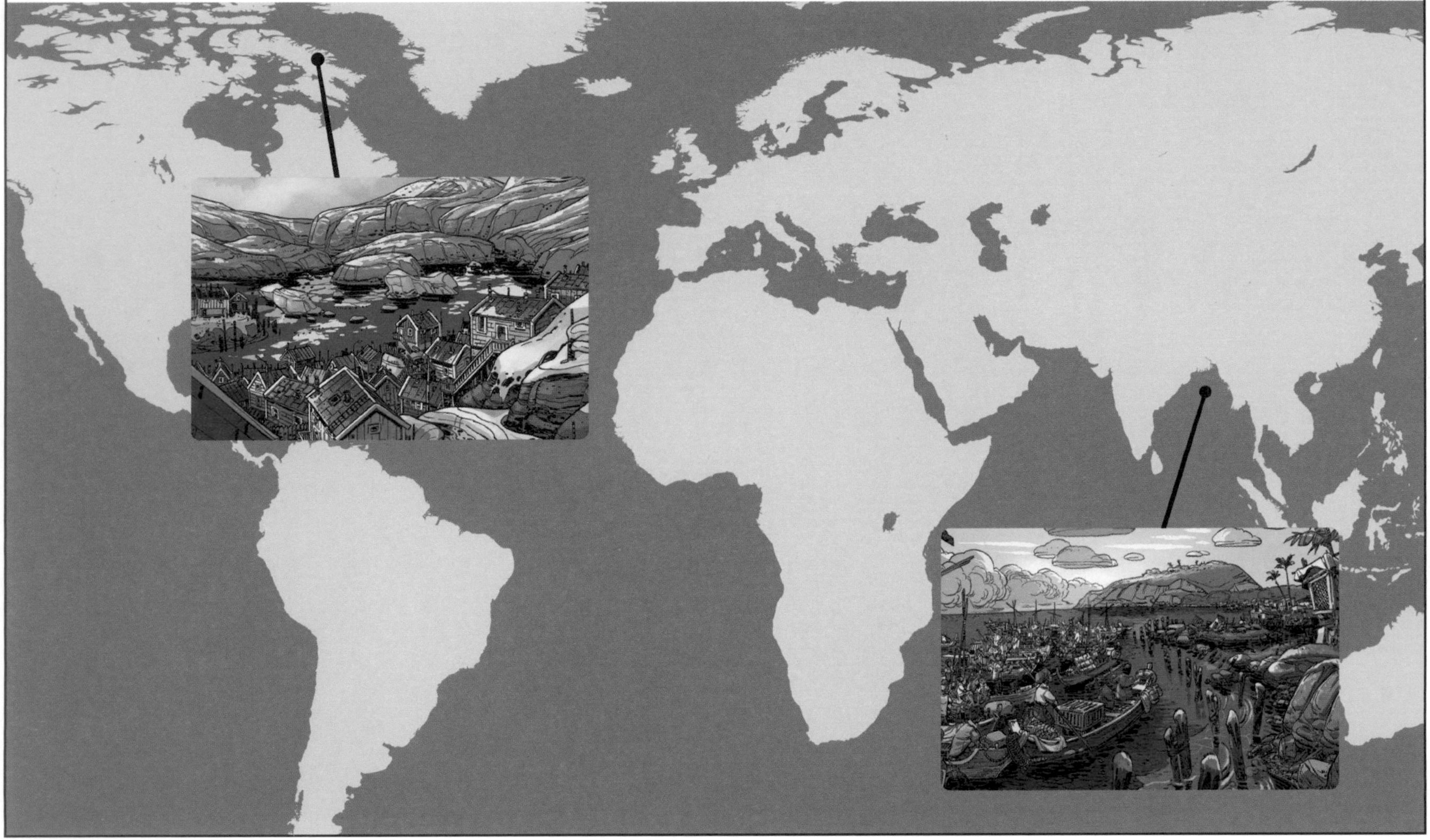

GLOBAL

The story you've just read about Sami and Yuki is a work of fiction, but every element in it that has to do with climate change is true.

GLOBAL is not a story about what might happen in the future; all the climate change issues in this book are real and they are all happening right now.

Every year, humans pump many millions of tons of carbon dioxide and other greenhouse gases into the Earth's atmosphere. These gases trap energy from the Sun, causing our climate to heat up. It is now heating to a dangerous extent, dramatically changing the environment around us.

Climate warming across the globe, caused directly by humans, is an established scientific fact.

Across the globe, UNICEF estimate that 1 billion children are at an "extremely high risk" of suffering the impacts of the climate crisis. These impacts include droughts, cyclones, river flooding, coastal flooding, heatwaves, wildfires, flash floods, sea level rise, and air, soil, and water pollution.

Children are always more vulnerable than adults to climate and environmental shocks. For children like Sami in our story, the impacts of climate change make an already difficult struggle to survive even harder: the impact pushes vulnerable children deeper into poverty.

We created GLOBAL because we believe climate change is the most critical issue facing children today. Each generation of humans are only custodians of the planet—temporary occupants looking after it, for whoever comes next.

Today's children are least responsible for the causes of climate change, but sadly they are often the first to suffer its impacts. It's up to all of us to make sure our children and grandchildren inherit a livable planet.

Eoin Colfer
Andrew Donkin
Giovanni Rigano

WHAT IS GLOBAL WARMING?

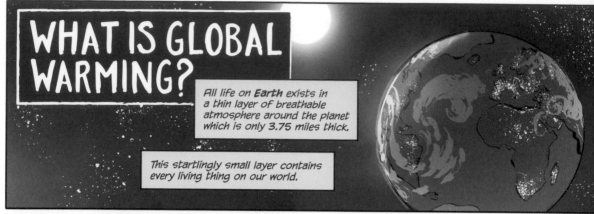

All life on **Earth** exists in a thin layer of breathable atmosphere around the planet which is only 3.75 miles thick.

This startlingly small layer contains every living thing on our world.

The Earth's atmosphere protects the surface of the planet from the most harmful rays of the Sun, allowing life to thrive.

When radiation from the Sun hits **the Earth**, some is absorbed by the surface and some is reflected back towards space.

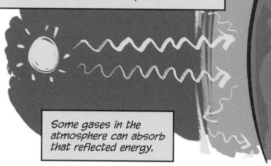

Some gases in the atmosphere can absorb that reflected energy.

Those gases are called greenhouse gases and the more of them that are present in the atmosphere, the more of the Sun's energy is absorbed and the warmer the atmosphere becomes.

This is known as the greenhouse effect.

CO_2

LIGHT

Climate records show that as the amount of greenhouse gases (like carbon dioxide) have increased in the atmosphere, the average temperature across the globe has increased too.

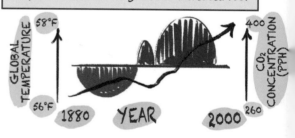

GLOBAL TEMPERATURE — 58°F ... 56°F — 1880 — YEAR — 2000

CO_2 CONCENTRATION (PPM) — 400 ... 260

The cause of the extra carbon dioxide in the atmosphere is human activity.

Burning fossil fuels like oil, gas, and coal over the last two hundred years has sent millions of tons of carbon dioxide into the atmosphere.

If humans keep burning fossil fuels at the current rate then the planet will continue to heat up and we will tip into irrevocable climate disaster.

All the climate change events shown in Sami and Yuki's story are real, and all of them are already happening to our planet today.

Rising temperatures across the globe are causing significant changes.

Around the world, higher temperatures are causing sea ice in the Arctic to melt, Antarctic ice sheets at the South Pole to collapse into the ocean, and mountain glaciers on land to melt and shrink.

As the water from melting ice sheets and glaciers pours into the oceans, sea levels continue to rise around the world.

Many low-lying cities on the coasts of countries are at risk of flooding.

Melting sea ice is very bad news for the animals that live on it, like polar bears.

With sea ice melting earlier in the year, polar bears find it difficult to hunt and have to swim much farther for food. This often forces them onto land and puts them in direct conflict with humans.

Climate change has driven polar bears south in search of food, at the same time as expanding the range of brown grizzly bears northwards.

Where the two have met, interbreeding has produced grolar bears—like the one in Yuki's story—a cross between the two breeds. Sadly they are not really suited to life in either region.

Along with melting ice, higher temperatures in the north are melting the permafrost—ground that is usually frozen all year round.

When these swamp-like areas of rotting plant matter thaw, they release large quantities of methane gas—another greenhouse gas that warms the atmosphere.

Rotting vegetation at the bottom of lakes also releases methane which can be frozen in place as bubbles, just like Yuki found.

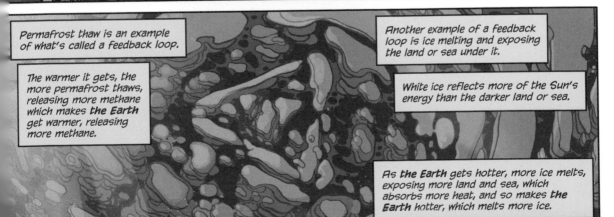

Permafrost thaw is an example of what's called a feedback loop.

The warmer it gets, the more permafrost thaws, releasing more methane which makes **the Earth** get warmer, releasing more methane.

Another example of a feedback loop is ice melting and exposing the land or sea under it.

White ice reflects more of the Sun's energy than the darker land or sea.

As **the Earth** gets hotter, more ice melts, exposing more land and sea, which absorbs more heat, and so makes **the Earth** hotter, which melts more ice.

Cold freshwater flowing into the oceans from melting ice sheets and glaciers can change deepwater currents, disrupting the global flow of the oceans.

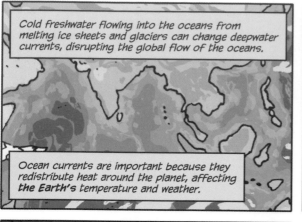

Ocean currents are important because they redistribute heat around the planet, affecting *the Earth's* temperature and weather.

As the world warms, so do *the Earth's* oceans.

Warmer water contains more energy than cooler water. This can lead to stronger and more frequent storms and cyclones as we saw in Sami's story.

Warmer oceans also become more acidic.

This means coral reefs bleaching and dying.

More acidic seawater means less plankton, the basis of all ocean food chains. Fewer plankton means less fish in the oceans.

As global warming increases, heatwaves are becoming more regular and more extreme around the world.

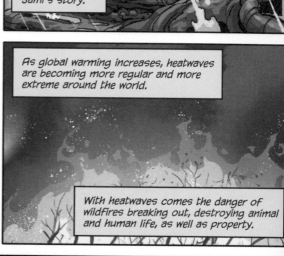

With heatwaves comes the danger of wildfires breaking out, destroying animal and human life, as well as property.

Many people rely on stable, predictable weather patterns, with rains coming at a particular time to grow their crops.

When global warming changes weather patterns—especially rains—crops can fail, leaving large numbers of people facing famine or drought.

Global warming will affect the world's most vulnerable people first and worst.

People in the developing world often have to cope with difficult and challenging climate conditions to begin with.

The number of climate refugees—people forced to move by extreme weather events—is increasing every year.

Climate change is also likely to increase the number of human conflicts and wars.

People will be driven to fight for dwindling resources like fresh water and food sources, as well as the land rights to dwindling mineral reserves.

Scientists agree that human activity is the cause of global warming and that if we don't act quickly to drastically reduce our fossil fuel use, then things will only get worse.

So what can we do to reduce emissions and stop climate change?

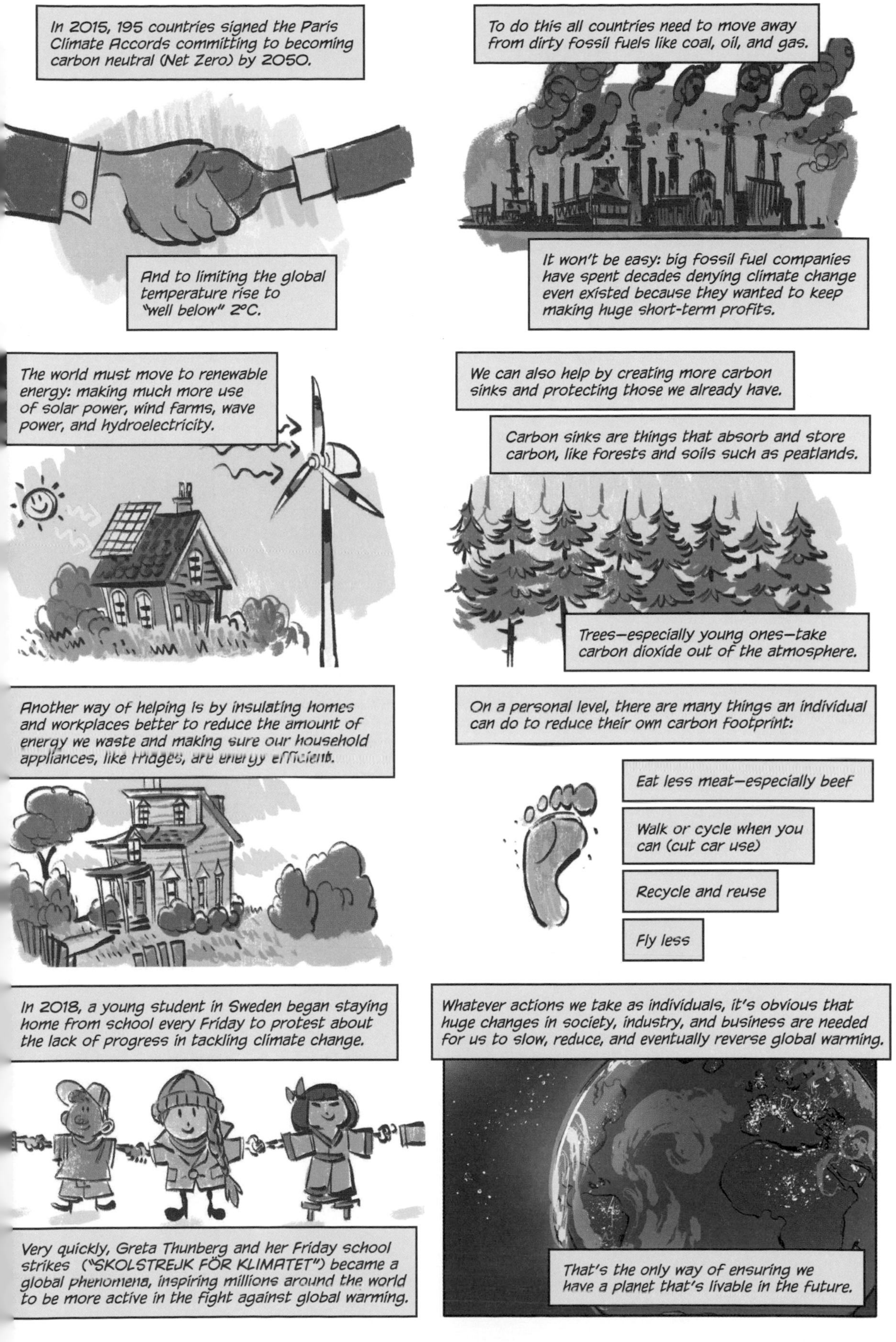
In 2015, 195 countries signed the Paris Climate Accords committing to becoming carbon neutral (Net Zero) by 2050.
And to limiting the global temperature rise to "well below" 2°C.
To do this all countries need to move away from dirty fossil fuels like coal, oil, and gas.
It won't be easy: big fossil fuel companies have spent decades denying climate change even existed because they wanted to keep making huge short-term profits.
The world must move to renewable energy: making much more use of solar power, wind farms, wave power, and hydroelectricity.
We can also help by creating more carbon sinks and protecting those we already have.
Carbon sinks are things that absorb and store carbon, like forests and soils such as peatlands.
Trees—especially young ones—take carbon dioxide out of the atmosphere.
Another way of helping is by insulating homes and workplaces better to reduce the amount of energy we waste and making sure our household appliances, like fridges, are energy efficient.
On a personal level, there are many things an individual can do to reduce their own carbon footprint:
Eat less meat—especially beef
Walk or cycle when you can (cut car use)
Recycle and reuse
Fly less
In 2018, a young student in Sweden began staying home from school every Friday to protest about the lack of progress in tackling climate change.
Very quickly, Greta Thunberg and her Friday school strikes ("SKOLSTREJK FÖR KLIMATET") became a global phenomena, inspiring millions around the world to be more active in the fight against global warming.
Whatever actions we take as individuals, it's obvious that huge changes in society, industry, and business are needed for us to slow, reduce, and eventually reverse global warming.
That's the only way of ensuring we have a planet that's livable in the future.

SKETCHBOOK

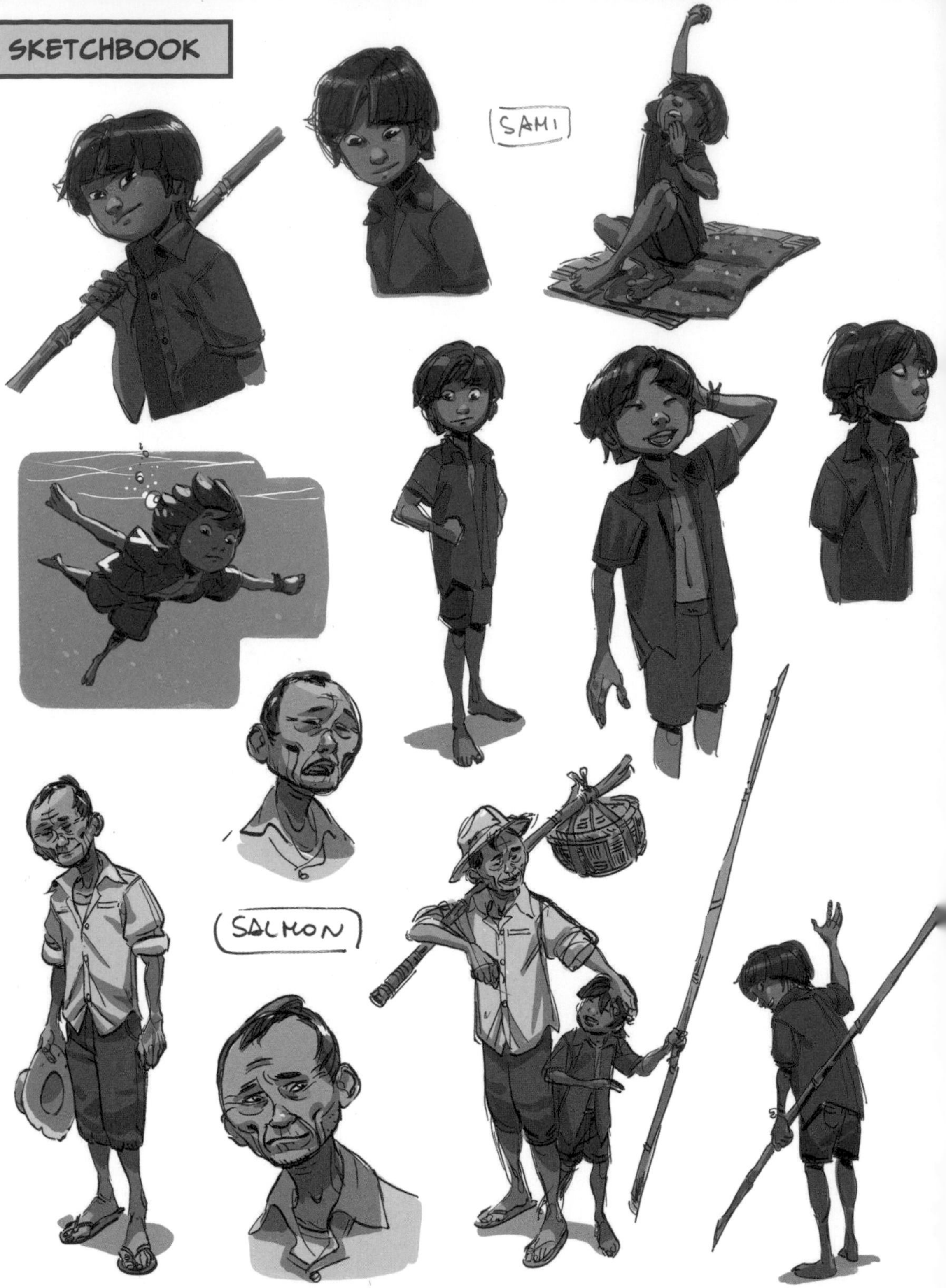
SAMI
SALMON

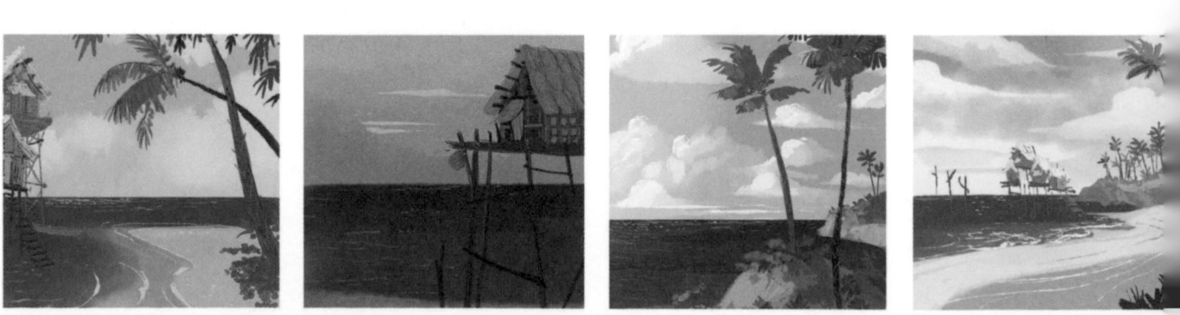

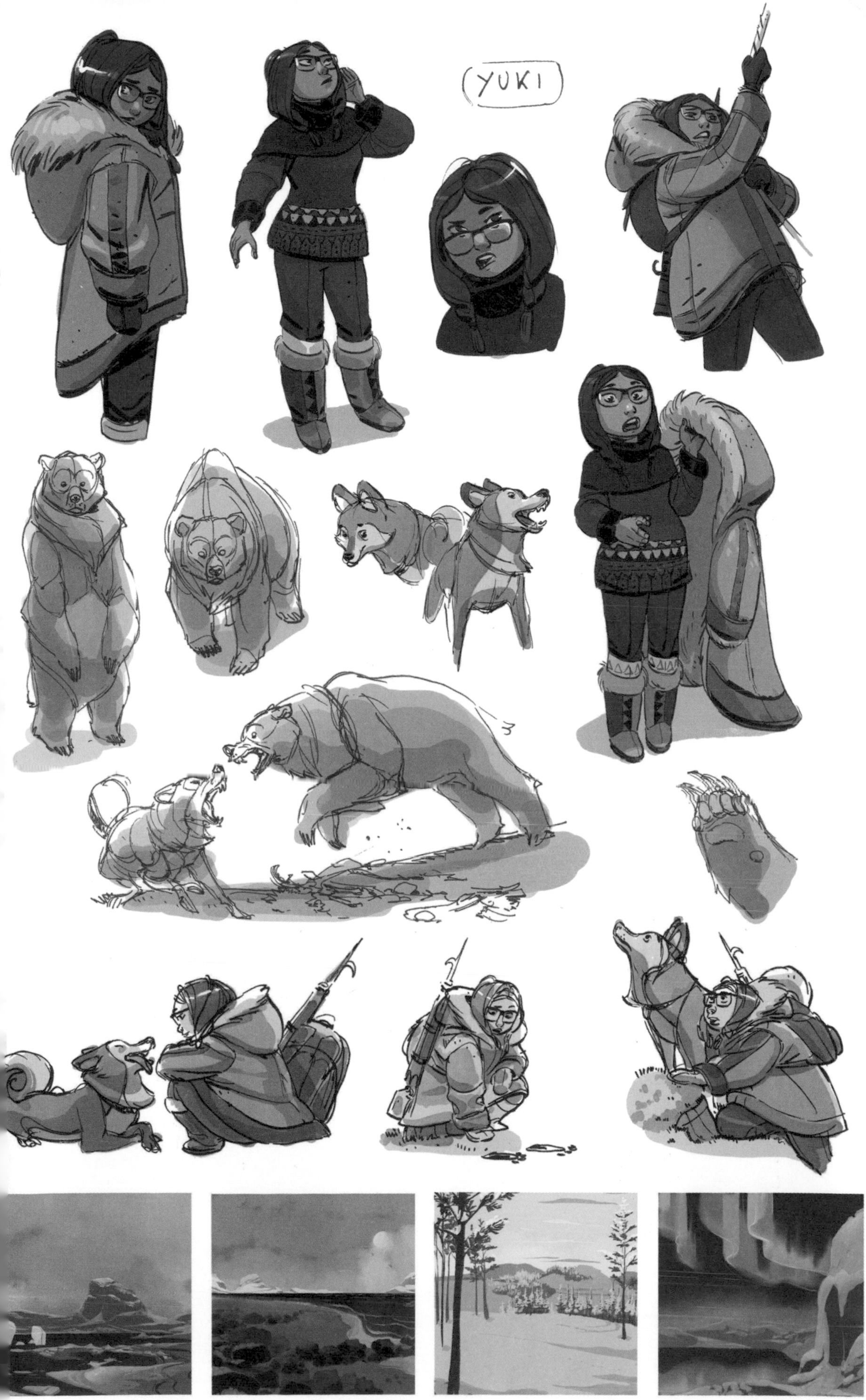
YUKI

OVER THE LAST DECADE, CO-WRITERS EOIN COLFER AND ANDREW DONKIN, AND ARTIST, GIOVANNI RIGANO HAVE CREATED MORE THAN A THOUSAND PAGES OF GRAPHIC NOVELS TOGETHER.

THE TEAM HAS ADAPTED FOUR OF EOIN'S SMASH HIT **ARTEMIS FOWL** BOOKS, AS WELL AS HIS FUTURISTIC NOVEL **THE SUPERNATURALIST**. THEY HAVE ALSO CREATED MANY SHORTER COMICS PROJECTS.

THEIR ORIGINAL GRAPHIC NOVEL, ILLEGAL, TELLING THE STORY OF TWO BROTHERS SEEKING A BETTER LIFE, WAS AN INTERNATIONAL BESTSELLER AND WAS TRANSLATED INTO OVER A DOZEN LANGUAGES. ILLEGAL WAS NOMINATED FOR OVER FORTY AWARDS AROUND THE WORLD INCLUDING THE CARNEGIE AND THE KATE GREENWAY MEDAL. THE MANY AWARDS THAT ILLEGAL WON INCLUDE A MEDAL FOR EXCELLENCE IN GRAPHIC LITERATURE, THE JUDGES' SPECIAL AWARD FROM CHILDREN'S BOOKS IRELAND, AND THE RED BOOK AWARD.

THE SUCCESS OF ILLEGAL TOOK THE TENACIOUS TRIO TO BOOK FESTIVALS, COMIC FESTIVALS, AND SCHOOL EVENTS ACROSS THE UK, IRELAND, ITALY, FRANCE, DENMARK, GERMANY, MEXICO, AND ALL OVER THE USA.

THEY ARE OPTIMISTIC ABOUT THE FUTURE AND LOOK FORWARD TO THE NEXT THOUSAND PAGES.

EOIN COLFER IS THE AUTHOR OF THE ARTEMIS FOWL BOOKS WHICH TELL THE STORY OF A LEPRECHAUN POLICE FORCE. HE DOES NOT HOWEVER LIMIT HIMSELF TO LEPRECHAUNS BUT ALSO WRITES ABOUT
TIME TRAVEL: **THE WARP SERIES**
DRAGONS: **HIGHFIRE**
PUPPIES: **THE DOG WHO LOST HIS BARK**, WITH P.J. LYNCH
IMAGINARY FRIENDS: **IMAGINARY FRED**, WITH OLIVER JEFFERS
AND IRON MEN: **IRON MAN: THE GAUNTLET**
HE HAS WON SEVERAL AWARDS (MOST WITH ANDREW DONKIN AND GIOVANNI RIGANO) THAT HE IS FAR TOO MODEST TO LIST HERE, AND HAS SOLD ENOUGH BOOKS TO KEEP HIS COMPUTER UP TO DATE. EOIN LIVES IN DUBLIN WITH HIS FAMILY. FIND HIM @EOINCOLFER ON TWITTER AND INSTAGRAM.

ANDREW DONKIN HAS SOLD OVER TEN MILLION COPIES OF HIS GRAPHIC NOVELS AND CHILDREN'S BOOKS WORLDWIDE. HE HAS WRITTEN OVER EIGHTY BOOKS, BOTH FICTION AND NONFICTION. HE LOVES TELLING STORIES, TEA, AND CAKE, BUT NOT NECESSARILY IN THAT ORDER. HE WAS DESCRIBED BY *THE SUNDAY TIMES* AS "THE GRAPHIC NOVEL SUPREMO"—A PHRASE HE'LL HAPPILY HAVE ON HIS TOMBSTONE IN THE UNLIKELY EVENT THAT HE EVER NEEDS ONE. HE HAS WON SEVERAL AWARDS AND, UNLIKE EOIN COLFER, IS NOT TOO MODEST TO LIST THEM ALL HERE BUT DOES NOT HAVE THE SPACE. ANDREW LIVES NEAR THE RIVER THAMES IN LONDON WITH HIS FAMILY. FIND HIM @ANDREWDONKIN ON TWITTER, INSTAGRAM, AND TIKTOK.

GIOVANNI RIGANO IS AN ITALIAN ARTIST AND THE CREATIVE VISIONARY BEHIND MANY BESTSELLING EUROPEAN GRAPHIC NOVELS. HE HAS PROVIDED ARTWORK FOR DISNEY-PIXAR'S **THE INCREDIBLES, PIRATES OF THE CARIBBEAN, ENCANTO, AND LIGHTYEAR**. HIS CREATOR-OWNED GRAPHIC NOVELS INCLUDE **DAFFODIL, CREEPY PAST,** AND MOST RECENTLY **LETTERS FROM ANIMALS** ADAPTED BY FREDERIC BRREMAUD FROM THE BOOK BY ALLAIN BOUGRAIN-DUBOURG. GIOVANNI LIVES WITH HIS PARTNER AND TWO CATS IN LAKE COMO, ITALY, WHERE HE ENJOYS A LIFESTYLE THAT MAKES EOIN AND ANDREW JEALOUS. FIND HIM @GIOVANNIRIGANO ON INSTAGRAM. GIOVANNI HAS ALSO WON MANY AWARDS AND, LIKE ANDREW, DOES NOT HAVE THE SPACE TO LIST THEM EITHER.